Claire Calman use [...] but gave it up when she re [...] adly paid and have a tough b [...] oyed and at least be allowed t [...]

I Like [...] [...] [...] is Calman's third novel. Her previous two books are *Love is a Four Letter Word*, a love story for people who wouldn't normally read a love story, and *Lessons for a Sunday Father*, which explores the break-up of a marriage from the viewpoints of husband, wife, teenage son and nine-year-old daughter – trust me, it's a lot less miserable than it sounds.

As well as writing novels and short stories, Calman sometimes does stuff on radio or performs her mercifully brief poems live. She lives in London with her partner and the world's tallest known stack of unfiled papers.

Acclaim for Claire Calman

LOVE IS A FOUR LETTER WORD

'A poignant and beautifully articulated tale of love and loss, memory and forgetting, grief and guilt, new love and letting go. I was engrossed, often tearful, and finally, uplifted. An unusual and very moving début novel'
Isobel Wolff, author of *The Trials of Tiffany Trott*

'Claire Calman's book is simply wonderful. I was totally enchanted, devoured it in a day, and have been raving about it ever since. I was so hooked that I flatly refused to break off to sign a vital document to do with the house move' Fiona Walker, author of *Snap Happy*

'Funny, clever and moving' *Sunday Mirror*

'This one is very special . . . A beautifully astute rendering of a mother/daughter relationship. It is quite simply excellent'
The Bookseller

'Claire Calman . . . mixes wit and pathos in exactly the right proportions so that you alternately laugh and weep throughout . . . She deals with profound and sensitive issues with a light, deft touch' Carol Smith, author of *Double Exposure*

LESSONS FOR A SUNDAY FATHER

Also by Claire Calman

LOVE IS A FOUR LETTER WORD
LESSONS FOR A SUNDAY FATHER

and published by Black Swan

I LIKE IT
LIKE THAT

Claire Calman

BLACK SWAN

I LIKE IT LIKE THAT
A BLACK SWAN BOOK : 0 552 77097 3

First publication in Great Britain

PRINTING HISTORY
Black Swan edition published 2002

1 3 5 7 9 10 8 6 4 2

Set in 11/12pt Melior by
Kestrel Data, Exeter, Devon.

Black Swan Books are published by Transworld Publishers,
61–63 Uxbridge Road, London W5 5SA,
a division of The Random House Group Ltd,
in Australia by Random House Australia (Pty) Ltd,
20 Alfred Street, Milsons Point, Sydney, NSW 2061, Australia,
in New Zealand by Random House New Zealand Ltd,
18 Poland Road, Glenfield, Auckland 10, New Zealand
and in South Africa by Random House (Pty) Ltd,
Endulini, 5a Jubilee Road, Parktown 2193, South Africa.

Printed and bound in Great Britain by
Clays Ltd, St Ives plc.

Dedication

```
F   R   L   R
E   O   A   R
V   H   W   Y
O   L   T   I
```

What took you so long?

I LIKE IT LIKE THAT

In the beginning . . .

'*Dear God,*'

wrote Georgia, aged ten, in her best, newly joined-up handwriting the week after her mother died,

'I am sorry but I do not beleive in you any more. What you did was something very wrong and you did not apologiese or anything. So when I die I will not come to see you. Actually in fact I will be going to the seaside instead.

Yours sincerley,
Georgia Abrams (Miss)
xxx

She had added the kisses automatically, because she always put three at the bottom, the way she would in a thank-you letter to Uncle Howard or Granny. God definitely did not deserve the kisses, she thought, but it would be rude to cross them out now that they were there, so she sealed up the letter and poked it through the letter box of the church at the end of their road.

1

A nice, normal family

So I'm standing in line at the orphanage and these prospective parents have turned up to choose a child. We're all stretching up straight and tall and remembering to keep our shoulders back like we've been told, and we've pulled up our socks and had our noses wiped so that we look like nice, clean children who'll be no trouble. Inside, we're all thinking the same thing and the air's thick with our thoughts, you can practically hear the words rushing out of us like the wind: 'Pick me! Me! Me! Pick *me*!' Then the couple stop right at the far end – they haven't even looked at all of us properly yet – and my shoulders slump: they're going to choose someone else. Someone smaller, younger, sweeter, blonder, cuter. Someone more lovable, someone more normal, someone who isn't *me*. But they turn then and come down this way a bit, stopping kindly to talk to each child, smiling and fussing over everyone, and making it worse – because now we all really, really want to be picked more than ever but we know that they only want one of us. And now it's my turn. I think I should do something adorable, something that would make me irresistible – perform a pirouette or an on-the-spot tap dance? Or just give them a dimply-cheeked smile instead of my usual serious face, a face that makes the man in the corner shop call me 'the undertaker's 'prentice'. But here they are now, right in front of me and I can't even seem to manage my own half-smile never mind a pirouette, so I just hold out my hand to shake theirs and say, 'Hello, I'm Georgia, how do you do?' And this is the best bit, because this is when the woman who's a bit chubby and nice-looking but definitely mumsy, you just know she's going to make apple pie and let you roll out the pastry and make hearts and stars to decorate the top – she turns to her husband and whispers into his ear and he smiles and nods and they each take one of my hands and draw me out of the parade and that's it, they've chosen me. *Me*.

Then they sign a piece of paper and my new *Daddy* picks up my small suitcase which has all of four things in it and we all get into their big, shiny car which has bouncy suspension and lovely slithery leather seats that you slide on when it goes sharply round a corner. The house is not especially grand or big, but completely perfect with a green front gate and a little wooden bird table with a tiny thatched roof on it. There's a straight path leading up to the front door, flanked by flowerbeds full of candy-pink roses and purple lavender with ladybirds clinging to the stems like bright red beads on a string. We go in and I wipe my feet on the mat without even having to be asked and they look at each other over my head and smile because they can see that I'm such a good girl and they know that they're going to love me. Then *Mummy* – she asks me if I'd like to call her that and I loop my arms round her neck and give her a big hug and she wipes a tear from her eye – says she must just pop in the kitchen and find me a nice treat.

And they've got a real fire and we sit and make toast at it using a proper long toasting fork, instead of a stupid, ordinary fork secured to the end of an undone wire coat hanger, and they give me a cup of tea like a grown-up instead of a babyish glass of milk or squash and we sit there and gradually the sky darkens outside and then it starts to rain and I can hear the wind ruffling the trees, but I don't care because I'm snug and warm and sitting by the fire with *Mummy* and *Daddy* and I'm the happiest, luckiest girl in the whole wide world.

And then the picture fades and that's the end.

That's it. That was my all-time favourite fantasy when I was growing up – that I was an orphan. I used to play it in my head like a videotape, exactly the same every single time, and if I was interrupted, I'd go right back to the very beginning and start again – because it just *had* to be the same, otherwise it felt as if the spell had been broken and the whole thing was spoiled. And sometimes, when I can't get to sleep or if I'm on a train journey and bored with my book, I push aside the anxieties and irritations of the day and let the fantasy return.

Now that I'm thirty-four, I presume that I've blown it on the being-adopted front. I don't suppose there'd be many broody prospective parents queuing up to have me unless I offered myself on the Net and posted a photo of me when I was about two and a half. I was moderately cute back then. But it's hard not to be cute when you're two and a half because you're all soft and dimpled and even when you fall over you look adorable whereas if you fall over when you're thirty-four, people think you're drunk and you have to walk round with holey tights and a bleeding knee and your best suede boots with sodding great scuff marks on them until you get home.

Also, I don't have angelic blond hair or appealing blue eyes or a cherubic smile. My hair is dark brown and what you could call curly if you were feeling generous, but not gorgeous film-star tumbling curls, like Ellen has – it resembles a nest of burnt noodles. If a man dared to run his hands through it, you'd have to call in the fire brigade to cut him free. To get it looking even halfway normal, I hire teams of minions whose sole task is to iron it day and night. OK, that's not true, but it would be if I could afford it; I wash it every morning then bludgeon it into submission with a big brush and a hairdryer so that I can go out in public without causing alarm. Left to its own devices, it reverts to its natural state and, believe me, that's not something you want to see staring back at you in the mirror first thing before you've even had a coffee. My eyes are brown, not blue, and I'm not sure what my smile is like because I tend to scowl when I look in the mirror, but my habitual expression is serious. I no longer see the man in the corner shop, but my face still says I'm the 'undertaker's 'prentice' – yes, that bit was real. When I'm walking down the street, total strangers call out to me, 'Give us a smile, darlin'!' or, worse, 'Cheer up, love! It might never happen!' A couple of times, I've said, 'Actually, my mother just died . . .' and done my ultra-sad face, then they look really guilty and feel compelled to apologize.

It sounds kind of horrible, the orphan fantasy, because I'm already half an orphan. Or should that be a semi-orphan? A demi-orphan? Anyway, my mother really is dead, she died when I was ten and no, I'm not playing for sympathy, I'm just telling you. My father's alive though and now I feel even worse about the orphan thing because it's not as if I don't love my dad. And I'm not an only child either. I've got a little sister, Ellen, she of the proper curls. She's twenty-seven now but she'll always be my little sister. And there's Matt, Matthew, my brother, who's thirty-one. That's my family, not counting Quinn, who's my stepmother so she's not real family, and Unc, who's Dad's brother, and a whole bunch of cousins too many to list here, then there's Quinn's daughter from her first marriage to this poxy artist, but we don't really count her. It's not that I don't love my family exactly – it's just that you've never met a bunch of people more guaranteed to drive you crazy. Other people's families always seem so nice and so, well, normal. Sometimes I just wish I could belong to a proper family like that, where everyone doesn't keep interrupting and interfering and taking the piss the whole time and where they say things like, 'Would you pass the potatoes, please?' instead of lunging across the table or nicking one from your plate. Is that too much to ask?

The sensible one

I wasn't always the sensible one, you know. At first I was a baby, of course, just like anyone else, with not a thought in my head for being sensible because all my time was taken up with more important matters – feeding and crying and weeing and gurgling and sicking up milk all over my mother's best silk blouse.

When I was two and a quarter, I clambered up onto the lavatory seat in the upstairs bathroom, then onto the cistern, and hurled Mumu, my toy monkey, out of the window 'to be a birdy'. Not being tall enough to see where – or even if – he'd landed, I was on the verge of following him when my mother rushed in and grabbed me, startling me so much that I burst into tears, she later told me, and could only be consoled by a jam tart and a ride on Daddy's back round and round the kitchen table until he lay flat on the floor and said horsey had to have a rest now. My mother clutched the chubby tops of my arms and told me that it was very, very bad to go near the open window and very bad to climb on things and I must not do it ever, ever again. Dad said that he went around for days cringing with guilt at having so foolishly left an upstairs window open, albeit one he didn't realize I could possibly reach, and berating himself for the near miss – what if . . . ? What if . . . ?

Then Matt was born and I wasn't the baby any more.

15

I was 'a big girl who must be ever-so-gentle with little Matthew'. I was always being told to shush and not to run up and down the landing for fear of waking him because he hardly ever slept and to 'please behave, because Mummy's far too tired to run round after you.' As far as I was concerned, he should have been taken right back to the hospital because all he did was cry and eat and pooh and be sick and take up Mummy and Daddy's time, so what was the point of him? It wasn't as if you could ride him round the garden like a tricycle or bounce him across the floor like a ball or even get under the kitchen table with him and play Being Invisible in the Magic Cave.

At the age of five, only two weeks into my first term at school, I dabbed green paint onto the nose of Martin, a boy I had a crush on; it was my first attempt at flirting. He retaliated with a blob of blue on my cheek and a riot of impressionistic brushwork soon covered our faces, arms, hair and grey school jumpers until the teacher extricated herself from the crisis at the other end of the room and stormed in to separate us. I was ordered to say I was very sorry, which I did, with my hands demurely behind my back, fingers crossed so I knew that it didn't really count. And the very next day, I refused to come in from the climbing frame at the end of break. I sat right at the very top, perched on the bar and swinging my legs and they had to send for Mum to come and talk me down, like a police negotiator with a person on a window ledge.

And then, when I was seven and three-quarters, things went from bad to worse – because that's when Ellen was born. It was bad enough having to share everything with Matthew, but at least I was used to him by then and he was a boy so I didn't have to give him all my toys the whole time and pretend to like it. When my mother told me, 'Soon there'll be another baby brother or sister for you,' apparently I uttered a single word: 'Why?'

'We thought it would be nice,' my father had said

lamely, though, as I later discovered, they were both as surprised by the prospect of another baby as I was.

Ellen was bound to make an enormous difference to my life, no matter what kind of a baby she was. But the fact that she was Ellen from Day One – irresistible, irrepressible, impossible – made it much, much worse. Ellen was cute and pretty almost at once in a way that babies rarely are. She had blue eyes like Mum's and, all too soon, soft curls rather than tangled frizz. Ellen smiled on cue and, as soon as she could sit up, clapped her hands when a new visitor arrived. She refused to sleep when out in her pram, preferring instead to bask in the admiration and sickening goo-goo talk – 'Who's a *boo-ful* baby? Yes, *you* are. You're a boo-ful baby, yes . . .' – of neighbours, shopkeepers, strangers.

It was also then that things started to change in the family. Anyway, no point droning on about it now, it's years ago. The key thing is that Mum died when Ellen was only three so she doesn't even remember her. Nothing – not her face, her voice or anything. She looks at the photos though and sometimes she says she thinks she can sort of remember her, but we both know that she can't, she just says it because nobody wants to feel that they've forgotten someone who must once have been the most important person in their life and maybe she thinks that if she says it often enough then she'll start to believe it and that'll make it true. Ellen still gets me to tell her stories about when she was little, sometimes the ones from before she was even born, but always the same. 'Tell me the bit when I was born and they brought me back from the hospital,' 'Tell me about when you cut off all my hair,' 'Tell me the time when I peed in Matt's wellie,' 'Tell me how Mum used to sing when you were out in the street with her,' and, endlessly, 'Tell me what Mummy was like.' Matt never does that. Never. He won't even talk about her. It's as if she never existed.

*   *   *

Anyway, Mum died. End of story. It happens to lots of people all the time.

A one-woman United Nations

I can't remember exactly how it happened, not Mum dying, I mean, I'll never forget that – but my becoming the sensible one in the family. All I know is that now it's been that way for so long that I can't even remember how not to be any more. Was it really me who was on the verge of hurling myself out of the bathroom window to fly like the birds? Could I have dared to smear paint on a boy I didn't know? It may not sound much to you, but no-one who knows me now would believe that I'd ever been naughty or even silly when I was growing up. I wasn't even wild as a teenager, when it's virtually obligatory. You're *supposed* to dye your hair jet black and wear too much eye make-up; you go to gigs in smoky pubs where the floor's awash with beer and sweat; you tell your parents to fuck off because they don't fucking understand you or what it's like to be young; you snog blokes at parties you've known all of ten minutes; you screw someone on a mattress on the floor without even using a condom; and you get pissed a lot. All this is bog-standard behaviour for the budding adolescent. Except for me. I did only the bare minimum of these things – a couple of token blond streaks in my hair for a few months, letting myself be groped by some creep in his car after a date, just enough so that I wouldn't be branded a complete swot – a geek I guess they'd say now. I got drunk precisely twice, once on vodka and lime at a friend's house where I threw up all over her mum's peach cushions – but, being me, I apologized profusely and took them to be dry-cleaned straight-away – and the second time when I'd gone to a gig with a friend and drunk quite a lot of lager and, weirdly, given that I can't remember ever having liked it, Southern Comfort and lemonade. Anyway, I walked home – I was so drunk I had no memory of it, I just trundled back on autopilot – finally managed to insert my key in the lock, which felt like something of a triumph as if I'd successfully completed one of those impossible puzzles you get in a perspex cube, only to find my father sitting at the kitchen table in his dressing gown, with his coat on top. I was sixteen. It was nearly two in the morning. To say that he was not happy would be an understatement. And remember, this is my dad we're talking about, the mildest, gentlest man you could ever hope to meet. He never went in for all that heavy father stuff – except on this one occasion. First of all he shouted at me because it was two a.m. and I hadn't phoned and that was the absolute Number One rule, wasn't it, that we'd agreed on and how could he trust me and let me have plenty of freedom if I was going to abuse it and behave like this? Then he noticed that I wasn't entirely as steady on my feet as I should be after two glasses of Coke and he went even more crazy. How could I? What was the one thing that I knew he minded about more than any other thing in the world? Did I want to flush my entire life down the drain, is that what I wanted? Then he grabbed a black Magic Marker from the dresser and drew a straight line all the way across the cork-tiled floor. Well, I got the giggles then and the more he stood there stony-faced, the worse it got. I was just doubled up, laughing and snorting, then I thought I was going to wet myself so I rushed off to the loo and he said, hurry up then and come straight back, we've not finished here yet. So I walked the line with exaggerated care as if it were a tightrope, and he said I was drunk and I said I wasn't I'd only had one half of lager and he said I was under age and shouldn't have even had that – and, more to the point, I was incredibly bloody stupid and I absolutely wasn't to drink again, he was dead serious about that, and did I understand? And, even though I was drunk, I could see that he was serious as hell and I never was much of a rebel anyway. It wasn't worth getting him all upset for. The black pen couldn't be washed off and it remained there for another three years – a one-line testament to my shame – until the floor was finally too scuffed and grotty even for us and was replaced.

These days, I don't even touch lager. A single glass of wine with dinner sometimes. When we're out, I order a glass of white and Stephen has a glass of red. He's my boyfriend, fiancé really, and he's not a great one for overdoing it either. We're very compatible. Stephen's very sensible, too, and reliable. That's one of the things I love most about him – you can always depend on Stephen. And, unlike everyone in my family, he doesn't expect me to come to the rescue all the time. When I'm with him, I feel I can have time off from being strong and sensible, because I'm not going to have to fix something or arbitrate in a row or solve anything.

When Matt and Ellen used to squabble or fight, it was always me who intervened and stood between them telling them they must make it up again. When Dad thundered upstairs and slammed his study door because some stupid client had changed her stupid mind for the forty-fifth time, it was me who waited ten minutes then tapped on his door to ask if he wanted a cup of tea. Even now, I guess it's me they all turn to in a crisis, real or imaginary – nearly always imaginary. Quinn phones to ask if she can use tomato ketchup in a meatloaf because they've run out of tomato purée (Yes) and do I think it would be interesting to add raisins? (No). Dad calls to get my thoughts on how to handle a client who is clearly colour blind but doesn't seem to know it. (Say the name of the colour when you point to it: 'This dark blue background works well with the yellow lettering, don't you think?'). Matt wants to know why his boss is suddenly picking holes in his work (Stress at home? Anxiety over flagging profits?) and, by the way, could I take a look at his speech for the presentation next Friday? He can fax it over now if I have a minute (I haven't, but go on, then). And Ellen, of course, Ellen most of all – have I come across her fake leopardskin gloves, her big silver hoop earrings, her pink bag, none of which she can find? (No. Has she checked the café, the bar, under her bed, under the pile of coats in her hallway?) What should she do about the man who gave her an enormous tip last Saturday and wrote his phone number on the back of his credit-card slip? (Ignore it.) Can she borrow the car because she's found a cheap source of silver but it's miles away and nowhere near a tube? (Yes, but absolutely only if she doesn't return it gasping for petrol like the last fifteen times or leave her cigarette butts in the ashtray.) Her horoscope says this month is a good time to explore new horizons and what do I think that means? (Nothing. Horoscopes are utter bollocks, she needs to start taking charge of her own destiny for the thousandth time.)

Still, all that early training – being the family peace-keeper (Matt calls me 'our one-woman UN') – has stood me in good stead. I'm a counsellor, so I listen to people talking about their problems all day long. Looking on the bright side, at least now I get paid for it.

2

Twenty-four years and one day . . .

Yesterday was the anniversary of Mum's death – and the first time in my memory that I haven't spent the day with Ellen. It's not a sacred ritual or anything, I don't want to sound too solemn about it; it's just a day when we do Mum-ish things like going to an exhibition then having tea and cream meringues afterwards while we argue about which pictures we liked and, much more fun, which ones we didn't. We don't go to the grave any more because that's not how we want to think of her, lying cold and alone beneath a slab of stone. 'Oh, you don't want to visit me – I'm just a bundle of old bones now!' That's what Mum would say if she was still alive – except then she wouldn't be bones, of course, would she? Mum had no time for sentiment or floaty notions that your soul lives on after you die, or you go to heaven, though she loved hymns and carols as much as any kind of song and used to sing in the house or even when we were out – 'There is a green hill far away . . .', 'For – all – the – s-a-i-n-t-s' and once on the way back from school, 'Jerusalem' at full blast. I ran ahead and kept five paces in front, pretending not to know her, the mad lady who sings in the street. She said when you die you become food for the worms and then part of the earth, it's a good thing, she said, because it means that, in a way, you're still part of the world even though you're dead, still around the people you loved, the people who loved you. You become the ground and the grass beneath their feet, the trees that shade them, the honeysuckle that makes them sniff deep and exhale 'aaah . . .' as they pass by, the water that trickles through the soil, the chalk, the rock, the water they drink, the sky, the clouds, the rain, even the air that they breathe.

Now, I realize that it *does* sound mystical, but that was the thing about Mum – I suppose she could be quite fey at times, but it never sounded affected, it was just the way she was, not like Quinn's out-to-lunch friend Tarka who keeps rearranging her furniture because if your bed's facing north-by-north-west and your bedroom's painted in 'yin colours', whatever they may be, it's supposed to be auspicious for good relationships, when in fact what's far more auspicious for a good relationship is not to be so fucking bonkers in the first place.

When I went through my brief pious phase, kneeling by my bed each night, praying for things to be different, and begging to be confirmed, Mum just smiled and didn't say anything even though there was no question of my being confirmed because a) Dad's Jewish so I'm not baptized and b) she knew I only wanted to do it so I could have a white dress and little white gloves; my second-best friend was a Catholic and I was seething with envy over her confirmation photos – her parents had one in a silver frame on their mantelpiece, with Martha affecting a sickly eyes-to-heaven smile. I bet she was only smiling because all her aunts and uncles gave her envelopes with money in.

And then Mum died and that pretty much put paid to my brief flirtation with God.

Last year on Mum's anniversary, on the actual *Day*, Ellen and I met up and went to an exhibition which included bizarre chandeliers that looked like something from a dream; they were constructed from cutlery and cheese graters and kids' lollipops and glass beads made from melted-down ginger-beer and 7-Up bottles. Over tea and cakes, we discussed which we'd pick if we *had* to live with one of them, day in day out, which was easier for Ellen because she thought they were wonderful so she was spoiled for choice, whereas I could see that they wouldn't be remotely practical because the one with the lollipops would get all sticky and then pretty soon it would be dusty and disgusting and encrusted with dead flies. Then we went on to the cinema, but we missed the first seven minutes because Ellen got the time of the film wrong. If I hadn't been with her, I wouldn't have bothered going in – I hate missing the beginning. But then, if I hadn't been with her, I'd have double-checked the time and I wouldn't have been late. With the exhibition, we try to go to something different, something I wouldn't choose otherwise, so we steer clear of the Impressionist paintings in the Courtauld Collection or the Flemish and Dutch works in the National, those clear, calm, ordered rectangles that I could happily lose myself in for an age. Instead, we go to view controversial photographs or angry installations or sculptures assembled from a conglomeration of scrap metal that look as if they're still waiting to become something, anything. Ellen's taste is more like Mum's, she loves things that are big and in-your-face, abstract, outsize, avant-garde. I like art that isn't trying desperately hard to be more than it really is – figurative, thoughtful, accomplished, small.

I don't know what went wrong with Mum's Day this year. Well, I do. Ellen forgot and went tootling off with a friend to some wholesale place miles away in quest of a particular type of crystal bead. Ellen makes jewellery. She doesn't earn a living at it because, well, because she's Ellen, so, despite the fact that she's bursting at the seams with talent and couldn't come up with an unoriginal idea if she tried, she manages to under-charge for her pieces and takes far too long to make them because she gets sidetracked halfway through or she leaves her best things behind at home when she rents a stall, so that there's not the slightest danger of her accidentally turning her talent and skill into a real career. 'In the meantime' – one of her favourite phrases – she works part-time in a wine bar called The Warm South. Ellen forgets things all the time, so that's nothing unusual, but she's never forgotten Mum's Day before. Even on the couple of occasions when one or other of us has been away, we've still spoken on the phone about Mum and that was different, because we knew we weren't going to have the Day – we didn't just forget.

It's not fair to blame it on Ellen though because, in fact, it was really *my* fault. I forgot last week, which is when I'd normally call Ellen to remind her and to fix up what we were doing. We see each other all the time in any case, but we always make a proper arrangement for Mum's Day and plan what we're going to see so the time doesn't just drift away from us. And Ellen always wants me to tell her favourite Mum stories. I suppose the Day is really more for Ellen than it is for me – it's my way of helping her to feel as though she remembers. So yesterday was the Day and I woke up and looked at my diary and I had three clients all in the morning, then one at seven p.m. and I saw the date and suddenly it clicked, 8th August, and I rang Ellen so that we could meet up in the afternoon and she wasn't there.

I sat through all my sessions, knowing that even if Ellen got my message and rang me back, she'd only get the machine. I know it doesn't sound like much, but I felt so twitchy about it, I couldn't wait for each person to leave and, in the few minutes' gap between them, I ran upstairs to check the machine, but there was nothing.

In the end, I went out after the last one had gone and had lunch in the café I go to all the time.

'Where's your sister today?' the waitress asked.

I shook my head.

'No idea, but if she comes in, tell her I was here, will you please?'

I thought about what we would have done if Ellen had been there, and I went to the Tate Modern. By myself. Mum would have got such a kick out of it – there's a vast open space when you go in and it's very unstuffy and unpompous, and everyone was talking at a normal level instead of in those special hushed, reverent whispers that people seem to reserve for when they're in the presence of Art, as if the pictures might be affronted if you speak too loudly. There was a huge stone abstract sculpture, a bit like a squashed circle with strange wooden spheres suspended in the central gap – the sort of thing I normally dislike because it makes me feel as if I'm missing something, that it *means* something only I don't know what it is and everyone else is looking at it and making little ah-I-see nods to themselves because they get it and I just stand there feeling like an idiot and telling myself that it's not really art, it's just a load of pretentious crap that isn't about anything at all, and I'm right not to understand it because there's nothing to understand. Still, despite the fact that I didn't know what it was or what it meant, I liked the way the stone was all smooth and curved, and, without thinking, I reached out and ran my hand down the cool inner slope of it until one of the guards scooted up to me and told me not to touch. I felt incredibly embarrassed, because I'm not at all the kind of person to step out of line like that, but afterwards I thought how proud of me Mum would have been because it was exactly the kind of thing she was always doing only she wouldn't have gone bright red or apologized – she'd have got into a discussion about the accessibility of art and why we should all be allowed, no, encouraged, to touch sculpture rather than just look at it. There were loads of other things I hated, inevitably, and I wished Ellen had been there because what's the point of looking at things you hate unless you can argue about them with someone else?

Eventually, Ellen rang me back.

'Oh, George, I'm so sorry! I can't believe I forgot. I feel so bad!'

'It's all right. Don't worry, babes. It doesn't matter.'

'It does! It does!'

'No, really, it's OK. We couldn't have gone on for ever, in any case.'

'Why couldn't we?' Sometimes Ellen sounds as if she's about four years old, just like my niece Bonnie.

'Ellie, come on. It doesn't mean we've forgotten her. Let's meet up tomorrow instead. At the café?'

'OK. And you don't hate me?'

'Don't be silly.' Ellen loves to dramatize everything. She is such an old ham sometimes. 'You're still my favourite sister.'

Stephen doesn't really get the 'favourite sister' thing. I love Stephen, but he's very . . . literal. He says, 'Well, of course she's your favourite sister – she's your only sister.' I hate having to explain stuff like that. I mean, that's the point, it's what you call a 'joke', a 'statement intended to cause amusement or arouse mirth, m'Lud' – sometimes you have to bring Stephen up to speed on certain things. I know, I know, I'm a mean bitch and it's unfair. He has got a sense of humour and he quite often tells jokes, but sometimes he's rather fazed if you say something that isn't exactly in a straight line. Anyway, in a way it isn't a joke because even if I had fourteen sisters, Ellen would definitely be my favourite. Even when she drives me crazy, she's still my favourite sister and I'd do anything for her. Anything.

When Joy was gone

Joy died on a Tuesday and was buried on Friday. David believed that Ellen was too little to attend the funeral, but he sat down with Georgia and Matt and asked them solemnly what they would like to do, it was up to them to decide. Matt, not quite eight, leapt up and kicked his father hard in the shin and said he wasn't going, no-one could make him, then he ran out to the garden and rode his bike round and round the garden and into the flowerbed. Georgia sat very still for a moment, then she said, yes, she thought it best if she went. David pulled her onto his lap, although by now she was ten, and said into her hair, 'You don't have to go, little chick, if you don't want to. Mummy wouldn't mind.' That's what he used to call her, when she was only small.

Georgia slid off his lap and nodded and said it was fine and she would go.

At the age of ten, Georgia does not have anything black to wear, but the night before the funeral she picks out her navy dress with the red ladybird buttons and hangs it on the knob of the wardrobe door, and puts her black patent party shoes beneath it on the floor. She also gets out her best purple knickers with the tiny pink flowers on, because these are the ones she wears for luck, like when she has a maths test at school or if she has to go to the dentist, hoping not to need a filling. Ellen and Matt are taken two doors down to Mrs McNeill who gives them fizzy orange and packets of Iced Gems and lets them watch TV, even though it is the middle of the day.

Georgia has never seen a real coffin before, only ones on the news and in the newspaper. She knows that her mother is in that box, and she knows that she is dead. Daddy says it is just like being asleep, only for ever and ever and that she couldn't wake up again. So that was what being dead was and then you got put in the ground like a daffodil bulb only you stayed there, you didn't come up in the spring, and then the worms got you and after ages and ages you became like earth, that was what Mummy said when their kitten died, and the terrapin, and the goldfish, and the snail, and even Daddy said that it was natural and not really a bad thing because, in a way, you were carrying on and, most of all, he said, you lived on in people's heads, their memories and thoughts, the way Mummy would, for ever and ever. Or you got burnt like a log or a piece of screwed-up newspaper and then they could fit you into a pot, like Lisa's granny who was in a nasty green thing called an urn with a lid and Lisa had said come on, let's have a look, and Georgia had half-expected to see two eyes staring back up at her from the pot and hadn't wanted to. But then she had and it was only like dust, like the stuff you get when you help change the Hoover bag, with no eyes or anything, but it was still yucky and sp-o–o-o-o–o-o–o-k-y, and she and Lisa had made *woo-woo-ooh* ghost noises to show that they weren't really scared at all.

Georgia knows that Mummy is not awake *in there*, but still she does not like the way the lid must be so close to her nose and there is no room even to turn over. Georgia holds Daddy's hand tight and her face is white as a shroud, but she does not shed a single tear.

Her father, by contrast, cries continuously from the moment the coffin appears. The tears just keep falling down his face, like the leaky tap in the kitchen. Every few minutes he blows his nose loudly and clears his throat and wipes his face, and then the tears leak out again, rolling down his face and inside his shirt collar.

Afterwards, people come back home and Georgia helps make cups of tea. Auntie Audrey puts sugar in Daddy's tea, 'to keep your strength up, it's good for shock,' and he drinks it even though he doesn't take sugar.

After the sweet peas

In the middle of the lawn there is a table, the sort with folding legs. In the middle of the table is a jug, the big glass jug Mummy used to fill with water to put on the table at suppertime. In the jug are sweet peas. Pink and mauve, purple and white, and one nearly the colour of red wine. The jug looks as if it has been besieged by butterflies, the sweet-pea petals in the wind fluttering and fragile like wings.

Georgia tips her head back to look at the sky; it is hot blue, the blue she has painted as a strip at the top of the paper a hundred times, a thousand times, a hundred thousand times. Around her, the grown-ups are talking and drinking and making lip-smacking noises when they kiss each other. It is rude to smack your lips when you are eating, but maybe it is allowed when you are kissing.

Matt and Ellen are brought back by the neighbour and Matt stands by the buffet table, cramming crisps into his face and throwing peanuts high up in the air and trying to catch them in his mouth, like the sealions being thrown fish at the zoo, then he goes outside and kicks his ball against the back wall again and again until Uncle Howard gives him 50p to stop and he goes upstairs to look at his comics. Ellen works the room, tugging at trouser legs and skirt hems and smiling until she receives attention and Amaretti biscuits, stuck out of her reach on the table.

Unc pats Georgia's head and pulls out a coin from behind her ear. She stands next to Daddy, half-hiding behind the tree-trunk of his leg, leaning against him. He looks down at her, rests his hand on her head, draws her closer. He is nodding, saying yes, yes, he knows, of course, it will get better in time, of course it will, of course.

Mummy's best friend Briony is there. She is wearing the most beautiful dress in the whole wide world. It has millions of colours in it, all in stripes, and there are glittery bits like the tinsel they put up in the classroom at Christmas. Georgia looks down at her own plain navy dress and wishes she were wearing something else. Briony's dress is like one great big ginormous long sock, but there is no heel and no toe. Briony knitted it herself. She taught Georgia how to knit last year only there wasn't time to do casting on or casting off so all Georgia can do is keep on adding rows to the bit Briony started off for her, a strip of colours so long that soon she'll be able to wrap herself up in it, winding it round and round from her ankles all the way up to her head, like an Egyptian mummy. Auntie Audrey must like the dress too because she is nudging Uncle Howard and pointing at it. Auntie does not knit her own dresses. Probably she is not such a good knitter as Briony, so she is wearing a black skirt and a matching jacket. Every time the wind blows, Auntie's hand goes to her head as if she is patting herself the way people keep patting Georgia and Matt and Ellen. Twice the hat has flown across the garden like a frisbee. Each time, Georgia runs to pick it up.

Auntie runs after her and says what a nice girl she is to fetch Auntie's hat and she must come and visit soon and bring Matthew and little Ellen too and they would have lots of treats so they wouldn't be sad any more, and wouldn't it be nice for Daddy to have a bit of a break? Georgia nods though she is not sure exactly what Auntie means, but it is the kind of thing grown-ups are always saying and it was best not to keep asking why all the time because after a while they got cross and told you to give it a rest. But if you were quiet and nodded and said thank you, they were nice to you and gave you money you could save up for going away in an aeroplane, like the one up there, leaving a trail like a white zip against the blue sky.

All is going as swimmingly as could possibly be expected given the nature of the event, until Ellen, catching sight of the jug of colourful sweet peas, runs towards the garden and takes a tumble on the back step. She is quickly scooped up, but she is crying now, really sobbing, and wailing: 'M-u–u-u-u–m-m-m-ee-e-eee! I want Mu-u-u-mm-eee-ee!', her breaths jerky and gulping. A cluster of women coo and fuss around her, soothing her and offering her cocktail cherries, toys, Amaretti dipped in wine, anything to make her stop.

And now the guests are starting to leave, and they are kissing each other all over again. Georgia is getting patted on the head so often she sticks her tongue out and pants like a dog and gives a small yelping bark until Daddy squeezes her and says, 'Not now, little chick, not now.'

Briony and Auntie Audrey stay behind to clear up while Uncle Howard and Daddy walk to the bottom of the garden. Georgia can see Unc light a cigarette then, after a moment, he holds out the packet to Daddy. He must be pretty silly because Daddy doesn't smoke. He gave up ages and ages ago when they found out that Mummy was going to have a baby. And when the baby was born, it turned out to be Georgia. Unc can't have forgotten, but maybe Daddy has because he takes a cigarette and dips his head towards the flame.

Georgia goes to the kitchen to ask Auntie why Daddy is smoking, but she stops at the door when she hears them talking.

'. . . manage with them all, I don't know,' Auntie is saying. 'How's he going to get any work done for a start? He'll have to get much more help.'

Daddy used to work in a proper office like everyone else's dads, but now he says he is going to work at home. He is called a designer and he does things like books and posters for exhibitions and he tells people what sort of lettering is best to have and how it's supposed to look, like when you do a project book at school and you make a cover for it and do a drawing or cut out pictures from a magazine to show people what's inside.

'Of course it'll be tough.' Briony is slotting plates into the dishwasher. 'But I'm most worried for Georgia. She seems so grown-up, so calm. I've not even seen her cry. It can't be healthy to bottle it all up.'

Georgia slides back into the hall.

Back in the garden, Briony comes out onto the lawn and takes away the jug of butterflies to put in the kitchen.

'I must have a big hug with my favourite girl before I go,' she says. 'You be sure to come see me with your dad, OK?'

Georgia nods and buries her face in Briony's neck.

'You smell like Mummy.'

Briony blinks hard, then smiles.

'Oh – what? Yes! You're right. Your mummy gave me this perfume. It's the same as hers. You clever thing. Fancy you noticing that.' She turns away then and runs back into the house. Probably she is going to the loo, it's best to go before you get in the car or when you're on the motorway everyone gets cross and says you should have gone before you left.

When she comes out, her face is all pink and she stands by her car talking to Daddy, saying she could stay, it's no trouble, Adam can survive without her for a day, she's worried about – and Daddy saying no, no, he won't hear of it, it's all right, he wants to be alone. Really he does. Honestly. Auntie Audrey is looking at her watch about fifty times a minute practically and saying they ought to be making a move too. Unc gives her a funny look and says for God's sake, there's no rush, of course there isn't, what can she be thinking of. And Daddy says, never mind now, they should go. Please go. Will they all just go now?

The table that was on the lawn has been folded up and is leaning against the wall in the hallway. Ellen has finally keeled over and is fast asleep on the sofa and Matt has gone back up to his room to play with his car-racing track. The jug of sweet peas sits on the kitchen table. There is no wind in the kitchen so the butterflies are still now. Daddy sits down in his chair and Georgia leans against him; he pulls her up onto his lap.

'Oof, you're getting heavy.'

'It's not me, it's my shoes.' She holds out her feet for him to see. The shiny patent leather is smeared with mud from the graveside.

'Have to polish those, won't we?' he says.

Daddy reaches across to pull out the dark sweet pea, the one like wine. It is drooping.

'They don't last long.' He presses the petals between his fingers.

'But they'll grow again next summer, won't they?'

He shakes his head.

'No, Squidge.' He kisses the top of her head. 'Once they're gone, they're gone.'

Georgia nods then she looks up at her father's face and lifts her arm, offering him the sleeve of her dress to wipe away his tears.

3

Queen of Communication

I nodded and clasped my hands loosely in my lap in my attentive-and-supportive-listening pose.

'Hmm-mm. And how did that make you *feel*?'

And hurry *up*, I thought, flicking my gaze to the carefully positioned clock on the side table. Three minutes and counting, I mentally intoned, like the villain's henchman in a Bond film.

'We-e-e-e-ll . . .' My client paused, as if unsure whether this might be a trick question and she might give the wrong answer. 'A bit hurt reelly . . . ?' She pulled a velvet cushion onto her lap and stroked it as if it were a small pet or a soft toy. 'And a teenthy bit – ' her voice dropped as if she were about to blaspheme in front of a priest – 'croth?'

Ah-hah! Now we were getting somewhere. I resisted the urge to punch the air in triumph. I bet there was a whole cauldron of rage and resentment bubbling away under all that girlie lisping. I notice that her lisp gets worse when she talks about anything that makes her uncomfortable.

'I *see*. And did you tell him how you felt?'

'We-e-e-e-ll – not reelly, I thuppothe, but . . .'

Oh, hurry up, will you? I'm meeting Ellen.

'. . . I did throw thomething at him . . .'

'*Mmm?*' One minute and thirty seconds. 'Which *was*?' I prompted. I must try harder not to be so impatient.

'Theodore.'

Theodore? Or was she trying to say *Seeodore*? Who the fuck was Theodore/Seeodore? Her son? Her ex-husband? Oh, bollocks. Bollockth. I should have checked my thodding notes.

'*Teddy*,' she added. Not 'a teddy bear' or even 'my teddy bear'. Just 'Teddy'. Oh dear. Not a good sign in a woman of forty-one.

'Well, we certainly need to come back to this next session . . .' the well-timed pause before sending the traumatized client out with all their emotions freshly unleashed, '. . . but I'm afraid we do have to end now . . .'

She gathered up her bag and jacket.

'Bye-bye.'

I nodded.

'See you next week.'

Now kindly beetle off so I can go and meet Ellen.

I stayed in my chair, a figure of perfect repose and calm wisdom, a bit like Buddha only with slightly less of a tummy. As soon as the door clicked behind her, I sprang to my feet, leapt with one bound to the sofa and began my post-client cushion-plumping ritual.

'And don't fondle my cushions!'

I tweaked a wrinkle out of the rug and gave a quick appraising look round the room. Went over to the screen that conceals the tiny kitchenette, and altered the angle so that it was just right, crossed to the window ledge and gave the pot plants there a quarter-turn each – it's important to do that otherwise they won't grow evenly. Straightened the items on my desk, tucking a stray paperclip back into the correct compartment of the drawer-divider, aligning the notepad so it was square to the edge. Then I hovered in the hall for a moment, straining my ear at the door to hear. Pulled it open a crack and peered out. Coast was clear. Closed it as quietly as possible and locked up, then tiptoed along the corridor. That's the trouble with a block like this – if you're not careful, the neighbours buttonhole you at every opportunity wanting to chat and tell you about their knee operations or ask you in for cups of tea every two minutes.

Thirty-two seconds and twenty-four steps later, I unlocked the front door of my flat on the floor above. Ah, home. An identical studio flat to the one I use as a consulting room on the fourth floor. Or rather, the layout's the same – a not-large-enough studio room that includes the world's smallest kitchen. But, whereas downstairs all I need is a kettle and a sink, and the rest of the room holds only a sofa bed, my armchair and a desk, my living accommodation has to be bedroom, sitting room and kitchen all rolled into one.

I had the bed specially designed for the room and it folds up each morning into a discreet cupboard. Aside from that, I've kept the furniture to a minimum – a boxy sofa like the one downstairs, a rectangular beech table and six pale chairs. Roman blinds in textured fabric the colour of caffé latte, cushions covered in velvet, bouclé and mohair in soft smoky greys, creams and milky chocolate colours. A beautiful parlour palm in a square ivory pot and a weeping fig that's getting too big for its boots. The bathroom is a cool haven of white and grey with sharp touches of turquoise and lapis lazuli. On the whole, considering that the flat is clearly too small for anyone with a normal amount of clutter to live in, I manage pretty well. This I achieve partly by being naturally tidy – or 'an anally-retentive control freak' as Ellen puts it with her usual charm – partly by storing half my clothes in the hall cupboard of my consulting flat downstairs, and partly by having a lot of stuff stored in the basement of the block and therefore beyond daily reach. The only major problem is the kitchen. Technically, it is referred to as a kitchenette, but I can never see why something smaller than a kitchen should have a longer name. Logically, it should only be a 'kit', surely? And that's what it is – a handy, almost pocket-sized kit for cooking. It consists of a cupboard – literally – in which lives a sink, draining board, a worktop the size of a table mat and storage space. To one side, I've added a diminutive fridge which doubles as a plinth for a mini cooker with two rings and a small oven. The area, like the one downstairs, is masked by a screen. It's an ideal set-up for a student or someone with a wild party-going lifestyle who never eats in. No, really it is. It's just that I *love* to cook. I'd have people round for dinner every night if I could, but cooking for six is a struggle when you have to kneel on the floor every time you want to chop a mushroom.

Never were there such devoted sisters . . .

I slowed my steps, trying not to be so predictably punctual – not that Ellen would know if I were punctual or not. Ellen was bound to be late herself, of course. Ellen is always late. It's a law of Nature, like gravity or the tides being governed by the moon. God knows I ought to be used to it by now, given that she has been unpunctual for all twenty-seven years of her existence. She was even born two weeks late. I can just imagine Ellen as a baby, popping her head out into the world, already talking. 'Sorry, sorry! I was just coming! I was held up . . .' And it's never only by five minutes either. If she's only twenty minutes late, you feel honoured because sometimes it's forty. Needless to say, it is never her fault, never that she was nattering on the phone to someone or was running round the flat looking for her pink mules; it's always the traffic, the tube, the bus, she had stopped to direct a lost tourist, got talking to a mime artist in Covent Garden.

It is almost as rare for me to be late as it is for Ellen to be on time. Sometimes, I deliberately try to be a little late – to prove to myself that I'm not some obsessively punctual, uptight control freak. I hover in my coat, fluttering round the flat watering the plants or plumping up the cushions to delay myself a few minutes. Then I take the stairs rather than the lift and dally at the newsagent's looking at the magazines on the way to the station. But, for some reason, the ticket machines will be working and I'll reach the platform just as a train's pulling in and for once there won't be a points failure or a signalling fault or a body on the line and I get whisked to my destination in record time and I'm the first one there. Again.

So yet again guess who arrived at our café first? It had become 'our' café, mine and Ellen's, although it was my discovery, and barely a day goes by when I don't pop in to read or make notes over a cup of tea away from the all too close confines of home. The waitress had served me many times before and I nearly always have the same thing, but still she stood there, pen poised over her order pad.

'Um, hi. A pot of English breakfast tea then please, *as usual*. With milk. And a plain croissant. Jam, no butter please. Apricot, if you have it. Or cherry. Thank you.'

I was deep in my book by the time Ellen finally put in an appearance, her first word, as it so often was, not 'hello' but 'sorry'.

'Sorry, sorry, sorry!' She kissed me and gave me a hug. 'I had to run half the way here – the tube—'

'Yeah, yeah. I know. You had to listen to the driver tell you all about his prostate problem before the train would move off and then you had to rescue a nun who'd fallen on the tracks . . . Never mind, you're here now.' She was wearing an orange tie-dye T-shirt and red velvet hipster trousers, a combination that only she could possibly carry off. Ellen's one of those people who can throw on a disgusting pair of jeans tugged from the bottom of her laundry basket and some manky old top that you wouldn't pay 20p for in a charity shop and she'll look gorgeous and funky and stylish but in a blasé, couldn't-care-less kind of way.

The waitress came over, deposited my tea on the table, and kissed Ellen on both cheeks.

'Ciao, Elena!'

'Ciao, Paola!'

'*Caffè latte?* Almond croissant?'

'*Si*, Paola. *Grazie*.' Ellen sank into her chair and started divesting herself of her usual array of baggage: hat, Filofax, magazine, two bags, mobile phone, sunglasses, cigarettes . . .

'How come I never get this?' I straightened my one, small handbag on the seat beside me as if it would magically tidy her chaos on the other side of the table. 'You go somewhere all of three times and already they know exactly what you want and the waitress treats you like her long-lost sister.'

'Oh, George. It's only because I got into a chat with her about her little boy and the problems he's been having at school.'

'How do you get into these conversations? I know you – you can't be on a bus for thirty seconds before the conductor's asking you whether he should tell his mother he's realized he's gay.'

'You do it too.'

'I don't.'

'You *do* – only you're intelligent enough to have made it into a grown-up career.'

'It's *so* not the same thing.'

Ellen tucked her hair behind her ears and sipped at her latte.

'Touchy toots. Why isn't it? You're good at listening, finding out what makes people tick. Any good?' she said, changing tack abruptly as she picked up the novel I'd been reading. She started to read the page where my bookmark was.

'No, you can't borrow it.'

'I'm only having a look.'

We've been through this one a thousand times. Never

leave your book unattended if Ellen's in the vicinity – not even for one minute. Perhaps you think it'll be fine while you nip to the loo but when you come back she says she's absolutely hooked and please can she borrow it – just for a day or two, you won't even miss it, she'll give it straight back. And then, three weeks later, you find it on her kitchen worktop, spreadeagled and smeary with butter like a spatchcocked chicken, and it turns out she got bored or she couldn't follow who was who so she gave up on it and, oh, was it yours? She'd forgotten, no she hadn't, she was just about to give it back to you but did you have anything else you could lend her instead? Something without so many things going on, something she didn't have to think about too much.

She lit a cigarette.

'And don't sigh at me, George. I need a fag after the journey I've had.'

'You said you were giving up.'

'I *am*.' She took an exaggeratedly long drag. 'But probably not today.'

I waved away the smoke and she gave me a look, the two of us slotting into our regular performance we have acted out a thousand times before, the way sisters do.

'Anyway . . .' I stirred my tea to make a questioning pause, 'so who are you in love with this week?'

'Bitch.' Ellen pretended to be aggrieved.

'Trollop.'

'That's so unfair!' But she laughed, scattering almonds and icing sugar from her croissant as she waved it around. 'Promise not to do your teacher-face? He's called José. He's one hundred per cent drop-dead gorgeous and—'

'Never mind his blazing brown eyes and cute bum – what's he *like*? That means personality, by the way, not penile dimensions.'

'Well, he writes poetry . . .'

41

'Oh. *Poetry*. So he's got a steady job then? I *am* glad. I thought for one second you might have gone for someone who had less career sense than a battery chicken.'

'Oh, shut up. He's got a real job, too.'

'No – let me guess. He's a top corporate lawyer? An international banker? A TV producer?'

'Ha ha. No, he's not some dull suit type . . .'

The words '*like Stephen*' hovered, unspoken, in the air between us.

'. . . He's a motorbike courier actually, but it's only temporary.'

I slid my teacup to one side and laid my head on the table.

'Call me when it's all over, will you?'

Ellen is clearly making some sort of world-record attempt in the 'Longest Succession of Unsuitable Boyfriends for One Woman' challenge. Mostly, they fall into one of two distinct categories, with her swinging pendulum-like between the two extremes; the earnest, intellectual ones who wear fleeces and talk about fractals, and the dumb, gorgeous ones who barely know what a fleece is, never mind a fractal, but they stroke bits of Ellen's anatomy in public and as long as they're good in bed she doesn't care that they don't attempt to make conversation. Neither type tend to be especially well endowed in the job department. Ellen claims she just doesn't fancy 'career types', insisting that they are boring, arrogant workaholics who 'don't have a real life and brown-nose their bosses'. I'm pretty sure she just can't handle the challenge of a relationship with anyone who is more sorted out on the career front than she is. And, given that, at the age of twenty-seven, she still doesn't seem to have a clue about what she wants to do 'when she grows up' or if she's going to make a serious go of her jewellery, this considerably reduces the pool of potential men.

'Not everyone is lucky enough to have Mr Perfect,

you know.' Ellen exhaled sharply. 'Anyway, how is Stephen-with-a-p-h?'

'Oh, behave.' When I first met Stephen, he tended to introduce himself as 'Stephen – with a "p-h" ', as if the other person was about to write his name down. I think it comes from having to spell it out for name tags at conferences and business courses. Ellen witnessed him in the act a couple of times and now calls him Stephen-with-a-p-h or Mr P-h or even *the* P-h – often right to his face. Stephen, being Stephen, is never quite sure whether Ellen means it as an affectionate joke or whether she's just taking the piss.

'He's fine. Stephen's always fine.'

'And . . . ?'

It was no longer even expressed as a full question. There was no need to fill in the blanks any more.

'And – nothing. We were thinking of looking at this hotel near Oxford next weekend.' I shrugged. 'Or the one after.' Going to Look at Prospective Wedding Venues is an activity we revive from time to time; I love it really, it's just I get depressed because they're never *exactly* what I had in mind.

'Ah, the blushing bride-to-be, all aflutter with nerves and excitement as the Big Day draws near . . . only another three and a half years to go.'

'Oh, fuck off.'

'Well, why don't you break it off, for fuck's sake? If you're not going to put the poor old P-h out of his misery, then get shot of him and at least have the fun of shagging someone new.'

'That's how you see men, isn't it? I've used this one up, now who's next in line?'

'Don't change the subject. If you really wanted to marry him, you wouldn't keep pissing about looking for the perfect venue and the perfect car and the perfect dress, would you? You could wear tartan pyjamas and hitch a ride on a rubbish lorry and it'd still be perfect.'

'I'm *so* glad I didn't ask you to organize the wedding. You know I *am* going to marry Stephen. At some point.

There will be a wedding, OK? Absolutely. Definitely. I just want everything to be exactly right, that's all. Why do I have to be in such a rush?'

'Er – because you're thirty-four and your eggs will soon be wanting little walking frames?'

'Thank you for that, sister dear. That's not an issue. I told you. I'm not having children.'

'Yes, I *know* you told me. A hundred times. I didn't believe you then and I don't believe you now.'

'I don't care whether you believe me or not. I've made a rational decision and I feel very comfortable with that.'

'Oh, puhleese. Spare me the therapy-speak, George. It's total pants. You'd be a lovely mum. I know you say you don't want sproglets because you might die and leave them motherless . . .'

'. . . like us, yes. That seems perfectly reasonable. It's not an emotional reaction. I've weighed up all the pros and cons.'

Ellen rolled her eyes.

'And what does the love of your life think about your *rational* decision?'

I paused for a moment. Ellen doesn't do pauses, not as such, so she always thinks you haven't heard her or you don't understand instead of that you might actually think for two seconds before you open your mouth.

'Mr *P-h*. Remember him?'

I sighed and fiddled with the lid of the teapot.

'We don't discuss it all that much . . .'

'But you have told him, right?'

'I'm pretty sure he knows how I feel, yes.'

'Eh, hello? Queen of Communication? – i.e. you haven't told him?'

'Well . . . I've made it crystal clear in my own way. Besides, it's not as if I'm dragging him into Mothercare every five minutes to gush over the little bootees, is it?'

'No, no, no. Have you said, "Stephen-with-a-p-h, there's something you should know – I, Georgia

44

Abrams, being of totally unsound mind, do not want to have any mini-Georgias or mini-Stephens-with-or-without-p-h's so please will you kindly keep your sperms at a safe distance from my eggs for evermore?"'

'You have such a charming way with words, you know that?'

She blew a raspberry.

'You're being mean. If you really loved the P-h, you'd tell him that little peeps are off the agenda and give him the chance to find someone else if he wanted to.'

'He knows. I told you.'

Ellen licked her finger and dabbed at the scattered flaked almonds on and around her plate, not saying a word.

'He *does*.'

Of course he does. You don't have to set everything out in black and white when you're a couple, do you? All sorts of things are just *understood*.

4

The Abrams Sunday Brunch

Every Sunday, whoever's around heads home to gather for brunch, which is something of a mixed blessing. On the plus side, there's seeing Dad and Quinn and Ellen and Matt and Izzy and the kids. And, on the minus side, there's seeing Dad and Quinn and Ellen and Matt and Izzy and the kids. I love the moment of anticipation when the doorbell rings and you don't know who it might be: Unc, with or without Audrey and the cousins in tow, or a neighbour or one of Quinn's friends or an entirely new face; but then comes the moment after that moment, when you see who it actually is. And if it's Unc, well then that's sort of nice because I love Unc to bits but, on the other hand, he does insist on asking me every single time when Stephen and I are going to name the day. And he always says, 'Shrunk anyone famous recently?' because he refuses to understand a) my explanations of the distinctions between psychiatrists, psychoanalysts, and psychotherapists and plain ordinary counsellors like myself, bundling us all together under the general heading of 'shrinks' and b) the concept of confidentiality, which means that I can't go around naming my clients to all and sundry. Or if it's one of Quinn's floaty friends, then you find your shoulders sinking because they're barely in the door before they're requesting soya milk for their coffee, only they've brought their own coffee and it's made of dandelion root or seaweed or hedge clippings and then they're off, wittering on about their auras or their chakras and complimenting Quinn on placing a curved object near the front door because it slows down the flow of chi as it has to go r-o-u-n-d it, when you know that all it means is that she left a jug or the flour jar on the hall table because she got caught up with something else and has forgotten about it. I mean, just because Quinn used to grow her own bean sprouts and has a set of rusty wind chimes in the garden doesn't mean she's a complete sucker, thank God.

Years ago, when my parents were first married, Mum used to cook Sunday lunch, with a roast and crispy potatoes and carrots and cabbage and gravy. I can only just about remember her doing it though, because, when I was five or so, Dad went to New York to see his sister Rachel and when he came back he was singing the praises of *brunch*. Once he explained that, with brunch, a) everyone helped themselves and b) you didn't need to make lunch as well, my mother became an instant convert.

Over the years, we've tinkered with the details, but the fundamentals of the original winning formula have remained unchanged. Any time from ten a.m. onwards – well, up until one-ish – you can turn up, eat, talk, squabble or just read the Sunday papers. You can bring anyone you like, an old friend or even someone you've only just met (that was my mother's particular speciality), so long as you phone before Dad has left to fetch the bagels. We have plain ones and poppyseed ones and onion ones (which I hate) – and smoked salmon and fresh cream cheese and those lovely, crunchy sweet-sour cucumbers. Everything is set out on platters on the big kitchen table and there's tea and coffee and orange juice and a massive bowl of fruit and, now, raisin bread. The raisin bread is a Quinn

47

addition because she makes it every Saturday and, even though as a general rule Quinn and fine cuisine – or even edible cuisine – are two notions that rarely rub shoulders in the same sentence, when it comes to raisin bread, she has no equal.

So the point of Sunday brunch is that it's supposed to be a family thing – but that it's always better if you have at least one non-family person there. Having a non-Abrams, Mum said, stopped squabbles getting out of hand because you had to behave at least half nicely in front of other people.

Once, years and years ago, a schoolfriend of Ellen's stayed over on Saturday night and gave our carefully laid-out brunch a sneering look.

'What's that supposed to be then?' she'd said, as if surveying a spread of sheeps' eyes and monkey brains.

'Brunch, of course, thicko. We always have it on Sundays.' Ellen, charming as ever.

'Don't you have Weetabix or anything *normal*?'

I flushed with shame, of course, but Ellen was entirely unperturbed.

'No, because we're not *boring* and *normal*. We—'

'Ellen!' Dad, frowning. 'There should be some cereal in the larder for your *guest*.' Abrams Family Rules: No. 1 – Be a good host.

The alleged 'proper' grown-up in my family is my dad, David, who's sixty-two. He's quite wise, I think – well – wiser than the rest of us, but no-one, least of all Dad, would call him a Real Grown-Up. He still lives in the same house he bought with Mum over thirty-five years ago, only now he lives in it with Quinn, my step-mother, who shares his deep, abiding love of never throwing anything away. Untidiness is almost a relig-ion to Dad. He equates any kind of neatness or order with being a) boring, b) conventional and c) repressed. He believes that it's simply not possible to be a truly creative person if you have a tidy desk. But he is brilliant; my dad has a way of looking at the world that's completely original – just when you feel you know exactly what you think about something, then he'll say something that makes you question it all over again.

So the worst thing about Sunday brunch, aside from the fact that no more than two Abrams can ever be in the same room for more than ten minutes without bickering, is the house itself, which acts as a kind of magnet for all known clutter in the northern hemisphere. Every time I go, I stand on the front path a moment, hoping that a magical transformation will have taken place and that I will enter a calm world of ordered papers and well-wiped surfaces, a beautiful place where things are put away after use and where a flat surface may remain empty for more than five seconds. Maybe, *this* time, it will be different.

The Abrams Family Ten Commandments
Regarding the Matter of Mess

1 Chaos is thy God. Thou shalt have no other gods before It.
2 Thou shalt not venerate tidiness, nor make it holy, for if thou dost, thou shalt be called 'uptight' and 'anally retentive' and be cast out even unto the suburbs to be amongst thine own kind wherein all things shall be put away rather than being scattered or piled in diverse heaps, according to the wishes of thy God, Chaos.
3 Thou shalt not abhor mess, but honour it as a holy sign that those who have made it thus have true creativity and artistic leanings, remembering this also that he who dwells in clutter wastes not his days in fretting on matters of dust nor in wiping his worktops.
4 Remember the Sabbath day. Thou shalt not tidy up even though thou mayst have guests turning up at any moment.
5 Honour thy father and stepmother for they dwell in the House of Chaos and have made thee welcome.

6 Thou shalt not throw anything away for it might come in handy later.

7 Thou shalt not file anything in a place where it might be easily found.

8 Thou shalt not take thy newspapers regularly for recycling but shalt let them accumulate in the hall until thou canst no longer get past.

9 Thou shalt not bear false witness against an untidy person by saying that he has 'lost' things, for know that these things are but only mislaid and will surely come to light before another moon has waxed and waned.

10 Thou shalt not covet thy neighbour's house nor his empty worktops, nor his unencumbered chairs nor his plumped-up cushions nor his polished taps for these things are a sign that he worships the false God of Order.

Sunday

Quinn answered the door. Quinn isn't her real name, but I presume you worked that out already because it's ridiculous. Her real name is Margaret, which she hates and most of the people in her life have called her Maggie, which she hates too. Then she met Dad about ten years ago, no, it was twelve, because someone brought her along to his surprise 50th birthday party and introduced her, saying 'This is Maggie Quinn,' and what with the music and everyone talking and my dad being a bit deaf in one ear, he only heard the Quinn bit, so he called her that and then they did awful, embarrassing, vague jiving round the sitting room and the next thing we knew they were saying they were deeply in love and snogging in the kitchen and generally making us all want to vomit. Quinn's not so bad, aside from her name and the fact that her hair is about fifteen shades too red for a woman of fifty-three and her cooking . . . and her clothes. Don't get me started on the clothes.

'Georgia! How nice.' She leaned forward to kiss me

on both cheeks and I turned my face so as not to be impaled on her lightning-bolt earrings. Quinn favours 'interesting' jewellery – strings of big, clunky beads, metal cuff-bracelets that look like they've been purloined from a suit of armour, and, most of all, outsize earrings that catch in your hair when she kisses you. The earrings are quite at odds with her clothes, which have that faded, comfy, worn-and-washed-a-thousand-times look. They're all slightly shapeless, skirts with no proper waistbands, jackets with no lapels, flat shoes that look like larger versions of the sort that children have so that their toes won't be squashed. This morning, she was wearing a green crushed velvet skirt – not a skirt made of crushed velvet but a velvet skirt that had obviously been scrunched up in the bottom of the wardrobe – a not-matching sludgy green long-sleeved T-shirt that had seen better days and, inevitably, her famous patch-work jacket from which she is rarely parted. The jacket has those wooden toggle buttons that you love when you're about six years old and it's made up of hundreds of tiny squares of material, in every colour you can think of (and some you can't). Quinn calls it her 'Joseph's coat' and claims that 'it goes with everything' because it contains so many colours whereas, in fact, it goes with absolutely nothing except possibly the contents of a skip. At a pinch, it might make passable cushion covers for a gestalt therapy centre.

'Is Stephen coming today?' Quinn really likes Stephen, a fact which makes me feel slightly beholden to her because she's the only one of our lot who is actively nice to him. Ellen and Matt take the piss out of Stephen as if it's a sport they must practise constantly or they'll lose their mastery of it. Stephen rarely comes to brunch in any case because his parents like to see him for Sunday lunch and they live much further out, so it's hard to fit in both.

'Yes, he is for once. Later though.' I came into the hallway.

My father was sitting on the stairs, peering at the spines of the books next to him. By his feet, perched on the bottom step, were a can of shaving foam and a packet of toothpaste.

There are narrow bookshelves that line the stairs all the way up, which in theory is a sensible use of space but in practice means my father spends endless hours trundling up and down the stairs, shouting to anyone who happens to be within earshot, 'Have you seen that Kowalski book? Paperback, brown jacket, white hand-lettering.' He can never remember the title of anything, but he always recalls what a book looks like. When Dad does manage to find the book he's looking for, he then loses it in the piles of papers in his study for a year or two until eventually it resurfaces and he thinks to put it back on a shelf. *A* shelf, not *the* shelf it came from, of course. No. That would be too easy, too straight-forward, too conventional. My family mock me because my books are arranged in a logical way – fiction separated from non-fiction, non-fiction divided by subject, fiction ordered alphabetically by author name. Why not? That's how they do it in a bookshop or a library. As I often point out to Dad, people who run bookshops don't arrange books that way because they're uptight or kowtowing to convention – they do it so that you can find the book you want in less than a minute. But he *likes* having everything mixed in together, he *likes* to be sidetracked. That's why you find him sitting on the stairs reading a dictionary or smelling the pages of an old, leather-bound volume of Byron or completely absorbed in one of our cherished childhood Tintin books. Dad always has a book or a newspaper in his hand. In fact, if by chance you catch sight of him and he's not clutching some form of reading matter, he doesn't look quite like himself – he looks slightly unfamiliar, in the way that a photograph that's been taken by a stranger often misses the moment when you most look like you.

'Hi, Dad. Have you done the bagel run yet?' I bent to

kiss him. Needless to say, as it's Dad who fetches the bagels, it does not involve any kind of a 'run'. He gets in the car – 'so that they're as fresh as possible' – but actually because it's a ten-minute walk each way and if he drives, he doesn't even need to put on shoes. He wears his slippers. He's even been known to go in his pyjamas with his awful old beige raincoat on top.

'Yes, I have, bossyboots. It's all in the kitchen.'

'Good.' I squeezed by him to go up to the bath-room.

'Hang on,' said Quinn. She handed me the toothpaste and shaving foam without comment.

The stairs, which in any normal household are just what they should be – a simple means of getting from one floor to another – double as a temporary resting place for all manner of objects. Any item that is meant to be taken upstairs is laid on the bottom step, so that you can't miss it. Even if you've never been in the house before and couldn't possibly be expected to know where said item is destined for, you're still supposed to carry it up at least as far as the small round table on the landing, a kind of base camp for stray objects. Things that are to go downstairs are also, confusingly, put on the round table so you have no way of knowing whether any given item is a) waiting to be taken down or b) in transit, on its way to a bedroom or bathroom. And don't think that you could work it out using some kind of everyday logic, like 'Ah-hah – a kebab skewer, I'll take that down to the kitchen,' because, inevitably, you then run into Quinn who informs you that she needs the skewer in the top bathroom because she thinks that something strange is blocking the plughole.

After I'd been to the loo, I came down again and into the kitchen, bracing myself to expect the worst, but it only registered about a 5 on the Abrams Chaos Scale. There were the inevitable papers on the table, the worktop was crowded with last night's dirty dishes, there were bowls of soaking pulses on the window ledge and the dishwasher door was open, waiting to trip someone up, but it can be a lot, lot worse.

Underneath the mess and the crumbs and the dirty dishes, there's quite an attractive kitchen, with wooden worktops and a quarry-tiled floor. There's an old dresser at one end packed with a plethora of odd crockery, each piece with its own story: there on the top shelf is the rosebud plate, sole survivor of a set of six, one of our parents' wedding presents; two mis-shapen pottery cats with pocked glaze I made when I was eleven in memory of Black Nose and White Nose, my grandmother's two cats, that's Granny, Dad's mother; four 1930s cocktail glasses that shine with rainbow colours when they catch the light – those had been Grandma's, Mum's mother; a peculiar earthen-ware cow Matt brought back from Morocco; a sludge-coloured mug with a black and white yin-yang symbol on one side, evidently a contribution from one of Quinn's friends; and, tucked out of harm's way near the top, the three eggcups from when we were little, with our names painted on by Mum: Georgia, Matthew, Ellen. Mine has a hen painted on it, Matthew's a cockerel, and Ellen's a little yellow chick. I even remember Mum painting them and me saying they were lovely, but really just feeling horribly envious; I wanted to have an eggcup with a little fluffy chick on it – especially as that was Dad's name for me – not a boring old stupid hen, but I couldn't say anything.

'Georgia, any chance you could do the scramblies?'

The only cooked element of our brunch is scrambled eggs – or 'scramblies' as they're known in our family, which sounds horribly self-conscious and cute, but it's just because that's what I called them when I was little and the name stuck, the same way we still call plums 'plungs' and lightbulbs 'blubs' as in 'this bloody blub on the landing's gone again!' There's nothing worse than other people's family expressions, is there? I hate it when Quinn uses our family words for things, it sets my teeth on edge, like people putting on a pretentious accent when they ask for *'filet'* steak in a restaurant. Also, I always do the scramblies, the scrambled eggs, I mean, whenever I come to brunch, so why does she always ask me as if it's a one-off and it's only just occurred to her to mention it?

'Of course. Perhaps we should clear the table first?' I said pointedly.

Dad was surrounded by his usual nest of papers. He looked up vaguely, like a tortoise waking from hibernation.

'Mm?'

'Dad! Table! Please, please, *please* can you clear off your papers? At least while I wipe it?'

He started slowly shuffling the bits together into something vaguely resembling a pile, then looked round and balanced them right on the edge of the dresser, the only surface close enough for him not to have to get up again.

'Or they could go in your study maybe?' The study's even worse than the rest of the house, but it's so bad that attempting to tidy it would be like trying to rake up autumn leaves in a high wind; a few more piles of paper here and there aren't going to make much difference. God knows how Dad manages to work in there, because it's more of a room-sized in-tray than a study. My father has some kind of allergy to empty surfaces – as soon as he sees one, he is under a compulsion to cover it up with many, many layers of papers – journals and correspondence and sketches and notes and jottings on the backs of old envelopes, all held in place by his collection of hardly-touched mugs of cold coffee. I've never, ever let Stephen in there. His parents' house is immaculate. And all the surfaces are not just empty, they're polished. And when you sit down, you don't have to check your chair first to make sure there isn't a book or a toast plate or a bit of left-behind Lego on it.

'Do I surmise correctly that Stephen will be turning up later?'

'I'm not asking you to roll out the red carpet, am I? Just make the place look passably civilized.'

Quinn, wiping the table and swooshing the crumbs straight onto the floor and all over the chairs instead of into her hand, looked up for a moment, but she didn't say anything.

'Oh – *civilized*? Well, of course, that's the most important thing.' My father leant back in his chair and laughed softly to himself.

'Don't be annoying.' I took out the eggs from the fridge and ventured into a cupboard for a large bowl.

Out of the corner of my eye I noticed Quinn piling the bagels into some awful dark brown palm-leaf basket. They've got a perfectly good set of plain white china which I prefer to use so that it all matches.

'Or we could use one of the white platters?' I said, cracking the eggs into the bowl, and not looking at her.

'*Georgia* . . .' Dad's voice came from behind his newspaper. He always clears up afterwards and loads the dishwasher, but keeps from under our feet while we're laying everything out.

'Oh,' said Quinn. 'Yes. A plate. If you like.'

I caught Dad looking at me.

'No. Sorry. The basket's fine.' Quinn favours tableware made out of old bits of dead twig wherever possible or wooden bowls that look as if they've been hand-hewn from fallen trees or strange, sludgy stoneware mugs made by her pottery friends – cups that seem to have been excavated from under a rock, the colours of moss and damp earth and mouldering leaves, their aimless markings like the slime trails left by a slug or a snail.

I delved under the sink for a new cloth and surreptitiously shoved the old one deep down into the bin while Quinn had her back turned, then I gave the worktop a proper wipe-down.

'I brought some flowers if you want to stick them in

a vase.' I gestured to Quinn. She drew out the bunch of white lilies from their paper and buried her face in them, emerging again with a streak of bright orange pollen on her nose.

'Oh, how lovely!' She held them for Dad to smell. 'Thank you, Georgia.'

'That's OK.' I don't know why she was thanking me; they weren't for her really, just for the house.

I was dishing out the eggs when my brother Matt arrived with his wife Isobel and their kids, Bonnie and Daniel, who came running up to me and clutched me round my legs.

'Auntie Gee! Auntie Gee!'

I squatted down to hug them. Being an auntie seems to me the best of both worlds: you get to spend a small amount of time with children, children you love enormously and who seem to be quite fond of you, then after an hour or two – just when you're thinking that's enough hilarity and riot for one day – you get to give them back and return to your nice, calm, ordered, non-sticky existence. Bonnie is four and destined to be a major captain of industry, I suspect. She's very good at telling other people what to do. Daniel is two and his main ambition in life so far is to be Bonnie.

Isobel came over and gave me a hug.

'Hi. D'you want a hand?'

'No, you need a break. Sit down. Matt – pour Izzy a coffee, will you?' Matt rarely helps unless he's prodded – no wonder Izzy looks so exhausted the whole time.

'Yes, ma'am!'

Matt is two and a half years younger than me and a lot less hopeless than Ellen, but that's not saying much. Unlike Ellen, he does at least have what passes for a normal job – he edits reference books and his office floor has even more piles of paper on it than Dad's does, so it must be a family trait.

More arrivals

At about eleven thirty Stephen appeared and, as there was no safe haven next to Quinn or Isobel, he was forced to sit next to Matt, who immediately started to quiz him.

'So, how's tricks? What's the latest news from the fascinating world of management consultancy?'

'Matt, bugger off! Stephen, just ignore him if he gets too annoying.' Matt's always winding people up about their jobs.

Stephen sat perched on the edge of his chair, as if he might make a run for it at any moment.

'Actually, you may mock but it really is rather interesting at the moment – ' I saw Matt doing his pretending-to-find-it-all-fascinating face, he furrows his brow slightly and gives a small nod every few seconds. I shot him a warning look. I wish Stephen would just give as good as he gets, but he's far too nice.

Then Ellen turned up.

'Hiya, everyone!' She breezed in, then came to kiss each of us in turn. 'Have I missed the scramblies? I'm *starved*.' Ellen rarely goes more than half an hour without eating so her idea of being 'starved' mustn't be taken too literally.

'They've all gone, babes . . . but I can do you some more if you really are hungry.'

'Oh, will you? Thanks, George. Budge up, P-h.' She squashed an extra chair in next to Stephen. 'So . . . what's occurring? What have I missed? Any news? Is there any coffee?' Ellen's always asking questions then not waiting for the answers because, despite the fact that she's always late herself, she's incredibly impatient with everyone else and doesn't listen properly. 'God, I feel completely wrecked. We went on *such* a bender last night. Frozen flavoured vodkas. Cranberry, lemon . . . everything.'

'Weren't you at work?' I caught Dad's eye. Ellen normally works at the wine bar on Saturday nights.

'Nah. I swapped shifts with Tony – but I forgot to tell Brian. He went totally apeshit, left about a thousand messages on my mobile.' Brian is Ellen's boss and we all think he's in love with her, but Ellen says he's 'too old' (he's thirty-six), 'too short' (he's about five foot eight) and 'called Brian' (which he is, but I don't see why that has to disqualify him).

'Aren't you a bit *old* to be going on benders?' Matt said.

'You're just envious because you've traded in your social life for a sofa, a video and a pair of comfy slippers.'

'*You're* the one who should be envious.' Matt squeezed Isobel's hand. 'At least I'm not still pretending to be a teenager at nearly thirty.'

'I'm not even twenty-eight yet!'

Stephen was looking from one to the other of them, then over at me, as if wanting to be rescued. You think he'd be used to it by now, but Stephen never knows quite how to take our family squabbles. His family don't believe in disagreements, all that raising your voice and getting heated, so even the most minor altercation he regards as the beginnings of World War Three.

I handed Ellen a cup of coffee and she stood up.

'Just going to check on the garden.' Dad hates the fact that Ellen smokes but he won't go so far as to stop her smoking in the house because that would go against all his most dearly held beliefs about the importance of personal freedom. Matt hasn't got time for such high-flown idealism but just insists that she's not to smoke in the same room as the children.

'Don't be long – your eggs are nearly ready.'

Matt gave me a look.

'What?'

He shrugged.

'You shouldn't run round after her the whole time. Let her cook her own eggs if she's missed them.'

'I cooked yours too, and I didn't notice you begging to make your own.'

'I was here before they ran out. Crucial difference. And I don't ask you to lend me money or do my tax return for me either.'

I noticed Isobel squeezing his arm.

'C'mon, Matty, don't give her a hard time. The eggs were delicious, Georgia – as always. Thank you.'

'Thanks.' I smiled at Izzy, then Matt came over and kissed the top of my head.

'I didn't mean to upset you, Gee. Just – you know – Ellen's old enough to take care of herself. Or she should be, at least.'

'Yeah,' I sighed. 'I know.' Then I tipped the scrambled eggs out onto a plate, laid two neat triangles of buttered toast alongside. 'Give her a shout, will you? Before it gets cold.'

5

Family matters

I was just getting ready for bed when the phone rang.

'What can they *possibly* want at this time of night?' Stephen said as he lay in bed reading the newspaper. For 'they', read my family. Stephen's parents never phone after nine forty-five p.m.

'It's only just after eleven.'

'Perhaps now would be a good time to check if your answerphone is working?' He smiled.

I ignored him and answered the phone. It was Matt. His birthday is this week, and he wanted to go out for dinner with Isobel on Saturday. Matt explained that Ellen had volunteered to babysit and he'd agreed.

'I think it's good for her to have to be the responsible one occasionally – but Iz can't believe I said yes. She said she'd sooner leave Bonnie in charge of Ellen than the other way round.'

'Can't you tell Ellie that Izzy had already booked a babysitter so you don't need her now?'

'No, because we've tried all the babysitters we know and none of them can do this Saturday. It's too short notice.'

'Why didn't you ring them earlier?'

'Because I'm not you. I'm not that organized and I thought Ellen would be OK.'

Stephen rustled his paper.

'I do hope your brother's not trying to get you to babysit,' he said, too loudly. I mouthed 'Sssh!'

'Is there any chance you could do it *with* Ellen? So she still thinks *she's* doing it but we'd have a proper grown-up there too?'

'Well, I don't know . . .' I lowered my voice. 'I always see Stephen on Saturday night.'

'Bring him too – you can snuggle up on the sofa like teenagers.'

'We were *supposed* to be going to see a film,' Stephen said.

'We could get a video instead? And have a takeaway?' Stephen shook his newspaper crossly. 'Crispy duck?' I said seductively. 'Stir-fried noodles with prawns and ginger?' I don't eat prawns and never cook them either, but Stephen loves them, so he jumps at every possible chance to have them. 'Lovely big TV,' I reminded him.

'All right, but I can't get there till eight and I'm not changing any nappies,' Stephen said from behind the paper.

'OK, Matt, I'll do it.'

'Thank you, thank you. Our table's at eight. Can you come by half seven?'

'Sure. I'll come at seven, then I can help with the kids.'

'You're a star. Thanks, Gee. I owe you one. Hang on—' I heard Izzy's voice in the background. 'Iz sends her love and thanks and says she doesn't know how you've turned out to be so wonderful when I'm such a pain in the bum – well, thank you for that, my dearest darling sweetheart . . . she loves me really.'

I said goodbye and hung up.

'And I get to have sweet-and-sour pork,' Stephen said.

'God, you're really going to milk this, aren't you?'

'Yes.' He looked over his paper at me and smiled. 'They don't deserve you.'

'Don't be daft. It's only one evening, no big deal. Anyway, it's always nice to see the kids.'

'You're very good with them. Bonnie's quite a handful.'

'Oh, she's not really. She just knows her own mind, that's all.'

'She's definitely an Abrams, that's for sure.'

'Meaning?'

'She's a character. She's selfish and stubborn.' He looked down at his paper again. 'Thank God you're not like your family.'

'Stephen! Don't say that.'

'What?' He kept one eye on the paper.

'Bonnie's sweet . . .' Stephen's expression was incredulous. 'She is – OK, she is a bit stubborn, but lots of kids that age are. And she's bright and sharp and funny and I love her, so please don't be like that about her. And another thing – I *am* like my family.'

Stephen laughed.

'Now, come on, darling, that really is ridiculous! You're always going on about how diferent you are – and you're absolutely right. They're all chaotic and unreliable and hopeless and you, thank the Lord, are the perfect model of order and reliability – my ideal woman.' He smiled and patted the bed. 'Come on, come to bed now. I've said I'll babysit with you, so don't be cross with me.'

An auntie in action

By seven on Saturday, I was upstairs, helping Matt give the kids their bath.

'You be the shark!' Bonnie bossed me. 'I'm the diver and Daniel is all eaten up.'

'I'm not eaten!' Daniel stood up in alarm. 'I'm a diver too!'

'Sit down, Daniel, or you'll slip.' Matt squeezed out the flannel and attempted to wash Daniel, who squirmed out of his grasp like a slithery fish.

'All divers have to have their wetsuits wiped with special anti-shark deterrent before diving,' I said to Bonnie. 'Chief Diver – present yourself for inspection.' Bonnie stood to attention and I seized my chance to wash her down with a soapy flannel. 'Chief Diver – Passed and Ready!'

'Me now! Me pass and ready!' Daniel pulled at my arm. I started to wash him, then caught Matt watching me.

'What?'

He smiled.

'You're good with them, you know. You should have your own.'

'No. This is easy. I'd go crazy doing it full-time. Come on, Daniel – out you get! Here's your special cloak.' I lifted him out and enfolded him in a towel.

'Why? You're good-tempered and very patient. You're miles better than I am and even I manage.' He got Bonnie out and started to dry her.

I shook my head.

'It doesn't have to be with Stephen, you know.'

I turned on him.

'It's nothing to do with Stephen. Why do you say that?'

Matt laughed.

'Well, it should be to do with Stephen as you're engaged to him, wouldn't you say?'

'I didn't mean that – don't be annoying.' I lowered my voice. 'I meant I don't want kids of my own, full stop. Stephen isn't the issue.' I stood Daniel up and started towelling him dry.

'Why don't you wan' kids, Auntie Gee?' Bonnie said.

I shot Matt a look.

'Because they couldn't possibly be as nice as you and Daniel,' I said.

'Daniel's not nice – he took my big fire engine and he won't eat his carrots.'

'He *borrowed* your fire engine, Bonnie – and you

must learn to share your things.' Matt sighed. 'Jim-jams on now, be a good girl.' He passed me Daniel's pyjamas. 'He'll need a nappy too, but I can do that. I don't want to use up all the auntie goodwill in one go.'

'It's fine. I'll do it.'

I laid Daniel down and dipped to kiss his tummy, then turned it into a raspberry, making him giggle. He smelled soft and clean and sweet. I put the nappy on then pulled his pyjama top half on over his head.

'Where's Daniel gone?' I said. Daniel laughed. He never tires of this; he thinks it's the most hilarious joke ever. 'Have you seen Daniel, Matt?'

'No. I wonder where he can be.' Matt smiled.

'He's under his *pyjamas*,' said Bonnie as if we were quite unbelievably stupid.

'Listen, Gee, all I'm saying is that I never thought I'd have kids either before I met Iz. If you're with the right person, suddenly it all slots into place and you start thinking, "God, I might actually be able to do this."'

'Well, Izzy's great, she'd be the right person for anyone – but I don't think it's practical for me to have kids with her too, is it?' I stood up, then scooped Daniel into my arms. 'Anyway, Stephen is exactly right for me,' I added. 'He really is.'

Once upon a time . . .

Stephen arrived just before eight, but Matt and Izzy had already left for the restaurant by then, of course. I was quite glad they'd gone – after my conversation with Matt, I knew he wouldn't be able to resist trying to winkle out Stephen's views on having children.

'Hello, darling. Are they in bed yet?'

'Only just. I'm about to read them a story.'

He came into the sitting room and switched on the TV.

'Just want to catch a bit of the cricket.'

'You're not tempted by the joys of Babar or the Cat in the Hat then?'

'Who could resist? Tell you what – you make a start, sweetie, and I'll come up in a minute.'

Daniel was settled into his cot with a final bottle. He seemed happy enough, so I went through to Bonnie's room. She had got out of bed again, not surprisingly, and was doing somersaults across the floor. I frog-marched her back to bed and asked her to pick a story but she claimed to have read them all.

'OK, let's make one up then, shall we? How shall we begin?'

'Don't know. *You* make it up.'

'Well, I'll start it off. Once upon a time, there was a clever and beautiful princess . . . and what do you suppose her name was?'

'Her name was Bonnie and then what happened was she had all magic powers and there was a really, really bad witch and then this prince—'

The doorbell rang once more. I hoped Stephen would answer it but it's hard to lever him away from a cricket match once he's engrossed, so I stood up.

'Lie still now and I'll be back in two minutes. No getting up.'

Stephen was opening the door as I came down the stairs. It was Ellen.

'Well, well – it's the P-h! This is an unexpected treat. Am I babysitting you too?' Ellen swept in, kissing Stephen on her way past.

A nervous laugh from Stephen as he said hello.

'Hi, babes.'

'Where are Matzo and Izzy? Have they gone?'

'Yes, of course. It's ten past eight.'

'God, I'm only a couple of minutes late – he said to come at eight.'

'Really?' Stephen dug his hands down into his pockets. 'I believe their dinner reservation was for eight. Georgia's been here since before seven.'

'It doesn't matter – you're here now.'

Ellen dropped her bag on the floor and thundered up the stairs to see the kids.

'Sssh, Ellen! Don't get them all hyper – please.'

Stephen rolled his eyes at me, then returned to the joys of the cricket.

I followed her up. She went into Bonnie's room, tiptoeing with elaborate care even though Bonnie was wide awake and sitting up in bed.

'Auntie Ell! Auntie Ell!' Bonnie leapt out of bed and started jumping up and down.

'*Ellen*. She was nearly settled.'

'Play a game with me!'

'No. No more games, Bonnie – back to bed.'

'What shall we play?' Ellen doesn't understand about being firm.

'We mustn't keep her up or she'll be awful in the morning.'

'Just five minutes. Come on.'

'Five minutes then. But that's it.'

Ellen made a face at Bonnie, as if I were the big bad wolf. Thanks, Ellen, that's really helpful.

'Dressing up,' said Bonnie. 'I'm the king and – ' she pointed at Ellen, 'you're the queen—'

'What about Daniel?'

'Daniel's the servant and he goes in the dungeon for being bad.'

'It's the servant's day off,' I told her. 'We're not to disturb Daniel, so this is to be a nice, quiet game.'

'And what about your Auntie Georgia?' Ellen asked. 'Is she the dungeon guard?'

'Hilarious.'

'Auntie Gee,' Bonnie corrected her. She thought for a moment. 'Auntie Gee's the queen.'

'But you said *I* could be Queen.' Ellen sounded aggrieved, as if she really were playing the game with the same seriousness as Bonnie.

'No.' Bonnie pointed at Ellen again, as if ordering a courtier. 'You're the little princess.'

'But I'm not little.'

Bonnie looked at her as if she were being dumb.

'You are more littler than Auntie Gee.'

'Yes, that's true.'

'And more littler than me.'

Ellen looked at me and laughed. Out of the mouths of babes . . . I thought. Bonnie marched over to the dressing-up box and fished out a battered crown that I'd made for her a couple of months ago. I cut it out from a dismantled gold cardboard cake box, then stapled the bits together and stuck on coloured fruit gums for the jewels – just the way my mum did for me when I wanted to be a princess. A couple of them had fallen off or, more likely, been chewed off glue and all.

'Five minutes and no more,' I said. 'You start – I'm just checking on Daniel.' I shut the door and went through to Daniel's room.

Daniel was deeply asleep, his arms flung back in total abandonment, his bottle lying beside him. I pulled up his cotton blanket then kissed my fingertips and gently touched his forehead.

I stood there, watching him for a minute, seeing the slight rise and fall of the blanket as he breathed, then I went back into Bonnie's room. She was drooping with tiredness.

'Hail, Majesty – it is dark and we must retire to our bedchambers.'

'But I was about to get my coronet,' Ellen said.

'The coronation has been adjourned until tomorrow,' I said firmly, bending down to pick up Bonnie. She reached her arms up around me. I squeezed her tight then tucked her under the covers.

'Night, night, King – sleep tight.'

'Ni-nigh.' Her voice was already sleepy.

I motioned to Ellen with my head to go, then stayed to stroke Bonnie's hair for a few moments, until she was asleep. I love her when she's awake but she does zap your energy in no time. Now, when she was like this, her eyelids fluttering as she drifted into sleep, I felt almost overwhelmed with love for her.

Dressing up

Sometimes, when Georgia comes home from school, she gets herself a glass of lemonade, if there is any, or 'fancy water' which is the way Mummy drinks water, with a slice of lemon and ice cubes going clink, just like a grown-up drink. Matt still prefers milk, like a baby, like Ellen. Georgia spreads two slices of bread with butter and thick honey, then folds each one over to make a sandwich. Passes one to Matt with instructions not to drip honey everywhere. Raises the sandwich to her mouth and nibbles her way delicately along the fold – the best bit; this keeps her going until proper supper when Daddy comes home. Ellen is too small for honey sandwiches.

Matt plays with his Bat Cave, a papier-mâché one which Mummy made before Ellen was born. There's a secret door and a trapdoor with a chute down which your most deadliest enemy falls when he comes to get you. Matt wheels his toy Batmobile in and out of the cave and makes screechy noises as it takes a corner at speed. If Mummy is not having a little lie-down before supper, she plays with Georgia for a while: they raid the dressing-up box or her own wardrobe, for Joy doesn't mind a jot about Georgia trying on her things; Georgia goes clack-clacking along the tiled hall floor in strappy gold sandals or black suede high heels, an antique fringed shawl cascading over her small frame, a curtain of black embroidered with crimson. They are princesses in the palace, sporting cardboard crowns and ordering people's heads to be chopped off. They are opera singers, waving their arms about and singing at the tops of their voices, bellowing in a mixture of fake Italian and mangled English – 'Un bel di . . .' sings Joy, while Matt presses his palms flat over his ears and sings his own aria 'La-la-lah!' to block them out, '. . . and a *sheep* appears,' Joy and Georgia sing together, '. . . on the far horizon!' They take their bows, receive bouquets, curtsey to each other and blow kisses at Matt, who refuses to clap. Or they shed their shoes and dance barefoot round the kitchen table and into the sitting room, leaping from the sofa in *grands jetés*, pointing their toes and making pouty faces, prima ballerinas at Covent Garden, pirouetting from one side of the stage to the other then falling, dizzy and delirious with giggles, onto the rug. They lie there, letting their limbs be used as ramps for Matt and his collection of vehicles. '*Ner-ner, ner-ner, ner-ner,*' he imitates a siren, 'here's the fire engine.' Georgia and Joy, softened by play and dancing, humour him.

'Help! Help!' Joy calls. 'Fire! Fire!'

'Rescue us!'

Ellen sits on the rug, watching the circus in full swing around her, and laughs and claps her hands.

In need of a change

'What are we having then? Pizza?' Ellen threw herself onto the sofa and put her feet up on the coffee table.

'Chinese,' said Stephen. 'We're just about to order.' He slid the menu across the table to her.

'I'm not sure I really fancy Chinese . . .'

'Order yourself a pizza instead if you like,' I said, at the same time as Stephen said, 'Well don't have it then.'

I scowled at him.

'Nah – can't be bothered to order separately. What are you guys having?'

I told her.

'Mmm – I *love* crispy duck.'

'Why don't you just order what *you'd* like?' I suggested, seeing Stephen was starting to be irritated.

She turned back to the menu.

'What do you think the chicken and cashew nuts is like?'

'I should think it's very like chicken,' said Stephen. 'Only with cashew nuts.'

'Why, Mr P-h, get back in the knife box!'

'*Ellen* . . .' I said warningly. 'Can we just order and skip the sparkling repartee for once?'

Ellen went into the kitchen to see if there was any wine.

'Did you get the kids off to sleep all right?' Stephen channel-hopped with the remote, now that the cricket had finally come to a halt.

'Yes. Fine. I thought you were going to come up?'

'I was. Then your sister turned up so I thought I'd better hang back or it'd have been like Piccadilly Circus up there.'

'There's some Chardonnay that's already open.' Ellen came back in, sniffing the neck of the bottle. 'D'you think it's OK?'

'We can't just drink all their wine,' I said.

Stephen looked at his lager with proprietorial concern, which made Ellen laugh.

'Don't worry, Stevie – you won't need to put up an electric fence round it. I promise not to touch it. I'll risk the wine I think – Matzo won't mind, they've got some more. George?'

'Uh-uh – I'm happy with water or juice.'

'You're an example to us all, you really are.' She poured herself a large glass of wine. 'I can never say no to anything.'

As we were halfway through our food, we heard crying coming from upstairs.

'Probably stop in a minute,' said Stephen.

'Izzy always says it's best to leave them sometimes,' said Ellen.

'I'll just have a quick look.'

It was Daniel. And it was my fault. I hadn't secured his nappy tightly enough and he'd leaked onto the sheet so he was all wet and cross and uncomfortable. I

71

lifted him out and carried him through to the bath-room.

Stephen popped his head round the door.

'All right, darling?'

'Me? I'm fine. Daniel's a bit wet, that's all.'

'Oh. Right.' He shifted from foot to foot, as if he also needed to wee. 'Erm, do you want a hand or anything?'

'No. I'm nearly done.' I bundled up the soggy nappy. 'Actually, I need to change his bottom sheet – can you have a look in that chest there?'

Stephen tentatively opened the top drawer.

'Oh. It's got – women's things in it.' He recoiled as if he'd discovered the contents crawling with maggots.

'Stephen, come on – you've seen tampons before. They won't bite you.'

He looked in the other drawers and eventually extracted a piece of white cotton.

'Is this it?'

'Well, I'm no expert either. Does it look like a sheet?'

'I don't know.' He shrugged. 'It's very small – maybe it's a type of pillowcase?'

I finished Daniel's nappy and gave him a cuddle.

'There we go, all clean and dry again.' I grabbed the sheet. 'It's supposed to be small – it's for a cot. If it were a pillowcase, it would have a space to put a pillow in it.'

I handed Daniel to Stephen while I remade the cot.

'Here. Hold him a sec, will you?'

Stephen held Daniel slightly away from him, as if Daniel might possibly explode or, worse, expel noxious fluids.

'Er, hello, baby. Baby Daniel. Er. *Hush-a-bye, baby.* Um, how's it go? On the tree top? *La-la-la-lah!* The cradle will rock?'

I took Daniel back again.

'Here we go, little one. Nighty-night. Sleep tight.' I kissed him and tucked him under the blanket once more.

'You're good at this baby stuff, aren't you? Where did you learn it?'

'I didn't learn it. You just do it.'

'Well.' Stephen put his arm around me as we stood by the cot for a minute. 'I suppose I'll pick it up eventually.' He turned to kiss me. 'You can teach me.'

6

Mr P-h

Stephen and I have been together for three and a half years, and engaged for two and a half years. In fact, we became engaged on the first anniversary of our very first date – 'so we'll only have one date to remember,' Stephen said. He was joking, of course, but actually it is kind of handy.

We first met at a truly hideous party. I was taken there by a brand new boyfriend who started knocking back the wine the second he stepped in the door then draped himself over some other woman and completely ignored me. I felt so angry and completely humiliated. I didn't know a single soul there aside from him, so I phoned for a taxi to make my escape. While I was waiting, I made myself a coffee in the kitchen and started clearing up a bit, wiping the worktops, rearranging the cook books in order of size, more to take my mind off how awful I was feeling than anything else. Then this very handsome, tall man came in and made some gentle joke about my being a sort of superheroine, swooping into parties late at night and clearing up the mess.

'I'm Stephen,' he said, 'with a p-h.'

'Georgia,' I replied. 'Without.'

And I made him a coffee and we stood there chatting

and he was so nice and unpushy that I found myself telling him what had happened.

'I guess now's not the time to ask for your phone number then? I hope it hasn't put you off men.'

As he said it, he took out his business card, then scribbled his home number on the back.

'We're not *all* bad,' he said.

'I *know*. I'm sure you're not.'

'Give me a call and I'll take you out to dinner, let you find out for yourself.' Then he escorted me downstairs when my taxi turned up and even held the door open for me.

The night we became engaged, we'd gone out to dinner, to what had quickly become 'our' restaurant, an old-fashioned Italian place five minutes' walk from his flat. Back then, there wasn't a particle of polenta in sight, but it's not like that any more. The gingham tablecloths and candles in Chianti bottles have gone. The food's better now, I admit, but why do people feel the need to *change* things all the time?

'Is everything OK? You seem a little on edge,' I remember pointing out, as Stephen, who isn't prone to fidgeting, tweaked at his cuffs yet again.

'I'm fine,' he said, stretching across to squeeze my hand. 'Shall I order a bottle of bubbly?'

'Why? Oh! You got that big client?'

He gave me a considered half-smile, a cautious nod.

'It's not one hundred per cent as yet. But I think it's in the bag.'

'Wonderful! And well deserved. I know how hard you've worked.'

'Thank you. Shall we have that champagne?'

'I hate to be a wet blanket, but you know I really can't drink all that much . . .'

'Not even this once? It is our anniversary after all.'

'Honestly not.' I smiled.

'A half-bottle then?'

'Lovely.'

After dinner, we'd walked back to his flat and I made us some coffee.

'Darling?'

'Yes?'

'Come and sit down.'

'In a sec. Let me just do the coffee.'

I came and sat by him on the sofa. He was looking at me and smiling in a very un-Stephenish way.

'What?'

'Well.' He paused, took my hands in his. 'We've been together a year now.' I smiled.

'And I think it's time to move on to the next square . . .'

At the time I thought he meant he was going to dump me. Good enough for a year, but now it's time to move on? I looked down at my hands in his, unable to meet his gaze. I thought everything had been going so well. We're so compatible, we're both reliable and tidy and punctual, we fit together.

'Oh.'

'Hang on – no point doing these things if one doesn't do them properly, eh?'

I still didn't get it.

'Georgia, you know how I feel about you – ' He slid off the sofa and balanced on one knee, wobbling slightly. 'I think it's time I asked you to marry me.'

I was so relieved that I wasn't being dumped right there and then that I gave him the most enormous smile.

'Oh, Stephen! I can't believe it! Are you sure?'

'Of course I'm sure.'

Then he took out this little box from his pocket and opened it at me. It was a diamond solitaire.

Call me a horrible person, but my first thought was, 'Eek – I never wear gold.' I mean, I know engagement rings are almost always gold, but why are they? What if you prefer silver? And I felt a tiny bit, well, disappointed, that Stephen had somehow not noticed that I never, ever wear gold. Anyway, I took out the ring and put it on my finger. It went on easily. Too easily.

'Does it fit? It's too big, isn't it?' Stephen slid the ring up and down my finger. 'Oh, sweetheart, I'm sorry.' He patted my arm.

'Don't be silly. It's not your fault. Still, I'd hate to lose it . . .' I tucked it snugly back into its box.

It turned out that he'd tried to get my size by borrowing the only ring of mine he could find, an old silver one I used to wear on my right hand, which explained why the new one was too big on my left. I keep the silver ring in my little shell box which lives at the back of my top drawer. I showed the box to Stephen once, but I wasn't at all happy at the thought of him ferreting in my drawer, his big fingers poking through the contents of my shell box. I don't like people touching my possessions. I admit that I'm neat, but that's a positive trait, isn't it? Don't you find that other people never put things back properly after they've borrowed them? I really hate that. Besides, the shell box is special because Mum gave it to me. I suppose people would find it pretty naff now, or call it post-ironic kitsch – it's completely encrusted with tiny periwinkles and other little shells and, when I unwrapped it, I fell utterly in love with it and thought it was the prettiest thing I had ever seen. A few of the shells have fallen off over the years, so it's far from perfect and that's partly why I keep it out of sight.

I knew that this probably wasn't the ideal moment to remind Stephen that I'm not keen on people going through my private stuff, so I made a mental note to mention it tactfully at some later point.

A symbol of everlasting love

So, the following weekend, Stephen took me back to the jewellers.

'I wonder if we could change this ring?' Stephen unfolded the receipt from his wallet.

'Different size or different style?' The assistant looked at me. He had one of those unpleasant smug faces, like he felt he knew what you were going to say before you said it.

'Well, we could look at some others maybe . . .' I avoided Stephen's eyes.

'I thought you *liked* it.'

'I *do*. Of course I do. I just thought, you know, now that we're here anyway . . .' my voice tailed off. 'I've never had the chance to look at engagement rings before.'

The assistant gestured to a display case.

'Aside from our extensive range in the window, these are the diamond solitaires,' he pronounced, as if customers might otherwise mistake them for marshmallows. 'Eternity rings over here. Then coloured stones, rubies, sapphires and so on – here.'

'Do you have anything in silver?' All the trays seemed to be full of gold.

'Silver?' He said it as if the word was 'Shit?' He gave Stephen one of those 'Women! What are they like?' expressions and Stephen smirked back with a 'Let's humour her for now!' look. 'Silver tarnishes, of course,' the assistant told me, as if now talking to someone incredibly stupid, 'and it's rarely used for those truly special items, betrothal rings and suchlike, because it's so *common*, you see.'

'Oh.'

'We do carry a limited selection of white gold pieces, of course. And platinum in our "Once in a Lifetime" range, though obviously they aren't in the same price range . . .' This last remark directed at Stephen.

'That's no problem—' Stephen began.

'May I see the white gold ones then?' Stephen's sweet, but they were a ridiculous amount of money as it was. You could have bought a reasonable second-hand car for the money or a gorgeous new sofa like this beautiful dove-grey suede one I saw when I first moved into my flat, which I couldn't afford. I even used to have fantasies about it, picturing it in my flat, mentally rearranging the rug and the plants to offset it, imagining myself sitting on it, reading, reclining on it, chatting to some presumably perfect man just sort of off-screen if you know what I mean; it was almost exactly like a sexual fantasy – only without the sex.

The assistant unlocked a case and brought out a tray. They were pretty enough, but so shiny and so, well, new. There was something soulless about them, like they'd been churned out on an assembly line, given a final polish, then – plonk, now they were going to end up on someone's finger. Mine.

'You haven't got anything a bit more . . .'

'Look at the platinum ones if you like, sweetie.'

'No, I mean, have you something more, sort of, battered? Er, old, I mean.' Another smirk from the assistant.

'We don't specialize in *used* rings, Miss.' He hissed on the 'Miss' as if the word pained him. 'Though we do have a small selection of *Heritage* rings. They're antique.' He locked the first tray away, then went to the back and returned with another.

'Antique? So these are *used* then?' I gave him a tight smile.

'Presumably so.'

'But, don't you mind having a second-hand ring?' Stephen rubbed the back of my hand.

'No. Why would I? Quite the opposite, actually. An old one has a history, like an heirloom.'

I wished I hadn't said that, because it set me off thinking of Mum's wedding ring, which Dad had kept for me. Dad hoards absolutely everything and the house is hopelessly cluttered, as you know. He never has a clue where anything is – except for the ring. He gets it out every now and then for me to try on and then he tells me all about the day they got married and about how I would have the ring whenever I marry because I'm the eldest and Mum always said I should have it. It's a plain gold band, and it's inscribed on the inside 'Jumping for Joy' with the date of their wedding, only after he'd had it done Dad said he thought he should have made it 'Jumping *with* Joy' but by then it was too late. The ring is wrapped up in a blue silk handkerchief and lives in a dark wine-coloured velvet pouch. Ellen is to have Mum's pearl earrings when she marries. I bit my lip, told myself *I* should be jumping for joy at being engaged, not being morbid and thinking about Mum, but now the thought was there and what could I do but think it? I was engaged and all I wanted to do was to ring up Mum and tell her but I couldn't and then I started thinking about how one day I'd get married and Mum wouldn't be there to cry or kiss me or do her awful, embarrassing dancing at the reception and there was no getting round it.

I fumbled in the tray and picked out one with tiny pearls and diamonds in it.

'Silver?' I asked, already knowing the answer.

The assistant nodded.

It was much cheaper than the other one but, needless to say, they weren't exactly falling over themselves to refund the difference, so we bought Stephen a new watch while we were there, and I felt much better after that because it seemed a bit fairer somehow even though it was still his money. The silver ring was also slightly too large, so the smarmy assistant checked my size and said they would have it altered and Stephen could go back and pick it up next week.

After that, we went for coffee and I kissed Stephen and thanked him.

'I want you to have whatever you want,' he said.

'Thank you for being so nice about it.'

Still, it's moments like that that make you sad when you should be being happy. On key occasions, like when I graduated from college, and when I first qualified as a counsellor, I wished so strongly that Mum could be there – even if only for a minute, just so

I could hug her and hear her tell me how proud she was. There's Quinn now, of course, but that's not the same thing, is it?

Stephen doesn't really understand all this stuff because he's never lost anyone except his grandfather and they weren't ever close. He's sympathetic and sweet because he's a nice person, but he doesn't really *know*. It's like being a virgin and trying to imagine what sex is like – you sort of understand the mechanics of it all right, but you can't know deep down in your gut until it's happened to you, can you?

Something to look forward to . . .

Last night, after we'd had supper at a Thai restaurant in Soho, Stephen came back to my place. He went to use the bathroom, while I pulled down the bed – you just give the fake cupboard door a tug and down it comes, complete with bedding. It has straps that hold the duvet on for when it's folded away or, if you're a bit of a perv, you could use them to keep your man in place while you take advantage of him. I can't quite see Stephen being up for that.

He came out of the bathroom as I was plumping up the pillows – they get a bit flattened by being in the cupboard.

'Herbal tea, sweetie?'

'Don't worry, I'll do it. You sound like you've had a tough week. Do you want a coffee?'

Stephen is the neatest man I've ever met, but he still looks so very large in my flat, sort of out of scale like an Action Man in a dolls' house. I prefer to do things myself. I put just enough water in the kettle for two mugs and flicked it on.

'Yes. I've barely been in the office more than two hours at a time.' He slumped down onto the sofa. 'I ought to do some work this weekend really.' I went and stood behind him and kneaded his shoulders to help him relax.

'Well, we don't have to go away. I don't mind.' We were supposed to be heading off to the Cotswolds on Saturday, to look at a potential wedding venue, a gorgeous-sounding country-house hotel, then stay the night there – make a weekend of it.

'Don't be silly, darling. That's sweet of you, but we've booked it now and they'll charge us if we cancel. Would you object if I take my laptop though?'

'Mmm. I'm not sure there's much point in going and spending all that money if you're going to be hunched over a hot keyboard all weekend.'

'Of course not. I only meant for an hour or two. Well – what say we come back by six or so on Sunday and I can work then?'

'Fine.'

Stephen took off his jacket and tie then patted the sofa cushion for me to come and sit by him.

'I'm desperate for a bath,' I said. 'I really need to unwind.'

He smiled and looked sympathetic.

'Hard day?'

'Not half as hard as yours, I'm sure.' I usually only work a half-day on Fridays. Originally, I vowed not to take clients on Friday afternoon so I could have a long weekend, but given that I then have two first thing on Saturday morning, we can never get away early anyway. 'Go on and get into bed, don't wait for me.' He looked so tired, poor thing.

'I'll do my best,' he said, starting to get undressed. 'I thought maybe we could, y'know . . .' Stephen put his arms round my waist. 'It feels like ages since we did.'

I bent to kiss him.

'Oh, it isn't. Silly. It was only – ' I thought for a moment. Only last weekend. Saturday – so, less than a week. 'Anyway, we'll be away tomorrow night. Just think – lovely crisp sheets, plumpfy pillows . . .' I pulled away from him. 'My bath.'

'I'll be in in a minute to do my teeth.'

*   *   *

It wasn't that I didn't want to make love exactly. It was just I thought that if we were going away tomorrow, I'd rather save it up and have it to look forward to. It feels more special if you're away somehow, especially if you're staying in a nice hotel. Like it's all part of the package – proper starched sheets instead of a duvet, old-fashioned poached eggs and toast in a toast rack, a delicious dinner with linen napkins – I love all that. Then sex before or after dinner or, even better, on Sunday morning, then you roll downstairs for a late breakfast and half the room have been at it too, they're all smirking at each other over their orange juices and being nice, pouring their partner's coffee and smiling instead of grunting at each other from behind the shield of the newspaper.

When you've been together as long as we have, it's rare to have sex two nights in a row. Not that it's ever been the be-all and end-all of our relationship. Ellen thinks there's nothing wrong in basing an entire relationship on sex, but then she also believes that four months counts as a long-term relationship, so she's not exactly what I'd call an authority on the subject. It's all very well for the first few weeks, but sooner or later you're going to have to detach yourselves from each other's private parts and get down to some serious business – having a conversation. It's just not realistic to expect life to be fun, fun, fun the whole time, is it? When you're in a relationship for the long haul, other things – compatibility, companionship, shared values – start to take on greater importance. Ellen says I've got no romance in my soul, but what's romantic about trying to shag yourselves senseless so that you'll go to sleep straightaway afterwards and won't have to lie there struggling to find something to talk about?

I did once have a relationship that consisted almost exclusively of sex – but it's years ago now; I was twenty-seven, Ellen's age. I met this guy, Rory, and the thing is, I didn't even *like* him all that much. But when he kissed me it made me want to throw my knickers into the air – and, when I did, believe me, it wasn't a let-down. And we did it three, four times a night. Seriously. More than I do now in a month sometimes. Looking back, I wonder if he might have had some kind of weird medical condition because he seemed to have a near-permanent erection – you could have used him as a coat hook. Anyway, we'd go to see a film or something – just as a sort of token date to make it seem as if we were having a proper relationship when we both knew we weren't – then we'd practically race back to his place and go straight to bed. I lost loads of weight – whenever I attempted to cook him a meal, he'd come rubbing up behind me like a dog against the leg of your primmest guest, practically panting and with his bulge digging into me. Then he'd slide his hands up under my top or start pressing me through my trousers until I crumpled against him and I'd have to turn off the stove and we'd do it right there on the floor or standing up against the wall. He even kept two phone directories at the ready for me to stand on so I'd be at the right height for him. Trouble was, once or twice I said, 'Why don't we go out to dinner?' so we did and we had absolutely nothing to say to each other. We only made it through the evening because he started making lewd suggestions to me over the main course about which foodstuffs he wanted to smear over various bits of me prior to licking them off again, then he pushed off his shoe and put his foot between my legs, fondling me with his toes. It's better than it sounds. We ate half our food, then skipped pudding and coffee and jumped in a cab to get home as fast as possible. I remember him putting his hand up my skirt in the cab, right in my knickers, with me squirming away while pathetically still trying to maintain a seemly demeanour, panicking about the driver seeing us in his mirror. Rory said they see that kind of stuff all the time and it's probably one of the perks in an otherwise boring job and why should they care so long as you don't spurt spunk all over their seats? He had a real way with words.

It's very different with Stephen – gentler and less rushed; we've gradually found a way of making love that seems to suit us. I'm not saying I don't miss the occasional passionate quickie – when your skin feels hot and sensitized to the slightest touch, your mouths are sucking on each other like limpets, and you're so desperate for him that you've just got to get his pants off and climb onto his cock right now or you'll spontaneously combust. But you can't expect to maintain that level over any length of time, can you?

I know I'm very lucky to have Stephen; as I've said to Ellen countless times, once you find someone who's really *right* for you, you can just relax and life's so much easier.

Getting away from it all

'Oh, yeah. Cooling. Mr and Mrs Cooling. You're in 206. Harry – take these bags up to 206.' The youthful hotel clerk called this last bit over my shoulder to another boy in a too-large uniform.

'*Mr* Cooling and *Miss* Abrams,' I pointed out, icily. 'We've arranged to look at your banqueting rooms for our *wedding* – it *should* say.' I peered over the ridiculously high counter to see if he had any notes. 'So, not Mr and Mrs Cooling – *yet*.' In fact, I'm planning to keep my own name in any case, but I wanted to make the point.

'Wooden hangers, not wire,' Stephen pronounced approvingly once we were installed in our room. 'And a decanter of sherry.'

'Bottles, not sachets,' I added, checking out the shampoo and bath foam. 'And cotton wool in a little china dish.'

He lay down on the bed and plumped up a couple of the numerous rose-spattered cushions behind him.

'Bed's not bad.'

'They've gone a bit overboard on the chintz. No surface left unflowered.'

Stephen patted the space on the bed beside him.

'Care to join me, Miss Abrams?'

I lay down next to him and he shifted onto his side and kissed me.

'Don't suppose you fancy a little . . . pre-dinner . . . appetizer?'

I smiled and put my arms around him.

'Aren't they expecting us downstairs to show us the Gainsborough Suite?' Why do these places always have these stupid names? I bet they don't have an actual Gainsborough painting gracing the wall.

He sighed and looked at his watch.

'OK . . . Now, darling?'

'Mmm-mm?'

'Promise me you'll give this one a fair chance.'

'Of *course* I will. Why wouldn't I?'

'Ssh-shh.' He put a finger to my lips. 'Just let's try not to get too bogged down in the *details*, eh? We can't keep ruling places out because the wallpaper's not a hundred per cent to your satisfaction.' He smiled at me.

I nodded.

'I promise to try to behave myself and not be too picky.'

'That's my girl.' He swung his legs round and stood up, put his jacket back on. 'Ready?'

We looked at the rooms and murmured appreciative noises at the ornate cornicing and the windows looking onto the rose garden, then the child-manager person asked us about our proposed dates.

'Late spring maybe?' Stephen said.

'Perhaps we should check our diaries and get back to you,' I suggested.

'Well, if you like, but we're getting well booked up for next year.' The youth rubbed his nose with the palm of his hand. 'You don't wanna leave it too late.'

*　　　*　　　*

'This is really very nice,' Stephen said as we stood outside in the garden, though only a few blooms still remained. 'And it's a good location, isn't it? Not too far for people to get to.'

'Yes. It really is pretty and the main room is lovely. Shame we can't do it here.'

'What? Georgia, why ever not? If it's about the cost—'

I shook my head. 'Well, aside from the reception staff who are all clearly incompetent and barely out of school, and the fact that they're really trying it on with the wine prices, the room's too small.'

'But he said it holds up to seventy.'

'Exactly. Darling – work it out – that's only thirty-five guests each – and by the time I count in my family, including the cousins and the aunts and the American contingent and everyone's children and my friends . . .'

'But we don't have to include all the children, do we? And your American relatives aren't likely to come all this way, are they? Do you have to ask them?'

'They're *family*.'

'OK.' Stephen sighed heavily. 'Well. *I* don't need thirty-five – if I only ask, say twenty-five, you can have forty-five. Is that enough?'

'You're so unselfish. Still . . . I'm not sure. We'll have to work it out.'

Stephen wanted us to draw up a list before dinner, so we could book a date while we were still at the hotel, but I was longing for a lovely deep bath. I was lying back in the bubbles, letting thoughts waft through my mind, picturing myself in the perfect dress, trying out different fabrics – heavy satin or sheer chiffon, silk dupion or layered organza. I was just adding Stephen into the picture, swapping around a traditional grey morning suit and a stylish linen number, when he tapped lightly on the door and came in.

'Fancy some company?'

'Sure.'

He handed me a small glass of sherry.

'Nice bath?'

'Gorgeous.'

He undid his cuff and rolled up his shirt sleeve, dangled his hand in the water, brushing along the side of my arm.

'I could get in too if you like?'

'Or wait a minute and I'll get out – then you can have it all to yourself.' I hate sharing a bath; I can never get comfortable – there always seem to be too many knees and too many elbows and you can't lie back properly.

'No. You stay in and enjoy it. Shall I do your back?'

'Would you? Thank you.'

I sat up and leaned forward while he slowly soaped my back, then rinsed it down with a thick white flannel.

'Mmm-mm.'

'You like that?'

'Mmmm. Lovely.'

He leaned in closer and I turned towards him. He kissed me softly then pulled away slightly, a question in his gaze. He held out a towel for me and I stepped onto the bathmat.

'Shall I dry you?'

'Uh-huh. Do we have enough time before dinner? We don't want to have to rush.'

'Nearly an hour.' He checked his watch. 'It won't take me two minutes to change.'

'Fine. You go through. I won't be a minute.'

When I went through to the bedroom, Stephen was already undressed and under the covers. He drew back the sheet for me to climb in.

We lay side by side, then we started kissing. It was nice to be away, with no thought that the phone might ring with some member of my family wanting me to solve their latest drummed-up crisis.

The good thing about having been with Stephen all this time is that we're completely familiar with each other's bodies and preferences. There's none of that awkwardness you get at the beginning of a relationship when you're having to find out what he likes and doesn't like, where and how he likes to be touched, all that stuff and you don't have the embarrassment of trying to show or tell him what you like either.

Having devoted a couple of minutes to my breasts, he slid his hand down between my legs. After a couple of minutes more, he said, 'Shall I get something?'

OK, I admit it, that's the one thing that drives me crazy about Stephen. He always pauses when I'm just beginning to get excited and says exactly the same thing: 'Shall I get something?' And it's usually several minutes before I'm ready. I don't know – am I especially slow to warm up? How can you tell? It's not really the level of detail you go into with your friends, is it? Even my closest single friends, Emma and Susie, might make a general comment about whether a boyfriend is any good or not, but they don't get out the flipcharts to make an in-depth analysis. Ellen doesn't hold back, of course, and it's all I can do to stop her from relating the ins and outs of some poor man's sexual performance, but she gives so much detail that you begin to feel you're listening in to some bizarre chat show. But, back to Stephen – why doesn't he just get a condom or say what he means, 'Shall I put on a condom now?' I know condoms are the most un-romantic, unsexy things in the world and the word itself is somewhere halfway between clinical and comical, but does he have to resort to euphemism? Sometimes I say, 'Oh, not just yet,' or, 'Can't we carry on just touching each other for a bit longer?' but then, after a while, you feel as if you're being mean and he's looking kind of impatient, so you think, 'Oh go on, might as well, even if I'm not quite ready.'

Anyway, given that we didn't have loads of time because I'd still need to change and do my face, I thought we'd better cut to the chase really. He rolled on the condom, then slowly eased into me with a sigh of relief.

His eyes were closed, as usual. Do other men do this? It's so long since I've slept with anyone else that I can't really remember. He's almost like one of those dolls – put him in a horizontal position and his eyes shut. I don't know why it bothers me – it's not as if I think he's fantasizing about doing it with someone else – it's only that sometimes I'd like him to look into my eyes, to linger on my face, just enjoying the fact that he's with *me*, making love to *me*, rather than concentrating so intently on the actual act.

'Darling?' I said.

'Hmm?' He opened his eyes. 'What? Is this OK? Am I going too fast?'

'No. It's fine. Just – hello – that's all.'

He smiled.

'Hello, beautiful.' Then his eyes closed again.

Do you ever have that thing when, suddenly, you just *know* you're not going to come no matter what? Well, I had that feeling.

I want to make it clear that I have never, ever faked an orgasm, but I do occasionally slightly *emphasize* my enjoyment a tiny bit more than is actually the case. But, given that, when I do come, you could still hear a mouse scratch its nose because I'm so quiet, it's fairly difficult for Stephen to tell whether I'm in the throes of extreme ecstasy or not. Don't get me wrong – it's not that Stephen doesn't know one end of a clitoris from another. He's really sweet in bed. And if we've got plenty of time and I'm in the mood, I usually come. Well, more often than not, at least. But don't you ever have times when you really can't be bothered, but you've started now so you can't ask him if he'd mind pulling out because you'd rather read another chapter of your book or could he just hurry up and come as quickly as possible because you can tell that it's not going to happen for you tonight and he shouldn't waste too much energy in trying? So you lie there, saying 'Mmm, mmm' in an encouraging sort of way every couple of minutes, thinking, 'If he comes in the next minute or so, I won't miss the start of the late-night film.'

It was a shame because, when you're spending all that money on a nice hotel room, you feel as if you deserve a seriously decent orgasm – to sort of *go* with the room, like getting early-morning coffee and a newspaper brought to you on a tray first thing. Anyway, so I didn't fake it, not at all, but I did make one or two extra mmm-mmm noises that were somewhat surplus to requirements. After a minute or two more he came, in any case, then he carefully pulled out and lay back next to me.

'That was wonderful.' He tilted his head to kiss me. 'I love you.'

'I love you too.'

'Was it nice for you?'

'Yes. It was lovely.'

When Stephen says, 'Was it nice for you?' what he really means is, 'Did you come?' which he can't bring himself to say for some reason. But it's not as if I was really lying to him – after all, it *was* perfectly nice. Very nice, in the way that lots of things are: the decanter of sherry on the polished wooden table, the window seat upholstered in rose fabric, the fluffy white towels in the bathroom. I don't mean it sneeringly at all – it was just what I needed – and lovely being held and kissed and I was pleased that it was so good for him, I really was, I hardly minded about not coming myself, and besides, we still had a delicious dinner to look forward to, so, all in all, I felt almost perfectly content.

7

An end to life as we know it . . .

'. . . and then I was being chased by a courgette . . .'

One of my new clients is prone to having peculiar dreams, which she likes to recount in some detail; often, they're miles more interesting than her waking life. This woman, Dream Woman – for confidentiality's sake – has got this really boring voice and when she's describing some dreary conversation she's had with her husband, it's all I can do to stay awake.

I imagined a giant courgette bouncing along the road – or perhaps it had legs? I mentally added a pair of stubby green limbs, sticking out on either side like stabilizer wheels on a child's bicycle.

'I think maybe it symbolized my mother.'

'Uh-um . . . and why do you think that?'

'Well, she was always making us eat ratatouille when I was a child . . .'

Why wasn't it accompanied by its old buddies then, I was tempted to ask, Messrs Aubergine & Capsicum, perhaps with a platoon of irate tomatoes marching behind? A rampant courgette seemed to me to indicate sexual anxiety, a classic phallic object running amok.

'Had you considered—' I began.

There was a sudden, violent crash against the outer door and both Dream Woman and I let out a simultaneous cry. For one moment, I imagined it might be the courgette on the rampage, questing for its quarry – in which case, I wasn't going to stand in its way. The woman looked terrified.

'I'm sure it's nothing major,' I reassured her, 'but if you'll excuse me for a second I think I'd better just check . . .' I smiled with considerably more confidence than I felt, opened the inner door, pulled it shut behind me, then opened the outer one.

'Holy fuck!' A man was sprawled on the floor, surrounded by various enormous bags and metal cases. 'Oh, for fuck's sake!'

'Sssh!' I said automatically, thinking of my client, then more softly, 'Are you all right?'

'Yes, I'm fine. I always like to lie down in the corridor with half a ton of equipment on top of me. Who needs a sodding duvet? God, that fucking hurt!' He rubbed his left knee.

I pulled the door to behind me, noticing a dent and a deep, long gouge in the wood.

'Have you broken anything?'

He leaned up on one arm and looked around him.

'I can't tell yet – I'll have to unpack and check it all.'

'No, I meant *you*. Bones, I mean.'

He sat up a bit more.

'I guess I'll live.' Suddenly, he smiled, a crazy, warm smile, displaying a chipped front tooth. 'Hello, by the way.'

'Right. Yes. Hello. Sorry – I really can't help you now – ' Session time is sacrosanct. 'I've got someone here. Sorry. But I must—' I started to open the door, catching sight of the damage again. 'Um, perhaps you could just leave your details at the front desk – with the porter?' I gestured at the scarred door, thinking can I trust him? He'll probably do a runner and I'll have to get it off the insurance.

'Oh God – I'm so sorry. Here, let me – ' He started to struggle to his feet.

'No, really. *Not now*. Leave your address. It's fine.'

I closed both doors behind me and nodded at Dream Woman.

'Nothing serious,' I said authoritatively. 'Nothing but a minor mishap.' I sat down again. 'I do think there might be a sexual element to your dream.'

'No, I don't think so. I'm not all that keen on sex, to be honest, so I don't think it could be sexual, could it?'

Later . . .

I was in another session when there was a knocking at my door. I have an outer door, then there's a little hallway – the bathroom leads off there – with a big storage cupboard, then the inner door to the main room. When I moved in, I had the doorbell removed to minimize unexpected interruptions, neighbours wanting to rope me onto the board of the residents' association or galvanize me into complaining about the person who plays their music loudly after nine o'clock at night. When both doors are closed, someone has to knock pretty loudly for me even to hear it, which suits me just fine. You can't have people interrupting every three minutes when a client is sitting there sobbing her eyes out, can you? At first, neighbours did knock on my door, but I ignored it, then I put up a discreet notice where the bell had been: 'Please knock only if you have an appointment; for any other purpose, please contact Flat 511.' Still, people can be quite slow to take the hint. Sometimes, one of the neighbours waylays me in the lobby or the corridor and it's hard to get away. Mr Rose is the worst. He signs his numerous notes Henry Rose, CRA, and when I asked him what the CRA stood for, he said, 'Chairman, Residents' Association' as if the honour had been conferred on him by the Queen. He's always fretting about the state of the building – have I noticed that one of the lights hasn't worked on the stairwell for over six weeks, could I join with him in complaining about the state of the mat by the main door, and please would I pop in my cheque for the association subscription, maybe stay for a sherry – Flat 21, same as his age, ha ha, grinning to show me that he knows that I know that he's old enough to have a grandchild of twenty-one, but that he had a bit of a way with the ladies in his day, oh yes, quite a twinkle he had and a spring in his step, there's more than one lady in the block who'd get out her rouge if she were invited in for sherry with Mr Rose. And there's Mrs Patterson, who's very sweet but very lonely. She must have some high-tech sensor laser beam by her front door because a mouse couldn't tiptoe across the corridor carpet without her opening a crack to see who it is. You really have to keep your distance in a block like this, otherwise you'd spend your entire life being dragged into flat after flat for yet another cup of tea.

Anyway, there was a knock at my door, and not the tentative tap-tapping of an elderly neighbour, but a more assertive, insistent kind of a knock.

'Just ignore it,' I told my client. 'Please, do go on.'

He glanced nervously at the door.

'. . . erm, OK, so then she said, "Well, *I* didn't come – were you in a rush or something?" and I, you know, wasn't sure if she was expecting me to do something about it, you know, and—'

Another knock, louder this time.

'I'm terribly sorry – please excuse me a moment while I just check the building's not on fire or anything.' I smiled brightly.

I pulled the inner door closed behind me and opened the outer one a little way.

'Yes?' It was that man from earlier, the one who'd taken a gouge out of my door.

'Ah, hello – you *are* there. Look – I hope I'm not disturbing you, but I just wanted to say—'

'Hang on a second.' I raised my hand, like Canute trying to hold back the waves; he spoke really quickly and I could tell if I didn't interrupt him at once, he'd be there babbling away all afternoon. 'Let me put you on pause for one moment. I have a *client* here. We *cannot* be interrupted. It may have escaped your notice but many people actually work for a living and cannot spend hours idly gossiping at the front door. You've already interrupted my work once today and, bizarrely, you seem to feel the need to do it again.'

He flushed.

'I was only trying—'

'I'm sure you were, but if it's about my door, please speak to the porter or leave your card there for me . . . if you have one. Georgia Abrams, Flat 411, as you can see.' I gestured to the number and the sign saying only to knock if you have an actual appointment.

'*Miss* Abrams?' he said tightly. I could tell he meant it as an insult.

'*Ms*. Thank you.' I started to close the door.

'All right, but it wouldn't take—'

'Sorry – was there some part of that sentence you didn't understand? Do I need a Do Not Disturb sign swinging from my doorknob?'

'Sorry – I – all right – keep your knickers on, *Ms* Abrams, there's no need to be so snotty. I was only trying to apologize, but forget it. For God's sake, who rattled your cage?'

I closed the door. Well, I half-slammed it. I stood in my tiny hall for a moment, trying to regain my composure. Nice and calm now, I said to myself, a couple of slow, deep breaths, calm, calm. I opened the inner door once more. I'd have to give my client another few minutes at the end of the session, it wasn't his fault.

'I'm *so* sorry for the interruption.' I sat and nodded for him to continue.

'So . . . d'you think she might have been expecting something else then?'

Uh? Who? What? About what?

'I'm sorry?' I flicked a look at the door once more.

'My new girlfriend, Lindsey, when she said, you know . . .' he tailed off.

Oh, I remember. The man who can't understand why

his girlfriend selfishly would like some pleasure in bed. Mr Speedy.

'Have you experienced similar problems before – with another partner?'

'Uh? No, no, well, I don't think so. I think it's just her. She's a bit uptight, you know?'

Well, there's a surprise.

'Hmm-mm. Do you see it as being somehow her fault?' I asked.

'I didn't say that.' He looked at his watch. 'Isn't it time?'

'We have a few more minutes in hand – because of the interruption earlier.' I paused. 'I notice you seem in a hurry. Do you think this might be how Lindsey felt when you were in bed together?'

He sat staring straight ahead, then he shrugged.

'Do you feel as if I'm criticizing you the way she did?'

He shrugged again.

'I find it hard to be . . . patient sometimes. I'm like always in a whirl for work, then I get to the end of the day and I don't know how to slow down.'

I smiled.

'Mmm – mm. Perhaps you could explain that to Lindsey – you might find she's more understanding than you imagine. She may be able to help you wind down and then you can work together on finding a pace that suits you both perhaps?'

He looked at his watch again.

'Well, that is all we have time for today,' I confirmed. 'See you next week.'

I shut the door behind him and rolled my head round first one way then the other. I felt so stiff and tense, my neck was tight, as if my spine were made of steel. I thought about the interruption. Could you believe the gall of that man? Some people just have no idea how to behave, do they?

97

'Love' is a four-letter word

'Hey, Georgy, love!' Barry, one of the porters, called out to me as I strode across the lobby on my way out. I've given up trying to explain to him that it's Georgia not Georgy, but I do hate to be called 'love'. I've told him before.

He was waving an envelope at me.

'It's from that new bloke, the photographer what just moved in on the fourth. Said he took a tumble with some gear against your door.'

'Oh, yes. Yes, he did.' Well, at least he hadn't disappeared without trace. Barry stood there eyeing the envelope. Everyone is so nosy around here. I don't know why he didn't just go ahead and open it, save him holding it up to the light for half an hour trying to read it.

'I could come up and take a look if you like, love.'

I sighed, but he misread my annoyance somehow.

'At your door,' he added. 'P'raps I can fix it?'

'Thanks. But I don't think so – there's a long, deep gouge out of the wood.' He hooked his thumbs into his waistband and hoiked up his trousers. He's always doing that.

'How'd he manage to do that then, love?'

'I can't imagine. You'd think it would be impossible to cause that much damage simply by walking along a corridor, wouldn't you?'

Barry rubbed his nose with the back of his hand.

'You don't think he's like a vandal or somethink?'

I tried not to seem impatient, but glanced down at my watch.

'No. I'm sure if he were a vandal, he'd have spray-painted his name in fluorescent colours floor to ceiling rather than just scraping one door, don't you think?'

Barry looked over my shoulder towards the stairwell, as if expecting to see an aerosol-crazed graffiti artist come bounding into the lobby at any moment. He pulled up his trousers again.

'Don't you worry, love. I'll keep an eye on him for you. If he starts being a nuisance, you just tip me the nod, OK love, and I'll see to it.'

The idea of Barry's seeing to anything more challenging than a defunct lightbulb is patently ridiculous, in fact he can barely manage that. I pretended to rummage in my handbag for something to suppress my urge to giggle.

'No, really, Barry. Thank you, but I can manage perfectly well. Really. And, er . . . I don't mean to be rude but do you mind not calling me "love"? Georgia is fine – but not love. OK?'

He looked down at the desk.

'Oh. Sorry, love. Oh – sorry. I mean . . . yeah, sorry.' His voice dropped to a mumble. 'Didn't mean to cause offence like.'

'No, of course not. Good.' Looked at my watch openly this time. 'Well, I must dash.'

I ran down the front steps, checked my watch again, quickened my pace. I can walk it in twenty minutes flat if I go at a fair lick. I often meet Stephen after work at a wine bar halfway between his office and my flat.

Started opening the envelope, thinking about my door. It was most annoying, and it looked so bad – as if one of my clients had gone bonkers and tried to attack me. The envelope, I noted, said Ms Abrams, Flat 411, with the *Ms* underlined, making a point. Why is it that if you call yourself Ms people automatically assume you're an embittered divorcee, a pursed-lipped spinster or a diehard feminist? OK, so I am a spinster, technically I suppose, and a feminist naturally enough, but I can't go around calling myself Miss at my age, it sounds ridiculous. And, anyway, it's no-one else's business whether I'm married or not, is it?

The note just plunged straight in, no hello or Dear Ms Abrams or anything:

'Sorry but somewhat baffled that my attempts to apologize for accidentally scraping your door have proved so offensive to you for some reason. Had no idea that you were in the middle of defusing a nuclear bomb or otherwise caught up in some matter of global importance. Perhaps, if it won't interrupt your pressing schedule too much, you could find out whether the damage to the door is covered by your buildings insurance. If not, I will, of course, be happy – no, ecstatic, over the moon, delirious with delight – to pay for it and, as you're too busy to speak to anyone for three seconds, I will also arrange for the work to be done. Let me know.

   Leo Kane'

It was a compliments slip, with Leo Kane, Photographer at the top and an address in Glasgow, which had been scored through and Flat 418, Weedon Court written in. Oh, marvellous, the rudest man on the planet has just moved in onto my floor. If he hadn't been so bloody foul, I would have welcomed having someone under seventy around for a change. Most of my neighbours are retired people; because the flats are so small, they really don't suit couples or families. Quite a few are let as pieds-à-terre to weekly commuters who obviously have some rambling great Tudor farmhouse out in the sticks somewhere, but you don't see them much because they work so late during the week. Still, at least my neighbours are mostly quiet – no loud music, no crying babies, no children trundling up and down the corridors on their bikes. It's peaceful and, mostly, people don't bother me.

I read the note again. No phone number. Well, I could drop a note back through his letter box, I suppose. As I was thinking about this, a man coming the other way barged straight into me, banging my elbow.

   'Oh!'

'Why don't you watch where you're going!' he shouted at me over his shoulder as he strode on.

I rubbed my arm. I don't know what's wrong with people today, everyone seemed to be in such a bad mood.

Stephen was already there when I arrived at Vats 'n' Vintages. God, I hate places that have that poor little amputated 'n' in the middle of their name. I mean, how hard is it to put 'and' or even '&'?

'Hi, sweetie! Good day?' He bent to kiss me.

'No, actually. Fucking awful.' Stephen raised his brows – he's kind of old-fashioned about women swearing. 'It's been one thing after another and then some stupid prat busted my office door.'

'No! Not a burglar? While you were there?'

'No, no, just some idiot. It was an accident.' I felt silly for being so melodramatic about it now. Stephen is very measured about everything – he doesn't exaggerate and he doesn't overreact. It's great, but it means he does tend to take everything you say a bit literally. 'Never mind anyway, I'll get it fixed. Tell me about *your* day.'

'First-rate.' He turned to the barman to order. 'Sparkling mineral water with a twist of lime and a glass of the Beaujolais.'

'Actually, hang on a sec – ' I said, 'I think I'll have a glass of wine too.'

Stephen looked surprised.

'Sorry, darling, I just assumed.' Normally, I only have wine when we're out for dinner.

'It's fine.'

'Two glasses of the Beaujolais?' said the barman.

'No. I prefer white . . . God, I don't feel up to making even the most trivial decision. It's pathetic.' I felt as if I'd been all used up, crumpled and falling apart at the edges, like an old tissue that's been crushed at the bottom of your handbag for months.

'The Pinot Grigio's good.' The barman smiled. Just a

friendly smile, I mean, I don't think he was flirting or anything.

'Fine. Thank you.' He was rather attractive actually. I smiled at him a second longer than was strictly necessary and he smiled back.

What are you doing? I said to myself. Here you are with lovely Stephen who's handsome and six foot two and you're very, very lucky. I turned away from the bar as if to scan the room for the remote possibility of two empty chairs, but it was packed as usual.

'So, can I tell you what happened?' Stephen loosened his tie and put his briefcase down on the floor, trapped between his ankles.

I could hardly blame him for not being eager to hear about my day of disasters.

'Of course,' I smiled. 'Tell me all about it.'

To the rescue . . .

I was already in bed at Stephen's place when the phone rang at about half eleven. He rolled over and said, 'Gosh, I wonder who that can possibly be at this time of night?'

I jabbed him affectionately in the ribs as I stretched over him to answer the phone.

'George – it's me.' Ellen – surprise, surprise. I was quite pleased though, I'd been longing to offload on someone about that rude man and my door; I'd tried to tell Stephen about it later, but he spoiled it by being immensely reasonable and talking about liability and insurance and saying he was sure it would all be sorted out satisfactorily.

'Hi, what's up?'

'I'm in Baker Street and I've lost my tube pass . . .'

'Haven't you got any money?'

'Well, that's the thing – my purse doesn't seem to be in my bag and—'

'Hang on a sec.' I covered the phone with my hand to speak to Stephen. 'It's Ellen – she's stranded and she

hasn't got any money to get home. She's not far.'
Stephen put his pillow over his face.

'She's twenty-seven for Pete's sake!' His voice was
muffled but not muffled enough, so I pressed the phone
close to my ear. 'Why doesn't she go out with money
like a normal person? And what does she want us to do
about it – as if I didn't know already?'

'I'd go on my own if I had my car here, you know I
would.' I rarely drive to Stephen's because the parking
is even more impossible than it is near me. Besides, for
once I'd found a residents' space right opposite my
block, and I was still relishing it. On the rare occasions
that I manage to grab a parking space within walking
distance of my building, I'm not going to do anything
stupid like actually use my car after all, am I? Stephen,
lucky sod, has an off-street parking space with his flat,
so he can afford to gloat about it – and believe me, he
does. I think he's more proud of it than of his entire
flat. Sometimes I suspect he may even be secretly in
love with the parking space; whenever he pulls into it,
he gets this little smirk right here at the corners of his
mouth. Then, as he digs into his pocket for his house
keys, he always gives this apparently casual glance
back at the car, but it's a proprietorial glance, the look
of the man who merely has to walk three steps from
his car to his front door rather than the disgruntled
frown of the man who has spent twenty minutes
driving round and round the neighbourhood and has
eventually found a space so far away that he's had to
get a bus home from his car.

'Never mind, Stephen – I'll get a cab.' I turned back to
the phone. 'Ellie? Still there?'

Stephen folded back his side of the duvet neatly and
swung his legs round onto the floor.

'Tell her we'll be ten minutes – and this is absolutely
the last time.'

'Thank you, darling. El? Give us ten minutes. Where
are you exactly?'

*   *   *

103

Stephen put on his trousers and sighed.

'You know this doesn't happen in normal families, don't you?'

He's right of course, I know that – but she's my little sister.

'I mean, what was it your brother felt the need to call about at practically midnight the other night?'

'Don't exaggerate – it was barely after eleven.'

'You ought to get paid as a consultant, the amount of times he phones you.'

'I don't mind.'

'No – but *I* do.'

I put my arms round him and stretched up to kiss him.

'I know they're a pain in the bum and you're a saint to put up with them. And with me. You're racking up Brownie points.'

He smiled and kissed me back.

'Anyone would count themselves lucky to have to put up with you. It's them that's the problem.' He pulled out his jacket from the hall closet. 'Ready?' I nodded and grabbed my bag.

'And please, please can we not have her staying over this time? I don't mind giving her a lift home, but we're not staying up half the night listening to her latest escapades.'

'Course not. Thank you. I really appreciate it.'

'Next time she can jolly well walk home. I mean it.'

8

It's fine – so long as it's perfect

On the way into my block the next morning, I stopped to talk to Vernon, another porter, to explain about my damaged door.

'Yeah, I know all about it. Leo had a word with us. First you got to notify the managing agents, then you have to get three quotes for the insurance, then you have to fill in—'

Leo? Vernon made him sound like an old friend. The man's hardly been in the building two minutes.

'And how long will that take?'

'Shouldn't be more than three, four weeks, I reckon, if you're lucky.'

'I can't possibly wait that long. Can't we just get it done *now*, then claim the money back?'

Vernon rubbed his chin.

'Well, no, see, you have to get three quotes for the . . .' Vernon is fond of repeating himself, so even the simplest exchange takes three times longer than it should do.

'Yes, I appreciate that,' I said firmly, trying to head him off at the pass. 'But if I can find a handyman . . .'

'To tender a quote, you mean? Like one of the three—'

'No. I mean to do the work, just to *get on* with it.'

'Hi there!'

I swung round. Oh, marvellous – the Door Destroyer.

'Ah, it's you. The man who doesn't know his own strength. A gentle knock should more than suffice in future.'

'I'll bear it in mind next time you invite me round for tea and scones. Now, about your door—'

'Vernon told me. It's far too slow. I can't let my clients see it like that. It looks *appalling*.'

'Hmm. You wouldn't say you were exaggerating just a tad? But . . . OK.' He checked his watch. 'What say I sort something out for later on today – four? Five? What suits you?'

'Really? Well. Four then. Thank you.'

I thought he was probably just saying it to get me off his back, and I must have looked as if I didn't believe him, because then he said, 'I *will* be there.'

He smiled suddenly and it was so unexpected that I found myself grinning back at him even though so far he'd done nothing but be rude and damage my property. Still, at least now he seemed to be trying to make amends.

'So. Um – did you – were you all right then?' I asked. 'You weren't hurt?'

'Nope. All in one piece.'

'Good. That's good. I'm—' I was on the verge of apologizing; I felt embarrassed that I'd been so brusque and wanted to explain that I can't just leave a session in the middle, but I felt suddenly very aware of Vernon hovering there.

'So, see you at four or so?'

'Yes. But don't come early, will you? I'll be in a meeting until ten to four.'

'That's very precise.'

'Yes.' I didn't want to launch into explanations about fifty-minute sessions in the middle of the lobby. 'Yes, it is.'

I headed for the stairs, hearing Vernon taking up his thread once more.

'We're really supposed to get three quotes, you see . . .'

Is this it?

'But how do I know if Donald really is *right* for me?' my client said.

'We've talked before about your difficulties in committing to a relationship in the past . . .'

'Yes. That's exactly the problem. How do I *know* whether it's just me getting cold feet again as soon as things start to get remotely serious or if he's simply the wrong person for me?'

'Well – let's look at this a little more closely. What makes you think that he's the *wrong* person, as you put it? How do you feel when you're together?'

She sighed and her shoulders drooped. She had one of my cushions on her lap and picked thoughtlessly at the seam – if I'd realized clients were going to use my soft furnishings as surrogate comfort objects, I'd have chosen something more robust.

'I do like him . . .'

I nodded. Well, it's a start.

'And I sometimes think that I really love him . . .'

I flicked my gaze over to the clock. It was coming up to quarter to four. The number of people who wait until near the end of a session to discuss their most pressing issues, you wouldn't believe. It's because that way it feels safe, of course, it's all right to delve into risky territory because they'll be saved by the bell before they get in too deep.

'But then we'll be walking in the park or having a meal out and I'll look across and see another couple and they'll be laughing or leaning in close, like they're desperate to hear what each other has to say, you know?'

'Mmm – mm.' I used my all-purpose mmm-mm. It's a basic, go-on-I'm-still-listening sort of noise.

'And they look like – well, proper couples – and

then I find myself looking at Donald and thinking, is this it?'

I raised my brows, a question.

'You know – *It*. I keep thinking I should be feeling more . . .'

'More . . . ?'

'Yes. *More*. More – more *everything*. More excited to see him, more interested in what he has to say, more pleased at the prospect of spending my entire life with him.'

'Relationships do go through a series of stages,' I pointed out. 'It isn't realistic to expect that first giddy in-love feeling to last for ever.'

'Yes. Of course. But if it was right, wouldn't I just *know*?' She put her hands up to her face. 'But I so don't want to be on my own again. I've done all that. Staying in with a video every bloody Saturday night and ordering too much Chinese takeaway because you don't even want the guy who takes your order to know that you're a sad cow sitting in on your own, or going out with a girlfriend who you don't like all that much but she's the only other woman you know who's free on a Saturday night, and the waiter gives you the worst table by the loos and you both drink way too much because you're surrounded by couples and if you had to look round the room stone cold sober, you'd attempt to stab yourself with your pudding fork. It's so fucking awful. I can't face it.'

'But do you believe that's a good reason to stay with Donald – out of fear? You were speaking earlier about wanting the best for him. Do you think that's fair on him?' Another practised glance at the clock. Two minutes left.

'No. It isn't fair. But he says I make him happy, so why not? If I'm lousy at relationships in any case, I may as well be with him and at least let him be happy rather than ditching him so we'll both end up miserable.'

She looked directly at me, for the first time beginning to acknowledge just how unhappy she was.

'I think you know that's not really the answer – you'd end up resenting him,' I said gently. 'And we do need to look at this further next time, but . . .'

She twisted to look at the clock, then stood up slowly and said goodbye.

Four o'clock came and went. Five past. Ten past. I might have known. The kind of person who damages your door then sends you a rude note is hardly likely to be punctual. I was on the verge of phoning the front desk to ask Vernon if he'd seen any sign of a handyman, when there was a firm rat-a-tat-tat knock at the door.

'Hi!' It was Mr Rude. No handyman in sight.

I peered past him into the corridor.

'I assumed you were bringing a handyman.'

'I am. That's me.'

'You're a handyman?'

'No, I'm a photographer. And you are?'

I ignored his question. 'I don't want someone to take a nice snapshot of my door – I want someone to mend it.'

'Look!' he said suddenly, slapping the door. 'Do you want this sorted or not?'

'Yes.' Then, as an afterthought, 'Please.'

'Right. Let's take a look. Sorry – can I just – ' He moved towards me, so I was forced to withdraw further into my hall. 'I need to see the back.'

He concluded that, as the door wasn't actually cracked or broken, he could probably hide the scrape with wood-filler.

'But won't that show?'

'Not if I sand it then paint it.'

Currently, aside from the scrape, the door is a rather nasty, institutional dark brown – a sort of shit-brown, to be honest. Originally, every door in the block was identical, but gradually the rules have been relaxed and now some doors have been painted white or black or even been replaced with ones that have glass panels to let in more light.

109

I stood there, thinking about it.

'Or wait for the insurance and have a new door. It's your call. Makes no odds to me.'

'And you think you can really make it look perfect?'

'It'll look fine. Better than fine. But *perfect*? Who knows?'

'I'm not sure . . .'

'It's only a door – what's the problem?'

'Well, I just want it to be *right*.'

He smiled and covered his mouth with his hand for a moment.

'Tell you what – I'll fill it and rub it down and paint it . . .'

'Yes . . .'

'Then, when you discover it's not quite *perfect*, give me a call and I'll come and smash it down – only I'll make a proper job of it this time, and then you can start over and call the insurers and get yourself a new door, OK?'

I looked at him and he stared back, unblinking.

'Well. What's it to be? Time's cracking on.'

'Filler then. Please. When can—'

He checked his watch.

'Bugger – I'm running late now. Tell you what – I'll do the filler tonight, then paint it at the weekend. No – not tonight – it might be late – after twelve – I don't want to keep you up . . .'

'It won't. I don't actually live here.'

'You're doing a bloody good impression of it. Are you house-sitting or something?'

'No. I do live *here* . . .' I waved an arm expansively to indicate the building as a whole. 'But I don't live *here*.' I slapped the door, as he had done.

'So – where do you live then?'

'Upstairs. On the fifth. The flat directly above this one, in fact.'

He made a face.

'What?'

'What?'

110

'You made a face. What did you mean by it?'

'Nothing. Just – bit weird, isn't it? *Two* flats, on different floors.'

'Not so different from having a house – besides, they're so small.'

'Tell me about it. By the time I got all my gear in, I realized there was no space for a bed. I'm sleeping on the window ledge.' His expression was perfectly deadpan.

'Hmm, well, nice for the summer . . . perhaps I should let mine out? Compact yet airy accommodation with open views? Anyway – ' God knows why I felt the need to justify myself. 'The two flats – it's just that I like to keep my work and home life separate. It's neater that way.'

'They're not that separate if you only live upstairs.' He was smiling.

'Psychologically separate,' I explained. 'More than geographically.'

'Ah-ha!'

Don't you hate it when people act as if they've got you sussed? I gave him what I hoped was a withering glance.

'Anyway. So – the *door*. It would be great if you could do it tonight. As long as you won't disturb my neighbours?'

'I'll wear slippers and muffle my spatula.'

I suppressed a smile.

'Oh – and get some paint, will you?' he called back down the corridor. 'We need undercoat and gloss. And for God's sake pick something jollier than this disgusting Hint of Turd!'

A good impression

I dragged poor old Stephen with me on Saturday to help me choose paint.

'Here's some undercoat,' he pronounced. 'Now, what colour are you having?'

'Well, black, I thought.'

He nodded slowly, considering.

'Yes. Professional. Authoritative. Serious. That should work.'

'Or white maybe?'

'Hmm – fresher, I suppose. Lighter. Still smart.' He nodded once more.

'Not a colour then?'

'Well, you don't want to look . . . trivial, do you?'

Heaven forbid.

'No, but . . .' I hesitated.

He smiled, waiting. Stephen's always so patient. I just love it that he doesn't interrupt me all the time, like my family.

'You don't think black's a bit – severe?' I asked him.

'Not really, no.'

'Oh.'

I picked up a small can of Ebony gloss.

'Or maybe I should go for navy blue or dark green?' I put it down again.

'Sweetie, have it dayglo pink if you like.' He laughed, tickled at the preposterous thought.

For a moment, I was tempted to pick something outlandish, to have my door dayglo pink or lime green or metallic silver just for the fun of seeing his face. But then, he rarely sees my office in any case, so what would be the point?

I walked my fingers along the rows of cans: Racing Green, Prussian Blue, Pillar Box Red, Ivory, Brilliant White . . .

'Sweetie . . .'

'Sorry, sorry!'

'We're seeing Mike and Liz at seven fifteen and I want to check my e-mail.'

'I know, I know – sorry, I'm coming.'

I grabbed a tin of paint and my tin of undercoat and hurried over to the till.

*   *   *

On Saturday night, if we're not away for the weekend and haven't booked cinema tickets, we sometimes meet up with Stephen's friends Mike and Liz. I usually see my own friends during the week; Stephen's not mad keen on most of them, to be honest. Liz and Mike are tremendously nice and it's great that we both get on so well with both of them. And they're very easy company, too – they don't keep interrupting each other or trying to probe your innermost thoughts the whole time – you can just chat away about nothing at all and then you look at your watch and realize that the whole evening's gone by.

We were having supper at their place, a small terraced house in Dalston or, as Liz and Mike call it, 'Islington Borders'.

'Of course, this area's really, *really* coming up now,' said Liz.

'Yes – you can get a proper cappuccino just down the road,' Mike added. 'And it's not that far from the tube. You can power-walk it in only twenty-eight minutes.'

'Gosh. How are the schools?' Stephen asked, although Mike and Liz don't have any children.

'We-e-e-ll. We're planning to go private.' Mike began topping up our glasses.

'Are you – thinking of starting a family then?'

'Of course.' Liz smiled. 'We thought we should have our first, say, end of next year, then the second about two and a half years after that. We'd like one of each, ideally.'

'Right. Great.'

She probably had it all scheduled in their joint diary: Conceive Baby No. 1 for delivery in November.

'And how about you two? C'mon, Stephen, I have mega-mega plans for the ultimate stag night!' Mike gave him a manly slap on the back.

'Don't you dare get married without us! No sneaking off to the Caribbean!' Liz laughed and gave me a conspiratorial look.

'We wouldn't dream of it,' Stephen assured them. 'Would we, darling?'

'No, of course not.'

'But we were rather thinking of next spring or summer, weren't we, sweetie?'

I took a sip of my wine.

'Mmm. But we still need to find the perfect place. We found somewhere nice recently but the room was too small.'

'OH!' Liz let out a squeal and clapped her hands together.

Then she launched into an account of the most perfect, perfect wedding venue. It was just absolutely super, to die for, she wished she'd seen it before they got married and she knew for sure that I would just love it, love it, love it. A friend of hers had taken her there to look at it last week and they'd been able to look round while the staff were preparing the tables for a wedding and everything – *everything* – the flowers – the room – the setting – beautiful gardens – fountains – the choice of menus – it was all perfect. *Completely perfect.*

'We must make an appointment. Why don't you note down the details, darling?'

'Yes, of course.' I fetched my handbag from the hall and fished out my notebook.

'It sounds ideal.' Stephen raised his glass. 'Here's to the *perfect* wedding.'

I raised my glass and smiled.

'I hope it's not too expensive,' I said.

Stephen fiddled with his signet ring, then winked at me.

'Let's not worry about that now.'

'Ooh – leave the finances to Stephen!' Liz nudged me. 'You're so lucky, Georgia. You wouldn't believe the fuss Mike makes every time I buy so much as a pair of shoes!'

'Why?' I was puzzled because Liz works and earns quite good money herself, not as much as Mike, but certainly enough to buy the occasional pair of shoes if she wants them. 'You don't expect him to pay for them, do you?' I laughed.

She looked at me as if I were being slightly stupid.

'It's a joint account.'

'Yes, but surely you each have your own too – for personal stuff?'

'No. Whatever for? We don't need one. It's so much easier this way.'

I tried not to look too horrified. I accept that, eventually, I suppose Stephen and I will have some sort of joint account, just for bills and so on, but I don't want to merge completely and have to explain myself because I've dared to take Ellen out for a meal. Not that Stephen's mean, he isn't, but I can't bear the thought of feeling someone might be checking up on me and I like my things to be separate.

'Just you wait and see,' Liz attempted to reassure me. 'Once you're married, you'll be the same.'

Mike waved the wine bottle over my glass once more. Normally, I refuse after the first glass, but he was so persistent and I was feeling quite thirsty for some reason.

'Thank you.'

'This must be good wine, Mike – you know Georgia's not normally much of a drinker.'

'Come on, Georgia, let's get you plastered!'

Don't you just hate people trying to tell you how to have a good time? I took two more sips, then deliberately left the rest.

9

The open door

I tried to coax Stephen to brunch on Sunday morning, but he said he wasn't in the mood and, anyway, he'd been really recently so he wasn't due to go again for weeks, was he?

'No need to make it sound like a penance. You don't have to go at all if you don't want to. It's supposed to be fun.'

'Don't be crotchety, you know I didn't mean it like that. You go, darling, and give everyone my best. I've got loads of work to do in any case.'

'OK. Sure you don't mind if I go?'

'No. Really. See you later – or tomorrow?'

'Tomorrow. I must do my laundry tonight.'

'Rightio.' He kissed me. 'I'll phone you later.'

I stayed at brunch until nearly one, but Ellen didn't show up. Unc came with Auntie Audrey, and a neighbour popped in, a rather interesting man with one of those shaggy, untrimmed beards that look as if they've been dug up from the bottom of an amateur dramatics props box; it was so big and dense that I found myself transfixed by it and had to keep consciously jerking my gaze away so I wouldn't seem to be staring rudely. But brunch is never the same without Ellen. I love Unc and

Auntie but she always frowns at you if you put your elbows on the table. Matt's got awful table manners – he's always eating with his mouth open, which I hate, but as soon as I see Audrey frowning at him, I start bristling with outrage on his behalf and I'm willing to defend to the death his right to eat disgustingly if he wants to. Also, she wears an unbelievable amount of make-up. Even at ten o'clock on a Sunday morning, she looks as if she's just heading off to the opera. I long to know just how deep the layer of gunge really is, you could set a whole team of archaeologists loose onto her cheeks and they could dig for days without getting down to actual skin. And her eyebrows have been zealously over-plucked, so that they seem merely sketched in as an afterthought, and they're too arched so she always looks rather surprised, as if she's just sat on something nasty. I kept looking round for Ellen, wanting to see her doing her Auntie Audrey face.

When I got back home, I found a note had been pushed under my door.

'Filler all done. Need to have door open to paint it and while it's drying. When's good for you? Or let me have the keys (if you can trust me not to demolish the rest of your flat).
   Leo the Barbarian.
PS – Did you get the paint?'

At least he'd thought to put his phone number this time.

'Hello, Mr Kane? Er . . . Leo?'

'Yup.'

'It's Georgia Abrams, about the—'

'Yup – now please don't tell me you're not happy with the door. It'll look fine when it's painted.'

I explained I hadn't even seen it yet, because I was in my upstairs flat, but that I'd bought the paint and he said he could do it tonight or I'd have to wait another week.

'Tonight? Well, I was planning . . .' It sounded pathetic to say I was planning on doing my laundry, but I didn't want to have the door open without my being there.

'Or leave it for now. I promise to come back.'

'Come back?'

'I'm going to Dublin tomorrow at the crack of dawn. But, don't worry – I wouldn't dream of emigrating until I've completed the door to your satisfaction.'

'Do you always take the piss out of people you barely know?'

'No. Only the ones I like.'

'You're very direct, aren't you?'

'I find it saves time. Why – does it bother you?'

'Not at all. No. Why should it?'

'Well, we could go on like this all night, I'm sure, but I'd better get on with it. So – you want to lend me the keys or what?'

'Oh, no – I'll let you in. I need to do some work down there anyway.'

'That's OK – can't blame you for not trusting me. You don't know me from Adam.'

'No, it's not that – ' I was trying to be polite.

'Yes, it is. It's OK. You're right not to trust people too quickly – I always trust everybody from Day One and I've had my fingers burned more than once. Well. Let's not dwell on me and my past mistakes or we really will be here all night. Bang on my door when you're ready – number 418.'

Crossed wires

'Hi!' He was holding a cordless phone and he mouthed 'Sorry' at me. 'Yup . . . Yup.' A sudden laugh. 'OK. Yup, I've got to go now, I've got someone here . . . No . . . no . . . yup, it's a she, but no, she isn't.' Another laugh. 'You're unbelievable . . . Yeah, I will . . . You too. Lots of love. Bye.'

I felt my cheeks flaming. How incredibly rude.

118

'No, she isn't'? What the hell did he mean by that? Presumably, that was his girlfriend on the phone and he was reassuring her that I wasn't any kind of threat – No, she isn't attractive? No, she isn't beautiful? No, she isn't remotely sexy? No, she isn't my type? Of course, there's no reason why I should give a toss about some stranger's opinion of me – and an extremely rude stranger at that – but *still* . . . I do have some feelings.

He put the phone down and looked at me. I was torn between wanting to appear entirely unconcerned and wanting to punch him.

'What?'

I looked back at him, unsmiling.

'What?' he repeated. 'You look cross.'

'How perceptive of you. Do you normally talk about people in that way as if they're not in the room?'

'In what way?'

I sighed. I could tell he was being deliberately obtuse.

'In that way: "It's a she, but no, she isn't." What the hell's that supposed to mean? If you want to bitch about me to your girlfriend, fine – but you might at least wait until I'm out of the room, don't you think?'

'Whoa – hold it right there. Is this all because of your door or what?'

'The door? No, what's that got to do with it? Excuse me but on the phone just now, you said—'

'I'm not talking about that. It's just that every time I say anything to you, you seem to plunge off into the deep end and take offence where absolutely none is intended.'

'You're saying I'm paranoid?'

He looked at me, then gave a cautious smile.

'Can't we just start again? I'm sorry if I've rubbed you up the wrong way – I know I have a tendency to speak first, think later, but . . .' He shrugged.

'I'm sorry, too. Perhaps I have been a little . . .

awkward,' I conceded. 'But, you must admit, on the phone—'

He laughed.

'Do you honestly think for one second that I'd be rude about you on the phone while you're standing right there? I might be rude to your face, sure – but not about you as if you weren't there. No way.'

'Fine. OK, I take your word for it.'

'No, you don't. I can see it in your face. That was my mother and, as she's just as nosy as every other member of my family, she wanted to know if you were a girlfriend, OK? And I was merely saying that you weren't – "no, she isn't" – a statement of fact, not an insult or a slanderous defamation of your character or person – you agree?'

'Oh. Sorry. Somehow, it just sounded . . .' I looked down at my feet. How could I have been so ridiculous? So embarrassing. 'It's really good of you to fix my door yourself,' I said, changing the subject. 'I do appreciate it.'

'No problem. I broke it – I'll fix it.' He picked up a set of keys. 'Right – let me at it then.'

I unlocked my door and gestured to the bag of paint and brushes.

'It's all in there. What about your clothes?'

'You're kidding?' He gestured to his, admittedly rather faded, shirt and well-washed jeans. 'I don't think I own a single item of clothing that wouldn't be improved by a fresh lick of paint. But – do you have a dust sheet or anything to protect your floor?'

'No, I don't think so. Hang on.' I opened one door of the large built-in cupboard in my hall just a crack and peered in.

'Is that where you've stashed the bodies of your exes? It's OK – I won't peek.'

I never let anyone see inside that cupboard – or the one in my other flat. I'd be less ashamed of them if they did contain the remains of my ex-boyfriends, to be honest.

'Strangely enough, no it isn't. It's just rather full at the moment and I don't want anything to fall out. My exes wouldn't fit in here – they're boxed up and in the basement.'

He nodded, his face serious.

'Very wise. Good solution.'

'Yes, I think so. Anyway – we can use newspapers, can't we?' I retrieved some from the cupboard, carefully sliding them out through the half-opened door, and started spreading them out.

'Here, I can do that. You get on with your work or whatever.'

I sat at my desk and took out my notebook so that I could write up my notes from yesterday's sessions properly. Fired up my laptop and switched on my printer.

'Hey – glad you resisted the dubious delights of Dried Turd!' he called through.

'Yes. It is better, isn't it?'

'Much. Perhaps you'll start a trend.'

'Perhaps.' I wasn't really listening, to be honest. I was hoping he'd just shut up and get on with it but he was obviously one of those people who have to keep talking the entire time, even if they don't have anything particular to say.

'Do you want a coffee or anything?' I called through.

'What's the anything?'

'Tea. Herb tea. Water.'

'Er, coffee then. Thanks. Black, no sugar.'

A couple of minutes later, he stuck his head round the door.

'Er, hi?' venturing a step into my inner sanctum.

'Yes? I'm just bringing the coffee.' I stood up, crossed to the kettle.

'Hey, isn't this great!' He came in uninvited, looking round at the room. 'How do you keep it so – empty?'

'I only use it for work. As I mentioned, the other half of my life's upstairs.'

'Oh, yes. Still – you're so tidy. This is like something out of a magazine.'

'Well, you have to be tidy in such a small space or it'd drive you crazy. Besides, it wouldn't be appropriate to be cluttered – I see my clients here.'

'Why – what do you do?'

'I'm a counsellor – as in counsel not council, as in trying to help people with their emotional and psychological problems, not trying to improve waste-collection services or push through dodgy planning applications.'

He raised his eyebrows but said nothing.

'Meaning?'

'Nothing.'

'What? You think counselling's not a real job, I suppose? That people should just pull their socks up and get on with their lives rather than coming to someone like me. That's so English – this ridiculous belief that it's fine to go to a doctor if you sprain your wrist or something but that if you're unhappy you should just soldier on regardless and never seek any kind of help. It really annoys me.'

'So I see. Have you finished now?' He looked like he was about to laugh.

'Yes. I suppose so.' I handed him his coffee. 'Biscuit?'

'Please. I can't imagine how you got it into your head that I'm anti-counselling. Quite the contrary – I've had – anyway, I'm not, not at all. I was simply intrigued as to why you seemed so cynical about the other sort – councillors. Course, now I'm also curious to know why you're so defensive about your own chosen profession.'

'Are you trying to analyse me? A lot of people seem to find it amusing to try and prove that a counsellor has problems too – they think it's a game they can catch you out on.'

'Well, it wouldn't be how I'd get my kicks, but if you say so. I can't imagine that being a counsellor means you never have a single problem – but I guess you're maybe a bit more mature than the rest of us in the way you deal with them.'

How annoying. Just when I thought I had him figured, he turns out to be quite thoughtful and intelligent after all.

'Well, I don't know about that . . .' I said modestly. Then I looked up to see two of my neighbours blatantly peering in at us through the open door. People can be so rude, it's quite unbelievable. I gave them a chilly look, which should have been enough to send them scurrying on their way, would have been I'm sure, had not this stupid Leo character waved at them, I mean *waved* for God's sake and called out, 'Hi there!' He went out to talk to them, and I hung back, watching. He was showing them the door, patting it, chatting away as if nothing could be more enjoyable than to stand there discussing the minutiae of door decoration with two old ladies. They were soon giggling away.

'So, you come and bang on my door anytime, OK? It's 418, just along the corridor there! Bye-bye girls – behave yourselves now! Don't talk to any strange men!' There were more shrieks of laughter then they moved on. I so wanted to close that door. I got up again to close the inner door, but as I neared it, he started again.

'You've got some great neighbours.'

'They're all right. They're fairly quiet, at least.'

He gave me another assessing sort of look, then he stared straight past me towards the window.

'Now this is fantastic! A balcony! I don't have one on my side.'

I'm quite proud of my little balcony, even though it's a stupid impractical shape. It runs along the width of the flat, but it's very narrow. All I have on it is a cluster of plants in pots, one chair which I've painted a soft grey-blue and a lantern.

'Far too small to have parties or anything out there though,' I said.

123

'No, but you could have a little table and another chair so two of you could eat out there.'

'No, you can't. It's too narrow.'

'No, it isn't. See – not if you moved those plants along that way, you could easily—'

'No, you couldn't. It's not possible.'

He looked at me again, as if puzzled. Why on earth did he think he could tell me how to start rearranging my flat? I'm very happy with it exactly the way it is.

'Well.' He retreated to the hallway. 'Most things *are* possible – *I* find – if you really want them to be.'

After that, I left the inner door open, partly so I could keep an eye on him. He continued to talk to me and to enter into conversation with every single person who went past him along the corridor, so that each time I attempted to settle back into my work, I'd be interrupted by the sound of people chattering away – 'Ooh, what's going on here then?' – 'Oh, you're the man who had the accident, aren't you?' – 'Have you moved in then?' It seemed as if there wasn't a single resident in the entire block who didn't know all about it; they'd probably got a taped announcement being broadcast in the lift. God, it's only a bloody door – I wanted to call out: 'Haven't you people got lives to go to?'

'Do you feel compelled to speak to every person you see?'

'Why – don't you?'

'No. Of course not. Why should I?'

'Because people are interesting? Because you might hear something you've never heard before? Because someone who starts out a total stranger might become a friend for life?'

'Oh, come on.'

'Why? Have you known all your friends for your entire lifetime?'

What a stupid question. I raised one eyebrow.

'Well then. So they were strangers at some point?'

'Yes. *Obviously*. But – '

He smiled.

'But?'

'It's hardly the same thing.' I turned back to my work.

'This undercoat's done now.' He came further into the room. 'Shouldn't take long to dry, but I'm desperate for a bite to eat, so I'll slope off now and get a pizza or something, then come back and do the gloss, OK?'

'Fine.' God, I could just murder a pizza. I wondered if I could possibly ask him to pick one up for me, seeing as he was going anyway. Maybe I should have been a bit more polite to him. I hate asking people for favours.

He paused by the door.

'Can I get you one? I'd say come with me, but it's better for the door to dry while it's open.'

'Um, no, of course. Actually, yes, could you get me one?' I reached for my handbag and took out my purse. 'Where are you going?'

He told me.

'There's a Pizza Express just a bit further, if you don't mind . . . the pizzas are miles better.' I described how to get there. 'Can I have a Giardiniera, only with artichokes instead of leeks and no black pepper please? Should I write that down or will you remember?'

He sucked in his breath through his teeth.

'God, I'm really not sure – what was it? Baked bean and pineapple pizza with extra garlic?'

I peeled off a yellow stickie and quickly wrote it down.

'I really don't need that. I'm not six, you know. Artichokes, not leeks – see?'

'Yes. And no black pepper – you must emphasize that or they get carried away with it. Please will you be sure to get it exactly right? I like it like that. Not any other way.' I started to hand over the money.

''s OK. I think I can stump up for a pizza.'

'It's not necessary. I can buy my own.'

'I'm sure you can but I would *like* to pay for it. We

don't have to argue about everything – we're not married, are we? Call it compensation for the door if you like.'

. . . and no black pepper

I passed him a plate, cutlery and cloth napkin, which were met with another of those lopsided smiles and the raised eyebrows. I don't know why I'd bothered with the napkin – if he wasn't worried about getting paint on his clothes, I doubted that the odd splash of tomato was going to vex him unduly.

'Pepperoni pizza with many, many extra anchovies,' he said, passing me a box. I opened the lid. Giardiniera. Artichokes, not leeks. I searched for telltale dark specks of black pepper, but by some miracle he seemed to have managed to order it correctly.

'Does it pass muster?'

'It does. Thank you.' I passed him a tumbler and a corkscrew for the wine he'd bought. 'I'm sorry I haven't got any proper wine glasses down here.'

'But cloth napkins?'

'I prefer them. Even if I'm just having a bowl of soup on my own.'

He laughed, then started to open the wine.

'I suppose you think that's very prissy?'

He shook his head while he swallowed a mouthful of pizza.

'It's not that. Don't get cross, but it reminds me of my mum, that's all. She always has proper napkins. Gets out the bone-handled fish knives and forks even if we're just having takeaway fish and chips.'

I asked him about his family and he explained that his parents had moved from London to the outskirts of Glasgow over fifteen years ago, when his father had taken early retirement.

'But he's dead now, alas. He died a couple of years ago.'

'I'm sorry – was it sudden?'

'Yeah. Stroke. He'd had two before so I guess it was on the cards – we sort of expected it.'

'That doesn't make it any easier. We imagine we can somehow protect ourselves by saying we expect the worst – '

'Then when it actually happens, you're still knocked for six. True. Too true.' He held out the wine to offer me some.

'Just half a glass, thank you.'

'And you – what about your parents?'

'My dad lives up in—'

My mobile started to ring.

'Sorry, please excuse me – hello?'

'George, hi, it's me.' Ellen. 'Where are you? You're not at home.'

'No. I am allowed out occasionally. Actually, I'm in my office.'

Leo stood up and made a walking movement with his fingers, jerked his thumb towards the door – a question.

'No, it's fine. It's only my sister.'

'*Only* your sister?' said Ellen, loud in my ear. 'I'm not an *only*.'

'Behave. What do you want?'

'Can I borrow the car tomorrow evening? Who've you got there? Not the P-h?'

'No, it isn't. What do you want it for? And, by the way, it's not *the* car – it's *my* car.'

'Yeah, yeah, we know. Why are you being mysterious? It's a man, isn't it?'

'Yes, it is, but—' I turned away from Leo. 'Anyway, yes you can borrow the car, but I want it returned with at least the same amount of petrol in it as there is now.'

'OK, OK, I promise. I'll come by at six or so tomorrow to get the keys, yeah?'

'Fine. See you then. Take care. Bye.'

Leo had stood up and had his back to me, washing the plates and cutlery at the sink.

'You don't need to do that.'

'Won't take a minute. I'd better get on with that gloss.'

There's no such thing as an accident . . .

'I think we may have a small problem,' Leo said, knocking at the inner door just as I was backing up my files.

'What kind of a small problem?'

'A should-have-read-the-paint-tin-first kind of problem.'

I frowned.

'It says to leave it sixteen hours between coats. It won't be properly dry till tomorrow morning so you shouldn't really shut the door.'

'I can't leave it open all night.' I stood up and went into the hall, then stopped dead in disbelief. 'Why is it *red*?'

'What do you mean – "why is it red?"? It's red because that's what you bought, see?' He held up the tin. A small label proclaimed it 'Pillar Box Red'.

'But that's not what I chose! I *know* I picked up the black.'

'Well . . .' He shrugged. 'No, you didn't. It's red.'

'Thank you. Yes. I can see that.'

'I like it. It's way better than the brown you had before.'

'But it's not what I was planning to have.'

'Maybe not, but it's what you've got. Look – I'm not going to get a second coat done before I go tomorrow in any case. Why not live with it for a week, then when I come back, I can either do a second coat of this or go over it in black?'

'I suppose so . . .' I stepped out into the corridor, looking up and down at the other doors, mostly brown, a varnished wood one, two white ones.

'Now, the bigger problem is the drying time. Obviously, we can't leave your flat unattended . . .'

128

'I can't sleep here with the door open – anyone could stroll in.'

'OK – so, either both of us stay up all night here, talking, reading, arguing, playing cards, trading insults or whatever – '

'I can't – I've got a session first thing. I'll be shattered.'

'Or I could sleep here.'

He read my silence.

'I know you don't know me. All I can say is that you can trust me, I promise. Take your laptop and anything else valuable if you like. OK – why don't I give you *my* spare keys as a hostage, then if I nick anything, you can confiscate my cameras and equipment while I'm away? Or we can just close the door tonight and it'll stick all round the frame, but so what? You'd only see it when it's open. Not exactly the end of the world.'

When I first furnished the office, I bought a sofa bed rather than an ordinary sofa because I thought it would be useful for guests, but as it's turned out, I've never had anyone to stay down there because I can't have the place looking like a tip filled with people's bags and shoes and belongings all over the place when clients are coming, so it's never been used. If Ellen stays over, she sleeps on the other sofa bed I have upstairs or, if we can't be bothered to open it out, she shares with me.

'Well, if you really don't mind . . .'

'Course not. It's my fault – I should have checked the tin first.'

'No, I should have.'

'You're right. It *is* your fault.' Then he laughed. 'But I must pack for Dublin.'

'Do you want a hand?' I said it automatically, without thinking, partly because I often help Stephen pack when he has to travel for work, I suppose.

'What – really? I loathe packing.'

129

It seemed mean to withdraw the offer, even though I'd sort of said it by accident.

'Sure.'

Strange man's underpants

We pulled my door to slightly, and wrote a 'Wet Paint' sign to put on the floor outside, then went to his flat. There was a long table against one wall and a couple of plain wooden chairs, an unexpectedly smart dark red sofa and a lot of equipment. He opened the built-in cupboard in the hall and took out a large holdall.

'Leave my door open too,' he said. 'Then we'll hear anyone coming along and you can stick your head out to check it's not burglars.'

'How will I know? What if they're not wearing stockings on their heads and carrying a jemmy?'

'You'll have to ask them. Now, what do I need?'

'What are you doing there? Work or pleasure?'

'Work *is* pleasure – well, on a good day. It's work. Pretty much non-stop – I'm doing some stuff for a travel guide to Dublin. Another photographer's done most of it, but they still had some gaps. You ever been?'

I nodded.

'So, tell me what to see. I've got a list from them, but it never does any harm to shoot extra stuff.'

I made a number of suggestions, while he pulled bits of clothing out of the cupboard.

'Right,' I said, sitting on the floor by the holdall. 'You're going for, what, a week?'

'Four or five days.'

'Right. Jeans? Trainers?'

He passed them down to me.

'Pants. Socks. Shaving things. Toilet bag plus razor, toothbrush etcetera. What else? Aftershave?'

I balled the pairs of socks and stuffed them well into the trainers, then suddenly felt embarrassed as he dropped five pairs of underpants into the bag in front of me. Briefs, not boxers like Stephen, I noticed. Nice

130

plain black ones and soft grey ones. I looked up at him then and we both laughed.

'Sorry – I don't normally throw my underwear at women I hardly know.'

'That's OK – I don't normally pack for strange men either.'

He smiled.

'Now what?'

'Do you need something smart? For meetings?'

'Dunno. I might go and see a couple of magazine bods while I'm there.'

'What've you got?'

He held up an awful old grey suit and a crushed linen jacket with too-narrow lapels.

I shook my head.

'What else?'

'Not a lot. Some of my stuff's still up in Scotland.'

'You ought to have a few decent things for when you see clients.'

'I know. I'm hopeless. I hate clothes shopping.'

'Now. Shirts . . . um, I could come with you some-time if you like. Shopping, I mean.'

'You're kidding?' He rummaged in the cupboard once more then emerged with an armful of shirts.

'No. Why not?'

'God, that'd be great. Here are my shirts.'

'Hold them up, one by one.'

He did.

'Yes, ma'am. Did you used to be in the army?'

'Do you want help or don't you? That one, not that one. Dear God – *no*. That shouldn't be let out of your wardrobe – ever. Charity shop. That's OK at a pinch. And I'd burn that one if I were you.'

He passed them to me and I folded each one, aligning the sleeves properly to minimize crushing.

'It'd be better if you had a suitcase with rigid sides.'

'I'll add it to my shopping list, shall I?' He tilted his head to one side, smiling.

131

'Sorry – I'm too used to organizing other people. It's become a habit.'

'No sweat. It doesn't bother me. Don't suppose you want to come to Dublin, by any wild chance?'

I wasn't sure if he meant it flirtatiously – or if he just needed someone to help him run his life. If his out-of-date wardrobe was anything to go by, he could definitely do with a live-in housekeeper-cum-manager.

'As your personal valet?'

Tell him, I thought, why haven't you told him about Stephen yet? This is all becoming far too flirty-flirty.

'I don't suppose my boyfriend would be too happy about it.'

'Oh. I guess not.'

'Fiancé, I should say.'

'Oh. Right. Congratulations. When's the happy day?'

God, I do wish people would stop asking me that.

'Whenever.' I waved my hand airily. 'There's no rush.'

'Really?' He disappeared into the bathroom and returned with a plastic carrier bag. 'This is my toilet bag for the moment. My proper one seems to have disappeared.' He folded the end over and handed it to me. 'Why no rush? Life's all too short.'

'It is. But that's no reason not to plan, is it?' I tucked the ad hoc toilet bag into a corner of the holdall and zipped it up. 'It's just like packing – plan properly and everything will be fine. No getting caught out. No surprises.'

He raised his brows and did his peculiar lopsided smile once more.

'No surprises? Now, where's the fun in that?'

Act with caution

There is a strange man sleeping in my consulting room. He could be prowling around, looking through my things or – dear God – my cupboard. He could have broken open the locked filing drawer and be reading my clients' confidential case notes. He could be eating toast and chocolate and jam doughnuts all through the night and leaving crumbs and sugar and chocolate smears on my sofa. He could be spilling coffee all over my carpet. At least I don't keep anything really personal down there – there's no underwear or diary or photographs or anything like that, but . . .

I must be bonkers. Why on earth have I let a complete stranger loose in my flat? It's the kind of thing Ellen would do. And I have a client coming first thing. What if he doesn't get up in time?

3.22 a.m. Perhaps I'll just nip down and check that the contents of my office are still there at least. That can't do any harm, can it? I know, I'm probably being neurotic, but I can't sleep without making sure.

I put on my dressing gown and pull the cord extra tight, knot it in a double bow. One good thing about this block is that you don't get any weirdos wandering around the corridors in the middle of the night.

I tiptoe down the stairs, although as I'm barefoot there's really no need and no-one could possibly hear me. Through the double doors and along the hallway. Slow down.

The front door is open, of course, and there's a dim light from within. Perhaps he's reading? I hover outside by the Wet Paint sign for a minute, trying to hear the turning of pages, but there's no sound. I push open the door a bit further – the paint's only very slightly tacky. I'm sure we could have locked it and it would have been absolutely fine, far more sensible than getting caught up in this ridiculous charade. What can I have been thinking of?

The inner door is shut. Of course. But I can see the light beneath it. He could have simply fallen asleep with the light on. Lots of people do that. I've even done it myself a couple of times. Or he could be reading. Or he could be going through my stuff. Or he could have left with all my things in a van. I quietly get down on my knees and crouch right down to the floor to listen at the gap. Maybe he snores? Wait – what was that? There was definitely – a noise. A small but distinct noise that could be – anything. Absolutely anything. Oh, for God's sake. I rest my head on the floor and try to peer under the door. Marvellous. I can see about two inches of carpet in front of my nose. And nothing else.

There! Definitely a noise. I *knew* I was right. I think I can hear him moving. A creak – is he by my desk? This was such a stupid idea. Now what the hell do I do? Throw open the door and demand an explanation? That'll scare him, won't it? Perhaps I should just creep back upstairs. He probably only got up to get a glass of water. Another creak.

Suddenly, the door flies open and he's standing over me brandishing the wine bottle.

I scream and he lets out a yell.

'Shit – it's you! What the hell are you doing, creeping around? You nearly gave me a heart attack!' He lowers the bottle. 'Why are you scuttling about on the floor? What *are* you doing?'

He puts out a hand to help me up.

'I thought you – I was just – checking,' I said feebly. 'I was, you know . . .'

'Hang on a tick.' He goes out into the corridor, standing there in just his jeans with no shirt on. Not surprisingly, the noise has roused a couple of the neighbours, who have opened their front doors a crack to peer out. 'Everything's fine,' he tells them, with solemn authority, as if he is used to handling this sort of thing all the time. 'No need to worry. Georgia saw a huge spider and had a bit of a panic. Sorry, folks. Very sorry.'

He turns and comes back inside.

'I can't believe you said that! I'm not even scared of spiders.' I try not to seem as if I'm looking at his chest.

'So? They don't know that, do they? It was all I could think of.' He stands back to let me in. 'Come in – come and see that I haven't damaged anything or bundled all your belongings out the window.'

'I feel incredibly embarrassed.'

He laughs.

'It's fine – you should have just banged on the door and said, "Oi, *you*! You're not messing with my stuff, are you?" You can't go creeping around a respectable block like this in your dressing gown, sneaking into strange men's bedrooms – whatever will your neighbours think?'

'I didn't think anyone was going to see me.'

'There, I told you. You can't plan for everything. Life is full of surprises.'

'Your life – maybe. Not mine.'

'That's fine as long as you live in a cocoon and never have any contact with anyone else – '

'Especially not peculiar photographers with a tendency towards clumsiness and a complete lack of regard for all social conventions – '

'Especially not anyone like that. Bound to cause no end of trouble. Do you want a well-after-dinner coffee now that you've – dropped by unexpectedly? Says he, blithely offering you your own coffee in your own flat.'

'I'd better not.' I clutch my dressing gown round me more tightly. It goes all the way down to my ankles, so it's not as if it's revealing, but I'm not wearing a bra, of course, and I'm beginning to feel extremely self-conscious. 'It's very late.'

'Good night then. See you in the morning.'

'Yes. Sorry. Sleep well.'

'You too. And don't worry. I only booked the van to remove all your stuff for half seven – you can get plenty of rest before then.'

10

A suitable mate?

'Ellie, I must tell you – I've met *such* a lovely man – ' I
said, when she finally arrived at our café.

'Ooh, who's this then?' She started shedding her
various belongings, creating a nest of jacket, scarf, and
numerous bags around her the way she always does.

'He's called Leo and he's a freelance photographer.
He's just moved in, on the same floor as my office.'

'Hang on – wasn't he the guy who bashed your door
down? The one you said was abominably rude?'

'He didn't bash it down – it was just a scrape. And,
he's not *that* rude, just direct. And he *has* fixed the
door. Do you want to hear about him or not?'

'Go on then. What's he like when he's not being
rude or demolishing the fixtures and fittings? Shag
potential?'

'Well, he's not exactly what you'd call handsome, not
in the conventional sense – '

'Is he what you'd call pig-ugly in the conventional
sense?'

'No!' I banged down my teacup. 'Absolutely not! He's
really attractive – just a bit crumpled-looking, you
know? He could probably shave a bit more often, and
his hair is slightly receding – well, retreating at a gallop
might be more accurate, but—'

'Wow – sounds gorgeous . . .'

'Oh, shut up! OK, so he's not good-looking in a boring, bland, film-starry way, so what? But you wouldn't push him out of bed. There's something really . . . moreish about him. And he's warm and bright and funny – you'd love him, I'm sure – and he's always in a whirl – I think he's a bit chaotic – '

'Just as well he's met you then. You'll soon sort him out.' She waved at the waitress, who mouthed, 'Latte?' at her.

'Will you let me tell you? He's sharp but not in a bad way, and very direct, always interrupting, bit like you really—'

'I don't interrupt!'

'You just did!'

'Only to defend myself, that doesn't count.'

'Shall I carry on or what?'

'Okey-doke, so not a ten on the looks front?'

'Don't be so shallow. No, more of a six. Maybe seven and a half in a dim light – '

'And you say *I'm* bitchy . . .'

'I'm not being bitchy, just honest. Anyway, you'd love his face – he's got gorgeous brown eyes and he looks at you really intensely as if he's trying to work out exactly what you're thinking at the same time as listening to what you're saying. And he smiles quite a lot only his smile's a bit lopsided, it's more of a slope than a smile – ' I raised my finger to my mouth. 'And this tooth here's got a chip out of it.'

'Bleugh.'

'No, it's not yucky – it's just you can't help noticing it. But you'll really like him, I know you will.'

Ellen had apparently stopped listening; she often did if she thought anyone was going on too long. She was digging around in her handbag, then her carrier bags.

'George, I've just got to nip next door . . .'

'For cigarettes? Oh, Ellen, for fuck's sake, you keep saying you're giving up but it's total bollocks! Aren't you even going to make an effort?'

138

'I *have* been! You've got no idea how hard it is. Stop lecturing me – I don't tell you how to live your life.' She scraped her chair back from the table. 'Won't be a minute.'

I could have kicked myself. Ellen is contrary by nature – the more I nag, the more she smokes, just to be awkward, to be rebellious, still, at the age of twenty-seven, enjoying the feeling of being naughty. It's ridiculous, but there it is. She knows that I only nag her because I care so much about her, but I really don't get it. I don't understand how anyone can wilfully commit slow suicide like that and still be so blasé about it, especially Ellen – who could be more full of life than Ellen? But then, as she always says, I'm not addicted so what do I know? I swear she gets the same thrill from smoking now that I did when I was fourteen and I used to sneak into the gap behind the gym with my two best friends to light up. But then you realize that it's disgusting and makes you horrible to kiss and you stop, don't you?

Ellen returned, puffing away.
    'Just *don't*, OK?' she said to me.
    I held up my hands, palms outwards.
    'I *wasn't*.'
    'Anyway, never mind all that. So? What are you planning to do?'
    'About what?'
    'The balding paparazzo, of course.'
    'He's not bald and he's not a paparazzo. He—'
    'Whatever.' She waved me away. 'What's the plan?'
    I shrugged.
    'Have him over for dinner at my place, I suppose, if you think that's a good idea? See how things go? Or maybe ask him to Sunday brunch?'
    'Good idea.' Ellen stubbed out her cigarette with exaggerated mashing movements, making a point. 'But what about Mr P-h? Have you told him?'

'No. Why should I? What's it got to do with Stephen?'

'I can't believe you're being so casual about this!'

'*I'm* being casual? *You* don't even seem all that excited. I thought you'd be really pleased.'

Ellen leant forward and took my hands.

'Oh, I *am*, George. I am. I'm *so* pleased. I can't think when I last saw you like this – it's just it's so not like you to go sneaking around—'

'What sneaking around? What are you on about?'

'Well – what you just said, of course. Surely it would be better to make a clean break first? You're always so honest. Or are you trying to keep Stephen on standby just in case things don't work out with Baldy? I can't believe you're *finally* going to get rid of the P-h after all this time . . . I may even miss him a bit. What? Why are you looking like you've swallowed a goldfish?'

I clunked down my cup with a bang.

'Haven't you been *listening*? Honestly, you *never* listen, it's so infuriating! What on earth makes you think that *I'm* interested in Baldy? In Leo I mean? I'm *immensely* happy with Stephen as you know.'

'But you—'

'I was telling you all about Leo because I thought *you* might like him. I was perfectly clear – it's only because you couldn't be bothered to listen properly – I was thinking of *you* – though God knows why I bother – you probably wouldn't like him because he's not some awful Peruvian-hatted geek or a ponytailed barman whose idea of stimulating conversation is saying, "You wan' sex?", so you wouldn't know what to do with him – I was going to invite him round to dinner to meet you, but forget it, just forget the whole thing—'

'But why the hell are you trying to pair him off with me when you're the one who's obviously bonkers about him?'

'I'm NOT!'

Faces turned towards us and I ducked my head and glared at Ellen.

'Well, you were doing a bloody good impression of it.

140

You looked all lit up and were going on and on about his gorgeous chipped teeth and his lovely shiny bald head—'

'*One* tooth has *one* small chip and he's not fucking bald for the fucking forty-fifth time, all right?'

Ellen sat back and lit another cigarette.

'Right. You're not in love with him even the tiniest bit – you're not in the least bit interested, you were only playing matchmaker for me, but you leap to defend him and his crumbling dentures and acres of naked scalp. Try taking all that bloody insight and wisdom you're so proud of and direct a bit of it at yourself, why don't you? You're gagging for him, just admit it.'

The thing was to remain calm. She had obviously completely got the wrong end of the stick.

'I can see now how you might have got the wrong impression. I shouldn't have gone on so long trying to sell him to you. My mistake. But – look – you'll see. Meet him. He's not even my type. Not remotely. He's disorganized and always dashing round in a frenzy. He'd drive me up the wall.'

'OK then.' Ellen took a dramatically deep drag on her cigarette. 'Have us both round to dinner or bring him to Sunday brunch and let's see if I like the look of him.'

'No problem.' I opened my bag to find my diary.

'And I take it Stephen will be coming too, of course?'

I paused, eyes down, toying with the ribbon marker of the diary.

'Mmm? Well, he's pretty busy right now. Probably easier with just us in any case.'

'Why?'

I shrugged.

'No reason really. No big deal. Just not sure that Leo would be Stephen's cup of tea, that's all.'

'I'm sure they'll cope now that they're both big boys.'

I clicked the point of my pen in and out.

'Give me some dates you can do, then I'll check when Leo's free.'

She rummaged in her various bags, then said she couldn't find her Filofax and would have to ring me later.

'And you won't have a problem with it if it's lust at first sight and we sit there with our tongues entwined all evening?'

She was only doing it to wind me up. Absolutely typical. Still, why should it bother me?

'Entwine away all you want – just retract your tongues long enough to eat something. I thought I might do that crispy chicken thing with the pesto in the middle.'

Ellen flung back her head and laughed.

'Right – ladies and gentlemen, take note. My sister's absolutely, definitely not in love with Old Shiny Head but she's just going to ever so casually rustle up her crispy chicken with her very own homemade pesto, which has been known to make men drool at her feet! Case closed. Bet you do your fruit bonfire thing, too.'

'*No*. Probably just put out a few bits of cheese. Anyway, it's not a fruit bonfire, it's *fruits flambés*.' Ellen made a face at me, which I ignored. 'I hadn't even thought about pudding. I'll just get some ice cream or something.'

Fruits flambés or flambéed fruit. She's right, it sounds pretentious in French. Fruit bonfire is better.

Whatever you call it, it is delicious. And it's piss easy, no more trouble than opening a tub of ice cream really. Yes. Some of those dark purple plums if I can get them, with ultra-fine slivers of orange peel and some blackberries. And maybe a few raspberries, all sealed in foil with a splash of Grand Marnier. Then you turn down the room lights and pour more of the flaming liqueur over the fruits. The scent is heavenly, intoxicating, the spectacle disproportionately impressive. Why is it that no-one can resist a pudding if you simply set light to it?

'Well, maybe a *bit* of fruit . . .' I said.

'If you really don't want him for yourself, you can tell him I did all the cooking. That'll prove it.'

I laughed. Ellen still has to be reminded to prick jacket potatoes before she puts them in the oven.

'Don't push your luck.'

The invitation

Leo was lying on the floor of my office, something he seemed to be doing quite a bit in the last few days because his studio was too full of equipment and there was nowhere to get comfortable. I was stretched out on the sofa, where my clients normally sit. I never sit there normally, so it felt fairly peculiar, the way it does if you borrow a jacket or something from a friend and catch sight of yourself in the mirror – and, just for a second, you feel that you know what it's like to be someone else.

'Any more coffee going?' He looked up at me.

'I'm not here just to wait on your every need, you know. Can you not navigate your way through the vast echoing recesses of my kitchen? You should be able to manage – kettle's due north once you come out of the east wing, OK? I have my water specially piped directly to my flat, it's very convenient, you should try it. If you get lost in there, just holler and I'll send in the troops to rescue you.'

He heaved himself up to his feet, suppressing a smile.

'D'you want another one?'

'Oh, all right then. God, I've done practically nothing this afternoon. You're a bad influence on me. Look, it's after five already. I'm supposed to be going out at seven.'

'Then it's miles too late to start messing about with your face now. You'll have to cancel.'

'Don't think anyone asked for your opinion, did they?' I got up and peered at my reflection in the small mirror in the hall. 'It's not that bad, is it?'

143

'Grotesque. I'm not playing this game. Why do women always do this? Anyway, even though you *are* clearly grotesque – are you up to anything this Sunday?'

Stephen is off at a conference on Monday, so was planning to stay in on Sunday to pack. He's terrifically organized about packing. Meticulous and efficient, more so than me even. He keeps a document on his laptop entitled 'Packing/list', which includes absolutely every single item of clothing or possession that he might possibly need; whenever he has to travel, he simply prints it out and highlights anything he wants to pack, then he ticks it off as he puts it into his case. It's a pleasure to help him pack – no, really it is. So nice to see someone who thinks ahead and plans for every eventuality. Makes me feel the world isn't such a chaotic place, being around him. I had been intending to go home for brunch, then see Stephen in the afternoon, go for a walk or see a film once he'd finished his packing, then listen to him practise his speech.

'Sort of. We have a kind of a family brunch thing at my dad's on Sundays, have done for years. We just talk and read the papers and eat bagels. Why don't you come too? It's very informal – Dad's always telling us to bring new people along. It stops us squabbling, gives us someone else to pick on.'

Suddenly, I very much wanted him to come. I couldn't remember the last time I'd brought a new guest to brunch. Stephen doesn't count, of course, because he isn't new any more and he always drags his feet about going, which takes the pleasure out of it. He usually visits 'the folks' for Sunday lunch and his stomach can't handle brunch as well. It isn't only that, I know. Being in the presence of my family isn't the most restful experience in the world. It isn't just that they talk all the time, *and* at the same time as each other; you can barely step inside the door before Ellen's off,

144

picking apart your clothes and your hair, or Matt's grilling you about your work and relationships. You start off thinking, isn't this nice to have someone so interested, then ten minutes later you're wondering whether you like your job as much as you thought you did. Matt has a knack of making you question everything when only half an hour before you'd been perfectly content. Or thought you were, at least.

'Please come. You can meet my sister, she's really gorgeous, and my dad would like you. He can't bear people who are too polite.'

'Thanks.'

'You know what I mean. And, if you get bored, you can always take a turn teasing my stepmother.'

He looked surprised.

'Don't you like her?'

I'd never really thought much about liking Quinn or not liking her – once she'd become ensconced in the household, I mean. She's just Quinn, who happens to have been married to Dad for over ten years. She isn't like a real mother, she never has been and never would be. Not that she's ever attempted to be maternal to any of us, she isn't stupid.

'Well – do you?' He stayed looking at me.

'I – I don't really know. She's just Quinn, you see? We've always teased her a bit because – well, that's just the way we are and she's such fair game. God, that sounds so mean. It's just that she wears these awful earrings and her clothes are peculiar – I don't know, coloured tights and strange, smocky dresses that nobody wears any more and patchwork jackets, like she's trying so desperately hard to be arty and bohemian when really she's quite ordinary and normal. And there's the cooking – her casseroles have always got things in them that you don't want – raisins or chickpeas or bits of kumquat or great big stalks of sage. You have to dredge all this sort of pond life out of the way until you can find this tiny bit of chicken or something normal at the bottom.'

'Ah, but do you *like* her?'

'You're very persistent, aren't you? Actually, I suppose I *do* – well, sort of. Quinn's fantastically fair. Same as Dad, come to think of it, though he's much ruder than she is. Also, she's not bitchy. Not like the rest of us. She's kind. Decent. Only a bit comical.' I felt ashamed. Am I really so low as to take the piss out of Quinn just because of her earrings and the fact that she puts chickpeas in everything? 'Anyway, you can see for yourself if you come on Sunday. Well – as you like. Not if you've got other plans of course.'

'No, that'd be great. It's just – ' he thrust his hands down into his pockets, suddenly looking embarrassed. 'Thing is – I dunno – it's kind of a bit – see, there's someone I have to see on Sunday. I think you'd get on, but – um – could I bring her too? No, sorry. Forget it. I've never even met your family. I shouldn't—'

'Um. No. Yes. Of course. That's fine! Brilliant! Do please bring her! How *nice*! Another new face. Dad'll be delighted!'

I had a horrible feeling in my insides, a heavy, churning feeling as if someone was tumble-drying a whole load of rocks in there. Why had I just said my father was always begging us to bring more guests? Why? Now I'd look rude and ridiculous if I tried to backtrack. Bugger. No – it would be fine. Why should it make any difference to me whether he brought anyone or not? Plus it would be an ideal opportunity for me to prove to Ellen that I'm not in the least bit romantically interested in him.

'Shall we meet here and go together – no – let's meet there, that'll be better.' I grabbed the notepad by the phone and scribbled down the address. 'There you go. Any time from ten on is fine.'

'Probably be about half past then, if that's OK? Because I have to go—'

'Yes! Great!' I felt I was sounding peculiar and falsely jolly, babbling on and getting carried away like a merry-go-round at speed, but I couldn't seem to stop myself. 'Half past! Excellent!' I dug my nails into the palms of my hands. 'God, I hate to throw you out, but I must get on – all that make-up to layer on with a trowel . . .'

Leo put down his mug and made for the door.

'Yes, of course. Sorry – do always feel free to chuck me out.'

'I will, don't you worry.'

He smiled, as if on the verge of laughing to himself.

Just like a normal person

I closed the door behind him and collected the mugs to wash up. Started singing to myself so I wouldn't have to think. Why do I feel like this? Please tell me it's not that I'm at all jealous. I'm not. Absolutely not. Just a bit disappointed on Ellen's behalf.

The annoying thing about all my training and experience as a counsellor is that I can only kid myself up to a point. You are such a pathetic liar, I told myself. OK, so I like him a little bit. So what? It's a very minor crush. This happens to people all the time. The important thing is to recognize it for what it is and not to make too much of it or let it get out of hand. Nothing would ever come of it, after all, so it really was quite unimportant. There was absolutely no question of my kissing him or sleeping with him or anything like that. Being naked with him, feeling his bare skin against mine. I wondered what it would be like to take off his clothes. First thing he does when he comes into my flat is shuck off his leather jacket, lets it fall to the floor in a single movement. What would it be like if he just kept on going? Unbuttoned his shirt, without even saying a word? Reached for me, pulling me close, his arm strong around my waist, his hand pressing me through the fabric of my skirt.

Come along now! You're being pathetic! Stop it at once! Still, it was good that I'd been able to be honest with myself about it. There was no need to mention it to Stephen, because that would only be making more of it than it was. By next week, I thought I'd be laughing about this with Ellen, saying, 'You know, I think you were right – I did have a little bit of a soft spot for Leo, but it was nothing and it wore off after a day or two.'

Well, now I'd admitted it, it wouldn't do any harm to think about it a bit more, try to analyse it in my mind, just out of interest really. That's one of the reasons why being a counsellor is so stimulating – I never stop learning and still constantly find parallels and echoes between the experiences of my clients and my own feelings. It really is a two-way process much more than people realize and you have to remain open to your own inner processes all the time. Fascinating.

Clearly, Leo already sees me as some trusty old friend whom he can rely on for a sensible, dispassionate opinion about all sorts of issues – which jacket to wear, which film to see. Perhaps I could sanction his choice of shirt, choice of car, choice of girlfriend? For fuck's sake. Next, he'd be asking my advice on the best way to propose. What on earth makes him think I'm interested in meeting some bimbo he's managed to chat up? Honestly. Well, I'm not going to lie just to flatter his ego. If he insists on asking for my opinion about this woman, then fine, I will give it, but there's no way I'm pretending I think she's suitable for him. 'I'm glad you asked me, Leo. Of course, as you know, I have to be honest – and I must say I do think you could do better. Yes, I suppose she is attractive in a humdrum, banal, supermodelish sort of a way, fine if you like that kind of thing, but I really can't see it lasting. Not exactly overburdened with brain, is she? Seems a little unstable as well, I'd say, and clearly extremely neurotic, very narcissistic, signalling emotional immaturity . . .'

I don't want to be his sodding pal, his good ol' buddy. Now I really am being ridiculous. What do I want then if not to be friends? Well, I do want him as a friend, of course I do. He's sparky and provocative and he makes me laugh and he's quick, too: I don't have to keep explaining what I mean the whole time – he can pick up the baton and run with it. And he's never boring. But it would be nice to think that he at least finds me vaguely attractive, attractive enough to wonder what it would be like to go to bed with me, attractive enough that he wouldn't dream of asking my advice about his stupid love life. God, you'd think he could show some sensitivity. Just because I'm a counsellor doesn't mean I don't have feelings like normal people, you know. I still feel hurt, jealous, anxious, ashamed, guilty, resentful just like everyone else. The only difference is that I'm supposed to keep recognizing my feelings, acknowledging them in a responsible, grown-up manner – 'Ah, I notice that I am feeling a little jealous. Hmm, what can I learn from this?' Perhaps I'd give myself a day off from being so bloody grown-up. Starting now and lasting the whole weekend. Maybe I'd just be unreasonable and jealous and pathetic about it all and wallow in it.

Bugger it, time was ticking on and I felt desperate for a shower; I usually have an extra one on Friday afternoon or evening; it's as if I'm cleansing my clients and everything they tell me out of my hair, washing their words from my ears, my skin, so that I can just be me again, not wise, not sensible, not objective, just myself with no expectations from anyone. I locked up and ran up the stairs to my flat above, quickly undressed and got in the shower, determining not to think about him at all while I was naked and wet. I wondered what I would do if there was a knock on the door right now. It could only be him. Normally, I never bother to answer the door or the phone while I'm in the bathroom, but maybe I would. It would be very inconvenient, of course, how selfish of him to come banging on my door when he knew I was getting ready to go out. I was starting to feel quite cross with him already when I pulled myself up short and reminded myself that a) he hadn't knocked on my door and b) he was very unlikely to as he'd only seen me half an hour ago. Still – if he were to be so selfish as to bother me yet again with some other pointless excuse, well, I might just go ahead and answer the door in my towel. Still see me as your good ol' pal? I'd drip onto the carpet, but that would be a small price to pay to register his expression of surprise, maybe even pleasure. My eyelashes would look all long and dewy from the shower. No, I thought, my face would be streaked with mascara. Even my fantasies are realistic. I rewound the images in my head like a videotape, and edited out the slatternly mascara, made my legs a little longer, my hair falling softly to my shoulders instead of hanging there like a soggy curtain. I'd answer the door, saying, 'Oh, Leo! I didn't realize it was you. I thought it must be Ellen. I wouldn't have dreamed of answering the door wearing only this impossibly small towel if I'd known . . .'

Wouldn't it be great to be a bimbo – if only for a day, an hour? To flirt and pout shamelessly and never feel guilty? Perhaps he wouldn't even be able to speak, would just tug the top of my towel where it was tucked in, so that it fell to the floor at my feet.

'Oops,' he'd say. That's the sort of thing Leo would say, I bet you. He isn't the kind of man who'd try to be macho or romantic; there'd be no 'Darling, you're so beautiful!' or 'God, how I've dreamed of this moment.' He wouldn't sweep me into his arms or any of that. He'd probably just—'

There was a rat-a-tat-tat on the door. For a moment, I thought I'd imagined it. You're becoming such a saddo, you're having auditory hallucinations now. But then it came again: a real knock.

No way was I actually going to answer the door in a small towel.

'Hang on a sec!'

I grabbed my robe.

'Who is it?' I called through the front door.

'Um. Me. Leo. Astonishingly. Sorry – I know you must be getting ready.'

'Yes. I am. Wait a—'

'No, don't worry. No need to open the door if you're – if you're, er, getting changed or whatever. I meant to say, to ask – what do I bring on Sunday? To the brunch? Not wine presumably?'

'No. Nothing. Honestly. Just yourself. Yourselves,' I corrected.

'Oh, OK. Well, thanks again then. Bye for now. Again.'

'Bye again.'

I stood there for a minute, dripping behind the door, wondering if he might say something else. There was a pause and then just the sound of his footsteps, padding back along the carpeted corridor.

11

And then it was Sunday . . .

Sunday. 7.55 a.m. according to my bedside clock –
which meant that it was actually 7.51. Or thereabouts.
I like to keep every clock and watch I own four minutes
fast so that I'm not late. I know, I know – seeing as I'm
never late in any case, this extra precaution is possibly
slightly redundant.

It was nice just lying there, sun filtering through the
pale blinds. Stephen was at a friend's stag night last
night, so I had my bed all to myself. In five minutes, no
– four minutes, I would get up and make some coffee,
then have a lovely long bath and annoy myself by
reading the style supplement of the Sunday paper. It's
the best thing to read in the bath because it's small and
glossy and I don't care if it gets wet because it's entirely
dreadful from front to back, but I enjoy being cross
with it and its pretentiousness and its preposterous
editorial posturings, its injunctions for you to shell out
£200 for some stupid stone bowl that would mark if
you put anything in it or £90 for a suede cushion that –
again – you clearly weren't supposed to touch. I'm as
neat as the next person, neater than the next person in
fact, but I refuse to get hyped up over a fucking
candlestick or some arrangement of stones that's
alleged to promote harmony in your household. What

utter bollocks – the only way to have a harmonious home is to live with people who don't drive you crazy. That's it – end of mystery. Pissing about rearranging your pot plants and hanging wind chimes in every doorway is missing the point. I realize that I don't actually live with anyone at the moment, so it's extremely easy for my household to be harmonious at all times. I could be living with Stephen if I chose to. I want to, naturally, but not right this minute. My flat really is looking rather good just now, despite its total lack of wind chimes, and it's so convenient to be able to nip downstairs to the office. Stephen and I will live together one day. Well, we'll have to if we're going to get married. *When* we get married.

Anyway. Brunch. Good, I could murder a bagel. Fresh and chewy and still warm. Weirdly, this brought Leo's face to mind Why did eating a bagel make me think of him? It didn't. It was just that he would be there. With some awful, giggling girlie – oh God, I could just imagine – skinny enough to wear one of those little strappy dresses and an itsy-bitsy cardigan perched on her shoulders. She'd laugh at his every utterance and he'd smirk and be insufferable. Well, thank God I don't care, I reminded myself. My crush was fading already, I knew it would. I wasn't in the least bit bothered if he wanted to make a complete fool of himself fawning over some girl who was bound to be half his age. He was, what, thirty-eight, thirty-nine? Hard to tell, what with the shortage of hair. Could be over forty. Well over. Bet his bit of arm candy would be twenty-two. Oh, that was disgusting, practically young enough to be his daughter, surely he wouldn't sink so low? Maybe twenty-six then. It was a shame for Ellen, of course, but at least I'd warned her. I phoned her yesterday to tell her that I'd invited Leo but that he was bringing someone else. She hadn't seemed remotely bothered, just said, 'Yeah, great, see you then,' in a rush to get off the phone. Mind you, once he sees Ellen, he'll realize how stupid he is to be fooling about with this other woman because Ellen is warm and bright and gorgeous, everyone thinks so. She is scatty, yes, and far from perfect, but that might well suit him. He probably loves scatty women. Lots of men do. It awakens their inner Neanderthal or something and they come over all protective. See? I said to myself. How could you have thought for a moment that you had a bit of a thing for him? It would never work. You're far too tidy and organized – that's not very lovable, is it? He probably thinks you're an uptight control freak and he'd be right. So it's just as well that nothing has happened. Nor is it likely to. Yes, he'll see Ellen and she'll be lovely and funny and flirty and he'll be completely captivated.

Funny how this wasn't making me feel any better.

Maybe I was coming down with something. My stomach definitely felt a bit – strange. I might have a bug. There was one going around. But I couldn't kid myself. There's nothing wrong with you, you just don't want to see him with another woman. It's truly pathetic. Beyond pathetic. You're jealous and you have absolutely no right to be. And what precisely would Stephen make of all this? You've got a wonderful, kind, sweet, handsome boyfriend who loves you and here you are getting yourself in a state over some ridiculous man who'll probably up sticks and troll off to New York tomorrow for work. And he probably sleeps with anyone who'll have him. He must be riddled with diseases – herpes, AIDS. How could I have thought for even a moment that I was interested in him? And, worse, I'd even tried to palm off this balding degenerate onto my own precious little sister!

Maybe I wouldn't go – but I'd have to phone Dad to warn him that Baldy 'n' Bimbo might be making an appearance. Dad wouldn't be fazed. He loves new people as long as it doesn't mean he has to do anything other than talk to them. Quinn could manage the scrambled eggs. She does them whenever I'm not there. And having to eat them would serve Leo right for taking some strange woman to our family brunch.

But *I* invited him.

All right. I would go – but only to be polite.

I got there just as my father was shuffling down the front path in his slippers to get in the car for the bagel run.

'Georgia!' He hugged me. 'Looking well and beautiful. You look like a woman in love – are you?'

'Oh, Dad! Of course not! Don't be ridiculous.'

Then I realized what I'd said. 'I mean, yes, of course. With *Stephen*. Of course. But not *like that*. Oh, you know what I mean.'

'Any special requests while I'm there?'

'Oh, I've invited my neighbour – you don't mind?'

'Course not. Long as she's not boring. Who is she? Is she a real *fresser* – shall I get extra bagels?'

'*He's* not boring but yes, I'd say he likes his food. And he's bringing someone, his girlfriend I presume. She probably won't eat a thing though. I bet she's one of those "Ooh – none for me thanks! I ate last Tuesday!" types.'

Dad smiled and scuttled off to the car.

'See you in a minute.'

I waved him goodbye and rang the bell. It was answered by Quinn, still wearing the black and white cotton kimono she uses as a dressing gown.

'Ah, Georgia, thank God it's only you. I mean, it's lovely that it's you, but I'm glad it's only family because I haven't had a moment – I was just tidying – just about to – you know – and then I said to David that he should be getting a move on – and you never know who's going to turn up – and I'd mentioned it to— oh! Coffee! I meant to tell David! Is he still – ? Shall I run after him?'

'No, he's gone.' I kissed Quinn on the cheek, narrowly missing having my eye poked out by an earring which looked like a small replica of a gladiatorial shield, with spikes sticking out of it. 'Don't worry about the coffee – I brought you some from the Algerian place.' I handed Quinn an aromatic package from my bag, along with some creamy-yellow roses.

Quinn thanked me, then led the way through to the kitchen.

'Now, let me make you some of this nice coffee . . .'

The supper dishes were still on the worktop from last night (or from the night before that? Best not to think about it). There were numerous mugs containing varying levels of coffee of varying vintages. The sink was full of pots and pans. At the back of the worktop, this week's selection of soaking pulses included red kidney beans, green lentils, and the inevitable chick-peas. The long kitchen table had stacks of papers at one end and a tray full of dirty crockery at the other. The fruit bowl was full at least, and looked reasonably presentable except for the presence of a lemon perched at the pinnacle which had gone mouldy at one end.

Quinn stood still, like a rabbit caught in the glare of headlights, unsure which way to jump.

She took a tentative step towards the dishwasher.

'Why don't you go upstairs and finish getting dressed?' I said, tactfully, although she had clearly not even started the process other than to put in her earrings, '. . . and I'll load the dishwasher.'

Quinn's face brightened.

'Would you really?' Virtually the same thing happens almost every time I visit but still Quinn seemed genuinely surprised and delighted by the suggestion. It wasn't even that she was angling for me to help, I thought. She probably had some vague idea that she would get round to doing it all, but then got flustered about where to start and so gave up. God knows what it's like when I'm not there.

I switched on the radio, emptied the murky contents of the coffee-maker, cleaned the jug, and scooped in fresh coffee, then I found a vase for the roses and began to empty the clean things from the dishwasher so I could reload it.

Despite, or perhaps because of, the mess, I still always feel so at home there. Of course, it is still home, the house where I grew up, more familiar in some ways than my own flat. No matter how much I hate the untidiness and the grunginess, I can't imagine not being able to turn up whenever I feel like it.

I plucked out a new cloth from the jumble under the sink and gave the table a serious wiping, extracted the mouldy lemon and a rather wizened plum from the fruit bowl and set it by the roses. The papers were bound to be Dad's; I moved them, stack by stack, onto the dresser. They looked messy, but the kitchen was never going to be perfect no matter what I did. Quinn's not tidy either, but at least she doesn't bring her work home and spread it out all over the place.

By the time Quinn re-emerged, wearing a maroon needlecord dress, bright yellow tights and flat black shoes with wide straps that seemed to have been designed to be as unsexy as possible, Dad had returned with the bagels and was sitting at the head of the table surrounded by newspapers.

The counter was as clear as it was ever going to be and the dishwasher was thrumming away. A stack of plates and a basket of cutlery and napkins were on the worktop and the bagels were piled on a platter. Quinn delved into the fridge and eventually came out with three jars of homemade jam, which I had tried to hide behind two large pots of organic yoghurt. Dad had brought cream cheese and smoked salmon from the deli. I added pots of honey and Marmite from the cupboard.

'Matt rang to say he's bringing croissants and the children,' said Quinn.

'No Izzy?' I started cracking eggs into a large bowl.

'No, don't think so. Oh, scramblies! Thank you for doing them. Yours are so much better than mine.'

I murmured a vague dissent, while gritting my teeth.

'Do people want salmon in the eggs, chopped up into little bits, or just on the side? Dad?' I sloshed in some milk and ground in just the right amount of sea salt.

'Mmm, lovely,' said Dad, not looking up from the paper. 'Did you hear about this exhibition of plastinated corpses?'

'What – real ones? People, you mean?' I said, whisking.

'Oh, no, David! Surely not?'

'Mmm – the so-called artist says it has enabled him to "democratize anatomy". What's that supposed to mean?' He looked up from the paper. 'Salmon's in the bag there. Huh – plastinated – I'm not sure that's even a real word. Is it the same as plasticized, do you think?'

'Actually, maybe I'll leave the salmon on the side, so people have the choice. Why would anyone want to look at dead bodies in an exhibition anyway? It doesn't make it art just because this bloke comes up with a whole load of bollocks about democratizing anatomy. You can't democratize anatomy. It just *is* what it *is*. Where's the butter?'

Quinn brought it over from the dresser.

'Still – no need to talk about dead, er, people, over breakfast, is there?' Quinn, for all her coloured tights and soaking pulses and Chinese herbs, frequently forgets how to pull off her bohemian eccentric act and betrays her upbringing. She's never quite got used to the way we all switch subjects mid-conversation or, worse, mid-sentence.

'It seems that any old scam merchant now thinks that he can shove his grubby sheets or his toenail clippings or the contents of his loo onto a plinth and – dah-*dah*, suddenly it's art and it's got a message – ' I said, ignoring Quinn.

'Well . . .' Dad leaned back in his chair and pushed his spectacles up onto his head. 'He could be saying something about the nature of the body, dehumanized and viewed purely as an object – at core, we're all equal, a collection of bones, muscles, tissues and so on . . .'

I knew my father didn't think the artist was saying anything of the kind, but he enjoyed playing devil's advocate or devil's avocado as Matt likes to say in his irritating, Matt-type way.

'Sorry – what does plastinated mean? Is it like covered in cling film or something like that?' Quinn said.

'No idea. Does it matter?' I poured the whisked eggs into the pan of foaming butter. 'No, he isn't, Dad. He's just yet another of those middle-aged would-be rebels who thinks that shocking people is the quick route to becoming rich and famous.'

'Does anyone want any of my homemade houmous with their scramblies?' said Quinn.

'No,' I said quickly. 'I mean, no thanks. Maybe after the eggs.' I felt mean. Why do I always end up snapping at people when I don't mean to? 'Quinn – sorry – can you pass a plate for the salmon?'

'Did you say you had a friend coming?' Dad looked up from the paper again. 'Who is he again?'

'Leo. He's a neighbour. And his girlfriend I think. Eggs coming up in *one minute*! Have your plate ready!'

'And Stephen? Is he coming?'

'Yes, how is Stephen? Working too hard?' Quinn said, shaking her head at the idea of his subjecting himself to such stress. 'Such a nice man.'

'No, he's going away yet again for work tomorrow – he has to pack.' I scooped out scrambled eggs onto three plates and left the remainder to keep warm over a large pan of hot water.

'Uh-huh,' said Dad.

'Meaning?'

'Meaning nothing. Just uh-huh.' He chewed slowly on a bagel and scooped up a forkful of scrambled egg.

'Dad, I know your uh-huhs and that was an *uh-huh?* sort of an uh-huh.'

'Now let's not get ourselves all worked up.' Quinn sat down with her eggs.

Matt arrived next with Bonnie and Daniel, who came running in, shouting, 'Auntie Gee! Auntie Gee!'

'Hey, everyone, how's it going? Iz sends her love.' He dropped a bag of croissants onto the table. 'She's having a much-needed lie-in and a bit of quiet time without the monsters.'

'I'm NOT a monster, Daddy!' Bonnie shouted. *'You're* a monster!'

'I'm a monster!' said Daniel.

'Yes you ARE!' Matt picked him up and turned him upside down until Daniel was shrieking with laughter. 'Which little monsters want scramblies?'

'I don't like eggs!' said Bonnie.

'I don' like eggs!' repeated Daniel.

'Yes, you do, Daniel. Don't be a pain. Scramblies aren't eggs in any case, they're scramblies. Bonnie is a bit off eggs just now, Gee, but she can have a croissant.' He took one out of the bag and broke it in two, put it on a plate. 'There you go, monster, do you want some jam?'

'Don't want a broken one!'

Matt sighed and plonked another croissant down in front of her.

Standing by the stove, spooning eggs into a dish for Daniel, I realized I hadn't noticed just how grown-up Matt could be. Yes, of course, technically he is a grown-up; he's thirty-two. It's just that I don't see him that way. He would always be my annoying baby brother. Usually, when I see him these days, it's with Isobel and she tends to sort out the children and help them with their food and fetch their water. But now, here was Matt, apparently quite capable of being a parent.

'Who else is coming? Mr Interesting?'

'Ho hum, Matt, that's original. Shall I lend you a fiver so you can run out and buy a couple of new jokes?' It isn't that Matt dislikes Stephen exactly, it's just that he once described him as 'a walking, talking cure for insomnia' and, seeing that it annoyed me so much, he hasn't been able to resist winding me up about Stephen ever since. 'Anyway, no he isn't. He has something important to do.'

'Whoo-oo!' Matt let out a whoop. 'Something *important*. Well, we can't possibly compete with that, can we? Lucky old Stephen, having such a grown-up life, full of important things.'

I turned to Bonnie,

'Bonnie, do please tell your dad to hurry up and grow up.'

'Mummy says Daddy's hopeless. Who's coming?'

'We don't know,' said Matt, 'Everyone except Stephen with a p-h.'

'Stephen-with-a-p-h!' echoed Bonnie.

'Steeph wiv p-a!' shouted Daniel.

'Oh, now look what you've done. He's *busy*! Now, will everyone stop talking about Stephen and just get on with their eggs?'

The arrival of the special guest

The doorbell rang. Oh God, this might be Leo. I bet it's him. Please don't let her be beautiful. Or bright. Please, God, let her be plain with a piggy nose and fat ankles and not even two brain cells to rub together.

It wasn't Leo. It was Unc.

'Greetings, all!' He handed a bag of satsumas and a pineapple to Quinn. 'Any eggs?' He came over and kissed me.

'Just making some more, Unc. Sit yourself down.'

'No young man today, Georgia? When are you two

161

going to name the day?' He prodded his stomach. 'Hurry up before I'm too fat for my best suit.'

'I gave him time off for good behaviour.'

'In fact, Georgia's got a *special guest* coming . . .' Dad said, as if announcing news of great significance.

'He's NOT a *special guest*. He's just a neighbour. No big deal. Please will you shut up about it.'

'Goodness!' Quinn's the only person I know who still uses the word. 'Are you not seeing Stephen any more, Georgia?' She gave me one of her concerned looks. 'I didn't know. I'm so sorry. When did all this happen? I can't believe it. No-one ever tells me anything – I'm always being kept out of the picture . . .' This is one of her fantasies, that there's some kind of conspiracy to keep her out of all our alleged family 'secrets'.

'Have you really ditched the P-h? Wow! And just when I was warming to the guy . . .' Matt spoke through a mouthful of croissant. 'So, who's this new man? That was fast – or was there an overlap?'

'Oh, just STOP, will you?'

The doorbell rang again.

'Well, I'm definitely not getting that.' I cracked open some more eggs and reached for the whisk.

Unc went to the door, with Bonnie tailing him.

I heard him opening the door, his booming 'Hello!' followed by Leo's, considerably quieter, then Bonnie saying, 'Who are *you*?' in her usual direct manner.

I feel sick. Please don't let me throw up. I should never have come. Why did I even ask him in the first place? Stupid, stupid woman. I'd go in a minute. Have one more quick cup of coffee, just to be polite, then say I had to be off, had to meet Stephen.

'No.' Unc's resonant tones again. 'I'm Georgia's uncle. I'm Howard – but you can call me Unc if you're Georgia's new man. Everyone in the family does.'

Oh, ground, please swallow me now. *Please*. What

on earth will he think? What must *she* think? How could Unc be such a blundering fool? Couldn't he see Leo was with someone? This is mortifying. Beyond mortifying. I might actually die from embarrassment. I've always thought people meant that figuratively, but now I'm sure it must be possible – I shall explode or implode or simply crumple into a small heap. Leo will think I've been going around claiming that he's my boyfriend. He'll believe I'm totally barking, clearly delusional – and who could blame him? Hang on a sec. I haven't heard a woman's voice. All I could hear was Unc, then Leo – surprisingly quiet – and Bonnie jumping and squealing. Maybe he has come on his own after all. I start to whisk the eggs, staring down into the bowl, telling myself I'm not bothered either way, keeping my back to the door where he would come in.

'So this is Leo, Georgia's *friend*,' Unc bellows.

'Hey, everyone. Hi.'

'. . . And this is his beautiful companion, Cora,' Unc concludes.

No, no, *no*. Oh shit – I can't bear it. Tears prick my eyes. Pull yourself together, for God's sake! I bite the inside of my cheek to focus on a different kind of pain, the way I used to when I was small. Now, just turn and smile and stretch out your hand, say how lovely to meet you. Be friendly, charming, the perfect hostess.

'Well, hello there!' Dad's voice, unexpectedly warm and interested. She must be devastating.

'Hey, Georgia!' Leo's voice, like a hand, warm and strong against my back. I can feel the beginning of a blush creeping over my face.

'Sorry – just at the crucial whisking stage. Give me a couple more secs!' Trying to compose my face before I turn round, crank a smile into place, not too much now or you'll look like the Cheshire cat. Just be normal.

Everyone around the table has fallen silent, a virtually unknown occurrence in Abrams land.

Dad clears his throat and rustles the paper.

'So, has anyone seen this new Brazilian film . . . ?'

'Hi there!' I twirl round, still holding the whisk and sending a trail of egg spinning out into the air in front of me.

His smile nearly knocks me over. The sight of his chipped tooth induces an inexplicable surge of tenderness. I desperately want to cup his cheek in my hand, touch his hair.

'And this is Cora . . .' She is indeed quite beautiful, with flawless skin, huge, dark eyes and shiny hair, and she's holding a big bunch of glorious sunflowers.

And she is no more than five years old.

'Cora, this is Georgia, the nice lady I told you about. Georgia – meet Cora, my daughter.'

12

Sardines

Needless to say, no-one believed my claim that I had burst into tears because I'd dropped the egg whisk onto my nice suede shoes. Nor did they believe me when I said I had a touch of PMT. But even Matt knows that there's a time for taking the piss and a time for shutting the fuck up and leaving things well alone. I can't even explain it myself – I'm probably just tired, I didn't sleep too well last night.

'I didn't realize you had a daughter,' I said quietly to Leo, as Bonnie took Cora's hand and towed her away: 'We're playing ships and *I'm* the captain. Watch out for sharks.'

'Join the club. Neither did I until very recently.'

'What? How? Surely even you must have noticed? Didn't you wonder why you had a small person tailing around after you and calling you Daddy? Did you think she was just a precocious stalker or what?'

He cocked his head on one side.

'Finished? I didn't *know*,' he lowered his voice, 'because Hazel, her mother, neglected to inform me of this minor development in my life until— Look, can we talk about it later? I don't want to discuss it while Cora's around.'

'Of course.' I laid my hand on his arm, then caught Matt looking at me, reading too much into everything as usual. I mouthed 'fuck off' at him and he grinned and mouthed it back.

Leo sat down and I gave him a plate so he could help himself.

'So . . . Georgia has managed to tell me very little about you other than that you're a neighbour.' Dad put down the newspaper and even folded it.

'You should feel honoured,' I said. 'It's rare for Dad to relinquish his paper. It may mean that he's even going to listen.'

One of us

The doorbell rang. It was Ellen, with yet another new man in tow.

'Hiya! This is Jürgen. Ooh, croissants! Jürgy, grab a plate and help yourself while I fill you in on who's who.' She seized a croissant and leant over to dunk it in Dad's coffee mug. 'OK – now this crumbly is my dad, David, that's his brother Howard but you can call him Unc. Quinn, my stepmother. Great tights, Quinny – are you auditioning for the part of Malvolio in *Twelfth Night*? Then that tall guy at the far end is Matt, my annoying brother, the person holding a tea towel and doing all the work as usual is my lovely sister, Georgia. Those are Matt's kids playing through there in the sitting room – Bonnie and Daniel and I don't know who that other gorgeous little girl is, friend of Bonnie's, presumably?'

'No, that's—'

'And who are *you*?' She turned to Leo. 'Are we related? I thought I'd met all the cousins by now.'

'No. Well, not as far as I know. I'm Leo. I'm—'

'Oh, *you're* Leo. But you're not *bald* at all. Well, not really. You've got loads more hair than Jürgy – hasn't he?' She addressed the entire room.

'Er, thank you.'

'Ellen, please feel free to shut up at any point, won't you?' I started collecting the used plates to give myself something to do.

Leo shoved me playfully.

'I see – so you said I was bald, did you? Remind me not to hire you as my PR manager.'

'I *didn't* say that – I said—'

'Anyway,' my father interrupted. 'Don't wait for the rare event of my children managing to shut up, Leo – do carry on with what you were saying. You're in Georgia's block?'

'Yes, I'm renting a flat on the same floor as her office. I'm a photographer so it's ideal being so central. The only trouble is that it seemed quite big before I filled it with all my equipment – I'm thinking of annexing a section of the corridor to sleep in.'

'You should get a fold-down wallbed, like I've got.'

'Don't let Gee start organizing your life, whatever you do,' Matt chipped in. 'Once she starts, she won't let up until you've been tidied within an inch of your life.'

'Sorry, was anyone asking for Matt's opinion?'

Matt flicked the stubby end of a croissant at me.

'I must apologize for my children, Leo.' Dad shrugged. 'I used to think that they would grow up eventually, but I know now that was just a foolish dream. Don't let the fact that they're no longer in nappies fool you into believing that they're anything remotely resembling actual adults.'

'That's so unfair!' Ellen spoke through a mouthful of croissant.

'Mouth!' I reminded her. She's always eating and talking at the same time.

'Shut up! I was just about to be nice about you. I was going to say that at least Georgia's a proper grown-up, but I shan't bother now.'

'Gee isn't anyway.' Matt turned to Leo. 'She's just as bad as Ellen—'

'And you. You're miles worse than me,' Ellen said.

'As bad as Ellen,' Matt continued, ignoring her. 'Worse in some ways because Georgia seems so sensible and well-behaved and all that on the outside—'

'But underneath she's passionate and deeply silly, thank God,' Leo added, turning to smile at me. 'I know. It's a well-kept secret, but bits of it do have a way of leaking out when she lets her guard down.'

'See, he's interrupting already. He's definitely one of us.' Ellen laughed.

'Apologies again, Leo.' Dad shook his head. 'I think Ellen meant that as a compliment.'

'I take it as one. You lot remind me of my own family. Well, what's left of us anyway.'

'Oh?' Quinn, getting a word in edgeways at last.

'Yeah, my father died a couple of years ago and my mum lives in Glasgow near my two sisters. I was living up there too, so I saw them all a lot, but I couldn't get enough freelance work so that's why I've moved back to London.'

'You must miss them.' Dad passed him a dish of pickled sweet-sour cucumbers, as if to compensate.

'Yeah, I really do.' Leo took one and crunched into it. 'I didn't realize how much. It seems a bit pathetic to be homesick at my age. And little things remind you – ' he held up his cucumber – 'my dad always loved these.'

There was a moment's silence then my father nodded.

'Well, you're very welcome here – come and see us anytime you fancy a bit of family life red in tooth and claw.'

'Quite. Hanging around us will probably make you miss your own family even more,' I added. 'We're not exactly your classic happy family, are we?'

'Oh, Georgia, that's a bit harsh.' Quinn, taking things too seriously as usual.

'Dissent is very healthy,' Dad pronounced. 'I've always been deeply suspicious of families where no-one ever argues – in my experience it usually means that they never talk much either.'

'But we *are* a happy family, aren't we?' Ellen's voice sounded very young. It does that sometimes, her voice suddenly regressing as if she's a child again.

'Of course we are.' Quinn, smoothing things over.

I snorted. 'Well, we seem to do way more shouting and crying than most other families I know.'

'Ah,' said Leo, 'but I bet you're there for each other when it really counts.'

Dad nodded.

'Yes,' said Matt. 'Unless Ellen wants to borrow money, in which case she can go to Georgia as far as I'm concerned, the bank that never shuts. Never lend Ellen anything, Leo, unless it's something you're keen to see the back of.'

Ellen and I turned as one to Matt.

'I haven't borrowed money from George for ages. Bugger off, Matt!'

'It's none of your business.' I scowled at Matt; there was no need to air absolutely everything in front of an outsider. 'Anyway, I'm sure our guest isn't interested in our petty squabbles.'

'Don't stop on my account.' Leo held up his hands. 'I feel right at home.'

'I don't still owe you any money, do I, George?'

'Well, actually, yes, you do. But it's fine. Don't worry about it now.'

'How much?' She reached for her bag, then began to forage in it.

'Um . . . it's sixty pounds. No big deal. Leave it for now.' It was more like a hundred actually, but I'd decided to let her off a bit.

'Sixty quid! When did I borrow sixty quid?'

'You didn't, not all at once. Look, can we do this later?'

'No.' Ellen started writing out a cheque. 'I'm not having Matt call me a sponger.'

Matt snorted.

'You said it, Ell. Bet you Gee doesn't cash the cheque in any case, she's always subsidizing you.'

'That's *so* not true. It isn't, is it, George?'

It *is* true, of course. If I go out to supper with Ellen, I nearly always treat her. But it makes sense, I earn a lot more than her and she's hopeless with money, and it's not as if I really mind. Matt only wants to stick his oar in and get involved because he thinks I'm over-protective of Ellen. Plus I suspect he's jealous because Ellen and I see each other so much and he feels left out.

'Please, please can we talk about something else. This is very boring.' I turned to Leo. 'Leo, tell us an amusing anecdote about one of your jobs.' I could see him suppressing the urge to laugh. 'Leo sometimes takes pictures of authors and celebs for the colour mags.'

'Yes, it's unbelievably glamorous and exciting. Now, can we get back to the arguing?'

I gave him a not-so-gentle punch.

'Will you not take the piss out of my family – that's my job.'

'Would you like some more coffee, Leo?' Quinn came forward with the coffee pot. 'Or would you prefer tea?'

He held up his cup for a refill.

'That's lovely, thanks. Georgia says you have a daughter, too?'

'Yes.' Quinn flushed, but whether with pride or shame I wasn't sure. 'Simone. She's in marketing, she's doing very well, but she works too hard. You young people all do. It's very stressful.'

'Oh, Quinn – you make it sound as if you're ninety-four,' I protested. 'You work hard too.' Quinn's involved in arts administration; I presume she's considerably more organized in her job than she is at home.

'And does she live close by? Is she a regular at your Sunday brunches?'

Quinn shook her head.

'Not really. She's further west – in Holland Park.' Simone's got a gorgeous flat with high ceilings and three bedrooms, she must be loaded, God knows how much she earns. 'But she's very busy,' Quinn added defensively.

'Can't be arsed more like,' Ellen said, not quite quietly enough. Ellen's never really mastered the art of whispering and she's always louder than she thinks she is. I gave her a kick under the table. Quinn pretended she hadn't heard but I could tell she had.

'Anyway,' I tried to turn the conversation around, 'Simone's very – um, lively, isn't she? You'd like her a lot, I'm sure.'

Quinn looked placated.

It's just a game

Cora came up and tugged shyly at Leo. He ducked his head so she could whisper to him.

'Well, perhaps we can play something else then, hmm?'

'Is Bonnie bossing her around?' asked Matt.

'Er . . .'

'Bonnie!' Matt got up and went through to the sitting room, and I saw him crouching down to speak to Bonnie.

'Let's all play something!' Ellen said, jumping up from her chair.

I rolled my eyes at Leo.

'I'm sorry. You don't have to join in. You probably want to sit and have a civilized conversation and enjoy your coffee in peace.'

He smiled, showing his chipped tooth.

'I can't remember the last time I had a *civilized* conversation, thank God. I'm up for it – what are we playing?'

'Charades!' said Ellen, who relishes the chance to show off.

'No!' Matt and I chorused, remembering last time. 'The Jumping Game?' said Matt. The Jumping Game is a family thing and it's very, very silly and involves everybody's bellowing at the tops of their voices and usually someone bangs themselves on the corner of a bookcase or the edge of the piano and it all ends in tears.

'No!' said Quinn and Dad together.

'What about Sardines?' I suggested.

'God, *Sardines* – ' Leo began. 'I haven't played that since I was—'

'A child?' I finished. 'Wow – aeons and aeons ago.'

'Thank you.' He reached out and suddenly squeezed my waist, making me yelp. 'Actually, no. I haven't played it since I was about twenty-five.'

'A late developer then?'

'Yup. Going to hit my prime any day now.'

'Call me when you do, won't you? I'd hate to look away for a second and miss it.'

'Don't worry – you'll be there.'

Dad and Quinn excused themselves, claiming that they were too old to fold themselves into cupboards.

The doorbell rang again.

'Oh, no.' Matt looked like a sulky child. 'New people. Bet they won't want to play Sardines.'

'Sardines! Sardines!' shouted Bonnie, jumping up and down.

It was only Tarka at the door, a friend of Quinn's, who said she'd prefer to sit with Quinn rather than get shaken up by running around the house so soon after her morning meditation. She took a packet of rooibos tea out of her horrible hessian bag and a small, wizened-looking wheat-free, yeast-free, fun-free loaf of bread to make her own toast.

Ellen started explaining the rules to Jürgen.

'So one person hides and then all the others look for him separately and one by one you all pile into the same tiny space and then the first person who found him hides . . .'

'My study's off limits, people,' Dad said, returning to his newspaper.

'Dad, you decide who's hiding first,' Ellen said.

'OK. Georgia hides. Two-minute head start. Everyone else stays in here. Talk loudly, everyone, so you can't hear her! Go!'

'As if you lot need to be told to talk loudly . . .' I said, slipping out of the kitchen.

My heart was pounding. We haven't played Sardines for ages but, when we do, Ellen usually finds me first because she knows the kind of place I'd choose, just the same way that I always find her before anyone else. But this time she'd probably hunt with Jürgen, or maybe with Bonnie or Daniel, so that should slow her down. Well, Matt would find me then. Or maybe Unc. Thoughts raced through my head as I rejected one potential hiding space after another. I didn't want to pick anywhere too obviously Georgia-ish. Ellen would look in the wardrobes first because she knows that I tend to avoid anywhere too dusty or grimy, which, frankly, rules out most of the house. Leo would never find me first. Couldn't do. He wasn't familiar with the house, for a start, and a newcomer was bound to be that much more tentative about poking around in someone else's home. In the shower? Too obvious. Stretched out behind the sofa cushions in the den? Behind the heavy bedroom curtains? Beneath the desk in Matt's old room? Could I fit in the chest on the top-floor landing? Hurry, hurry.

It wasn't ideal, but it would have to do.

Footsteps on the stairs, the sound of the door opening. I am trying not to breathe, keeping as still as I can, but my heart is thumping and it seems as if I can actually feel the blood racing round my body, I can almost hear it, surging like a stream after heavy rain.

'No, Daniel – she won't be in here. It's too grubby. There's dust everywhere.' Ellen's voice. 'Come on – quick! – let's look in the shower.'

Thundering footsteps going back downstairs to Dad and Quinn's bedroom.

The door opens again.

'Do you think she's in here?' Leo. He must be hunting with Cora. Of course. I feel myself sag a little with disappointment. Just stop it, will you? I dig my nails into my palms, telling myself I can feel nothing, nothing except the slight, satisfying pain of my own nails pushing into my skin.

Cora's reply is so quiet that I can't hear it.

'What about behind that curtain? No? Too scary? Go on – I'm right here . . . Not there . . . Hmm . . . what about under that cushion? You think it's too small? Yes, I guess she is *much too big* to hide there . . .'

He knows I'm in here, the rude sod.

'That's a strange lump, isn't it? What about under . . . here?' A glimpse of legs close by, then he ducks down and I am looking straight into his eyes. 'Cora, you've found her!'

'We found you!'

'Sssh!' says Leo. 'We all have to be quiet as mice until everyone else finds us.'

'Sssh.' Cora puts her finger to her lips.

'Well, isn't this cosy?' Leo pulls aside the roll of carpet, the cardboard boxes and the old manual typewriter that I had dragged across to conceal my hiding place beneath a faded camp bed. 'Shove up a bit.' He leans over Cora to pull the boxes and typewriter back in place. 'Cora – are you in properly?'

'Sssh, Daddy!'

I have never been so close to him before, so close that I can smell him, so close that I am touching him whether I want to or not. That is his shirtsleeve against the flesh of my bare arm, his leg pressing against mine. He is lying next to me, the way he would if . . . No, I must stop this. But now he is looking at me, here in the half-dark, his eyes shining. Why doesn't he look away? There is no need to stare. He's just doing it to make me uncomfortable. I scowl at him.

He isn't smiling, yet still I notice his mouth. It's so

174

close to mine, you see, our faces barely more than a hand's width apart. I can't believe I picked such a ridiculously small place to hide. Well, it is Sardines. You're supposed to be squashed, that's the point. Yes, but I thought Ellen or Matt would find me first, someone else, anyone else. His breathing sounds as loud as my own, Cora's much lighter and slightly faster on the other side of Leo. His hand is resting down by his side.

'Are you OK?' he whispers.

I nod, although I'm not remotely OK. I try to move then but there isn't a speck of space to move to. I slide my own hand down, mirroring his posture. The edge of my hand brushes his. It's an accident, of course. I didn't mean that to happen. It just – did. Then, in the half-light, his little finger hooks itself around mine. I should move my finger, unhook it and shove his hand back. That's what I should do. And I would. In a minute. There's no need to be rude. And, besides, it doesn't really count or anything – it's only because here we are, playing Sardines and squashed close together. You can't avoid touching, it's part of the game, a little playful, totally harmless flirtation – less than that.

Downstairs, on another floor, in another world, the doorbell rings once more. Dad would have to get it. I would go, but I can't move right now. We mustn't move until we are found. Those are the rules, everyone knows that, there is nothing I can do about it.

Footsteps running up the stairs now and Bonnie comes hurtling in with Matt.

'Gee, are you in here?'

'Let me find her! Let me! Grandad says we've all got to come down now.'

'Gee?' Matt's voice again. 'It's not a trick. Game's over.'

Bonnie's face then, peering in at us.

'Found you!'

We crawl out.

Matt looks at me, then down at my clothes. My black trousers look as though they've been used as a duster.

'We'd better go down,' he says. 'Guess who's just shown up?'

13

A wonderful surprise

It wasn't at all like Stephen to turn up out of the blue. Of course, he knows that brunch is always open house; of course, he knows that he's more than welcome; of course, he knows that I would be only too delighted to see him. But, the point is, it wasn't a Stephen-ish thing to do. I found myself feeling decidedly cross about his impromptu appearance, and it was nothing to do with Leo. It's just that the whole thing about Stephen, the essence of Stephen, is that he is predictable. In a good way. A way I like, rely on, depend on.

'Hello, darling.' By the time I had extricated myself from under the bed and brushed off the worst of the dust, Stephen was sitting in the kitchen, perched on the edge of a chair, and still wearing his jacket.

'Hi!' I said brightly. 'Well, what a nice surprise!' I bent to kiss him. 'I thought you'd be having a lie-in. We weren't expecting you.' He gave me a rather sharp look, I thought, that said, 'Apparently not . . .' but I ignored it.

'I did try calling you on your mobile. You look like you've been spring cleaning.' He swept some dust off my trousers. 'Here, turn round and I'll do your back.' Brushed the dust off my bum, the intimacy taken for granted. I felt like a child who'd been caught out playing somewhere forbidden

'We were playing Sardines. You know, for the children.'

As I said this, I looked around and what do you know? No-one else – except for Leo and Cora – had even a particle of dust on them, and Cora looked significantly cleaner than Leo, as if she'd been hiding in an entirely different location from us.

'What fun,' said Stephen, sounding like he couldn't imagine any activity on the planet that could conceivably be less fun. 'I'm sorry I missed it.'

'Hi,' Leo took a step forward. 'I'm Leo, by the way.'

'Stephen. With a—' Stephen cut himself short, with a nervous glance at Ellen. 'Georgia's *fiancé*,' he added.

'Oh, yes, sorry, haven't you two met yet?' I tucked my hair behind my ears. 'I was sure you had. Leo's recently moved into my block – you remember, Stephen, I did mention it? So he doesn't really know anyone . . .' I made it sound as though Leo was a refugee, in need of food parcels and introductions.

'And this is my daughter, Cora.' Leo rested his hands on Cora's shoulders, looking at me over her head.

'Hello, Cora,' said Stephen, visibly relaxing. 'Well, I woke up earlier than I thought, darling, and packed in no time, so decided to come and whisk you away for lunch.' He turned to the rest of the company. 'With my folks,' he explained.

'Oh, but I'm stuffed!' I waved a hand at the table.

'That's all right. Mum won't mind.' He rebuttoned his jacket. 'You *are* coming, aren't you?'

A glance at Ellen, at Matt, at Dad. A final one at Leo.

'Of course,' I said, feeling like a kid who's been dragged away from the party before they've even served up the birthday cake. 'Of course I'll come.'

Stephen was pretty quiet in the car. I felt as if he was waiting for some kind of explanation, almost as if I was expected to justify myself for some imagined sin. And, yes, I did feel guilty – but for what exactly? For having my little finger touch Leo's for all of five seconds? Oh, come on, people bonk their husband's best friend without so much as a twinge of guilt. I conducted a debate in my head, trying to be rational; there was really nothing to make a fuss about.

'You seem very quiet,' Stephen said, keeping his eyes on the road. He's a very safe driver.

'Do I?'

'You didn't have to come, you know.' He checked his mirror and indicated, then pulled onto the roundabout. 'You shouldn't have let me drag you away if you were having . . .' he paused briefly, as if the word were obscene, '*fun*.'

'Don't be silly. Of course I wanted to come with you. We were only playing Sardines.' I felt as if I were saying, 'We were only mud-wrestling in the nude.' 'The children were desperate to play.'

Yes, it was nothing to do with me, your Honour, they made me do it.

'I'm so dusty,' I added, unnecessarily, trying to move the conversation on a notch and brushing at my trousers once more. 'You wouldn't believe how grubby the house is.'

'Perhaps they should hire a cleaner?'

'They already *do*. But she never has a chance to clean anything. Quinn feels so guilty about having a cleaner that she spends the whole time making Mrs Atkins cups of tea and calling her Mrs Atkins even though Mrs Atkins calls her Quinn like the rest of us, and talking to her non-stop to show that she regards her as an equal. Which is incredibly patronizing – and ridiculous too because I bet Mrs Atkins would much rather just get on with trying to scrape the gunge off the kitchen table

179

than have to listen to Quinn wittering on about under-funding in the arts.'

Stephen tilted his chin up in that sort of half-nodding way he does, so you can't tell if he's agreeing or being cross.

'That Leo chap certainly seems friendly.'

It was one of those sentences that sounds innocuous enough, but you just know there's a snake slithering about underneath it waiting to bite you. That's the trouble with Stephen: he'll never come right out and say what's bothering him, we always have to go through this tippy-toeing round the houses approach to get to the point. Well, I wasn't going to rise to the bait.

'Yes, he is, isn't he?' I said in my neutral, mildly enthusiastic but not suspiciously so voice. La-la-la, blasé as can be. 'And his daughter seems very sweet,' I added as an afterthought. 'Rather shy and quiet, but then, who isn't next to Bonnie?'

Stephen smiled then and I noticed his shoulders relax slightly.

'Yes indeed. Divorced, is he? A part-time father?'

'No!' I knew it was meant as a dig. His tone suggested that Leo must be somehow inadequate, someone who couldn't cut it as a real parent. Stephen raised his brows, waiting for me to complete my defence.

'Actually, I don't know,' I admitted. 'He's only a neighbour. I haven't grilled him for his entire life story, you know.'

'No-one's saying you should, are they? I was merely showing an interest.'

I turned and looked out of the window.

'Shall we stop and pick up some flowers?' I suggested, suddenly wanting to be outside and not in the car with him.

'Tick,' he said, the way he does, as if he's filling out a form. 'They're in the back.' Stephen thinks of everything.

'Oh. Great. What did you get?' I asked, turning round in my seat to see at the same time.

'Those orange ones Mum likes. They last for ages.'

'Oh, yes. Chrysanthemums. Yes, they do.' I nodded. 'Ages and ages.' Never mind that they've got no scent and the leaves are horrible and that orange doesn't go with anything else. At least they'll last. What a boon.

I shouldn't have come. You kind of have to be in the mood for Stephen's parents and I so wasn't. That's unfair. They're ever so nice, really they are – very welcoming and wonderfully normal. When we go there for lunch, you know you're going to have a proper meal with meat and potatoes and two veg and pudding too. His mother's cooking is the absolute antithesis of Quinn's. Quinn's approach to culinary matters is what she would regard as 'creative' and anyone else would regard as 'disastrous': she delves in the fridge and cupboards then flings the foragings all together in the hope of discovering some exciting fusion of flavours that has never been arrived at before. But the reason people don't combine olives with pineapple or feta cheese with kumquats or chickpeas and Quorn with prunes is not because they're unadventurous – it's because the result is revolting and no-one but Quinn would even waste their time or ingredients on trying it. Trish, Stephen's mother, isn't impressed by novelty. She cooks sprouts for twenty minutes because that's the way she's always done them, thank you, and she's no time for all these fancy cooking programmes and that man who mixes the salad with his hands, it's not hygienic and she's got ever such a lovely pair of salad servers so why anyone would want to use their hands she'll never know. At least you know where you are with her cooking. There are no surprises. Also, you can eat uninterrupted – you don't have to fend off Ellen lunging across the table at you trying to nick your crispy chicken skin or Matt saying can you give that bit to Bonnie or Dad asking, 'Are you not having that potato?' when you were only saving it till last. And no-one asks you annoying questions about you or your life or your innermost self that you were trying not to think about just now. In Stephen's family, they ask if you're well and then they just sit and eat. Occasionally, someone comments on the neighbour's bindweed or the shocking price of petrol or the never-ending roadworks on the M25 or Stephen shares some amusing anecdote about one of his colleagues, but that's it. It's very restful. Really.

One of the family

The front door opened as we were getting out of the car. I'm sure Trish must hover by the glazed panels in the porch whenever she's expecting someone so she can open the door before they've even reached the front gate.

'Stephen!' She tilted her face up as he bent to kiss her, looking up at him as if he were a Greek god. She picked an invisible piece of nothing off his sleeve.

'And Georgia! 'Scuse me still in my apron!' I laughed automatically, knowing that I was expected to. Trish has a way of talking, her voice rising as if she's telling you a joke even when – which is always – she's telling you something completely prosaic. But then she laughs in this rather girlish way and you feel mean if you don't join in. 'Ted's through in the lounge. Ted! Ted! They're here!'

'I hope it's not putting you out, having me as well. I wasn't expecting to come for lunch today.'

'Putting me out! You're one of the family! And I popped in a couple of extra potatoes as soon as Stephen phoned me, so we won't be sending you away hungry, will we!' She laughed again.

'I won't eat all that much actually, because you know I just had brunch at—'

'Oh, I know. Your family! Breakfast all the day long! It must be like running a restaurant, I don't know how your, how your father's wife manages. She must be run off her feet!'

Trish, as you'll have gathered, doesn't like the word 'stepmother'. She thinks it's a new invention, and is therefore suspicious of it, as if it's 'the wide-world web' or microwaveable chips. I once pointed out to her that Elizabeth the First had four stepmothers in quick succession and she gave me a little pursed-lips smile as if to say, 'Well, you have your beliefs, dear, and I'll have mine.' Also, she's never met Quinn, so she doesn't realize just how ludicrous the idea is of Quinn's being 'run off her feet'. Quinn never runs – she says it raises your adrenaline levels and puts stress on your joints.

'Now. Nice cup of tea, Georgia? Or will you be naughty and take a sherry?' What I really fancied was a glass of wine. A big fat glass of chilled Pinot Grigio or Sauvignon Blanc. I've long since given up saying yes to any wine offered in the Cooling household after a couple of how-can-I-tip-this-into-the-aspidistra experiences. I've tried bringing a bottle too, of course, but then she says, 'Ooh, lovely!' and puts it away for best, never to be seen again. The sherry was on the sticky side, too, I remembered, but by then I'd have snapped off the tops of a boxful of chocolate liqueurs and swigged back the contents if she'd offered them.

'Well . . . a sherry would be nice. Yes, let's live dangerously.' God, I'd started talking like her; it was rubbing off on me.

'Ooh, shall I join you?' She looked as if she might just explode from the excitement of it all.

'Ted, dear!' she screeched, suddenly whapping up the volume of her voice to shout to him in the other room. He came shuffling through, smiled warmly, then waited passively for me to kiss him hello as usual.

'We girls are having a sherry!'

'I'll do the honours then, will I?'

Trish rolled her eyes at me like the villain in a Charlie Chaplin film.

'Well, I can't be messing about with drinks when I've all the dinner to get ready.'

'That's two sherries then? Coming right up.'

'And Ted! Ted!'

He paused in the doorway.

'Use the proper glasses, Ted.'

He looked blank.

'Not the wine glasses, the sherry schooners. In the cabinet! At the back!' She marched through to the sitting room.

'Honestly, I don't know why I bother, Georgia!' She opened the drop-down leaf of the drinks cabinet. 'These ones, Ted! See? Here, by the sherry?'

'I'd have found them.'

'Well, we don't want to be still waiting on our drinks at midnight, do we?' She rolled her eyes again and ushered me through to the kitchen.

'Let's leave the boys to themselves and us girls have a nice chat.'

All the food had been prepared, of course. Trish is very organized, just like Stephen. I didn't have to lift the saucepan lids to know that the sprouts would all be trimmed and crossed, waiting in their cold, salted water, the carrots peeled and thinly sliced, the frozen peas slowly separating. The joint was in the oven, the plates were stacked on the worktop. Everything was immaculate. Even though she'd prepared a whole meal, there wasn't so much as a potato peeling in sight. Of course, I try to clear away as I cook – well, I have to, given that my kitchen's so tiny – but even I can't compete with Trish for tidiness. The chopping board had been wiped down and set upright in its place behind the dishrack as always. The gravy boat was set by the hob.

I used to love coming here. I remember my very first visit. Trish was so kind, so solicitous, topping up my teacup and pressing de luxe selection chocolate biscuits on me rather than leaving me to fend for myself the way Stephen has to with my family. She fussed over me and said, 'Here's the downstairs cloak-room,' and pointed out the fresh guest towel, which I could tell she'd put out just because I was coming. And everything was so clean and tidy and polished. It wasn't that it was my taste – it wasn't at all, but I loved it that their window ledges weren't piled high with stacks of books or old newspapers or lamps that didn't work any more. I loved the fact that I could sit down without checking my chair for pens or keys or mouldering fruit. I loved it that Stephen came from such a family, such a house, I really did.

But, suddenly, I desperately wanted to be away from this well-ordered, brightly lit room. I wanted to be at home again – so much so that I almost cried out. Not my flat, I mean, but *home* home. I wanted to be sitting at the big old kitchen table with Dad reading out bits of the paper. I wanted to be listening to Ellen bitching about her customers at the wine bar and making me laugh. I wanted to have Bonnie and Daniel tugging at me and calling me 'Auntie Gee!' I even wanted to see Quinn with her patchwork jacket and her earrings swinging wildly as she talks. And I thought of our house, our home, with its crammed to bursting book-shelves and its sprawling houseplants, the stacks of newspapers and magazines and piles of theatre pro-grammes and exhibition catalogues, the unlabelled videotapes, that battered old enamel breadbin, the lamp with the shade made of string during Quinn's macramé phase, the cracked tiles in the top bathroom and the numerous progeny of the veteran spider plant on the landing, the strange dishes you seem to find on every surface containing coins no longer in circulation and old matchbooks and single earrings and odd screws and curtain hooks and dice and stray shirt buttons that are never, ever going to be reunited with a shirt. So many things, so much stuff, clogging every flat surface that dared to be a space. Suddenly, I craved the sheer, chaotic, ridiculous excess of it all, the prodigiousness of it. And I wanted to be back in the midst of it, eating with my elbows on the crumb-spattered table and Ellen nicking the end of my croissant or Matt bouncing his hand casually on the top of my head as he passed.

I just wanted to be There with Us and not Here with . . . Them, with these strangers, aliens. Kind people, good people, but not connected to me. They weren't part of me and I wasn't part of them, we just happened to be temporarily in the same building.

I thought of Leo then, too, and Cora – and how hard it must have been for Cora to step into a houseful of strangers. I remembered his face close to mine as we hid beneath the camp bed and his finger hooking round mine, his eyes in the half-darkness. My heart sounded loud in my head. I thought, 'I could stand up now and just walk out.' I pictured myself doing it, closing the front door quietly behind me, boldly striding away down the front path, through the gate, walking faster now, then breaking into a run, heading for the station, heading for home.

'. . . top up?'

'Mmm? Sorry?'

'You were miles away! I was thinking I'd have to wave a flag and ring a bell at you!'

'Sorry.'

'Not at all. Don't you think of it. Get Ted to top your glass up. Ted! Georgia's glass is empty! It must be going all the way down to your ankles, Georgia, I can't keep up with you! Oh, where's that Ted? Ted!'

I could do it. I could. I remember how to stand up, don't I? Lean forward, exert pressure downwards through the legs, that's not so very hard. Then walking, well I remember how to do that bit, too. Been doing it most of my life. It's no harder than it was before. Maybe I really could—

Stephen came in, holding the bottle of sherry. He poured some into my glass.

'Not like you to drink in the day, sweetie. Still, no harm in it. Do you good to relax a bit more.'

'I'll be under the table by teatime,' I said flatly.

Trish, who had just come back in, exploded into great gales of laughter.

'D'you hear that, Ted? Hear what Georgia just said?' She went through to repeat my stunning witticism. No wonder I always feel so amusing when I come to visit.

I leant back in my chair and shut my eyes. I could feel a headache gathering behind my eyebrows, brewing like a storm.

Mummies and Daddies

Georgia is playing at her new friend Josie's house. It is the first time she has been invited there.

'Let's play Mummies and Daddies.' Josie leads the way out to her Wendy house in the garden. 'I'm the daddy coming home on the train from the office. You're the mummy, making the dinner.'

Georgia mimes opening the fridge and stands there, hand on hip, frowning.

Josie peers at her over the top of her pretend newspaper.

'What are you *doing*?'

'Seeing if there's anything for supper, of course. You can't see me yet in any case. You're still on the train.'

'I'm here now.' Josie presents herself at the door. 'Ding-dong!'

'Haven't you got a key if you're the daddy?'

'Yes – but you're s'posed to open the door and take my coat and everything.'

'Why am I? I'm a *mummy*, not a – a butler,' says Georgia, pleased that she knows what a butler is.

'Ding-dong,' Josie says again.

Georgia opens the door and they make loud kissing noises and Georgia helps Josie off with her pristine white cardigan. Georgia dreams of owning one exactly like it, with little pearly buttons.

'Supper won't be ready for ages and ages.'

Josie frowns.

'I am *rather* hungry. I shall have to sit down in my chair – pour me a whisky.'

'There isn't any. I'll have to go to the shop.'

'There *is*. You're spoiling it.'

The pair stare at each other for a moment.

'Let's do skipping instead,' says Josie. They take it in turns to use her skipping rope at first, then they skip together, face to face, encircled by the whirring arc of rope, jumping in synch, grinning with the sheer pleasure of it as they count:

'. . . twenty-one, twenty-two, twenty-three . . .' seeing how many they can do before one of them makes a mistake.

Then Josie's mother calls them in to eat. They sit at the round kitchen table, eating fried chicken and chips – proper, crinkle-cut ones that come in a bag – and peas. Georgia sips her lemonade, trying to make it last, and looks round the room at the brightly patterned tiles and shiny taps, the scoopy-edged blind at the window, the yellow wall-clock, shaped like a teapot, the wooden mug tree, with its set of six matching yellow coffee mugs. It is the nicest, brightest, shiniest kitchen that she has ever seen. Mrs Taylor stands at the sink, drying the last of the washing-up, then puts every single thing away. Georgia watches her as she stacks plates, cups and bowls neatly in cupboards, assigns knives, forks and spoons to their allotted places in a drawer.

'Nice to see you're not a picky eater.' Mrs Taylor nods approvingly. '*You* can certainly come again.'

Georgia, too pleased to remember to smile politely, looks up at her in absolute adoration.

*   *   *

'You OK?' Stephen's hand on my shoulder, firm and comforting, holding me steady, keeping me in my chair.

'Mmm. Just a bit tired, that's all. It's been a long week.' I reached up my hand to his. 'You know – work and stuff.'

He bent to kiss the top of my head. I closed my eyes.

'We won't stay too long. Have an early night tonight, eh?'

I nodded weakly.

'You have a nice long soak in the tub when we get back while I work on my speech.'

'I said I'd help.'

'It's all right.' He spoke into my hair and looped his arms around me from the back. 'I'll let you off.'

'You're so sweet to me. I don't deserve you.' I felt my eyes fill with tears. I didn't know what was the matter with me. You're a mean, ungrateful person, I told myself, you're nothing but a snide bitch, silently sneering at Trish when she's been so kind to you and always offered you the fancy guest towel. So why was I feeling so awful now? Had they really changed? The house was no different: still immaculate, still clean and orderly. Trish would call it 'being out of sorts' and I can't think of a better phrase. I felt as if everything was just all wrong, as if I'd opened the wrong door and entered somebody else's life.

14

About Cora

I rang Leo the next day, desperate to find out more about his mystery daughter. He suggested we hook up in the evening because he had a real live job to do, photographing some author in a club in Soho, but he claimed that he would be back by seven.

'I can't, I've got my supervision then and I'm not usually home till ten. What about then – or is that too late?'

'Not for me, but if you still need supervision in the early evening, can you be trusted out on your own after ten?'

'I won't be on my own though, will I?' As Leo well knows, it's not that kind of supervision. No matter how many years you've been counselling, you still regularly discuss your cases with a supervisor if you've got any sense. 'You can supervise me.'

'Me?' He laughed. 'I couldn't supervise a paper clip.'

'You must have a responsible side tucked away in you somewhere, or how else do you manage with Cora?'

There was a brief silence.

'Leo?'

'Yup. Good question. I'm not exactly the most responsible parent – look, let's talk about this later if

190

we're meeting up. Just bang on my door when you're back.'

In my supervision session, I talked about various issues that had come up with clients, my response to them and how I had handled them. Supervision isn't therapy, and I was tempted not to mention the events of the weekend, but I couldn't stop thinking about it all and, frankly, I don't know anyone who has more sense than Marian does in these matters. The main thing that was bugging me was my reaction when I first saw Cora.

'Why do *you* think you burst into tears?' asked Marian.

'I don't know! I haven't a clue!'

She smiled, but remained silent, waiting for me to find my own answers. I breathed out, felt my ribcage soften and fall as if I were letting out more than simply breath.

'Maybe because I did have a bit of a tiny, insignificant crush on Leo and . . . oh, I don't know – his having a child puts him off limits because I don't want to be a stepmother. Hell, I don't even want to have kids of my own, as you know.'

The silence continued. The gentle smile. God, it's infuriating when she does that.

'You don't think that's it?'

'Do you?'

I cupped my face in my hands and looked at her.

'I guess – if that was really all it was, then I might have been disappointed – frustrated – even angry . . . but I don't think I'd have cried.' A small nod from Marian. 'I suppose that I was upset because my emotions were in conflict – which means that – in some way – as well as being surprised or upset or angry or all of those things – it means . . .'

Marian remained impassive, her expression unreadable, waiting for me to go on.

'I don't understand why it should be – but the tears

indicate that I was ambivalent in some way. At some level, I was also – excited – maybe even happy. It doesn't make sense.' I shook my head. 'Can't you just tell me and put me out of my misery?'

Marian laughed.

'Now, Georgia, you know it's not like giving you a solution to a crossword puzzle. There's nothing I could possibly tell you that you don't know already.'

'But I *don't* know . . . you're saying I should go away and think about it?'

'No.' She shook her head. 'You do more than enough thinking. I'm saying you should go away and let yourself *feel* about it. Not the same thing at all.'

God's views on pepperoni

It was a clear night and I wanted some fresh air, so I walked home afterwards rather than getting the bus. I couldn't stop *thinking* about it, of course, turning it over and over in my head as if it were some nonsensical 3-D puzzle that I couldn't solve. I felt buzzing with energy, even after my brisk walk, so I took the stairs two at a time until I got to the fourth floor. I drummed a rat-a-tat-tat tattoo on Leo's door.

'Hey, you – come in.' He looked past me into the corridor. 'Has your supervisor let you off the leash?'

'No, I did a bunk while she was looking the other way.'

He smiled. 'I'm starving – have you eaten?'

'Pizza?'

He nodded and reached for his jacket.

'Let's get a takeaway.'

As we went through the lobby, Barry called out hello to us.

'Hey, Baz – how's it hanging?' Leo shouted back, while I opted for a polite nod. Barry squared his shoulders.

'Great, Leo. Hanging loose. Have fun you two!'

'How's it *hanging*?' I said, as we descended the steps to the street. 'What are you – *fifteen*?'

'Oh, shut up. Barry gets a big kick out of my calling him Baz and pretending we're both still *yoofs* instead of totally uncool, balding gits heading for forty.'

'That is so deeply sad.'

'Where's the harm in it?'

I shrugged, thinking, well, it's obvious, isn't it? It's ridiculous. It's slightly pathetic. It's pandering to Barry's self-delusions.

'Well, it's . . .' I paused, suddenly realizing that perhaps there really was no harm in it. 'You're right. Who cares?'

'Did you just agree with me about something or am I dreaming?'

'You're dreaming.'

'It's a good dream – I'm walking down the road, it's a clear night and if I half-close my eyes I can make believe the lights in the office blocks are stars . . . and I even have a moderately attractive woman by my side . . .'

I nudged him in the ribs. 'And in your dream, you say, "Perhaps we should get ice-cream too . . ." '

'Mmm – are we talking *serious* ice-cream here?'

'Naturally. Now, look, you. I want to hear all about Cora. Stop messing about and fill me in.'

'But we're there now.' He opened the door of Pizza Express and waved for me to go ahead of him.

'OK, let's order first, but you're not sneaking out of this. I want to know.'

'OK, OK. Let's see . . .' He looked down the menu. 'You want a Giardiniera, but with artichokes instead of leeks, right? And no black pepper.'

I always have the same thing, but even Stephen forgets about the substitution unless I remind him. Still, I hate feeling that I'm quite so predictable.

'No, I'll have the – ' I scanned the menu, but nothing else seemed half as nice, then looked back at him. Leo was smiling knowingly. 'OK, I give in. I'm a boring old fart. I accept it. Same as usual.'

He ordered.

'. . . and a Four Seasons with extra cheese and extra garlic please.'

We sat by the counter to wait.

'Doesn't that have pepperoni on it?' I said. 'I thought you didn't eat sausage – aren't you vaguely semi-kosher?'

'Ah, good question. I'm sort of semi-kosher but on an erratic part-time basis, I don't generally eat pork or shellfish but I've decided pepperoni's OK very occasionally because for one thing, it's called "pepperoni" not "pork" and for another, God can't see it when it's on a pizza covered in mozzarella and stuff.'

'I see. That certainly sounds consistent.'

He laughed. 'I make no claims to be consistent. About anything. All I will say is that at least I'm consistently inconsistent.'

'True.'

'And – surely God's got better things to worry about than whether some poor schmuck is having pepperoni on his pizza? I mean, aren't there a few minor wars and things going on to occupy him?'

'Maybe the world's in a mess precisely because he's too preoccupied with you and your pepperoni . . . He's sitting up there, head in his hands, moaning, "Oy-yoy-yoy – that Leo Kane, such a nice boy, I thought maybe he'd become a doctor, settle down with a good woman, keep the sabbath – now here he is, nearly forty and still no sign of a regular salary – eating *trayf* goy food when he thinks I'm not looking—" '

'Ah, that explains it. You ever thought of becoming a rabbi? That makes a lot more sense than the God moves in mysterious ways schtick.'

'Anyway . . . I don't think I've ever known any-one quite like you for changing the subject – about Cora—'

'I didn't change the subject, for once. It was you.

194

You started interrogating me on my stomach's non-observance of the dietary laws.'

I thought back.

'OK, you're right. I did. Now tell me about Cora.'

'Too late – here are our pizzas.'

'So, let's start with the basics . . .' I said, as we walked back. 'Who is Cora's mother? Hazel, you said?'

'Yes – we had a brief thing over five years ago.'

'How brief?'

'Four, five months maybe. It was never serious. We were so different – Hazel was quite . . . floaty . . . I think is how you'd put it. She drifted from one creative phase to another – making candles, batik wall-hangings. Also, she never got up till about noon and she used to smoke dope during the day and speak really slowly, like she had to think about everything for half an hour before she said it, drove me up the wall. Sorry if I sound like an old fogey but it just got really boring. I wanted to get up and get on and *do* things and she didn't.'

'Was this in Glasgow?'

'No. She lived in Edinburgh, so I used to drive there at weekends to see her.' He turned to look at me as we walked. 'Don't go putting on your counsellor face at me – I know it wasn't a proper relationship, but it was fine at the time. Hazel was OK – despite the dope and the candles with bits of dead leaf entombed in them – she was a nice person. Kind. Well-intentioned. Decent.'

'And where is she now? Presumably Cora lives with her?' We'd reached our block.

'No. Cora lives with Hazel's sister in Cricklewood. Look – maybe I should show you her letter – that explains it. Well – better than I can, at any rate.'

The letter

Leo handed me a sharp knife to cut the pizza while he looked for the letter. We sat side by side on his sofa, eating straight from the boxes.

'Here it is.'

'Hang on – I'd better wash my hands.' I started to get up.

'Wipe them on my jeans.' He proffered his leg and I rubbed my hands over the denim near his knee.

'Feel free to carry on,' he said.

I ignored him and picked up the letter.

Dear Leo,

I hope this letter reaches you. I wrote before to the last address I had for you but there was no response – so I still don't know whether you received it or not. If you did – and chose to ignore it – please, please reply to this one because it has now become urgent.

It seems so strange to be writing to you after all this time. All I have to remind me of you is one photo of us together that you took on your automatic timer – remember how impressed I was! – and your black woollen scarf that you wrapped round me one day when we were out walking and it was cold. I'm afraid the moths got at it, so it has a few holes in it now, but I have kept it.

Please don't think me weird for writing to you out of the blue like this – I know what we had, our affair, relationship or whatever you like to call it, lasted only a few months and wasn't even what you'd call serious. I don't remember even saying 'I love you' though I feel as if I did in my own way. You see – still I am spinning it out, avoiding coming to the point – just like I used to lie in bed, putting off the moment when I had to get up – remember?

Leo – you got me pregnant. Or should I say, I got myself pregnant with you as my unwitting helper? Remember that time – just a week or two before we split up? It was the middle of the night and my room was hot and stuffy and neither of us could sleep. I turned to you then, pulled you towards me and, half in a dream it seemed, we made love. Did I know I would get pregnant? No. Of course not. Did I hope for it? I was scared, but yes, I have to say I did. Even though I was pretty sure it would mean bringing up the baby on my own. My fortieth birthday was round the corner and, Leo, with my history of men, who could blame me for thinking it might be my last chance?

I know we'd never have lasted as a couple – less so with a child, I truly believe that. As soon as I knew, I moved back south, out to south Devon where I grew up. I stayed with an old friend for a few months, then rented a tiny cottage by the sea. I used to think of you sometimes, when I walked by the water's edge with my – our – baby in a sling, thinking of how you would have loved to photograph it there – the views across the water to the other side of the bay, the light changing hour by hour.

Forgive me for not telling you sooner, for waiting until it was too late. Leo, I – we – had a beautiful baby girl. Her name is Cora Anne – I hope you like it. Anne after your mother – though I never met her, I remembered her name. If you work out the dates, you'll know that she is nearly five now. She's a daily delight – sweet-natured though rather shy, with bright, sparkling eyes like your own. She has been my joy, Leo, so thank you for that. I didn't tell you before because I was sure you'd show up, determined to 'do the decent thing' and I didn't want that. I didn't want you to be with me out of a sense of duty and I didn't really want to be with you – not really, not in the way it should be when you are raising a child. So, selfishly, I know, I kept her all to myself. I supported us both (just about) by hand-knitting jumpers and painting silk scarves, and my sister helped me out when she could.

But now I'm so angry with myself. Ashamed too

for not letting you know because – remember what you used to say? 'Life doesn't go according to plan'? How right you were.

I'll be blunt. Too late for anything else now. I'm dying, Leo. I'm bloody dying and there's not a bloody thing I can do about it. I've got ovarian cancer and they tell me that if they'd caught it earlier, perhaps they'd have been able to save me. You'll no doubt be pleased to know that I didn't waste time with my crystals but went straight for the chemo. We've moved back to London, and we're staying with my sister in Cricklewood (I know, after all my sneers about the suburbs!) and Cora's started school – I'm saving all her pictures for you to see.

I've given Cora the photo of us together and told her that you live a long, long way away – in case you don't want to see her or don't get this letter. I'm sorry – but what else could I say? I have no idea where you're living now, so I may even be right. It would be good for her to know she still has one parent to turn to. Please, please get in touch as soon as you get this – if you get this – for Cora's sake, for yours – if not for mine. This is my sister's phone number and address . . .

I'm so sorry.

With love and many regrets,
Hazel

I swallowed hard and looked up at him as I finished the letter. His eyes met mine.

'Yup.' He clicked his tongue, the way he does sometimes when he's feeling stressed or doesn't know what to do next. 'Quite a letter, hmm?'

I nodded.

'So, what happened?'

'See the date there? The letter didn't reach me for over three months. By the time I phoned her sister,

Hazel had been dead for a month.'

'Oh – how awful. I'm so sorry. Poor Cora.'

'Yup. Poor little mite. I felt pretty gutted. I thought maybe I'd have been able to do something. Anything. Maybe I could have *saved* Hazel – made her hang on longer, *made* her live.'

I laid my hand on his.

'No-one can do that.'

'I know.' He turned his hand palm up to hold mine. 'But you know what I'm like – what can I *do*? How can I *make* it *happen*?' He laughed at himself, shook his head. 'So much for the power of action.' He sank back into the cushions. 'And now all Cora's got is me – and her aunt's family, of course – at least they're pretty steady.'

'Hey – you're not so bad yourself. She's lucky to have you.'

That lopsided smile again.

'Thank you, but I'm totally new to this. Shit, I haven't got a clue how to be a dad. I've barely got my own life together – look at me, for God's sake.' He waved an arm at the sea of semi-unpacked boxes, the tripods and cases of equipment.

'You can learn. That's only what every parent has to do anyway. You're lucky – at least you've managed to skip the crappy nappies and sleepless nights . . .' Watching his face, his eyes. 'I'm sorry, now is not the time to be flippant.'

'That's OK. Sometimes flippancy is more useful than sympathy.'

The weekend father

I leant back on the sofa.

'So what happens now?'

'Now I'm a weekend dad – I get to take Cora out for the day on Saturday or Sunday – only I don't even have an ex-wife to bitch about. Now who's being inappropriately flippant? But, boy, do I know I'm on probation. Hazel may have been floaty, but her sister is one tough cookie – pick her up on time, bring her back on time, don't buy her sweets, don't fill her up with fizzy drinks, hold her hand when you're crossing the road, cross at a proper crossing, don't let go of her for one single second if you're in the West End—'

'Most of that's pretty sensible, surely?'

He twisted round to look at me.

'Oh, sensible, schmensible. I want Cora to have fun – I want her to know that the world's wonderful and exciting and weird and surprising – I don't want her to feel that everything beyond the zebra crossing is dangerous and scary.'

'She *will* have fun. She can discover how wonderful the world is – but you have to be sensible for her, don't you see that? Just think – she's had this huge loss and a massive upheaval – she's lost her mother, her home, everything – it'll be all she can do just to keep her head above water – but you can help her by being the rock in her life. You need to be one hundred per cent solid and reliable for her – that's the way to help her get as much fun out of life as you obviously do. The more grown-up you are, the less she'll have to be.'

He looked at me, assessing.

'You're not just a pretty face, are you?'

'Oh, hush – or I'll start taking myself seriously and then where will I be?'

'God knows. I haven't taken myself seriously since 1987.'

He stood up then and cleared away the pizza boxes, offered me a coffee.

I looked at my watch.

'No thanks, it's past my caffeine deadline. I can't believe how late it is. I must go. I've got a client at eight a.m. tomorrow.'

Leo made a face.

'OK.' He showed me out. 'Hey – and thank you. For what you said.' He leant forward suddenly and kissed me on the cheek.

'Anytime.'

'Maybe you could come with us sometime?' He dug his hands deep into his pockets. 'Cora and me, I mean.' I looked into his eyes and saw that it wasn't just a casual invitation. 'She liked you,' he said.

15

Close to the edge

'I meant to say – I had a good chat with your dad on Sunday, after you left,' Leo told me.

'Good. He's great, isn't he? Well, great if he's someone else's dad, I imagine.'

Leo frowned.

'I thought you got on well with him? You seem so close.'

'We do OK – I just get a bit exasperated by him at times. When he doesn't listen properly because he's reading the paper at the same time as ostensibly having a conversation or when he plays devil's advocate just to keep an argument going. And you should see his study – it looks like a paper-recycling depot. He never, ever files anything when he's finished with it. I once attempted to set up a proper system for him and the only three categories he could come up with were Urgent, Boring, and Aggravating but Pays.'

'What if he was working on something that was both boring and urgent?'

'Exactly! What kind of system is that?'

'Still – he's the one who has to live with it. If it doesn't bother him, why should it bother you?'

'Oh – *because* it just does – because I have to look at it and I can't bear it. Sometimes I think he's creating chaos deliberately, I really do – he says he can't work if everything's tidy around him, but that doesn't make sense, does it?'

'Maybe it does for him? Why don't you just not go in his study if it annoys you so much?'

I made a face.

'Will you please not be so rational and sensible? That's my job. And I suppose you and your family never exchange a cross word? You never find them annoying?'

'Of course I do. We talk, we argue, we give each other unasked-for advice – we're a family. It drives me bonkers the way my mother insists on keeping every single leftover item of food, even one lone boiled potato. Her fridge looks like a Tupperware catalogue.'

'She sounds wonderful.' And I meant it. I loathe waste. 'Perhaps she could adopt me?'

'I'm sure she'd love to, she's had enough of us lot by now.' He stood up and crossed to the sink. 'OK if I make myself some more coffee or, if I'm using all yours up, we can switch to my place?'

'No. Too untidy. Aren't you ever going to unpack properly?'

'Probably not. I've been quite busy recently, strangely enough – I don't think unpacking stuff I hardly ever use is exactly top priority – especially as I don't have anywhere else to put it. What's the point? I'll probably have to move quite soon anyway.'

'Really? Why? You only just moved in.'

'Think about it.'

'What?'

'Cora. There's nowhere for her to sleep. At the moment, I only have her for the day, but . . .'

'Of course. Sorry, I wasn't thinking.'

Talking about Joy

'So, is your mum still on the scene or what?' Leo settled back into my sofa. 'I started to ask you once but we got sidetracked – most unlike us . . .'

'On the scene?'

'Sorry – I mean, did your parents divorce, I didn't like to ask your dad, or – '

'She's dead.'

'I'm sorry, I didn't mean to sound flip about it – was it recently?' He sat forward again, his face serious.

'God, no. Years and years ago. I was ten.'

'That must have been awful.' He shook his head, as if remembering it himself. 'And how old was she? She must have been pretty young.'

'Yes. She was forty-two. What is this – *Newsnight*?'

'Sorry, I'm interested that's all.'

'Why are you?' I looked at him directly.

'Because I'm carrying out a scientific study of women who live in stupidly small studio flats, especially those who live in two of them at once.' He tilted his head to one side. 'Because I'm a deeply nosy person and I want to know all about you, your whole family, what makes you tick, everything.'

The trouble with Leo is that you can never tell when he's taking the piss.

'No, you don't.'

'Yes, I do.'

'Don't,' I said childishly, sticking out my bottom lip as if I were sulking.

'Do.'

'*N't.*'

'Oh, *shut up.*' He smiled. 'And you say *I'm* childish? I didn't mean to upset you, talking about your mum.'

I shrugged.

'It doesn't. It's ages ago.'

'Well, OK then.' He relaxed back into the sofa a little. 'So, do you mind my asking – what did she die of? Was it cancer?'

I shook my head.

'Funny how people tend to assume it was cancer – mostly they don't ask. I think they're worried that it might be embarrassing or that it might remind me that she's dead.'

'I can't imagine that you'd be likely to forget.'

'Quite – it's kind of nice to be asked in a way. I mean, I talk about Mum a lot to Ellen – she doesn't remember her at all, you see? – but not otherwise. I can't with Dad much because of Quinn, it wouldn't be fair.'

He was looking at me expectantly.

'Oh. Yes. Right. No. Not cancer.' I smiled and stood up, walked over to my rubber plant and dipped to feel how dry the compost was. 'Must give this a water.' Crossed back to the sink, started filling a jug. 'Oh, it sounds so silly. Ridiculous even. Look – please don't laugh – she – well, she fell down the stairs at home, the ones down to her studio and – ' I shrugged. 'Well, that was it. Her neck was broken. At least it was quick. She had these slippers, you see, we called them her "misery slippers" because they were these awful sloppy leather mules, the sort you can't walk properly in, you have to shuffle in a kind of gloomy way . . . anyway, she was wearing them and it looks as if she just slipped and . . . there you go – '

He stood up and came nearer, but I avoided his eye and started watering the rubber plant.

'I'm sorry.'

I moved away to put the jug back by the sink, dug out a new cloth and wetted it under the tap – that plant's leaves were getting so dusty. I used to be so good about wiping it, I don't know what's happened to me recently, I'm letting everything go.

'No need to be. Really.' I supported a leaf with my hand and wiped its surface with the cloth, getting rid of all the grime and dust. 'You're being very sweet about it.'

He scrunched up his nose at my use of the word 'sweet'. Men never like to be told they're sweet, do they? They think it's a euphemism for 'not sexy'.

'Honestly, it's just it's ages ago, and I dealt with it all in my training – I had therapy a-go-go – I'm not saying I never miss her or that I don't care. I've just . . . moved on, that's all.' I nodded. Subject closed.

'OK. If you say so.' He stood fingering the edge of one of the plant's now glossy leaves. 'I'm a bit surprised your dad didn't want to sell the house afterwards – it must be a painful reminder for you all.'

'He did want to, but I – we – asked him not to. In any case, he had his hands full trying to bring up us lot.' I stood back to survey the plant, see if I'd missed anything. 'It has lots of good memories, too. And we don't have much else that's connected to her.'

'Oh?'

'Well, there are photos, of course, and a handful of her paintings and prints but most of those were— but home is still home – that's the house she first bought and decorated with Dad. And very little's changed really. That big dresser in the kitchen – Mum found it in a junk shop, it was painted bright blue and she stripped off all the paint to get back to the wood. Things like that – they hold your memories, don't they?'

He nodded, considering. 'And don't you find – ' he began, his voice serious. 'I notice – in myself, I mean – traits I've got from my dad, I don't know – yes, all sorts of things – like the fact that I can whistle really well but can't sing to save my life and I love sweet-sour cucumbers but don't like olives and find people endlessly, endlessly fascinating but get ridiculously impatient with people who are boring—'

'But surely most of that's just because you grew up around him?'

'Ye-es, you'd think so, wouldn't you? But what's weird is that I didn't used to be like that. I could never whistle before and I didn't like sweet-sour—'

'You think it's mystical? What?'

He shook his head firmly.

'No. You know me – arch-sceptic most of the time. I don't know what I think really – maybe some of the things were already there in me, but I just didn't recognize them until after he died?'

'But I'm not like my mother at all, so bang goes your theory.'

'You must be. Even if you don't look like her, there must be qualities . . .'

'No. Not at all. I take after Dad's side more. My mother was very attractive – Ellen looks quite like her.'

'Yes, it's a shame you're so ugly . . .' he smiled.

'Go away. I mean she was very – very sparkly, you know? Full of life. Well, she was – anyway – not exactly beautiful, but charismatic, bubbly.

'And you're plain, repellent and dull? So Ellen got all the breaks? What a shame . . .'

'Hilarious. I'm just *saying* you can't assume that children always take after their parents. I'm completely different. You've seen what the others are like – I'm the inexplicable white sheep in the family.'

'Can you please stop pacing about and wiping things, you're driving me crazy! Come and sit down.'

'And you say I'm bossy!' Still, I went and joined him on the sofa, perched at the other end.

'But – I'm not sure you are that different . . . granted, I can see you're tidy and they're not—'

'Understatement of the century—'

'And you're fiendishly organized and they're not – but you're all – how can I put it? You're all – cut from the same bale of cloth. At your brunch, sure you were teasing each other—'

'Sniping at each other more like.'

'Not really. Even when you're arguing, you can tell there's a lot of affection underneath and you're all on the same wavelength. It was good to feel a part of it even as an outsider.'

'Ha! You're not an outsider!'

I flushed. I hadn't meant to say that. Don't you hate it

when words just slip out and you can't get them back again?

'I mean, of course you are – technically, but you're someone who obviously fits in easily in most social situations.' It sounded ridiculous, formal and limp.

He smiled and stood up.

'Anyway, I ought to make at least a show of doing some kind of work, justify my existence on the planet.' He took his cup over to the sink and held his hand out for mine. 'But I bet, if you think about it, there'll be some way in which you take after your mum – like your cooking maybe or your amazing eyes or – or the way you half-poke your tongue out when you're really concentrating on something—'

'I don't do that!'

'Yes, you do. You did it the other day when you were chopping something very finely with that big scary kitchen knife of yours.'

I paused, remembering.

'She used to do that when she was painting.'

'There then. You see?'

'Mmm.' I cleared my throat. 'Still, that's only one tiny thing. I'm not like her in anything significant.'

He looked into my eyes for a moment, seemed about to say something, then he simply smiled and reached for his jacket.

'See you tomorrow then?'

'Yes. Tomorrow.'

Breadsticks

Half-term. Thursday. Georgia, now nine and a half, and Ellen, nearly three, are hungry. Matt, as usual, has sloped off to a friend's house, something he does at every possible opportunity. It is well past lunchtime.

Georgia knocks timidly at the door of their mother's studio and, when there is no answer, puts her head round. As always, this room smells like no other in the house. Paint and turpentine and linseed oil, suffused with the smell of the slim cigars Joy smokes in the early stages of a painting.

'Mummy? What's for lunch?'

Joy is painting. Tongue poised between her lips in concentration, she scrunches her eyes half-closed at the canvas in front of her. Every inch of the table next to her is crowded with jars jammed with old brushes, dirty coffee cups, bottles, tubes of paint bent in the middle like sad old men, half of them with their tops missing.

'Hmmm?'

'*Lunch*. We're hungry. *Ellen's* hungry.'

Joy's brow puckers and she peers at Georgia as if about to transfer her dimensions to the canvas.

'You can find something, can't you? There's plenty of food.'

'No.' Georgia, patiently. 'There *isn't*.'

'Oh, well, there must be *something*. Make yourselves cheese on toast, you're good at that. Mummy's painting just now.'

'There isn't any cheese.'

Joy turns away again, back to the fragments of light and dark, the play of shadows demanding her attention once more.

'Well – just toast for now then, hmm? Put some jam on it to keep you going and Mummy will take you both out later somewhere nice. Special treat.'

Georgia doesn't bother to ask where or at what time because she knows there is no point. Joy stabs her brush into an extrusion of burnt umber on the dinner plate she is using as a palette. Georgia thinks it looks like a small pooh. She goes back up to the kitchen, tells Ellen to sit up properly in her chair, and heads for the breadbin. There are three slices of bread left and two of them are ends. Georgia fishes down into the wrapper, then recoils as if she has been stung. The bread is spotted with blue mould circles ringed with white as neat as if they had been painted too. She pushes the lot down into the rubbish bin, covering it up with a squashed cereal packet so that it won't be retrieved and the mould scraped off, it's fine, after all, not poisonous or anything, honestly you children are all getting so spoilt.

In the larder, Georgia finds a packet of breadsticks and, on the table, the much-gouged butter from breakfast is still out, as are jars of jam and honey. Georgia shows Ellen what to do, dipping the end of a breadstick first in the butter then directly in the jam jar. Ellen, who resists all attempts to get her to use a knife and fork, is delighted.

'You're very lucky,' Georgia informs her. 'Breadsticks are what people have for lunch in posh restaurants.'

Up on the roof

'Tell me when you sunbathe topless on the roof – so I can be sure to respect your privacy and stay away.' Leo was sitting out on my balcony, attempting to soak up the last of the sun – fully dressed, of course.

'a) I never sunbathe because it's bad for you and I find it boring, b) even if I did, I wouldn't go topless because if you don't have any pale bits left, how is anyone to know that you have a tan, if you wanted one – which I don't and c) I don't think you can get up on the roof in any case.'

'Course you can.'

'How?'

'Well, let me see – do you think it involves, a) going down to the basement, b) going to my flat and passing through the back of the wardrobe to a secret passage or c) going up, towards the direction of the roof? You're fond of this a, b, c approach to things, aren't you?'

'Not so's I've noticed. Am I? All right, so it's *up*. Obviously. I meant, how do you get out onto it? Is it safe?'

'It's incredibly difficult and dangerous – you have to shinny up this drainpipe first, then clamber along a narrow ledge clinging on only by your fingernails, then you have to leap across a *huuuuge* gap with a dizzying drop beneath you – come on, I'll show you.'

I looked down at my skirt.

'What – now? Do I need to change?'

'I think you could let yourself be a bit more spontaneous, but other than that – no, I like you the way you are.'

'Ah, what a thing it is to have a well-developed sense of humour.'

'Are you coming or not? If you're seriously worried about your smart skirt, you can take it off.'

'Can I really? How have I managed all these years without your helpful suggestions?'

He led the way to the top floor by the back stairs, then paused by a door marked 'Fire Exit'.

'Ready?'

He leaned on the lever and opened the door, picked up an odd brick and set it in the doorway.

'Always wedge the door unless you want to spend the night under the stars. You can't open it from the outside. And, if you do want to spend the night under the stars, I suggest you bring up a duvet, a pillow and a warm companion – all of which I may be able to supply at a moment's notice – the nights are getting quite nippy now, aren't they?'

I stepped out onto the roof.

'But this is amazing! I had no idea you could see all this. It's breathtaking.' I turn to look at him.

'You've really never been up here?'

'No. I didn't know you were allowed.'

'Allowed? Are you in nursery school?' He laughs. 'Look!' He sweeps his arm out and round. 'There – see St Paul's? And Canary Wharf? Now this way.' He stands behind me and swivels me round. 'Look – the London Eye? Big Ben! Isn't it fantastic!'

'What's that hideous one there? The round thing?'

'The Civil Aviation Authority. Don't home in on the ugly bits – don't you think it's wonderful?'

'Yes, it is. But how did you know you could even get up here? You still count as the new boy.'

'First thing I checked out. Always check out the fire stairs and the roof.'

'Really?'

'Yup – I was in a fire when I was a kid.'

'What happened?'

'Why – so you can analyse me and my childhood and tell me what's wrong with me?'

'No. I think analysing you would take a lifetime and I'm going out at eight with my friend Susie. Why do people always get so defensive as soon as they know what I do for a living? I'm not an analyst, for a start, and I don't usually explore people's childhoods in great depth. I'm just interested – making conversation, almost as if we were normal people.'

He laughs.

'Fair enough. Sorry if I was prickly. The fire – it was a chip-pan blaze when I was about six. The whole kitchen went up. Yup. My mum grabbed my two sisters one under each arm and shouted at me to get out too. But – see – at that age, whenever I went outside, I always went via the kitchen – to try and sneak a biscuit from the tin to eat while I was playing. And I didn't have a clue what was going on. So instead of following Mum out the front, I went the other way towards the back where the kitchen was – and there was this *wall* of flame right in front of me. I could feel the heat of it on my skin, but I couldn't move. It must have been ten feet high. I just stood there, rooted to the spot. Then – it felt like ten minutes but probably all of three seconds later, Mum came rushing back and yanked me off my feet and ran through the house with me to the street.'

'Very scary for a small person.'

He shrugs.

'Couldn't light a match till I was eleven. But then – this is kind of weird, don't you think? – I became absolutely fascinated by fire. When I was twelve, thirteen or so, any time we had candles on the table, I couldn't stop fiddling with them – playing with the wax – seeing how close I could get to the flame – passing my hand through it – dripping wax onto the back of my hand then peeling it off. Is that peculiar?'

'It's not uncommon to be both attracted to and afraid of the same thing at the same time. Especially things we can't control. Lots of people are.'

'Are they? Are you?'

'No. Of course not.'

'Why of course not? Are you on a higher plane than the rest of us just because you're a counsellor?'

'No. God, you remind me of my brother – a source of endless irritating questions. I'm not saying I'm even remotely more sorted out than anyone else . . . but I don't see myself as being torn by ambivalence. I pretty much know my own mind on most things.'

He moves closer to the edge of the roof. There's no railing there because, of course, it's not been designed with the intention of having the residents wandering about up here admiring the view. He takes another step.

'Be careful!'

He turns round, smiling.

'See?'

'What?' I look past him, presuming that he's pointing out another landmark.

'Just a few weeks ago, when I fell against your door, I'm sure you'd have quite gladly let me walk right off the edge of this roof if I'd been so inclined. Now, here you are, concerned for my safety. You have mixed feelings.'

'No, I don't. It was just a reflex – I'd be exactly the same if you were a complete stranger.'

'Thanks.'

'Anyway – that's not ambivalence. My feelings have changed, that's all. Before, I thought you were, well . . .'

'Rude? Irritating? Arrogant?'

'Yes, yes and yes – keep going.'

'Watch it, you. Only now . . . ?'

'Now I *know* you're all those things, but I think I quite like you anyway.'

'There you are then – mixed feelings. Like I said.'

I laugh.

'D'you fancy some ice cream?' he asks.

'I've only got vanilla in my icebox.'

'Vanilla? Vanilla! The world is full of double-treble-chocolate-chip and maple-pecan-fudge-ripple and strawberry-'n'-clotted-cream-'n'-clotted-arteries and you're dabbling about with vanilla? What's wrong with you, woman?'

'Well, it goes with everything. Puddings. Apple pie.'

'Goes with everything? What kind of argument is that? Following that logic, I suppose you only ever buy clothes that are black or white?'

'Actually – yes. Pretty much.' I let my gaze linger on his peculiar green shirt, without comment. 'I own a couple of things in navy. Cream.'

'Navy – now there's living it up! Don't you dare be rude about this shirt. I love this shirt.'

'I didn't say a word!'

'You didn't need to. Anyway – stay right there and I'll fetch the ice cream from my vast selection, OK? What flavour – oh, what's the point? I'll choose for you. A woman who thinks vanilla is the be-all and end-all of ice-cream flavours clearly can't be trusted to make that kind of important decision.'

What if . . . ?

'So what would you do if you were my counsellor and I was your patient?' Leo digs his spoon deep into the tub of Belgian chocolate ice cream and offers it to me. 'Look – have that bit with the big chunk of chocolate, see?'

We sit side by side on his jacket, looking out at the lights of the city.

'Client, not patient. And you wouldn't be.'

214

'Why? Am I beyond help?'

'Undoubtedly, but that's not why. I couldn't take you on because I'm—' I stop myself short. It's weird – whenever I'm around Leo, I find myself thinking out loud, saying things I would never say normally. You know how it is – even when you're talking to someone, you often have a whole separate track of thoughts going on at the same time underneath. Or is that just me? Anyway, when I'm talking to him, the two strands seem to get all intertwined and confused and I end up saying things out loud that I thought I had neatly tucked away at the back of my head.

'. . . because I'm your neighbour.' It sounds lame, even to me. 'It's a boundaries issue, you see,' I add with what I hope is a professional crispness.

'But we don't share a boundary – I'm right at the far end of the corridor.' He's doing his serious face, but he's pissing about as usual.

'You know that's not what I meant. It's just as I see you socially already, it wouldn't be – appropriate.'

'Why?' He's like a child sometimes, he really is. Why, why, why, all the time. 'That could be seen as a good thing, because it means I'm already relaxed with you. So why is it?'

'Questions, questions. *I* don't make the rules. But you can see it makes sense. If you already have some kind of relationship with the prospective client—'

'That would be me.'

'Yes, you or whoever – some sort of relationship, no matter how *slight or superficial*, there's a risk that the client may already have some feelings regarding the counsellor that are not part of the process and—'

'And what about the counsellor?'

'What? What *about* the counsellor?'

'What about the *counsellor*? Is the counsellor immune to all this or . . .'

'No, that's right. Exactly. The counsellor is also human, of course, so he or she may not be able to be one hundred per cent professional and impartial either.'

He swings round to look at me.

'I see. And is she?'

'Is she what? Who?'

Yes, I know what he means, but now I'm wishing I'd never got caught up in this conversation.

'She, the counsellor – you, then. Impartial, I mean.'

'Impartial as regards . . . ?'

'The potential client. Um – me.'

I could answer this in a purely professional, detached way. I could say how much I value our growing friendship, how I find him so easy to talk to. I could do that. That's probably what I should do. I get up and take a few steps towards the edge of the roof, stand there with my back to him – but whether it's so I can't see his face or he can't see mine, I'm not sure.

'Not one hundred per cent impartial. No, I'm not.'

'And you're announcing this vital fact to the deaf dome of St Paul's for what reason exactly?'

'It's important to keep significant landmarks well informed, I always feel, don't you? Most people neglect to, but . . .' I rub my upper arms briskly with my hands. 'I should've brought a jacket.'

'When you've finished chatting to the rooftops, do you think you might turn round and look at me?' I hear him stand up.

'I've still got Big Ben, the Houses of Parliament, and the Civil Aviation Authority to talk to.'

'What say you talk to me about this not quite hundred per cent impartiality and we notify the architectural highlights of Central London a bit later? How would that be?'

I nod slowly, then turn to face him.

'So – if you're not a hundred per cent impartial, just how impartial are you?' He comes one step closer. 'Ninety-seven per cent? Eighty-nine per cent?'

'Bit less than that.' I step towards him.

'Seventy-two per cent? Sixty-three?'

'Mm – lower.'

'Thirty-one per cent?' Now he seems to be standing right in front of me.

'I think it might be more of a fraction of a percentage.' I look up into his eyes. 'More like, say, two-fifths.'

'Two-fifths? So you're about two-fifths impartial, and three-fifths partial? This is getting complicated.' He takes his jacket and puts it round my shoulders, reaches his hands behind my neck to free my hair, lift it clear of the collar.

'No. I'm two-fifths of one per cent impartial. That makes me—'

'Ninety-nine per cent and three-fifths . . . ?'

'Partial. Yes. I'm afraid it does.'

Maybe it's still not too late to walk away.

'Didn't your teacher tell you never to mix fractions and percentages?'

'Yes. They're too different. You mustn't mix them. It doesn't work.'

'Except . . .' He puts his hand on my waist and pulls me gently towards him. I think it might be too late now.

'Except?' I echo, tilting my face up to his.

'Except when it does.'

16

The longest minute in the history of time

A minute later – or perhaps it's an hour? – I pull away.

'This isn't right.' I shake my head. 'I can't do this.'

'Well – why *are* you doing it then?' He is smiling that funny lopsided half-smile of his, but the question is serious.

'I don't know.'

'Cheers – flattery will get you nowhere.'

'I'm sorry.' I rest my head against his chest for a moment, feeling his arms around me.

'Is it because of Stephen? Or because of Cora?'

'Stephen, of course. What on earth has Cora got to do with it?'

'I don't know – just a feeling. I mean, you seemed really good with her, but you told me that you can't see yourself ever having kids and – you know – I come as a package deal now.'

'I really can't see how having one kiss with you has got anything to do with—'

'Of *course* it has. Come on, we're not fifteen any more. It *matters*.'

'Don't have a go at me.' I pull away from him.

'Hey, hey.' He takes my hand between his own. 'Look, you know I'm not the kind of person who goes round busting up other people's relationships – but you and Stephen – I mean – you've been engaged all this time yet you haven't—'

'So?' I pull my hand away. 'What's wrong with that? If more people took their time and didn't rush into marriage, there'd be a much lower divorce rate, wouldn't there? Besides, we want it to be done properly – not everyone likes to plunge in without any kind of plan, you know. There are so many things to go wrong.'

'True.' He nods as if he knows all about it. 'Such as who you choose to marry.'

'That's a really nasty thing to say. You don't know Stephen, you don't know anything about him. He's a wonderful person.'

'So why are you kissing another man on a rooftop?'

'I'm not.' I take another step back. 'It was a mistake. I'm sorry.'

'And you see no reason why you shouldn't carry on with Stephen as if nothing's happened between us?'

'Nothing *has* happened – just *one* kiss. It doesn't necessarily *mean* anything. I'm surprised you read so much into it – I thought you were Mr Fly-by-night, not ready to settle down and dashing from pillar to post—'

'I wasn't asking you to marry me this second, no, of course not, but I do—'

'Who was expecting you to? What on earth makes you imagine I'd even want someone like you?'

'Thanks. So what am I then? Did you just think you could have one last fling before you get that ring on your finger? One quick fuck, then you could forget me and play the blushing bride? Thanks a million.'

'Don't be ridiculous – you know I'm not like that!'

'Well, what are you up to then? I'm not being the understudy. You want Stephen? Fine – you've got him. If you only wanted to be friends with me, Georgia, that would've been OK, you know. I'm not going to be moping about outside your door – but if you're not interested, then don't bloody keep looking at me like that with those great big eyes of yours, don't melt into my arms as if you were meant to be there and don't go

219

kissing me as if you—' He clamps his lips shut, then opens them again only to make that soft clucking noise he does with his tongue. 'I'm sorry, why am I having a go at you? As you say, it's only a kiss. People are shagging each other left, right and centre without a second thought and here we are – here *I* am – getting all strung up over a meaningless little kiss.'

He nods towards the door.

'Coming?'

'Mmm.' I check my watch. 'Oh, I'm late. I'm never late!' I cannot meet his eye as I hand back his jacket. 'I *am* sorry. I wasn't thinking – '

'Hey, no big deal, OK?' He laughs it off. 'Forget it – it's just a kiss. Kids of ten get up to more mischief than that these days.'

I nod. He's right, of course. No big deal, no big deal at all.

The B-word

'And don't forget Ellen's birthday party on the 10th,' I said to Stephen as we went through our diaries.

He made a face, which I ignored.

'It's not at her flat, is it?'

Ellen's flat is on the wrong side of the Students/ Human Beings Divide as regards mess, which might be acceptable if she and her two flatmates were nearer twenty than thirty. To give you a taste, they used to have a coat rack in the hall but it collapsed under the weight of their combined clobber – mostly Ellen's, her carpet coat was probably the final straw. Naturally, putting the rack up again or hiring someone else to do it is beyond the capabilities of three intelligent, able people – so now they have a sort of compost heap of outerwear beside the front door. If I go there to pick up Ellen, I have to stand with my arms held out as she plunges into the pile and heaps things on top of me – 'Hang on! Hang on! Can you see a pink suede jacket?'

'No – at the wine bar. Brian's letting her have the

upstairs room for nothing. And giving her the wine at cost. And throwing in free bruschettas and stuff.'

'Which he's doing purely out of the goodness of his heart?' Stephen smiled knowingly.

'Quite. It's strange, actually, because Ellen's not usually slow to notice men being besotted with her. I think she just can't picture herself having sex with anyone called Brian.'

'That's a bit unfair, surely?'

'Of course it's unfair. When has fairness ever been even remotely in the picture when it comes to love and sex? Anyway, you know what she's like – if a man's halfway decent and suitable, then she's not interested.'

'I'm glad you're not like that.' He patted my leg and smiled. 'We don't have to stay long, do we?'

'Don't force yourself if it's that much of a penance. I can go on my own.'

'Silly. Course I'll go. I just don't want some *barman* having a go at me because I do a job that involves wearing a suit. Her friends all act as if working in an office means you've sold out to the big, bad capitalist oppressors.'

'Don't exaggerate. And what's wrong with being a barman – you snob!'

'That's rich. You're the one who's always saying that Ellen's "wasting herself" working at the wine bar.'

'Well, she *is*.'

'So, what's good enough for some people isn't good enough for your family?' He laughed.

'Well, if you had a child, wouldn't you want it to grow up to be – an MP, say, rather than a barman?'

He laughed again. I hate it when he laughs during an argument. It makes me feel he's just indulging me, and waiting for me to stop being stroppy, the moody little woman.

'Can I just point out that MPs don't earn particularly good money, so that wouldn't be my first choice – going into the law or, if he were creative, perhaps advertising, would be preferable. Of course I'm ambitious – why shouldn't I be? Unlike Ellen, I don't think having a proper job makes me a boring person and, by the way, in case you hadn't noticed, Ellen isn't actually your child, so it's not really a valid comparison, is it?'

God, he can be infuriating.

'You know that's not what I meant. Don't deliberately misunderstand.'

'I'm not. It's sweet that you want to protect her, very sweet – you're a lovely, kind person – and I do understand, but—'

'No.' I shook my head. 'I don't think you do.'

'Well. I do my best. All I'm saying – and don't get cross – is if you stopped bailing her out every time she has some trumped-up crisis, she might start growing up a bit. Who knows, she might even get herself a real job?'

I dug my fingers into my thigh in an effort to combat a strong urge to punch him.

'Come on, darling.' He put his arm around me, but I shook it off. 'I'm only saying what you've more or less said yourself enough times.'

'Stephen – everybody occasionally gets irritated by their own family. It's normal.'

Stephen, of course, though certainly the most 'normal' person I know and possibly the most normal person on the entire planet, never, ever criticizes his family. Not his mother, who never stops talking, she's like one of those self-winding watches, and you just have to hope and pray that eventually she'll get a sore throat or lose her voice due to an exhausted larynx or bore herself to sleep; not his father, who hardly says a word so it's hard to maintain a conversation with him – probably after thirty-eight years of being married to Trish, he's forgotten that conversation is supposed to involve *two* people; not even his Auntie Jean who refuses to wear her dentures because she's convinced they've been impregnated with drugs to shut her up so when she eats she sits there sucking the goodness out of the food, like a spider slurping the innards of a fly, then she leaves the revolting, sucked-dry remains in a neat semicircle around the rim of her plate.

'Anyway,' I continued. 'The point is that it doesn't give outsiders a licence to join in. It's not Free Admission – everybody welcome. I never criticize Trish or Ted, never.'

The other B-word

Stephen sighed. Sometimes I feel like a naughty child in his company.

'Sweetie, you don't *occasionally* get *irritated* by your family. You should tape yourself: you're always on about what a mess the house is, about Quinn's awful cooking and weird clothes—'

'Well, her cooking *is* awful and she does wear dreadful— anyway, Quinn's not really family, so that's different.'

'She's been married to your father for over ten years. She's family. And you complain about Ellen borrowing your stuff. And about Matt talking to his kids at the same time as talking to you on the phone so he never listens properly. You're always moaning about them. Of course it's not the same with my family.'

He was exaggerating ridiculously. Everybody whinges a little about their family, don't they?

'Why isn't it? Because they're so perfect, I suppose?'

He smiled.

'No, course not. But, well, we're just normal, aren't we? Average. There's nothing to get annoyed about.'

I managed not to snort.

'Is there?' he added, apparently as an afterthought.

I shrugged.

Don't get started on this, I told myself.

'Come on – let's have it.' He sat back. 'I won't be offended. It is possible to listen to criticism without getting oneself all worked up, you know.'

'It's not a criticism of *you*.'

'I know that. That's exactly my point. Just because I

223

think Ellen's got a lot of growing up to do doesn't mean I love *you* any less. Anyway. My family. Their less positive traits. Carry on.'

'Well . . .' It wasn't as if there was any shortage of material, God knows, but let's not get carried away. I hesitated and I could see him thinking I was having trouble coming up with anything. 'You know I'm fond of both your parents . . .'

'But?' he prompted.

'It's just that . . . sometimes . . . I mean, not all the time – obviously – but you know – occasionally – I find – don't you think? – I mean – '

'You're babbling, sweetie.'

'Right. Yes, I know that. Right. Just – don't you ever find them just the tiniest bit . . . boring?'

He looked at me for a moment, and then he laughed. A great big, hearty laugh.

'Is that all? Everyone's parents are boring sometimes. So what? It's hardly a big deal.'

Mine aren't, I thought. Mum wasn't, that's for sure. God knows, she wasn't perfect, far from it, but she wasn't boring. Dad isn't. Ellen and Matt aren't. Nor is Quinn, for that matter. She's a bit earnest sometimes, true, and she does come out with some bollocks about the benefits of drinking cabbage water or dabbing your pulse points with a tincture of wind chimes, but she isn't boring.

'I thought you were going to come up with something serious for a moment, you looked so solemn. Ah, dear, that's funny.' He patted me as if I were an errant puppy and stood up. 'Come on, let's hit the hay.'

It really gives me the creeps when he says that. It's like he's *trying* to be old before his time.

Hardly a big deal? Not serious? If you'd accused anyone in my family of being boring – Bonnie, Daniel even – they'd have been distraught. Dad once walked out of a dinner party because everyone was going on about property prices. He tried to change the subject several times, but he said it was as if the conversation was on elastic, and it kept springing back. 'Oh – Kilburn. That's up-and-coming, you should get in now while you still can.' 'You're too late for Hoxton – a loft conversion there is silly money.' On and on. Eventually, once the conversation reached Willesden, he stood up and shouted, 'God, you're all so fucking boring!' and walked out. Poor old Quinn just about died of embarrassment, and she apologized then scurried out after him, but now she tells the story with a flush of pride.

Don't forget to be spontaneous

Ellen's birthday falls on a Thursday this year, but the party is on the Saturday after. She always asks Dad and Quinn to her parties, but this time we'd just found out that Quinn's daughter Simone would be around too. Simone's been off working in New York, so she's let her flat for six months, which means she sometimes descends on Dad's house when she comes over. I bet her friends screen their calls when they know she's back in town.

'George, save me from the dragon!' Ellen said on the phone. Scary though Simone is, the dragon tag in fact relates to her habit of exhaling very emphatically through her nostrils when she's smoking – i.e. all the time. Sometimes you do almost expect to see a few flames come flaring out at you with the smoke.

'Remain calm. Just don't invite Dad and Quinn then she can't expect to come. Normal people of your age don't ask their parents to their parties in any case.'

'Too late, I already asked them and I don't give a toss what normal people do. They always come.'

Ellen's probably the rudest person I know, but she wouldn't ever withdraw an invitation once issued.

'Dad'll understand.'

'Yes, I know, and he'll be infuriatingly sweet about it. He's always so bloody understanding and tolerant, he makes me feel guilty and bad.'

'No-one else can *make* you feel guilty.'

'Skip the session, George, I won't be sending you a cheque.'

'Look – Simone's bound to be busy anyhow. She won't want to hang out anywhere that doesn't serve non-stop champagne and bring you a little dish of coke on the side. She's not going to drag over to some celeb-free wine bar for two glasses of Rioja and a tomato bruschetta, is she?'

'Yes, she is. She's not busy – Quinn said so.'

'Well, you're having how many people? Thirty? Forty?'

'Fifty-eight and rising. Brian's going to throw a major wobbly. I swore I'd keep it to no more than forty-five.'

'I think you'll manage to swing it. He's so in love with you, you could invite everyone you know to doss down in the bar for a week and he'd probably end up tucking them in.'

'So untrue!' But she laughed. 'He gave me a total bollocking last week because he said I'd been late three nights in a row.'

'And had you?'

'No. I don't work Wednesday nights, so I was only late Tuesday, Thursday and Friday – that's not in a row, is it?'

I sighed. I can't believe he puts up with her.

'Don't worry – with that many guests, you won't even notice Simone. With any luck, she'll spend the whole evening standing outside bellowing into her mobile and you won't even see her.'

'I know! Let's keep phoning her so she has to rush outside! You get a lousy signal in the bar – I think Brian had the place lined with lead or something deliberately. By the way, I asked Leo too – you don't mind?'

'No. No. Why should I?'

There was no reason to mind. It's just that Ellen has this habit of 'adopting' people she's met all of once, which is fine unless it's one of your friends. So far, I'd managed to fight the urge to confide in her about the kiss. Knowing her, she'd make a huge deal out of it then casually let it slip in front of Stephen. I've slightly been avoiding Leo the last few days. I can't think why I let him kiss me. Ha! So much for taking responsibility for one's actions. I kissed him back, I know I did. It was just being on the rooftop, the lights all around us, like being in a different world. How pathetic. Real life isn't like that, is it? You can have your head in the clouds, caught up in some ridiculous romantic fantasy, but, sooner or later, you've got to come back down to earth and face your obligations, get back to normal life and accept what you have, what you *know* is best for you – no matter how giggly and moonstruck you might have been for a few seconds.

'Good. He's nice, isn't he? Quite sexy, too, despite the lack of hair.'

'Mmm. Suppose so. I haven't really thought about it.'

Ellen laughed.

'You are the world's most crap liar, George, you really are. Don't worry, I won't tell Stephen about your secret lust for your next-door neighbour—'

'He's not next door – and I don't have—'

'Yeah, yeah, we know. I just meant that even though he's not your off-the-peg handsome type, like . . .' she paused, while we both thought 'like Stephen', but, being Ellen, the pause was too abrupt, too noticeable, so it would have been better if she'd simply gone ahead and said it '. . . like Jimmy or whoever.' Jimmy is one of Ellen's numerous exes, who fell into the gorgeous-but-not-your-first-choice-if-you-want-to-talk-about-the-meaning-of-life category.

'With Leo, the more you see him, the more you find yourself thinking you'd quite like to rip off his jeans, y'know?'

I cleared my throat.

'I wouldn't know.'

'Right. I bet you've thought about it. He looks like

he'd be really – dirty, I think. In a good way. Like he'd give you a bloody good fuck.'

'Ellen! For God's sake! I know you pride yourself on being *direct*, but you don't have to play up to your own myth quite so much, do you?'

'I'm only saying what you think.'

'You have no idea what I think. And, seeing as you're not exactly known for being a shrewd and perceptive judge of men, perhaps you'll let me form my own opinion? You must wonder how I ever manage without you.'

'Oh, shut up. I know what I know. Never mind – see you on Saturday and . . .' She paused again, two pauses in one phone call, that's practically a record for Ellen.

'What? Is this about Leo again?'

'No. Oh, just try and get Stephen to relax a bit this time, will you? Last time, he looked like a mannequin that had been nicked from Austin Reed. Get plenty of wine down him – there'll be loads.'

'Not everyone needs to get drunk to relax, you know. Stephen will be fine. He can be very laid-back when he decides to be.'

'*Exactly*. Only Stephen thinks you have to decide two years in advance that you might want to be laid-back on a Saturday night.'

17

Just a phase

'Please, please, please come early,' Ellen begged me down the phone. 'I need you to be rent-a-crowd at the start, otherwise it looks all sad and empty.'

'Then we can piss off when your real friends arrive, you mean?'

'No way – you've got to stick it out till the bitter end. Till the last guest is lying in the gutter.'

'How lovely. But I'll head for the hills the second I get trapped by scores of your exes wanting to tell me how they've never managed to get over you.' That's what happened last year.

'Hardly *scores* – it was only Luis.'

'And that very thin guy with the shaggy hair, the one who looks like a mop. The "lesbian" one.'

'Oh God – you mean Jaz?'

'That's the one. Can't you find men who have normal names like everyone else? Remember – he said, "I must have been a lesbian in a former life because I'm, like, *so* obsessed with women."'

'Yes, Jaz was a bit of a twat.'

'Why did you ask him to your party then? It's only because you love being surrounded by adoring acolytes, isn't it?'

'No it's not!' she practically shouted. Ellen always

protests way too much when you're right on the button. 'I mainly asked him to wind up the P-h.'

'Well, it worked. We sloped off early, remember?'

'You *said* you had a period pain.'

'I lied.'

'I can't believe you lied to me.' For once, she sounded genuinely outraged and upset, not just hamming it up.

'Oh, come on – it's not such a big deal.'

'It is, it *is*. I never lie to you.'

'You do. What about when I lend you something, such as my good leather gloves, and you lose them but keep saying you'll give them back.'

'That's not lying. I don't lose things, not really, it's just I put them down and then forget where I put them – but I always find them in the end. And I do mean to give them back. I *never* lie to you – I always tell you everything.'

'Well.' I was starting to feel uncomfortable. 'Don't feel obliged to if you don't want to. God, it's not such a big deal, is it?'

'It is to *me* – now, promise you'll come early? The P-h can come later if he needs more time to prepare for having fun.'

Expert advice

'Hi, Georgia. On your own?' Brian, Ellen's boss, waved me over.

'Yes. Stephen's not coming till later.' I was surprised Brian remembered him actually. It's not really Stephen's kind of place and he finds it hideously embarrassing to be served by Ellen.

'Oh. I meant Ellen.'

'She's not here yet? I knew I was stupid to get here so early.'

'It's fine. Come on up and have a glass of wine.'

The room looked great, with two huge vases of flowers, chairs and tables pulled back around the edges so there would be a small area of floor for dancing later, and a long table covered with a brightly patterned cloth for the food.

'Red or white?'

'Perhaps I'd better start with water. I don't want to get carried away.'

'Very sensible. Some of my customers think they've entered some kind of drinkathon the second they walk in the door . . . but there's a nice Pouilly Fumé if you fancy it?'

'Bit swish for one of Ellen's parties?'

'Too right. It's not what we're having later. Grab it now while you have the chance.'

I laughed.

'It's really kind of you to do all this for her.'

'Ah, get away. She's a good worker.'

God, he must be seriously in love.

I laughed again, then he laughed too.

'OK, no she's not, but she is good with customers and that counts for a lot. Quite a few of the guys fancy her, so they order more and keep coming back.' He looked away from me, concentrating on opening the wine. 'She's very attractive, isn't she? You can't blame them. I mean, I think she is.'

'She *is* very fond of you.'

He snorted.

'Great. I'll crack open the Dom Perignon, will I?' He poured me a glass of mineral water, and offered me the wine once more. 'So, drop me a few pearls of wisdom then, Georgia. How do I hook myself a soulmate? Tell me that it's just a matter of time before she— before some wonderful woman realizes she can't live without me. Ellen says you're the expert on all this.'

'Hardly.' I smiled. 'Though it's always easier to be wise about other people's relationships, isn't it? All I would say is that I think you're a lovely man and any woman in her right mind would count herself lucky to have you. If I weren't already spoken for, I'd be joining the queue myself.'

'What if she's not in her right mind?'

'Ah, then you may have a problem.' I laid a hand on his arm for a moment. 'Who knows what may happen? All I know about love is that you can never predict how things will turn out – you can't even count on remaining miserable. Sometimes, just when you think it's all hopeless and you let go – that's enough. You relax and something shifts and the next thing you know you're walking up and down the landing at two in the morning trying to coax your baby to sleep.'

'Dinner for two would do to start with.' He sighed and topped up our glasses. 'So, how's your love life then, Georgia? Cheer me up – tell me it can be done.'

'Oh, well – you remember Stephen?'

'Tall, handsome bastard, right?'

'That's him. Well, we're still together. I mean, of course we are. We're engaged. We have been for a while.'

Over two and a half years in fact, but people don't want you to drone on about all the details of these things, do they?

'Good on you – when's the Big Day and do you want someone to do the bar?'

'Never miss an opportunity, do you?'

'Course not.'

'We haven't finalized the actual date yet.'

'Yeah, but when – roughly? Next couple of months? Or wait for spring? Summer?'

'We haven't quite decided. There's so much to arrange. I want everything to be absolutely right. Well, one's only going to do it the once, presumably . . .'

'Oh, rightio. Always thought I'd go back to Ireland myself, have a big do with all my family – you know, everybody, the drunk uncles, the old grandads sitting in the corner, sucking Murphy's through their gums, little kids running round scoffing the cake, I love it.'

'I didn't even know you were Irish. You don't have an accent.'

'I came over when I was a baby, but I've more

cousins and aunts over there than you can count. County Cork, couple of miles from the coast. Beautiful place. I'd love to take— it's great for a holiday. What about you – you wanting the big family do, or you planning to run off to Las Vegas just the two of you?'

'I couldn't get married without my family. Well, they're more important than the groom, aren't they?'

He laughed and I did too, though a moment later I realized how weird it sounded.

'I'll tell him that when he turns up, will I?'

'Brian!' One of the bar staff called over to him. 'Phone! It's Ellen!'

'You'd think she'd manage to get here on time if she wasn't having to work, wouldn't you?'

A few moments later he beckoned me and handed me the phone.

'She's having a crisis, she says. Probably can't find the other shoe or something.'

'George – can you come round?'

'Why aren't you here?'

'I'm having a problem. Please come – get Brian to bring you if you don't have your car.'

'I'm not asking him for favours.'

'Give the phone back to him then and I'll ask him.'

A dire emergency

Two minutes later, we were on our way to Ellen's flat. It's barely more than a ten-minute walk, but you can do it in no time by car.

'Shall I come up too?'

'Better not in case it's a girlie-type crisis.'

'Give her a boot up the arse and tell her to get cracking. Tell her I'll wait ten minutes, no more.'

When I got up to the flat, Ellen was running around like a headless chicken, still in her underwear and struggling to put up a dilapidated ironing board.

'It won't go up! What can I do?' Her voice was

starting to take on the note of hysteria Ellen reserves for completely minor setbacks or mishaps.

'Phone the Fire Brigade? I'm sure they won't mind dropping everything to come and sort out your domestic accoutrements. Oh, give it here – I'll have a go while you get the rest of your clothes on or we'll be here all day.'

'What rest of clothes?' She held up an extremely crumpled dress.

I battled with the ironing board, but it was like trying to set up a deckchair in a Force 10 gale.

'Anyway, I thought ironing was against your religion? You never buy anything that needs ironing.'

'I know. This is Siobhan's.'

Ah-ha, the flatmate's.

'And does she know you're borrowing it?' The catch suddenly loosened and I managed to release the legs – but only to get the board up at knee-height.

'She's not fussed. Unlike *some* people, she doesn't go into a total strop if I borrow something of hers for a couple of hours.' She paused, looking at the ironing board. 'Is that so I can iron lying down?'

'Or Quinn's yoga pals drop by to iron in the lotus position . . .'

'Or if I have Bonnie round to help . . .'

'Or you invite some geishas over for tea . . .'

'Maybe I should just wear it crushed.' She held it up against her body.

'Uh-huh – it looks like you've slept in it.'

'I *did*. I wore it one night last week then I was too knackered to undress. Honestly, you'd think Siobhan would have washed and ironed it by now though.'

'Thank God I don't have to live with you. I'd have to put a combination lock on the wardrobe.'

Ellen knelt down at the semi-prostrate ironing board and spread out the dress.

'This is *really* hard, you know.' She said it the way she used to when she was about seven or eight and struggling to wrap a present neatly or wipe the table, wanting someone else to take over and do it for her.

'It's not exactly scaling Everest in stilettos, is it? It's *ironing*.'

'But you're *so* much better at it than me.'

'Yes, but I'm still not doing it.' I flung myself onto the sofa, and put my feet up on the arm, partly to stop myself grabbing the iron.

'It's all right for you . . .' she said, somehow managing to iron a crease into the shoulder strap. 'Oh, now look!'

'Oh woe! Oh woe! Just go over that bit again. Dear God – surely you can iron a bloody frock without turning it into a global disaster? Why is it all right for me?'

'Because you're so neat. Naturally – you don't even have to try.' She pouted at the dress, as if it might suddenly be won over and resolve to be smooth just to please her.

'Of course I try. What makes you think I don't?'

'Because it's just how you *are*. Georgia equals tidy plus neat plus . . . whatever.'

'Plus uptight plus controlling plus bossy plus . . . ?' Is that really the sum of me? How other people see me? 'What a wonderful equation.'

'Don't be daft.' Ellen stood up and put the dress on. 'You could say plus warm-hearted plus clever plus funny plus unselfish plus longing to do her little sister's hair in a French plait.'

'Go on then. Sit down. Where's your brush – or is that a stupid question?'

'It was in the kitchen, but someone moved it. Siobhan's is on the table there – you can use that. She won't mind.'

I reached for the brush and started taming Ellen's hair.

'Tell me about the time you cut my hair,' she said.

'What – again? You know it better than I do by now.'

She nodded.

'Good grief. Well, it was a few months after Mum died and we were playing hairdressers, taking it in turns to brush each other's hair and plaiting it, then you said—'

'Cut my hair! Cut it! Cut it!'

'So I *did* but . . .'

'. . . it was all crooked . . .'

'. . . and it looked really silly. And I thought you'd start crying, but when you looked in the mirror you thought it was funny.'

'Yes, and you thought it was hysterical too, didn't you? And we both laughed and laughed. And then Dad came down and—'

'Your plait's done. We'd better get going.' I held the end tight in my fingers. 'Have you got an elastic thingy?'

Haircut

Ellen is crawling on the floor, being a doggy. What used to be her fringe is now down to her chin and has to be kept out of her eyes with kirby grips. For the last three weeks, every morning Daddy has looked at Ellen and said, 'We really must get you a haircut.' Daddy works from home now but he never has time even to brush their hair, so it is left to Georgia or one of the string of young women who comes to help for a month, a week, a day, half a day – however long they last before Ellen bites them or Matt kicks them or Georgia tells them off for cooking the spaghetti the wrong way. Georgia helps Ellen get dressed first, then dresses herself while Daddy puts out boxes of cereal for the children to help themselves. Georgia shakes out Rice Crispies into a bowl for Ellen, pours milk on top and tucks a napkin round her. Then Georgia pours milk into her own bowl before adding her cereal and bending her head to listen: 'Snap! Crackle! Pop!' it says on the box but no, that is not right, it is more of a soft *pock-pock-pock* noise she thinks. Georgia always eats her cereal 'upside down' in this way so that it doesn't go soggy too quickly. That is the way she likes it.

Saturday: Daddy is still in his studio. He has promised them cakes for tea, proper chocolate eclairs not just iced buns, if they can all just keep out of his hair for two hours and let him get some work done. That means no coming into his studio every three minutes to tell him 'Knock-knock' jokes or ask him questions: 'Daddy, why do cats like milk?' 'What would happen if everyone started walking backwards?' 'What makes pink *pink?*' 'If the world's really turning, how come we're not dizzy the whole time?' Matt has gone next door to play with a friend. The French windows are open and Georgia can hear them in the neighbouring garden, shooting each other: 'You're dead!' 'No, you're dead – I shot you first!'

'Play with me!' Ellen orders, wanting her own way as usual.

'All right then,' Georgia says, cross at being stuck with such a baby all the time. 'I know. Let's play hairdressers. You're a grown-up lady having your hair done and I'm the hair – I'm the *stylist*.' This is a word Georgia has only learnt last week, and she likes the sound of it. 'I'm the *top* stylist,' she adds, in case there should be any doubt about her place in the hierarchy. Ellen will fall in with any plan that involves her pretending to be a grown-up lady. Georgia ties an apron round Ellen, 'Your gown, Modom,' and seats her on one of the kitchen chairs. 'Does Modom want a shampoo and set today or a cut by the top stylist?'

'Cut! Cut!'

'I've got to wash it first.'

'No!' Ellen tries to climb down from the chair. She hates, hates, hates having her hair washed and screams with fury every time her father attempts it in the bath. Now she will only have it done if Daddy sprays her head with a water pistol to get it wet and she's allowed to splash him to make it fair.

237

'All right. Don't be such a baby. No water, OK?'

Georgia takes out the kitchen scissors from the drawer and grabs a stray hairbrush which is sitting on the dresser in a pile of papers. She is only going to give Ellen a little tiny trim. She brushes Ellen's hair, or rather, attempts to, since at each stroke Ellen squeals and wriggles like crazy. Georgia holds a hank of hair between two fingers, the way she has seen hairdressers do it, then slowly eases the scissor blades closed. The trimmings fall in clumps down Ellen's back. It is the noise that is the most satisfying thing, the sound of the blades slicing through the hair. But now the hair is noticeably shorter in one place at the back. She'll just even it up all the way round so it's tidy. And Daddy will be pleased. Now he won't have to take Ellen to the barber with him when he goes and they'll have saved lots of money too. She snips the right-hand side, then the left, to make it even, but when she comes round to look at Ellen from the front, the left-hand side is clearly shorter. Ellen must have had her head tilted when she was cutting.

'Stop moving all the time! Keep your head still!'

'I *am*!'

Georgia trims the right side again, and now the back needs doing. And there's still the problem of Ellen's grown-out fringe. Georgia stands back, assessing, hands on hips, the way Mummy used to look at a painting-in-progress, narrowing her eyes.

'Shall I do your fringe?'

'Can I have a sweet?'

'There aren't any, but we're having cakes later. He promised.'

'When later?'

'Soon later. Sit still.'

Georgia brushes the ex-fringe down over Ellen's eyes and Ellen giggles.

'Now keep really still. I mean it.'

She traps the hair between her fingers once more and, tongue poking out in concentration, cuts it.

It is rather more than she meant to take off, but it was miles too long before. Also, it is still not straight. She snips here and there to attempt to even it up, then she stands back to survey her handiwork.

The back is still uneven. The fringe is too short and so stubby it won't lie flat but sticks out like a small ledge way above her eyes.

'Mirror! Mirror! *I* want to see!'

'In a minute. Stylists always give it one last brush.' Georgia reaches for the brush, but it is too late. Ellen is off the chair and heading for the stairs and Dad's study.

'Ellie! No! You mustn't!'

Suddenly, Georgia feels doubtful that her father is going to be as overjoyed at this saving of time and money as she'd first thought. He is not often cross but when he is the whole house seems to shudder and for days afterwards they are all on their best behaviour, trying to dispel the air of gloom. She grabs the scissors and brush and locks herself in the downstairs loo. Stares at her serious face in the mirror there. Her own hair now falls nearly halfway down her back. It, too, hasn't been cut for nearly a year, but she brushes it brutally each morning and tames it into a tight plait for school. Now, on a Saturday, it is pulled into a ponytail. Georgia pulls off the band securing it, a purple covered elastic with two small butterflies attached that cling close to her hair as if it is rich in nectar. She glances at it for a moment then drops it next to the soap, looking at it as if it is some childish thing that has nothing to do with her.

She presses her lips firmly shut, as if to stop herself from crying out loud or shouting. Then she lifts the scissors and, quickly, begins to cut.

Does he or doesn't he?

'Tell him two minutes!' Ellen said, when the bell rang. I picked up the entryphone as she ran from room to room in search of shoes.

'He says he must get back. It's not fair to leave him hanging about outside.'

'God, it's only Brian!'

'Ellen! How can you be like that? He's such a lovely man – I'm beginning to think he's too good for you.'

'You like him so much, you have him. He's way more fun than the P-h at least.'

'He's not a Bounty bar – I don't fancy this just now, here, you have it.'

'Too true. If Brian were a Bounty, I'd be slobbering all over him.'

'Yeuch, you're so revolting sometimes.'

'Why?' She ran into the bathroom and out again. 'Where the fuck is my fucking mascara for fuck's sake! Sex does involve slobbering – surely even the P-h gets down and gives you a good slobbering from time to time – oh, shit, where is it?'

'Here, use mine – do it at the bar, we ought to go.'

'Oh, cheers, can I?' She shoved her feet into a pair of red beaded mules, which she took off again as soon as we attempted to go downstairs. 'Who can walk in these things?'

'Why wear them then?'

'Because they make me feel gorgeous and grown-up and fuckable – if I wear sensible shoes to a party, I don't have any fun. Anyway – does he?'

'Does he what?'

'Slobber? Stephen.'

'No, he kisses very nicely. Not too schlurpy at all.'

'So not what I meant – as you very well know. Does Mr P-h like to – *eat in*?'

'I'm not going into the ins and outs – ha-ha – of our love life. It's private.'

'That's a no then.'

'It doesn't mean that at all.' We were at the ground-floor outer street door now. 'Don't make assumptions. And can you please shut up – I'm not talking about this in front of Brian.'

'You've always said to me that people should talk

240

about *everything*. You always say the reason most of your clients have problems in relationships is because they won't communicate properly.' She went round to the front. 'I need to sit in front so I can do my make-up on the way.'

'With *each other*, I meant – not with their *nosy* siblings.' I handed her the mascara. 'You shouldn't do it in the car, you could poke your eye out.'

'Hi, Brian! Thank you for waiting – you're my hero!' She leant over and kissed him on the cheek.

'Another thirty seconds and you'd have come out to nothing but the whiff of exhaust fumes.'

'You wouldn't have gone without me!' She flapped down the passenger visor to use the mirror.

'Don't count on it. I'm not your unpaid chauffeur.' Brian pulled out and winked at me in the mirror. 'I'm supposed to be your bloody boss – let's see a bit of respect, for Christ's sake.'

'Yes, boss. Not too fast – I'm doing my eyes.'

Brian took the corner at some speed.

'You did that deliberately!'

'Did I?' He accelerated away. 'You don't need all that anyway. You're not so ugly just as you are.'

'Well, thanks a bunch. I'm glad you're not the type of bloke who thinks he can get me into bed by showering me with compliments.'

Brian smiled but said nothing.

'George, have you got any lippy?'

'Where's yours? Why don't you ever have anything you need?' I handed it over. 'Don't make it all blunt.'

'Yeah, yeah. Is this the only colour you've got?'

'Yes, I'm not a portable Max Factor counter. You want something else – try bringing it with you.'

'Well, you were making me rush.' She applied it in the mirror. 'God, I'll never get a snog wearing this.'

'I wouldn't count on it,' Brian said, not looking at her. 'It's better than that bright red gloop you wear. Less obvious.'

Ellen twisted round in her seat and made a face at me, mouthed 'ooh' and did a petulant pout,

'Now, Brian – you're a man—'

'You've noticed then?'

'Now, don't you think that – in general – men who really *like* women and who are good in bed—'

'Ellen! Shut up!' I could guess where she was heading.

'Sssh! I'm getting an opinion from the other side.'

'Aren't we on the same side?' Brian said, pulling over to a space near the wine bar.

'Don't you think,' Ellen carried on, 'that men who are good in bed like going down on women? And the ones that don't – well, they're always the ones who taste of soap and neatly put the condom on the bedside table an hour beforehand and have sex like it's shagging-by-numbers: Kiss, two, three, four. Tweak nipples, two, three, four—'

'Ellen, give it a rest.' I got out of the car. 'Lipstick?'

'Ellen, I wouldn't know what other men get up to. To be honest, I don't give it much thought.'

'God, well you two are being no fun at all.' She handed me my make-up and skipped merrily into the bar without waiting for us.

I looked at Brian and he smiled and took my arm as if we were a long-established couple.

'Ah, well,' he said. 'Perhaps she's just going through a phase.'

'Some phase – twenty-eight years and counting . . .'

18

Fun, fun, fun

'Do you realize,' said Stephen, 'that there are well over a hundred piercings in this room?'

'Don't forget my two.' I waggled my earrings. 'You're not really counting?'

'Yes. That girl over there has got five in her left ear and one in her tongue!'

'And that's only the ones you can see.'

Stephen winced at the thought.

'Can we go yet?' It wasn't even half past ten.

'I really can't. You go if you like. I don't mind.' What was the point of making him stay if he was going to stand there looking like he'd rather be having root-canal work.

Just then, Leo appeared. I watched him saying hello to Dad, Quinn and Simone, then he got scooped up by Ellen.

'Leo! Leo!' She threw her arms around him and gave him a kiss, then started introducing him to her coterie, clutching him as if he were one of her oldest friends.

'You never said *he* was coming.'

'I didn't know.' Which was partly true at least, because although Ellen *had* told me that she'd invited him, I didn't know he'd turn up. I saw him half-craning his neck round, trying to catch my eye.

'We probably ought to go and say hello,' I said, as if Leo were some tedious distant relative I hadn't seen for some years.

'I dare say he'll come over if he can bear to tear himself away from that gaggle of semi-naked women.'

Three of Ellen's friends were clustered close around him, wearing various skimpy, strappy garments that revealed their navels. The volume of shrieking and giggling noticeably increased.

'Well, if I'm not going I might as well have another drink,' Stephen said, as if I'd insisted he stay. 'Sweetie?'

'I'd better switch to water now. Thanks.'

While Stephen was at the bar, Leo appeared by my side. I peered to either side of him, pretending to be surprised.

'No groupies?'

'I chucked them some jelly babies then ran the other way.'

'They do seem *so* young, don't they?'

'Everybody seems young to me. I must be the oldest person here apart from your dad and Quinn. So . . . do I get a kiss hello or what?'

I smiled and he leaned in close. I turned my face slightly so he'd kiss my cheek.

'You smell gorgeous.'

'Thank you. Stephen's here by the way.'

'So? Does he smell gorgeous too?'

I punched his arm lightly.

Stephen came rushing back with the drinks, handed me my water.

'Stephen! Good to see you again!' Leo held out his hand.

'Wasn't expecting to see you here.' Stephen shook his hand. 'Glad you could make it.' It was hard to imagine anyone sounding less glad.

There was an awkward silence.

'I was just saying to Georgia how incredibly young

everyone here seems,' Leo said, swigging his beer from the bottle. 'I feel like I ought to be seeing them all safely home.'

'Yes. Very true. We feel like that too, don't we, darling? But of course, Ellen's rather young for her age, isn't she?'

'She *isn't*! She's just got lots of energy. I wish I was like that.'

'Now, darling, don't always do that.' Stephen put his arm round my waist and pulled me closer. 'She's always moaning about her family, but as soon as someone says a word against any of them, she comes rushing out with all guns blazing, don't you, darling?'

I gave him a tight smile.

'I'm just the same.' Leo took off his jacket and slung it on a nearby chair. 'My mother's always on the phone, driving me crazy – am I eating properly, not just crisps and Mars bars? Am I getting enough sleep? Do I always observe the speed limit? Have I been to the dentist yet to have my tooth fixed? My sisters and I ring each other up to let off steam about her – but if anyone else said anything, we'd soon take up our swords, I imagine. It's natural enough. Defending your tribe.'

Ellen came over and dragged me away.

'Just borrowing George. You two boys can manage without her, can't you? Good.'

'What are you doing? You can't leave those two alone together. You could cut the atmosphere with a knife.'

'Good – let them fight it out between them, then you can swoop in and claim the victor.'

'I don't want the victor – I want – I don't want all this tension. There's no reason for them not to get on – no reason at all. It's not rational.'

Ellen rolled her eyes.

'This isn't about being rational. It's about biology – whose sperms will be successful?'

'I don't want anybody's sperm – successful or otherwise. Where are you dragging me?'

'Simone's had a go at Quinn. Come and make them play nicely.'

'Why *me*?'

'Because you're *you*.' She manoeuvred me towards their table. 'I've got to get Brian to whap the music up – I want to dance.'

'You're looking very nice,' I said to Quinn, hoping to cheer her up a bit. 'Um, interesting earrings – are they new?'

Simone sat there silently, taking deep drags on her cigarette, alternating with large gulps of wine. She stood up to go to the bar for a refill, vaguely gesturing at the rest of us in a half-hearted way. We all three shook our heads.

'You OK, Dad?'

He smiled as the music suddenly got a lot louder and Ellen bellowed:

'Come on, everyone! Dance!' She started dancing at once, pulling people away from the small groups where they were standing to make them join in.

'Feeling a bit old for all this,' Dad shouted in my ear.

'Same here.'

'Not at your age. Come and have one dance with your old dad before we head off.'

I felt a bit self-conscious – Dad's not too bad, really, but you can tell he's not in his natural element on the dance floor; he'd be much happier sitting at home behind the paper.

I looked around the room. Stephen, I noticed, was now talking to the pierced-tongue woman, apparently deep in conversation. Then Dad spun me round, doing the strange, slow, all-purpose jazz-jive type dancing he performs to every sort of music, and I spotted Leo behind me, dancing with Quinn. Ellen was gyrating madly and thrusting as if she were on show in some seedy lap joint, but I couldn't tell at that point if she was hyper just from excitement or if she'd had too much to drink.

'Why don't you dance with Quinn, Dad?'

'Good idea.' He sashayed over to her in an embarrassing, Dad-ish way, did a silly mock bow, then took her hand.

Leo took a step towards me, brows raised.

Stephen joined us.

'Hi! Saw you'd been abandoned – so I've come to your rescue!' He held my elbow, then started to dance. Usually, Stephen only dances to one or two slow numbers at the end of a party. He looked like a doll whose limbs had been glued in too tightly.

Leo backed off and I saw him go to the bar and stand next to Ellen. She was half-dancing while apparently having some kind of altercation with Brian. She was pawing him, evidently trying to talk him into something, but he remained stony-faced.

'I think there's some kind of problem,' I said to Stephen, nodding my head towards the bar.

'Well, I'm sure it's not *your* problem. Just leave them to it.'

I carried on dancing, but keeping an eye on things.

Then Ellen came over. Leo remained by the bar, talking to Brian.

'I want to dance with George,' Ellen announced. 'We have to do our sisters thing.'

No inhibitions

Ellen loves this. Every time we have an opportunity to dance, she drags me onto the floor. We know each other so well and we've danced together so many times that we have lots of the same moves and we can pretty much dance in synch – it's not a routine or anything like that but I have to admit it looks quite good when we get it right. I love it too.

At the end of the track, a slow one came on and Ellen swooped in on Stephen, like a hawk to a dormouse.

247

'Mr P-h! I'm sorry I dragged George away – dance with me now! Come on! Dance with me!' She looped her arms round his neck and he put his arms round her waist.

Leo is standing by the bar next to Brian. They are both looking at me, smiling. Suddenly, I feel as if I'm fifteen again, waiting to be asked to dance. This is silly. I could dance with either of them. It would be perfectly natural. Rude not to really. I could ask one of them, instead of standing here as if my feet are stuck to the floor. I could ask Brian. That would be fine. Or Leo. Either one. Or I could sit this one out. Give my feet a rest. Have some water. That would be the sensible thing to do.

Now Leo is standing next to me. He doesn't say a word, just takes my hand, pulls me closer, his hand on my waist. And we are dancing. He is holding me the old-fashioned way, not the way Ellen is clamped onto Stephen. It is perfectly respectable; aside from my hand on his shoulder, his hand firm at the dip of my waist, our other hands sealed together, we are barely touching – just the occasional accidental bump of hip against hip, my breasts almost brushing his chest as we turn. I can feel him looking at me, then – very softly – I feel his breath in my hair and I look up at him. He gives me the smallest of smiles and squeezes my hand but so slightly that I am not sure whether he really has or if I have imagined it.

The track ended, then glided seamlessly into another. Dad tapped me on the shoulder.

'We're just off.'

Ellen broke away from Stephen to hug Dad. She was unsteady on her feet, hanging on his arm. Dad looked at me, frowning, for reassurance. I nodded and mouthed, 'It's OK,' and shooed him away.

*　　　*　　　*

I was talking to Brian, when Ellen came up to me.

'George – tell Brian he should serve some frozen vodka. It's fantastic.'

'I'm not doing it, Ellen, so save your breath.' Brian cleared some glasses and wiped down the bar. 'Half of them are well pissed as it is. And it's not in your budget.'

'Oh – so it's not in the fucking budget? Who cares? I'll pay you back. You can take it out of my wages.' Ellen put on her sulky face.

'Ellen! Stop it!' I was mortified, knowing Brian had already provided all the drink at cost price. 'There's plenty to drink. No-one needs vodka as well. Brian's been incredibly generous as it is.'

'Needs? What's that got to do with it? It's not about needs – it's about having a good time.'

'And you certainly shouldn't be having any vodka – you're drunk.'

'I'm s'posed to be drunk! It's my birthday! You should be drunk too. Ev'rybody should be drunk!' Her voice was getting louder.

I turned to Brian.

'I'm so sorry – she's just awful when she's like this. I know you—'

'But George doesn't get drunk, does she?' Ellen was practically shouting, ignoring my attempts to get her to be quiet. 'Does you? Do you? No. No – George *doesn't* drink. George *doesn'* have fun. George *doesn'* get good sex – doesn' get licked out by the P-h, do you? No wonder she's so uptight.'

'Ellen! For God's sake.'

'Ellen – ' Brian laid a hand on her arm. 'Enough now. C'mon – come and sit and have a coffee with me.' She shook him away and returned to the dance floor, joining three or four of her friends who had also had way too much.

A couple of people cast sympathetic glances at me.

'Did Ellen just say what I thought she said?' Stephen said. He looked furious.

'Yes. I can't believe it. Can we go now?'

'Why did she say that?'

'Why are you sounding cross with *me*? She said it because she's Ellen, that's all. It's not my fucking fault. It's not because of anything *I've* ever said to her – if that's what you're worried about.'

'Where's your jacket?'

I pointed to the back of a chair beside the bar.

Leo came over.

'You OK?'

I nodded dumbly.

'Take care of yourself,' he said quietly. He bent to kiss my cheek, his hand holding the flesh of my bare arm for no more than a moment, skin on skin. 'I'll call you.'

Stephen came back and held out my jacket for me, I waved goodbye to Brian, and we left.

19

The morning after

I rang Dad and told him I couldn't make brunch because I'd be going to Stephen's parents. I know Ellen – she'll have conveniently forgotten all about last night and won't even apologize, then I'll look like I'm mean and pathetic for still being cross about it. And, here we go again, she's the laid-back one and I'm the uptight bitch, so what else is new?

'Dad?'

'Mmm?'

'You know at the party last night – did you notice Ellen? She'd had a lot to drink.'

'I wasn't paying much attention – I could barely hear myself think. You mustn't worry so much . . .'

'I know, I can't help it.'

'It'll be all right. Don't you fret, promise me?'

'OK. I promise.'

'Good. Take care now out among them English.'

A hand on the tiller

I took Stephen breakfast in bed, poached eggs on toast.

'Thank you for spoiling me. Aren't you having any?'

'I've had some toast. I'm saving myself for lunch.'

'Good.' He nodded. 'Mum's really pleased you're

251

coming. You haven't been for ages, she says.' As if he hadn't noticed one way or the other himself.

'Um – I'm very sorry about the way Ellen behaved – what she said – last night – it wasn't because – I hadn't said anything – I'm completely content with our sex life, you know that . . .'

'Georgia, I know you share everything with Ellen. Almost everything,' he amended, seeing I was about to protest. 'But if you swear that you never tell her . . . personal things about our . . . what happens between us in the bedroom, then I'm content with that. I take your word for it, of course I do.'

'Good. But I'm sorry she said it. She can be so embarrassing sometimes.'

'But darling – are you going to spend your whole life apologizing for Ellen all the time? Christ knows, I suppose I should be used to her by now but last night – ' he shook his head. 'She was totally out of order. And being drunk is absolutely no excuse—'

'I never said it was. I don't think it is at—'

'Plenty of people manage to hold their liquor without becoming offensive.'

'Yes, of course. I don't—'

'She carries on as if she's still seventeen or something. If she was a member of my family, there's no way I'd let her carry on like that.'

'Hang on a sec – one minute you're saying I shouldn't be apologizing for her, then the next you seem to be implying that it's somehow my problem and I ought to be able to control her.'

'I'm not saying that at all. But surely your father could have a word with her? As the head of the family.' He pushed the last crust of toast into his mouth, as if that ended the matter.

'I can really see Dad laying down the law as the stern patriarch. She'd laugh in his face.'

'Well, he should have instituted a bit more respect earlier on. It was probably your mother who did all that, eh? That's why you're always so polite and well-mannered and Ellen . . . isn't. She didn't have the benefit of your mother's guiding hand on the tiller.'

'My mother wasn't exactly – she wasn't very keen on rules.'

'Really? Well, lucky for me that you've turned out so well then. But we're not going to let our kids be like Ellen, are we, darling?' Stephen frowned. 'Children need a bit of discipline, you know.'

'Stephen . . . um – you know when you talk about having kids . . . ?'

'Yes.' He smiled.

'How much do you want them? I mean, do you really, really want them because you think having them would be the most important, amazing thing you could ever do and that your life would be incomplete without them or—'

He laughed.

'Hardly that, darling. Not incomplete, no, of course not.' He wiped his mouth neatly then scrunched up his paper napkin. 'They're just part of normal life, aren't they? Meet someone you like, fall in love, settle down, get married and so on and so forth, have two or three kids, then watch your life savings get eaten away by nappies then school fees then uni!' He laughed again.

'It's just – you know – I thought you knew – I did say before – I've always said – that I'm really not – I don't know – I'm not sure, you see – if I want to have any . . .' My voice faded away.

'Don't be silly!' Stephen waggled my knee to and fro. 'We can hire lots of help – a live-in nanny, au pair, whatever you like.'

'No, it's not that. It's just—' I shrugged, unable to explain myself to him. 'I don't think I want them.'

'Oh.'

This is it. He's going to say, well, that's that then. I couldn't expect him to make such a major sacrifice just to be with me. I wouldn't expect it. I really wouldn't.

'I'm sorry. I should have spelled it out more clearly before. It was selfish. I'll understand if—'

'Of course, we don't *have* to have children.'

'What?'

He took my hand and rubbed his thumb across the knuckles. I looked down at my pale hand, lying there like a dying shellfish scooped from the safety of its shell, as if it did not belong to me.

'I'm not one hundred per cent dead set on it, darling, if that's what you're worried about. You sweet thing – you've been giving yourself a hard time over it, I can tell. I'm not saying I didn't think I'd have kids. I *assumed* I'd have them, yes. And I *assume* I'll have a six-bed detached house and a top-of-the-range Mercedes, but I'm not broody or whatever chaps get, honestly. I don't see kids as being the be-all and end-all of my purpose in life. We can make a great life for ourselves, just the two of us. To be honest . . .' he rubbed his thumb back and forth over my hand, 'if anything, I'd say I'm quite relieved. I can't *quite* see myself dragging myself out of bed at two in the morning, can you? And I can certainly live without dirty nappies and – ' he waved his hand about, 'all that mess. Just think,' his voice brightened, as if he were trying to sell me the idea, 'no school fees, so we can have top-notch holidays – the Caribbean, the Seychelles, wherever we fancy. Looks like I'll be getting my Merc sooner than I thought.'

'You're just trying to be nice. I can't possibly deprive you of children, it wouldn't be fair.'

'You're *not* depriving me, I swear. The more I think about it, the more it makes sense.' He pulled back the covers and leapt out of bed. 'Best not mention it to my folks for now though, eh? I'll have to get Mum used to the idea gradually. Leave it to me.'

I nodded, barely able to speak.

'Right then. Let me at that shower. Why not put on a skirt today, sweetie? You should wear skirts more, they suit you.'

'Mmm,' I said, knowing I would wear my black trousers.

Out among them English

I have an unwritten rule not to venture into certain subjects when I'm in the confines of Stephen's family: religion, politics and sex are just for starters. We don't exactly see eye to eye on these things and, if I want to have an argument, what's the point of paddling in the shallows with amateurs when I can go home and get properly, deeply aggravated in the bosom of my own family? Normally, the taboo subjects are easy to avoid because Trish would rather talk about less contentious topics in any case, such as what she cooked for Ted each night this week, starting with macaroni cheese and going through to lamb chops with chips and peas, what the chiropodist said to her about her bunions, what her hairdresser told her about Marbella, how much Jif she gets through in a single week, why you should put a teaspoon of sugar in the final rinse when you're washing your nets, and what Mrs Winstanley had said to her about Mr Winstanley. In fact, the closest she comes to talking about sex is when she relates what problems Mrs Winstanley is having in the 'downstairs department', but seeing as I've never even met Mrs Winstanley, I'm not all that fascinated by her departments, downstairs or otherwise. As for religion, although Trish is sort of dimly aware that I'm half-Jewish and knows that Stephen and I will have a civil ceremony rather than a church wedding, she seems to find it all a little embarrassing for some reason so I've never really seen the point of discussing it.

We were drinking tea after lunch when Trish made some slightly unpleasant remark about refugees. Part of me was thinking, *leave it, don't cause trouble, it's not worth it.* Unfortunately, the other part of me wasn't listening. I pointed out that my father's parents had come to England not long before the Second World War and that I wouldn't be sitting there drinking tea right now if they hadn't been allowed in.

'I didn't realize your family were – that they came from abroad.'

'Oh? Surely I mentioned it before? This is my dad's side, of course, the Jewish side. My mother's family come from Wiltshire.'

'We had a lovely holiday in that part of the world, didn't we, Ted? Remember? Ever such a good cream tea, we had. Where was that tea room? Proper clotted cream like you get in Devon. Ted?'

Ted turned to me.

'So, where were your father's parents from then?'

It's so rare to hear Ted actually utter an entire sentence or say much more than 'Yes, dear' that I practically splurted my tea all over the nest of tables.

'Lithuania. Of course, it's just as well they left when they did or they'd almost certainly have been killed.'

Trish reached for the teapot and started topping up everyone's cup.

'Bit more for you, Georgia? Still, it's nice to be good with money, isn't it? Stephen's always said you've got your head screwed on right. And we've always been careful, Ted and I, haven't we, Ted? Not mean, I hope, no, but we're not ones to be buying things on the never-never, are we?'

'I'm sorry?'

I felt the pressure of Stephen's hand on my leg, but whether it was meant to comfort me or to stop me from taking issue with his mother, I wasn't sure.

Trish stopped pouring.

'Well, you know . . . it's just what they say, isn't it? What people say. You know. About Jews. No offence.'

Have you noticed how people always say 'no offence' just after they've said something unspeakably offensive? I could sense Stephen desperately willing me to leave the subject alone.

'Oh, what's that?' I feigned ignorance. 'What do *they* say?'

256

She stood up briskly then, and lifted the lid of the teapot, as if she was thinking of adding some more hot water.

'You know, that Jews are mean. I'm not saying *I* think that – *I* think it's good to be careful with your money, it doesn't grow on trees, does it? Don't drink that if it's stewed, Stephen love, I'll make fresh.'

Stephen patted me again, trying to pacify me.

'Leave it, darling,' he said under his breath. 'You know she doesn't mean it – it's just her generation—'

I shook his hand away.

'Really? And why do you suppose they say that then?'

'Well, I wouldn't know. It's just one of those things, isn't it? Like a saying or what have you, that Jews are mean, same with the Scots, it's like the French being – you know – ' she dropped her voice, 'dirty, or the Irish being stupid.'

I sat there open-mouthed and aghast. Dear God, where would you even start?

'Mum. Come along now.' Stephen chipped in. 'It's really not acceptable to say those kinds of things any more.'

Not acceptable to say them? But fine to think them presumably?

I shook my head.

'I'm sorry, but I really don't know what to say . . . I can't *believe* you really think that. Every time you meet someone who's Jewish – or Scottish, French or Irish – I mean, you must *notice* the huge gulf between the stereotype and the reality? You do *see* that they're just stereotypes based on prejudice and ignorance and fear, don't you?' I realized there was no point even attempting to go into an in-depth historical account of the origins of Jews' becoming bankers and money-lenders because Trish would never grasp it anyway. 'You do see that it's simply racist and wrong?'

Stephen's hand pressed firmly into my leg.

'Now, steady on—'

Trish's cheeks flushed red.

'But I'm not racist, am I, Ted? What about that coloured nurse I had when I was in hospital having my – you know? I always said good morning to her and everything. She was a nice lady, always a smile and a kind word for everybody.' She started towards the kitchen, avoiding meeting my eyes. 'I'll just put the kettle on.'

Roots

Ted gave me a sympathetic smile while she was out of the room, but he didn't say anything. I refused to look at Stephen but stood up and focused my attention on the pair of framed Japanese-style silk pictures by the window. I heard Trish come back in and start fussing around with the cups and saucers. I came and sat down again, perched on the edge of an armchair, rather than on the sofa where I'd been before.

'Yes, but you're not really a *Jew*, are you, Georgia dear? I mean, you don't go to the – the – you know, like church, but on Saturdays?'

'Synagogue. No, I don't.' I tried to breathe slowly. I don't think punching Stephen's mother is the best way to improve our relationship. I breathed out a little too loudly so it sounded like a heavy sigh. 'But it's not as black and white as that. It's not just about religious belief or practice – there are other things – tradition, culture, history, blood. Of course, I'm only half-Jewish and, technically, I don't even count – you know it follows the maternal line? But it's still there – *here*,' I added, thumping myself in the centre of my chest a shade dramatically. 'You can't erase it, no matter what you do – even if you wanted to, even if you never set foot inside a synagogue and ate nothing but bacon sandwiches every day, it's like—'

'Ooh, I know!' Trish was excited, as if she'd guessed the answer to a question on a game show. 'It's like that stain on the lounge carpet, Ted, remember? In the corner there. And, you know, we never found out what it was, did we?'

'Um, that's not quite what I meant.' I clutched my teacup tight to stop myself hurling it across the room to create another ineradicable stain on the textured wallpaper, the pale carpet. I tried to think how I might explain it to Bonnie, or to Cora, but either of them would probably latch on a lot faster. Trish isn't exactly the sharpest knife in the drawer. 'It's more like . . . well, you know how my hair is actually really curly – sort of frizzy . . .'

'But it's straight.'

'Only because I straighten it every morning. But—'

'Do you? Ooh, what do you use for that? That Sandra used to straighten her hair – remember, Ted? The woman in the baker's?'

'*Anyway,*' I persisted, giving Ted a look. He smiled back. How does he stand it? 'See, my point is that, even though I faff about every morning trying to straighten it – ultimately, it makes no difference. I'm still a curly-haired person. My DNA, my genetic inheritance, determines that I have curly hair so it's part of me. Not my whole identity – but part of me.'

Trish sat there blinking, like a rabbit wondering which way to run. Then she nodded.

'You know . . .' she said, sounding thoughtful.

'Yes?'

'I must say, your hair always looks lovely to me – but I think I saw something in Boots for frizzy hair – p'raps you should try that?' She smiled, relieved to have been able to offer a helpful suggestion. I am mean, I thought, she can't help it. She is who she is too.

I forced a smile.

'Thank you,' I said, glancing at my watch. 'Gosh, we really ought to be going, shouldn't we?' I said, turning to Stephen.

Trish paused, clutching the teapot close to her like a lifebelt.

'Stephen?'

'Yes.' He got to his feet. 'We ought to be off in any case. Thanks for lunch, Mum. Top nosh, as usual.'

'Yes, thank you. It was delicious. Lovely apple pie.'

'Oh, it was no trouble.' She turned away, took the teapot through to the kitchen. 'Now – coats! Ted!'

Ted stood up on cue and went through to the hall. As he helped me on with my coat, he held my shoulders for a moment and spoke quietly into my ear.

'I'm sorry.'

I patted his hand.

'Bye then. Thank you.' I stood behind Stephen so I wouldn't have to kiss Trish goodbye.

'Bye-bye,' she said, her voice bright and chirpy once more, waving at me as I backed out onto the front path. 'See you both soon. Take care, Stephen love. Give us a call.'

A difference of opinion

We walked in silence to the car and I waited until we'd been driving for a few minutes before I spoke.

'Well,' I said, 'that was fun.'

He sighed.

'I'm sorry if Mum upset you, sweetheart, but you must make allowances. It's just that generation, they say things like that. They haven't got the hang of the whole PC thing.'

'The whole PC thing? What the fuck's being PC got to do with it? I'm talking about being a decent human being. And, excuse me, but her generation should be more understanding, not less – it's not history for them, it's in living memory. I know she was only a small child in the war, but Quinn wasn't born till after the war and look at her – Quinn's the least racist person I've ever met.'

'Steady on, now. My mother's not a racist.'

'Well, what would you call it then?'

He sighed again and paused while he concentrated on checking his rear-view mirror.

260

'It's just the kind of thing people say without thinking about it. You are a bit oversensitive about this stuff, you know. You should learn just to laugh it off, you shouldn't let every little thing bug you.'

'Stephen! This is exactly why these things get out of hand – it starts with *harmless* little jokes and stereotypes and people who should know better saying it doesn't matter, then pretty soon you've got people turning their neighbours in or burning crosses on their front lawn.'

Stephen was silent. I could tell he'd decided to end the conversation. He does that sometimes, when he thinks the other person is being irrational and there's no point wasting his energy in trying to get them to see sense, i.e. agree with him.

'Stephen?'

'Yes?'

'I really don't think I'm overreacting about this.'

'Mmm-mm.'

'Can you stop the car, please.'

'What? Why?'

'I want to get out.'

'Now, let's not be silly. I'm sorry if Mum upset you, but—'

'*Please – stop – the – car.*'

'Let's all calm down and talk—'

'Oh – which *all* is this? Are you not calm? You sound reasonably calm. I'm fucking angry and upset, so perhaps you meant me? Stop the car now.' I started to open the door.

'Hey! Hey! That's dangerous! Don't be stupid. Let me at least drop you at the station – then you can hop on a train and not endure my repulsive, fascist company, OK?'

'Stephen, don't be like that – of course I'm not saying *you're* a fascist. I'm just saying it's important to me, I don't want these things swept under the carpet or have to pretend I don't mind.'

'I know you don't.' He pulled over by the station.

261

'Let's not fight, eh? I'm sorry, OK?' He smiled. 'Come on, sweetie – kiss and make up?'

I leant forward to kiss him.

'Of course. I'm not cross with you, really I'm not, but I just want to be in my own place.' I opened the car door.

'All right. Call me later then?'

'Yes. Take care. Bye.'

There was a train drawing in as I was buying my ticket, so I had to run for it. I hurtled down the stairs, but slipped near the bottom and fell headlong onto the platform.

'Hold the train!' I shouted to the guard. 'Please!'

A man came over to help me up.

'Thank you, but I *must* catch that train.' He helped me to the open doors.

'Mind the doors!' the guard called.

During the interminable journey back to town, I had time to inspect the damage: my hands were badly grazed and stinging like crazy, my trousers were filthy, with the fabric ripped at one knee, and my ankle hurt from where I'd twisted my foot as I fell.

A woman sitting opposite gave me a sympathetic smile, then everyone returned to their newspapers, their books, their Walkmans, and ignored me. I can't think when I was last on a train without a book. I felt almost naked. I rubbed at my ankle and thought about Trish – how on earth was I going to get out of seeing her in future? It's not practical. Obviously. If you're going to marry someone, you can't avoid their family for ever, can you? You can't live in a cocoon. That reminds me of something, I can't think what. Of course, Stephen would gladly not see my family for – ever. If he could. It's not that he dislikes them exactly, though given how obnoxious Ellie and Matt are to him, I couldn't blame him if he did. It's just . . . What was it Leo said about my family? I know – that we're all cut from the same bale of cloth. And Stephen's family –

262

well, they're not just a different bale, they're in a whole different warehouse, aren't they?

I *know* my family aren't the easiest people in the world. I *know* they're hard work. But I do love them and I'm used to them. And they're used to me. I don't have to worry about being polite or remembering not to swear. I don't need to comment on how nice the house is looking, because it never is and no-one expects me to. I can eat as much or as little as I like, without being handed a plate with Trish's idea of how much I should eat on it (less than Stephen, of course, because he's a man). I don't have to smile politely when Trish rolls her eyes over some supposed misdemeanour of Ted's, such as that he's left the seat up in the downstairs cloakroom again even though if she's told him once she's told him a thousand times, or he's used the guest hand towel when he knows she's put it out only for guests. Whereas I am not just allowed but *encouraged* to use the guest towel, which is soft and peachy and far cleaner and fluffier than any of the aged, faded towels that are slumped over the towel rails at Dad's, because I am a *guest* after all. And that's what's so depressing – I could know them for a lifetime – be their daughter-in-law for a lifetime – but I'd *always* be a guest. With my family, it's hard to remain a guest for any length of time, even if you wanted to be. After you've been there once, that's it, you've lost your guest status and you have to pitch in like everyone else. OK, so no-one runs round after you, offering you coffee or plumping up the cushions before you sit down, but then no-one bats an eyelid if you lie on the floor to read the paper or forage in the fridge to see if there's anything you fancy. You can do what you like. You can just *be* and that's enough.

20

The two a.m. test

The phone's ringing. Dear God – it must be the middle of the night. I fumble for the phone in the dark.

'Hello?'

There is someone crying at the other end. Not just someone. I sit bolt upright, wide awake.

'Ellie?'

'Ge-g-George?'

'What is it? Are you all right? What's happened?'

'N-n-no.' She's hiccuping with sobs. 'Can you come? I need you to come.'

'Yes, of course. Tell me what's happened.'

'I – I – there was a— I *can't* – please come.'

'I will, of course I will. Are you at the flat?'

'Yes. There's no-one else here.'

'I'm on my way, Ellie. Sit tight.'

I leap out of bed – straight onto my dodgy ankle, and crumple to the floor as it gives way beneath me. The pain is so bad I cry out. I can't possibly drive like this. Stephen? No. I can't phone him, not after yesterday.

I haul myself back onto the bed and call the taxi firm I always use. Sure, I can have a car, they say. In an hour. Very busy tonight – most of their cars are doing pickups at some big corporate do out in Docklands. Account clients, top priority. Shit, shit, shit.

I'll *have* to ask Stephen. I hate asking people for favours at the best of times. But this isn't for me.

His voice is sleepy. And cross.

'Stephen! Darling. I'm so sorry to wake you—'

'What time is it?'

'Just after two – but, the thing is—'

'What's the matter? Are you ill?'

'No, no. *I'm* fine. It's Ellen—'

'Oh, *Georgia*! Not really? Not *again*? What is it this time? We're not running a minicab service. She's unbelievable.'

'No. She sounds seriously upset. I wouldn't ask if—'

'Sweetheart.' He's got his being-patient voice on. 'Don't you see, if you keep running to her rescue every five minutes, she's never going to get her act together and grow up. She's just using you.'

'I'm not arguing about this now. I'm sorry I phoned you – I shouldn't try and drag you into my family's messes, but . . .'

There is a heavy sigh down the line.

'I'd come for *you*, of course – but why don't you find out what all the fuss is about? She's probably forgotten she even phoned you by now. You know what she's like.'

'I have to go. I'll call you tomorrow.'

'Good. I'll speak to you then. Night, sweetie. Just ring her. I'm sure she's perfectly all right. Honestly.'

But there is someone else. Someone who won't give me a hard time, someone who might even still be up. Leo.

'Urgh?' Oops. Not still up then.

'Leo. I'm sorry—'

'Georgia? What is it? Are you OK?'

'Yes. No. It's Ellen. I need to get to her now and I can't drive because I've hurt my ankle – and I can't get a taxi – and I phoned—'

'Give me two minutes.'

265

To the rescue

I crawl round the room, dragging on yesterday's clothes. A knock at the door. I hop to answer it.

'Sheesh – what the hell happened to your ankle?' He sees how unsteady I am and puts his arm round me. I tell him.

'Shoes?'

I sit down while he kneels in front of me to ease them onto my feet.

'My van's right outside. Lean on me.'

I take a tentative step, clutching his shoulder, but even that sends shooting pains up my leg. I must have made it worse by jumping out of bed onto it and I draw breath sharply.

'I take it we're in a hurry?'

I nod, feeling too faint and sick even to speak.

'Okey-doke. Hold onto your bag, lady. Prepare for lift-off.'

'Wha—'

With that, he crouches quickly and bends me over his shoulder in a fireman's lift.

'Oh, God – Leo! You can't!'

'Sorry. I know it's undignified, but I'll do my back in if I try to carry you bridegroom-style . . .'

He half-jogs along the corridor to the lift.

'All right there?'

'I can't believe you're really doing this. Can't you put me down for this bit?'

'No point. I'll only have to pick you up again to get you out to the van. So – tell me – where are we headed?'

'Ellen's flat. It's near Swiss Cottage, off Finchley Road.'

The lift arrives and he carries me in.

'I'm sorry I'm so heavy.'

'*You're* sorry? Thank God I'm used to hefting all my equipment around. Will you pay for me to go private if I get a hernia?'

I thwack his bum.

'Ow! Tell me what's going on – is Ellen all right? Stupid question. Presumably not – what's happened?'

'I don't know. Of course, I know she can be a bit of a drama queen, but she sounded so upset. She was really, really sobbing and – and – ' I start to cry myself then, 'she's m-my little sister . . .'

'Hey – it's all right.' He pats me on the bum, but in a comforting way. 'We'll get you there faster than you can say snotty handkerchief.'

As we cross the lobby, Vernon calls, out, 'Is that you, Georgia?' He gets to his feet. 'Are you being kid-napped?'

'Yes – but willingly!' I call back as we bounce past.

Leo unfolds me into the passenger seat of his van and carefully tucks my hopeless leg in after me.

'Buckle up tight.'

I reach into my bag for my mobile as he pulls away sharply and swiftly accelerates, heading north.

'Bugger – I've left my phone upstairs – it's charging. I wanted to phone Ellen to say we're on our way.'

'Use mine. Left-hand pocket – inside.'

I have to feel under his seat belt and work my hand round and under his jacket to get to it.

'No tickling,' he says, taking a corner at speed.

I dial Ellen's number.

'George?'

'Yes, how're you doing?'

'Are you still coming?' She's not crying now, but she sounds afraid and very, very young.

'Of course. I said I would. We're on our way.'

'We? Is Stephen bringing you?'

'No. He's – no, he isn't. I'm with Leo.'

'Really? Did you wake him up? Tell him I'm sorry.'

'Don't worry for now. Can you tell me what's happened?'

'Can I wait till you get here? But don't hang up.'

'I won't. I promise.'

'I – I just don't want to be alone.'

'I'm know. I'm right here.'

'Won't be long now,' says Leo. 'Which bit of the Finchley Road do we want?'

I break off talking to Ellen to give him directions.

Ellen's voice again.

'Talk to me. Tell me something nice. Tell me the time after Mum died and you made the brunch.'

'That's not all that nice.'

'Tell it to me. Please.'

'OK.' We stop at the lights then and Leo reaches for my hand and squeezes it.

'Well, after Mum died . . .' I squeeze his hand back and carry on. 'When it came to that first Sunday, I got up and came downstairs . . .'

'And Mummy wasn't there because she'd already been buried by then.'

God, this was some weird conversation.

'Yes, that's right. So I came down and got a cloth and wiped the kitchen table.'

'And then you went and fetched the plates . . .' Ellen prompts.

'I did. And the cutlery and the paper napkins and I set them out just the way Mum used to.'

'And then I came down . . .'

'Yes. I heard you because you were dragging that little wheelie dog you had and it went thunk-thunk-thunk down the stairs.'

'Yes, he was called Mr Bum.'

I laugh then at the memory.

'God, yes – whatever happened to Mr Bum? I always thought you called him that so you could shout the word bum loudly whenever you lost him.'

'I did.'

I break off to direct Leo again.

'And then?' Ellen prompted.

'You came into the kitchen, and you said . . .' I pause, knowing she likes to do this bit.

'Gee-gee – cannive scramblies?'

'And I told you to get up onto your chair and then I got the eggs out. We're nearly there, babes.'

'And then Daddy came down.'

'And into the kitchen. And, when he saw you sitting all up and ready with a napkin tucked under your chin and me trying to whisk the eggs . . .'

'He started to cry.'

'Yes,' I say. 'Yes, he did.'

We are both silent for a moment. I gesture to Leo to pull over.

'We're here.'

Leo comes round to my side and gets ready to haul me over his shoulder again.

'You can't. Her flat's up on the third floor and there's no lift. It'll kill you.'

'Well, you can't hop all the way up there, can you? I'll survive. Come on, get over here, woman.'

'What if I'm too heavy?'

'Then I'll drop you and you'll bounce all the way down to the bottom.' He crouches to heft me onto his back again. 'Oof! Have you put on weight in the car? Were you downing my secret stash of Mars bars? They're supposed to be for emergency lunches when I don't have time to eat.'

'That's not lunch. Don't you know anything about nutrition? No wonder you're losing your hair—'

'Watch it, Missy – I don't imagine you'd bounce well on this pavement. Top bell is it?'

'Yup.' He turns me round so I can speak into the entryphone.

Ellen buzzes us in and we begin the slow climb to the top.

'Ohmygod!' Ellen said. 'What happened to you?'

'It's nothing – I sprained my ankle, that's all – fortunately, I never travel without Sherpa Leo . . .'

He unloaded me – rather hastily, I thought – onto the sofa and Ellen came and sat down for a long hug while Leo went into the kitchen to make some tea.

'Do you want to tell me?' I asked her.

'This, this man – f-followed me . . .' she began, crying again as I cuddled her close. She and her flatmate Siobhan both work at the wine bar, so they usually walk home together, or, if it's raining, Brian sometimes drops them off in his car. But Siobhan had swapped her shift. Ellen's never been bothered by walking on her own late at night and it wasn't too cold, so when Brian offered her a lift if she wanted to hang on another half an hour for him, she said no thanks and set off.

'There was a bunch of blokes shouting and walking in front of cars in the road so I ducked down a side street to steer clear of them – but then I heard footsteps behind me. I turned round to look – but there was only a man some way back down the street, who'd stopped to light a fag, so I thought it was OK. I carried on but then I heard him again – faster this time – I speeded up and dug down into my bag for my mobile – but it wasn't there – I must have left it at the bar. And all I could think was, "George will be so cross with me because I've left my phone behind again. She'll say it was all my fault." '

'No, no. I wouldn't. Don't be silly. We all do things like that.'

'And then he started to run.'

'Oh, babes.' My hands felt clammy, as if I was reliving it all myself.

'So I ran too – as fast as I could – I could hear him panting and I tried to scream but I couldn't – I was running so hard I couldn't make a sound – I cut left into another street, trying to head back to the main road – but then – then he caught up with me. He grabbed the hood of my coat and yanked it back hard against my throat – I couldn't breathe – then he pushed me against this wall. He was – just *horrible*. So horrible. I *can't*—' I stroked her hair back from her face and then she sat up straight. 'He started kissing me, pushing his tongue into my mouth – and he *reeked* of beer and sweat – I kept trying to push him off, but he was stronger – and then he jammed his knee between my legs – and I was so *scared*. I managed to scream then – just once – but he pressed his hand over my mouth so I could hardly breathe. And the worst thing was, he kept saying, "I love you, I really love you," as if he thought that would somehow make it all right.'

'And then what happened? Did he—?'

'No – I – you know that pencil you gave me?'

'What?'

'The purple glittery one, with the silly purple dog on the end of it? It was in the pocket of my coat and I managed to reach in and grab it and then – I stabbed him with it as hard as I could.'

'My God – well done! Where did you get him?'

'Only in the cheek – but he jumped back and it gave me a couple of seconds to run for it. He shouted, "You fucking bitch!" after me, but I ran and ran until I made it to the garage. And they rang the police.'

The police had come and driven her home and taken her statement and a description. Then they'd asked if she wanted to talk to a counsellor.

'And I laughed,' Ellen said. 'I think they thought I must be a bit loopy. I said, "No thanks, I've got one at home." And then they left. And then I went to the loo and I felt sick but I couldn't get off the loo 'cause I had the runs, so I threw up into the bath. And then I rang you.'

'I'm sorry I wasn't here. I hate the thought of you having to be on your own after that.'

She snuggled up against me.

'You are now. That's what counts.'

Leo brought the tea and we ate all of Siobhan's chocolate digestives.

'I wish I'd got him in the eye. I bet he tries to attack someone else. I think I was lucky.'

'Maybe he'll die of graphite poisoning.'

'George?'

'Yes?'

'I feel a bit weird about being on my own. It's just I keep thinking he's going to find me somehow and climb in through the window or break down the door. Is that silly?'

'Not at all. Of course I wouldn't leave you on your own. You're staying with me. It'll be fun. We can have midnight feasts and talk in the dark until we fall asleep the way we used to.'

'Can we have popcorn?'

'Of course. And cheesy Wotsits and Toblerone and Iced Gems if they still make them and everything that's bad for us.'

I turned to look at Leo.

'Can I come?' he said.

It was after three by the time we got back to my flat and we were all pretty wiped out. I offered Ellen the sofa bed, but she wanted to come in with me – the way she did when she was little after she'd woken up from a nightmare.

Leo said good night.

'Just yell if you need me.' He stepped forward to kiss me on the cheek and I put my arms round him for a moment. He felt warm and solid and immensely comforting. I pulled away almost at once, though I could have clung to him for hours. He looked down at me, then at Ellen, and I knew he was wondering whether he should kiss her too or whether she might not welcome a man near her just then.

She smiled and gave him a hug.

'Thank you. For being our white knight.'

'No sweat. Anyone would have done the same.'

The following morning

Stephen phoned a little after nine, while Ellen was in the shower.

'Oh, hi.'

'You sound a bit off. Sorry – did I wake you?'

'No. We haven't slept much though.'

'We?' He cleared his throat.

'Ellen came back here.'

I could sense rather than hear his slight sigh at the other end of the line.

'Why? What happened? Is she all right?'

'No. She was attacked by some revolting drunk on her way home last night.'

'Attacked! How awful! Was she injured? Did he hurt her?'

'Not that kind of attack. It was attempted rape.' The phrase sounded odd, what they'd say in a court of law or in a newspaper, but more bearable somehow than saying, 'A man tried to rape my little sister.'

'I'm really sorry. I would have come if I'd known, of course. You know I would.'

'Yes. Anyway, she's physically OK, but pretty shaken up, I think.'

'How did it happen?'

I told him.

'What was she doing walking on her own at that hour?'

'Er, excuse me? She was minding her own bloody business, going home from work.'

'Well, come on – that's a bit silly in this day and age with all these muggers and nutters about.'

'Are you saying it's her fault?'

'No, of course not. C'mon, sweetie, you don't go wandering about the streets at midnight, do you? You can see—'

'Stephen! She wasn't "wandering about" as you so amiably put it, she was walking home. I suppose you think all women should have a curfew after eight p.m.?'

'Now you're just being silly. Don't go jumping on the feminist bandwagon just when it suits you.'

I managed to suppress the urge to scream and keep my voice low.

'It's not a matter of being a *feminist*. It's a matter of being a *decent human being*. Everyone should have the right to—'

'Darling, *darling*. Calm down. Of course, no-one's questioning anybody's rights. This isn't about rights. It's about acting with due caution. You must admit, Ellen's not exactly the most sensible person in the world – you've said so yourself enough times.' His tone was insufferably calm, as if he was being the rational one, trying to calm down the silly, hysterical woman.

'How dare you try and turn her into the guilty party! And don't fucking tell me to calm down!'

'I don't think we should talk about this now. I can tell you're upset.'

'Can you really? Well, how fucking sensitive of you to pick up on that, Stephen.'

'Give me a call a bit later when you're feeling more like yourself.'

'I *am* feeling like myself! I've never felt so like myself. Don't tell me how I am or who I am.'

'We'll talk a bit later then,' he said calmly and hung up. I slammed the phone down with a crash.

Ellen was standing in the doorway, pale and silent.

'What's going on?'

'Oh. Nothing. I just lost my rag a bit with Stephen.'

'You were shouting,' Ellen pointed out. 'You never shout.'

'Everybody needs to shout sometimes.' I could hear my counsellor voice spinning away inside my head: *It's healthy to express your anger by non-violent means* . . .

'But you *never* do.'

'Well.' I pushed my hair back from my face. My scalp felt sort of tingly and prickly all over as if I had pins and needles in my head. 'I do now.'

21

Sisters

'Do you want to talk about it any more?' I asked Ellen in bed the next night.

'Not really. I can't stop thinking about it as it is.'

'It might help. Or I can find you someone else if you like – another counsellor who's experienced in—'

'Nah.' She shook her head. 'I don't think that's what I need right now – I need . . .' Her voice faded away, as if she had simply run out of the energy it takes to speak.

'I'm sorry. It's not for me to tell you what to do. What do I know in any case?'

'You know lots, twitto – you know you do.' She got out of bed again. 'D'you want a herby?'

'Please.'

She flicked on the small light over the kitchenette and I could hear her overfilling the kettle as usual.

'Just boil enough for two mugs. Please.'

'Oh, ssssh. *I'm* making it.'

'It's *so* wasteful.'

'Yes, dear. The trouble is,' she craned her head round the screen to talk to me, 'I feel like a sitting duck and that he's out there, lurking in the bushes waiting to pounce on me – I feel like I've got no say in what happens to me.'

I don't remember her ever worrying about being passive before. I mean, Ellen's always just drifted from one thing to another as if she were being swept along with the current – she's never acted as if she might have the power to choose a direction.

'You have. You *have* – besides, I won't let him get you.' If only I'd been with her – I should have taken better care of her; then it would never have happened.

'Oh, George, how can you protect me? Twenty-four hours a day? You *can't*.'

'Maybe I could—'

'You *can't*. It's not possible. At least he doesn't know where I live.'

'And he wasn't out to get you personally, was he? I mean, he wasn't a customer at the wine bar, someone you knew?'

'No. Definitely not. I was just in the wrong place at the wrong time, I think.'

'Maybe you could do a self-defence course?'

'What – me? Hit him with my mobile phone? I'd be hopeless.'

'No, you wouldn't.'

'Brian does some kind of martial arts thing – ju-jitsu I think.'

She carried the two mugs of chamomile tea over to the bed.

'Thanks.' I took one and set it on my book by the bed. 'Mat!' I ordered, seeing she was about to put hers straight onto my polished wooden bookshelves. 'Why don't you ask him about it then?'

'Might do. God – do you remember that strange guy I went out with a couple of years ago?'

'Couldn't narrow it down a bit, could you?'

She gave me a look.

'Tee-hee. The *strange* one – who was totally fascinated when he discovered that I was half-Jewish? He kept wanting to talk about my roots and calling it *Judo*-ism, instead of Jud*ais*m – remember?'

'Yes! Judo-ism! – the ancient art of self-defence using only a bagel and a small accountant from Hendon.'

'Learn to survive armed only with your wits and a side order of latkes!'

'Subdue your foe by urging him to eat fifteen portions of lokshen pudding so he can't move . . .'

'Bore him to death by subjecting him to hours of Why Things Were Better in the Old Days . . .'

'Embarrass him to death with lectures on How You Could Have Really Made Something of Yourself if You'd Only Studied Harder . . .'

Ellen laughed and flumped back against the pillows.

'Aaah – I never have half this much fun when I'm with a bloke.'

'No. Me neither. Except—'

'You mean the P-h doesn't keep you up giggling half the night?' Ellen affected a look of astonishment.

'Oh yes, we roll around the floor night after night, weeping with laughter.'

'*I'm* supposed to be the bitchy one.'

'I'm just cross with him. I'll get over it. Giggling isn't everything. Stephen's very . . . he's very *good* for me. Very stable. Trustworthy. I know where I am with him and he doesn't let me down . . . mostly. I know, I know – it all sounds desperately dull to you, but it's what matters to me.'

'Hey, I'm no judge, am I? You're the expert.'

'Ha! I don't feel like it.'

'So what are you going to do once you're married? About the giggling. You can't keep having me over to stay then desert the marital bed because you want to sit up talking all night, can you?'

'But you'll come often, won't you? You *must*.'

'Oh yeah – like Stephen's really going to want me turning up on your doorstep every week. He's not exactly thrilled to bits at the prospect of having me for a sister-in-law.'

'He does like you – anyway, it's mutual – he's not in your Top Five Favourite People on the Planet, is he?'

278

She shrugged and wrinkled her nose.

'Can't you marry Leo instead?'

'What – would that suit you better?'

'Yeah.'

'No problem. Whatever you say. Stick it down on my "To do" list.'

Inappropriate attire

A couple of days later, I was getting ready to go out with my friends Emma and Susie. I was standing in front of the bathroom mirror, attempting to wipe off Ellen's toothpaste spittle-spray at the same time as trying to pin up my hair. Ever since that awful lunch at Stephen's parents, I've stopped straightening my hair. I'm beginning to get used to seeing my new, curly-haired reflection, but I still can't seem to achieve that soft, tousled look that Ellen always manages to create without even trying. There was a knock at the door – rat-a-tat-tat – Leo's signature knock.

'Get that will you, babes?' I called through. 'Might be Leo.'

Through the closed bathroom door, I could hear them saying hello to each other, an exchange of kisses.

'Hi! Leo? I'm going out,' I called through. 'Just finishing my face.'

'Shall I come back in three hours then?'

'Gosh, that's amusing and original! You must tell me who writes your jokes . . .'

'Sure – give him a call – he could do with the work.'

As I came into the main room, Ellen emerged from where she'd been half-hidden by the screen.

'Coffee, George?' She was wearing a pair of black jeans and a bra. No top. My face must have fallen as far as the carpet, because then she said, 'What? What is it?'

I went right up to her and mouthed, 'Why aren't you *dressed*?' pulling her back behind the screen.

'What?' she mouthed back, then, out loud: 'Why are you whispering?'

'What are you two up to behind there?' Leo called out. 'Are you preparing a puppet show for me?'

'Yes! Yes! Yes!' said Ellen in a squeaky, Mr Punch voice.

'No. No. *No*.' Then I dropped my voice to a whisper. 'Ellen, will you please go and get *dressed*? I can't believe you're *parading* around in front of Leo with no top on. What do you think you're doing?'

'Oh, for God's sake!' Ellen made no attempt to keep her voice down. 'He doesn't care – he's just like another brother or something. He doesn't count.'

'*Ssssh!*'

Ellen stepped out from behind the screen defiantly, as if striding out onto a stage.

'George is giving me a hard time about the fact that I'm *improperly dressed*, apparently – but a bra's no worse than a bikini, is it? No worse than you'd see on any beach – even in the park.'

'Er, no. I guess not.' Leo had been sitting back on the sofa, but was now perched on the edge looking decidedly uncomfortable.

'Ellen! Don't embarrass him. Of course he now feels he *has* to agree with you – to be polite.'

'No, he *doesn't*. He's not polite.'

'Don't mind me, will you? I *am* still here, in case you—'

'Leo – tell me,' Ellen demanded. 'Do you honestly care about seeing me in my bra?'

'Why can't you just put a top on – like a normal person?' I asked. 'All this time you're arguing – how long does it take to put on a top? Two seconds?'

'I couldn't decide what to wear – I haven't got anything I like here.'

'Well – *ask* then. You can borrow something of mine. Not my cream silk shirt. Or the white linen. Or the black thing with the see-through sleeves.'

'Jeez, what does that leave?' Ellen slid open the

wardrobe door and started to rifle through the contents. 'Don't you have anything with some bloody colour in it? This is all so boring.'

'I don't buy my clothes to please you, strangely enough—'

'Or anyone else, looking at this lot.' She plucked out a black stretchy top. 'So, Leo – you didn't answer my question – does it bother you seeing me in my bra, as George said?' She stood there, deliberately not putting on the top.

'Actually, no it doesn't.' But I noticed that he wasn't looking directly at her. 'I can take any amount of women waltzing around in various states of undress. Doesn't bother me a bit.'

'See?' Ellen made a face at me, then pulled on the top. Less than two seconds.

'Don't pull it out of shape. What do you mean *see*? That proves my point, not yours! You were being deliberately provocative.'

'I wasn't.'

'You absolutely were.'

'I absolutely was not. I don't see Leo that way. He's *so* not my type.'

'Still here in the room!' Leo waved.

'I'm not going to argue with you about this now. I'm late as it is. Leo – I'm sorry you got dragged into our immensely tedious sisterly squabbles.'

He stood up and headed for the door.

'No sweat. I only dropped by to say hi; I'm off out myself shortly.'

'Ellen, don't forget to lock up properly please. And take your keys – I may not be back till after eleven.'

'After eleven! Golly! You wild and crazy gal!'

We stood for a moment in the corridor. I felt I should say something.

'It's OK,' he said, as if I had spoken. 'She's bound to be acting a bit oddly – she's had a hell of a shock and maybe this is her way of dealing with it. Don't worry about me – I can handle it. Just look after yourself, hmm? You look tired.'

'I *am* tired. I've barely slept for three nights. I'd sooner be sinking into a deep bath with a good book and a glass of wine, not heading out for pasta and the latest instalment of Decent Men, Are They All Hiding In a Cave Somewhere?'

He smiled, then squeezed my arm.

'Not as bad as going to some awful magazine bash in a trendy bar.'

'Why are you going then?'

He curled his lip.

'Might be useful. I've got to get some new clients and earn more money if I'm ever going to be able to afford somewhere bigger.'

'Oh.' I looked up at him. 'You're going to get rich then swan off to a swanky loft with twenty-foot-high ceilings and those minimalist cupboards with no handles, aren't you?'

'Yup. Soon as I make my first couple of million. Then you won't see me for dust.'

'You won't be in too big a rush, will you?'

He smiled and bent to kiss my cheek.

'What do you think?'

Make a wish . . .

Georgia and her friend Ruth are outside in the garden. They are playing Spells, standing either side of a large stone urn as their cauldron. Ellen is in the sandpit, flicking sand out onto the grass with her yellow plastic spade.

Georgia has dug deep into the dressing-up box to find her magic silver wand, which has been ineptly mended with Sellotape. She has to hold the stem exactly on the join to stop it breaking again as she waves it to and fro over the ivy and periwinkle, which spill down the sides of the urn like potion boiling over.

'*Abracadabra – fabracadabra . . .*' she intones. 'Put a

pebble in the pot – ' Georgia nods sternly at Ruth, who throws in the stone she has been clutching hotly in her right fist – 'then you get to wish – a *lot*.'

Ruth shuts her eyes to make her wish.

'I wish,' says Georgia, 'that Mark Evans kisses Ruth in the playground.'

'No! Take it back. It's not your wish!' Ruth's cheeks are flushed, as bright as if she had dabbed cochineal on them, the way Georgia and Mummy did once when they were making marzipan apples.

'Too late now. You can't undo the spell.'

'You can. *You* can, Georgia. *Please* undo the spell.' Ruth's face, as she looks up at Georgia, who is tall for her year, is full of trust and absolute belief that Georgia has the power to grant or undo wishes.

Georgia relents and chants once more to reverse the spell.

'Have you got any lemonade?'

'Don't know,' says Georgia, knowing they haven't.

'Squash then?' Everyone has a bottle of orange squash in the cupboard, don't they?

They hear the doorbell as they near the French windows to go back inside, a long, insistent ring.

'It must be my dad, come to fetch me.'

Georgia runs through the kitchen to answer the door, but she is too late. Her mother is thundering down the stairs.

'I've got it!'

Before Georgia can speak, the door is open. Ruth's father stands on the path.

'Oh – I'm so sorry. I didn't – I wasn't sure if the bell was working – I was ringing – sorry, perhaps I have the wrong house . . .' He addresses most of this to the front step, with the occasional glance flicked up at Joy.

'Perhaps you have.' Joy, laughing. 'The bell does work, but I was just upstairs – ' She is standing by the front door in her tights, waist slip and bra. No blouse, no skirt, no shoes.

'Er, yes. Sorry. I'm Max, Ruth's father. Is she here?'

283

'Who knows? We may have to hunt for her, you know what children are like!' She laughs again. 'Do please come in.' She turns then and sees Georgia. 'Georgia, darling, who's your nice little friend you're playing with? Ruth, is it?'

Georgia nods.

'Hello, Georgia,' says Ruth's father. 'How are you?'

'Hello.' Ruth's parents have told Georgia that she can call them Max and Judith, but she doesn't like to, so she avoids using their names altogether. 'I'm very well, thank you.'

'You must come in and have a little something,' Joy urges, tugging at Max's jacket sleeve.

Georgia is praying silently inside her head, *Dear God, please, please, PLEASE make her go back upstairs.*

'Well, that's very nice of you, but we'd best be making a move, hadn't we, poppet?' He pats Ruth on the head. Ruth is looking at Joy's lacy bra, wide-eyed and open-mouthed.

'Ruth has such a pretty face,' Joy smiled at Max, 'and she's just adorable when she blushes.'

Max smiles while Ruth, on cue, goes bright red and presses her face into her daddy's jacket.

'Bye then,' says Georgia.

'Bye,' says Ruth.

'No – I *insist* you come in.' Joy laughs, leaning against the door frame.

'Another time perhaps?' Max gives Ruth a discreet nudge.

'Thank you for having me,' she says.

Georgia waves at Ruth and then the front door is closed once more.

'Well then – did you girls help yourselves to lemonade?'

'There isn't any.'

'Oh. Isn't there?' Frowning, then thoughtful. 'We could go and get some now.'

'It's too late now.'

'Don't be silly.' Joy checks the kitchen clock. 'The off-licence doesn't shut for ages.'

Georgia leans over the table and rolls the lone wizened apple around at the bottom of the fruit bowl.

'I don't want any lemonade.'

'You can't just think of yourself. What about Matt and Ellie?' Ellen is only two and does not yet know the grown-up delights of fizzy drinks. 'I'm sure *they'd* love some.'

Georgia winds a strand of her hair round and round her finger.

Joy looks down at herself.

'Oh! Look at me – about to go out half-dressed! Give me a minute and I'll be right down.'

Joy reappears, pulling on a black satin evening blouse as she descends the stairs.

'Ready?'

Georgia shakes her head.

'I'm not coming.'

'Of course you are.'

'I need to tidy up after our game.'

'Oh, you – little Miss Houseproud!' Joy picks up her purse from the dresser and checks the wallet part, fingers feeling the notes. 'Lord knows why the suffragettes bothered chaining themselves to the railings if your generation is just going to undo it all again.' She sees Georgia's face. 'Oh, come on, darling! Mummy's only teasing, don't look so serious all the time.'

Joy pauses in the hall.

'Promise me you'll be all right and that you'll look after Ellie,' she says, lightly touching the end of Georgia's nose with her fingertip, the way she used to, their family way of making a promise.

'I promise.' Georgia touches her mother's nose briefly.

'I'll be five minutes tops!'

The door bangs shut. Georgia stands in the hall for

a minute, running her finger up and down the door frame, then she goes back out to the garden, dips to pick up something from the ground. Closing her eyes, she puts her pebble in the magic urn and makes a wish.

22

Being together

I can't live like this. She's driving me crazy. Oh, I know Ellen's doing her best to be good – tiptoeing round the room like a cartoon burglar when I'm on the phone, watering the plants two hours after I've done them so all the water overspills their saucers and slops onto the carpet, bringing back treats such as croissants or marshmallows or overpriced, out-of-season strawberries to appease me because it's clear that I can't just rub along and live with another human being full-time like everyone else. I'm beginning to understand why when a person is murdered, the No. 1 suspect is their spouse. If this is what being married is like, then I may just stay engaged for the rest of my life. Of course, Stephen's not nearly as annoying as Ellen. At least he can manage to cross from one side of a room to the other without leaving a trail of devastation in his wake. Why can't she put anything away? She picks up the coffee jar from where she's left it on the draining board, opens the cupboard and I think, 'yes, yes, that's right – in the cupboard, keep going, don't stop now, just lift the jar, that's it, that's it – oh' – then she spots something else of interest in the cupboard, so what does she do? Does she put the coffee away, then take out the other item? Of course not. What would be the point of that? Why put something away when you know you're bound to want coffee again at some point during the day – leave it out on the draining board where it's handy, along with the forty-five other things you might want to use in the next week, even though it's now already so crowded with stuff you couldn't even find a gap big enough to fit a grain of rice on. No. Put the coffee back down, preferably precariously balanced on two other items of unequal heights, then take out the other thing that caught your eye. Oh. Not as interesting as you thought? Put it down on the cooker hob. Drift off to do something else. Even something as simple as making a cup of tea becomes this long-running tedious domestic soap. Any normal person can manage it; you know how it goes:

- Put correct amount of water in kettle.
- Place one tea bag in mug.
- Pour boiling water on tea bag, stir and wait a minute or two.
- Remove tea bag and discard in bin.
- Use milk from fridge and return fucking milk to fucking fridge.

How hard can it be? It's not brain surgery, is it? It's not trying to split the atom with a butter knife. It's making a cup of tea. But, of course to Ellen, nothing is ever that simple.

How to make tea, Ellen-style

- Announce to world that you fancy a cup of tea.
- Fill kettle right to the top in case fifteen guests pop by unannounced.
- Open all cupboards to look for mugs, banging doors with gusto.
- Remove mugs from cupboard to find one with stars on that is your favourite.
- Pile half of mugs back any old how.

- Interrupt older sister while she is reading or working to question her re origin of star-spangled mug.
- Open all cupboards again in quest of tea bags.
- Ask older sister if she has any other tea bags as those in cupboard not kind you like best.
- Poke around in cupboards *again*, then ask if there are any biscuits or, if not, then chocolate would do but not if it's that boring, plain stuff.
- Remark how very slow kettle is in coming to boil.
- Wander off to bathroom to carry out essential tasks, such as removing tops from bottles of shampoo and conditioner and placing towels in crumpled heaps on floor. Also remember to slop water liberally around room and in soap dish so sister's prized bluebell soap goes all gungy.
- Return to find kettle has boiled. Click it on again to return to boil.
- Point out diminutive dimensions of kitchenette in case sister has not noticed this during five years of residence.
- Pour water on tea bag and mash vigorously with any kitchen utensil to hand, eg handle of knife, potato peeler, etc.
- Remove tea bag and lay in white enamel sink to leave stubborn brown stain.
- Open fridge and comment on contents and lack of personal favourites, eg Kit Kats, squashy Brie, child-size pots of fromage frais.
- Stand there with fridge door open until sound of sister's gnashing teeth prompts you to close it.
- Ask in mock-humble manner if allowed to open fridge again in order to have milk in tea.
- Open fridge and remove milk.
- Bang fridge door shut at once, checking sister has noticed.
- Add milk to mug and slosh around for maximum spillage on worktop/draining board/floor etc.
- Leave milk on draining board for sister to put away.
- Take tea across room and set on table, ignoring chic

leather mat placed there for that purpose, leaving persistent ring on wooden surface.
- Take one sip of tea and exclaim on excessive temperature.
- Go off and do something else.
- Leave tea undrunk on table to get cold.
- Repeat whole process as desired.

How have her flatmates put up with her all this time? Clearly, they must be just as bad as she is – their kitchen makes Dad and Quinn's look like a show home.

While Ellen was having a bath, I rang Leo.

'Hey, you! How's it going?'

'Not so great. I think I'm in danger of doing serious damage to my house guest.'

'Come down for a break? I could do with a second opinion on some pictures.'

I banged on the bathroom door, called through to Ellen.

'Just nipping downstairs. Won't be long!'

Contacts

I stand at Leo's table, looking at contact sheets of photographs through a magnifying lens.

'Just pick out the ones you like best. How's Ellen doing?'

'She's OK, I think, but still pretty jumpy understandably – I wish I could somehow magic away all the shock and fear and anxiety overnight. But – I know I'm mean, but I just find it so hard having her in my flat. I wish I could be more relaxed and not keep whizzing round after her with a damp cloth – but I'm not.'

'It's tricky to have someone else suddenly in your space when you're used to living alone.'

'I know – but she's my sister. It should be easier with someone in your family – at least I knew all her faults already. It's not like it's a big surprise or anything.'

'Why do you have to be so reasonable all the time? It's OK to be annoyed – it doesn't mean you don't love her. I couldn't live with either of my sisters – they're both terrific and I love them to pieces, but we wouldn't last more than forty-eight hours under the same roof.'

'Why? They can't be worse than Ellen.'

'Because when it's family, every single thing you say has got thirty-odd years of subtext to it. If a friend asked me about the state of my love life, I'd say, "Crap, thanks, how's yours?" but if my sister Linda asked me, I'd think, "Here she goes again, getting at me about not being married yet," and I'd probably say, "Get off my back – I'm happy being single!" '

I laugh.

'And are you?'

'What do you think?'

'Do you always answer a question with another question? You're worse than my dad.'

'Does it bother you?' He is smiling now.

'You're doing it *again*! You're like a bloody politician.' I look away from him back at the images.

'In answer to your question, Ms Abrams, that would have to be a straight no.'

'So why are you then?' I point to some of the frames in the contact sheets. 'I like these two here, and that one, this, this and this.' He follows my finger and hunches over them with the lens.

'It's one of life's little mysteries.' He twirls his chinagraph pencil round and round between his fingers, then bends over the contacts once more. 'Was that supposed to be a serious question?'

'No, I'm asking because I love to engage in polite small talk. I'm interested, you dope.'

'These two are fine, that one's not so hot, this is OK, and I agree – that one, that one and that one. Good.'

I like the way he looks when he is concentrating. When I first met him, my impression of him was that he was disorganized, dashing round permanently ten minutes late for everything, trying to fit too many things into too short a day, always running to catch up with himself, but when he's working – taking pictures, or selecting which frames to print up, or even just looking at something – an old lady resting on a bench, a toddler throwing bread to the birds in the park, he suddenly acquires this wonderful sort of stillness and all the rushing and the frenzy drops away and then it seems as if there is nothing but him and whatever he's doing.

He straightens up again, marks the images we've picked out.

'I'm single because I'm too old to pick women up in bars, too proud to tout myself in the lonely hearts columns, don't want to face the fact that my days of messing about in a series of cul-de-sac affairs are over, and too irresponsible to feel ready to settle down – only now I've got a child so I'm not exactly No. 1 on every wonderful, single woman's wish list when they're look-ing for the man of their dreams.'

'Oh, come on! Lots of women wouldn't be put off by your having a child.'

'No. But I'm not interested in lots of women.'

'And Cora's lovely,' I carry on. 'If anything, she's one of your chief selling points. Possibly your only one.'

'Oh, ha ha.'

'Yes. Thank heavens she takes after her mother.'

He smiles then his face becomes serious again. 'Don't you think she takes after me a bit?'

'Of course she does – look at those gorgeous big eyes, for a start! And the way she's always drawing in that little book you gave her – she's obviously artistic.'

'Her mother was too.'

'Well – perhaps it comes from both of you.'

'Yup. Maybe.'

'Anyway – I'm sure you won't be single for long. There are always tons and tons of gorgeous, bright, single women and hardly any decent single men – it's a known fact.'

'I don't want tons of women.' He looks at me directly. 'I just want one.'

'Well, there you are then. That shouldn't be too hard. If you're not looking for an entire collection, just the one – I mean – well – that's not difficult, is it?' I am babbling, I know, but cannot seem to stop. 'God, I've got some great women friends, Emma's lovely and not really all that neurotic – and Susie, she's very attractive and amusing – and look at Ellen, she's terrific – and you've even seen her in her underwear already, so you—'

'Georgia.'

'Yes.'

'I'm not interested in your women friends.'

'No.'

'And, much though I like Ellen, I think you can cross that off your "Things to Arrange" list too.'

'Right.'

'The other reason I'm single . . .'

I want to hear this and I don't want to hear this. I eye the door, as if I might make a run for it.

'. . . is that I've become rather attached to someone already and I'm trying not to think about her, but it's proving rather difficult.'

'Oh. Is she – OK-looking?'

'Well . . . so-so if you like that kind of thing.' He sighs. 'No. She's rather beautiful, I think – but I'm not sure she even knows it. Her skin's so soft that some-times I have to shove my hands down into my pockets to stop myself from touching her. And when I look into her eyes, I forget what I'm saying and end up sounding like an idiot.'

I try to swallow.

'Nothing new there then,' I say, but my heart's not in it.

'And she's bright but without shoving her intellect in your face – opinionated and passionate – strong and fierce but also sensitive – full of warmth – '

'Huh. She doesn't sound real to me.'

He laughs.

'She's very real. And she's tough too – tough on the people she loves, but no tougher than she is on herself. She knows what she likes and she doesn't want it any other way. She can be inflexible, judgemental, hard to please, even shrewish, pedantic.'

'Now she sounds like a bitch.'

'Not at all. But she's not perfect – and thank God for that, say I.'

'Weird person – why should you be thankful that someone isn't perfect? Isn't that what everyone wants?'

'No. Of course not. Imperfection is part of what makes us human.'

'That's just trying to turn cod philosophy into an excuse for not trying harder to be a better person.'

He sucks in his breath through his teeth.

'That's a bit severe. And I don't think it's true. Our flaws are what make us vulnerable.'

'Well, that's not good.'

'It is. Our vulnerability is part of what makes us lovable. Look how much you love Bonnie and Daniel – children are immensely vulnerable and we love them effortlessly, unconditionally. Think how you felt when Ellen was attacked – did you love her any less? Or did it remind you just how much you love her?'

I nod.

'So – this all-too-imperfect individual . . . ?'

'Yes. I'm trying to get her out of my system because, if I can't, then I'm in danger of gathering her into my arms and my bed and peeling off all her clothes, her silky shirt, her slinky black trousers and getting the pair of us extremely hot and sweaty and, given that she's engaged to marry another man, I don't think that would be at all – what would you say? Appropriate, I believe is the term. It wouldn't be appropriate. Or, in my book, seducing someone else's fiancée just wouldn't be right.'

I nod again.

'No. It wouldn't be.' I could barely speak.

'Which – right or appropriate?'

'Either.'

'No.'

I move towards the door.

'Well . . .'

'Georgia?'

'Yes.' I cannot look at him.

'I – I'm sorry if I – I shouldn't have said – but. Oh, shit. Still – it's not exactly as if it were much of a secret anyway.' He waves me away. 'Go on, get out of here before my principles run out on me.' He turns back to the photographs, holding them close as if he were indeed completely absorbed in them once more.

23

Under a green sky

Ellen's moved out at last. In the end, I found I kept rushing down to my office 'to look for something' but really only so I could just be alone in my own uncluttered space. Part of me wanted to hug and protect her twenty-four hours a day – she had to stop me tagging along if she even nipped out for cigarettes – and part of me wanted to shout at her the whole time because she *never* picks up after herself. It was like living with Bonnie or Daniel, only without the charm. I felt like a chambermaid. I know, I know – it's not her, it's me. Maybe I'll never be able to live with another human being; I should just get a canary or something. No – too noisy. A goldfish then. Ellen's easy-going, she gets on with everyone, so it must be me that's the problem. I've paid to have someone fit a spyhole in their flat door so that she can feel more secure and I bought her one of those shriek-alarms to carry. More usefully, Brian has signed her up for a beginners' class at his ju-jitsu club and insists on driving her home after her evening shift at work. I know he blames himself for having let her walk home alone that night.

On Saturday, Stephen and I spent most of the day peering in estate agents' windows at houses we can't afford. We weren't seriously *looking* looking of course, because we haven't put our flats on the market yet – we just wanted to get an idea of what we can't have so we can have the illusion that we're making some progress. I don't see the point until we're ready, but Stephen says it's vital to recce in advance because it'll save loads of time later and we won't waste our energies looking at houses in streets that are a no-no. He's blown up pages of the A-Z on the photocopier then he marks any possible streets with a yellow highlighter pen.

Brunch, bagels and bananas

On Sunday, Stephen went off to his parents and I went to brunch on my own. Then Leo and Cora turned up too – Dad's issued a standing invitation to them. Leo settled in as naturally as if he'd been coming every week for years, while Cora was as quiet as before, watching everything going on around her with saucer eyes as if she were at a pantomime.

Leo was trying to coax her to eat something, but she refused scrambled eggs, smoked salmon, even a plain bagel with a solemn shake of the head and a polite 'no, thank you'. Quinn, putting yet more pulses in bowls of water to soak, then said, 'How about a banana sandwich? Anyone?'

How revolting, I thought, but I noticed that Cora didn't immediately shake her head as she had done before.

'Will you help me make it, Cora?' Quinn smiled. 'I'm hopeless at doing sandwiches.'

Cora nodded and stood by the worktop.

Leo bent to pick her up.

'Let's make you big as a giant so you can see, hmm?'

'Sit up here.' Quinn patted the worktop.

Cora, I noticed, was watching Leo's face, checking it was all right with him.

'There you go,' he said. 'A front-row seat.'

'Do you like plain brown bread or raisin bread?'

Quinn held up the two loaves so Cora could see.

'No bits please.'

'No bits, OK. Now, the banana – some people like it cut this way . . .' Quinn laid the edge of her hand along the banana's length. 'And some people like it cut that way . . .'

Cora smiled and pointed.

'That way! That way!'

'And some people have just butter on the bread . . .' Quinn's voice had taken on the mesmerizing tone of a fairy tale. 'And some people have a little bit of honey . . .'

Cora smiled and nodded.

'Can I have honey?' She swung her legs. 'Please,' she added quickly. She really is almost spookily polite. Doesn't get that from her dad, that's for sure.

Leo sidled over to me.

'Quinn's great, isn't she?' he said quietly. 'I can never get Cora to eat anything other than apples and crisps – I never thought of banana sandwiches.'

'Yes, Quinn's very patient.'

'So are you.'

'No, I'm not – look how horrible I was when I had Ellen staying? Every single thing she did drove me up the wall. How on earth would I manage with a child? You need to be patient and attentive and tolerant all the time. I wouldn't be able to do it properly. And children create so much chaos – I'd go bonkers.'

'I don't think there's any such thing as doing it properly – I think you just do the best job you can. Anyway – you can't compare the two things. Living with Ellen isn't the same as looking after a child – not the same at all.'

'Ha! There speaks someone who's never had to live with Ellen.'

'I bet you'd find you could deal with it when it came to it – and you'd be bound to get more laid-back after a while – you can't be obsessively tidy when you've got kids. It's just not possible.'

'Fortunately, we'll never know, because I won't *have* to deal with it. You know it's not part of my master plan. Also – I am not obsessively tidy, just averagely tidy – you're as bad as my family, you think just because someone hangs up their jacket when they come in rather than throwing it over a chair, that means they're obsessional.'

'You're right. You're completely normal and average in every way. Happy now?'

'Yes. Chuck me a bagel, fat-face.'

'Still,' he said, peering at me through the hole of the bagel as if it were a monocle, 'for someone who claims not to be keen on kids, you seem to do all right with them. No chance of your coming to the park with us later, is there? Just to have a go on the swings and stuff.'

'Aren't you too old for swings?' I took the bagel, tore it in two and handed him half back again.

'Nope. Never too old for swings. However – definitely too heavy for swings. I will limit my fun to doing the pushing.'

'Won't Cora mind?'

'Mind what?'

'My tagging along. She might want you all to herself, you know. You should think about these things.'

'I could ask her.'

'Uh-huh – then she might feel she has to say OK to be polite.'

'Not if she takes after me, she won't.'

Cora had a go on the slide and the swings, but she couldn't do the see-saw properly because of course Leo and I were both way too heavy to sit on the other end without catapulting her right over the fence, and it's never the same when you just push the other end down by hand. Then I tried to show her some clapping games, from when I was a child, but I couldn't remember the words properly. It was funny, though, I hadn't done them for – what? – twenty-five years or so

– but, as soon as I started, all the hand movements came back to me perfectly. It was just the words that seemed to elude me.

Inevitably, it started to rain, so we ran back to the block and they both came up to my flat for tea and orange juice. It was getting on for half five by then and Leo had to take her back by seven.

'Are you hungry?' Leo asked her. 'You should have something to eat before we go.'

Cora nodded shyly.

'I haven't got much in, I'm afraid – I could do pasta though?'

'I wasn't expecting you to cook for us – I just thought I'd go and get a takeaway. What would you like, Cora? Hamburger and chips? Pizza?'

She nodded again.

Almost like a mummy

'So,' I said, once Leo had left to fetch the pizzas. 'What would you like to do?' I suddenly felt ridiculously nervous, as if I'd been left alone in charge of a grizzly bear or a sabre-toothed tiger rather than a small, shy five-year-old girl.

'Don't mind.'

If it were Bonnie, she'd have been wanting to trampoline on my bed, play Shops by taking every single thing out of my kitchen cupboards, or make a camp in the wardrobe and generally create as much havoc and mess as she possibly could.

'You could jump up and down on my bed if you like.'

'No, thank you.'

'Or we could . . . I've got paper if you want to draw?'

'OK.'

I couldn't find any felt-tip pens, so she had to make do with some old crayons that Bonnie and Daniel had left behind. She sat at the table, hunched over her drawing.

'Is he coming back?' she asked after a little while, without looking up.

'Who? Your daddy? Yes – of *course* he is.'

'OK.' She sorted through the crayons. 'There's no blue,' she said. 'For the sky.'

'Oh, I'm sorry.' I sat down at the table. 'I think that one must have got lost. Maybe you could pick another colour?'

'Sky's supposed to be blue.'

'Well – ye-e-e-e-s. But it isn't always – look, now, when it's rainy, it's more a sort of grey really. And, you know when the sun sets, then it goes all sorts of colours, doesn't it? Pink and red and orange, even purple.'

'Can it be green?'

'It can be any colour you want it to be – it's *your* picture. You could have a beautiful green sky – the colour of grass, the colour of an apple, or an emerald.'

'What's an emerald?'

'It's a kind of precious stone – a jewel – sparkly like a diamond, only a lovely deep green.'

'When is he coming back?'

I checked my watch and showed her.

'See – your daddy left twenty minutes ago, when the big hand was here. See – that's five, ten, fifteen, twenty minutes,' I pointed it out with my fingertip. 'So he'll be back any minute now.'

I got her another glass of juice. Checked my watch again. I know it's not as if we made an exact time, but how long does it take to fetch a couple of pizzas?

Five minutes ticked by. Another five. Cora finished her picture.

'Sometimes when people go away they don't come back,' she said.

'That's true. But mostly they do.' I sat down at the table, half-facing her. 'Your mummy went into the hospital and didn't come back home – is that right?'

She nodded.

301

'But I knew she wasn't coming back because she told me she was going to die. I had a kitten and it died and we put it in the ground in a shoebox and put flowers on it and I couldn't play with it anymore.'

She drew a girl on the ground beneath the green sky. Picked out a pink crayon to draw flowers around her, swapping it over carefully with the green one to draw the stalks.

'Even when we *know* that someone isn't coming back, we can still be sad.'

'I'm not sad. I'm drawing. Was that your mummy, who made the banana sandwich? The red-hair lady.'

'No. That's Quinn – she's my – she's married to my daddy, but . . . I haven't got a mummy. My mummy died – like yours – but it was a long, long time ago.'

'Did she die in the hospital?'

'No. She was at home.'

'Is the red-hair lady like a mummy?'

'Not really. Well. Sort of. Um. A bit.'

'She looks like a mummy.'

'Does she?'

Cora nodded. 'Only older.' She added a cat in the garden, next to the girl. 'Are you a mummy?'

'No. I – no, I'm not.' I stood up again. 'Not yet anyway.'

'I don't think he's coming back,' she said.

Waiting

School finishes at three forty-five. Georgia is supposed to collect Matt from his cloakroom and make sure he has his coat and bag, then they wait together inside the gates for Joy to pick them up. Ellen goes to a child-minder. Most of the mothers are already there before the children come spilling out, swarming like ants to honeycomb, clutching at their mothers' offerings – a tube of Smarties, a two-fingered Kit Kat, a packet of cheese-and-onion crisps. Joy, when she remembers, brings a handful of raisins – 'I couldn't find a bag' – still warm from her hand on the walk there; ahead of her time, she refuses to give them sweets other than as a rare treat: 'They'll rot your teeth, like acid on a copper plate.' She uses acid when she makes etchings, big trays of blue liquid, the colour of swimming pools, tempting, forbidden to touch.

Two minutes to four and Matt and Georgia stand alone. Mr Dawson comes out and asks if they want to wait inside.

Matt sits on a chair, swinging his legs.

'When is Mummy coming?'

'In a minute.' Georgia gets up and walks to and fro on her heels, then on tiptoes.

'*Why* isn't she here *now*?' Matt is near tears, Georgia can tell.

'Because she got held up. Maybe she'll bring us some chocolate.'

'Everyone else has gone.' Matt's voice takes on a tragic note. He has a knack, at present, for pointing out the obvious.

'No, they haven't. The teachers are still here, silly.'

On cue, Mr Dawson comes out of the office.

'Ah – Georgia, yes. Just spoken to your mother. She's been a little bit delayed, but she's on her way.'

'I need to do a wee,' says Matt.

Georgia looks up at Mr Dawson. Mr Dawson looks down at Georgia.

'You can take him, can't you? Use the Junior one here. I'll keep an eye out for your mother.'

'I can't go in the Boys.'

'Well, take him in the Girls then. There's no-one else around anyway.'

Matt stops dead outside the door.

'That's the Girls.'

'No-one'll see.'

Matt shakes his head.

Georgia pushes open the door marked Boys.

'Go on. Hurry up.'

Matt crosses to the bank of diminutive urinals, then

303

peers back at Georgia and heads instead for one of the cubicles. Georgia stands, arms folded like a teacher, then goes over to the urinals. She wrinkles her nose; it is miles smellier in here than in the Girls. Still, she'd like to be able to wee standing up. And much better for when you're outside and having to go behind a tree or a bush, crouching awkwardly with bracken scratching at your bum, trying not to wee all over your shoe or down your leg.

When they come out, their mother is there, standing talking to Mr Dawson. They are laughing, Joy's laugh echoing round the empty hallway.

'You're late,' says Georgia.

'I had to do a wee,' says Matt.

'I know. I'm sorry, folks. I had a really bad headache and then I fell asleep.'

Georgia looks up at her mother, unsmiling.

'I had to go in the *Boys* with Matt.'

'Can we have some chocolate?'

'Maybe.' Joy takes Matt's hand and reaches for Georgia's on her other side, but Georgia keeps her arms folded. 'Well, OK then.' She turns back to smile at Mr Dawson. 'Thanks so much for looking after the little horrors! I hope it didn't put you out too much!'

'Not at all, not at all!' Mr Dawson adjusts his tie and shifts from foot to foot. 'And I hope you're feeling better, Mrs Abrams.'

'I am. And it's Joy!' She calls over her shoulder. 'Joy!'

Rock solid

Rat-a-tat-tat – Leo's knock. At last.

'Where have you *been*?' I pull the inner door to behind me.

'I couldn't find anywhere to park.'

'Why didn't you walk?'

'I thought it would be faster – wrong again – still, no harm done – Cora's all right, isn't she?'

'Yes – but we were *worried* – you could have phoned or something.'

'I didn't think. Come on – it's no big deal. So it took a few minutes longer than normal . . .'

'You don't understand!' I try to keep my voice down to a hoarse whisper so that Cora won't hear. 'You can't just swan about taking as long as you like – she was getting very anxious, worrying whether you were coming back.'

He comes into the main room and starts admiring her drawing.

'I'm sorry I was longer than I said I would be.' He puts his arm round her. 'Let's put your drawing here so it doesn't get pizza on it, OK?'

She nods and I show her the bathroom so she can wash her hands.

Leo comes over to me as I'm getting out the plates and cutlery.

'I think she's OK. Maybe *you're* the one who was worrying?'

'Me! Why should *I* worry? Don't attempt to play counsellor to me, puh-lease – anything but that. I'm just saying you need to be rock-solid reliable – for *her*. It's no good being late all the time.'

'I am not late all the time. I took a bit longer than I thought. I never let people down. Ever. I'm a *reliable* person.'

'Well – start acting like it then!' I thrust the plates at him, then begin to set the table.

Time for bed . . .

'Hey,' says Leo, turning up again after he'd taken Cora back. 'Sorry about earlier. I know you were only thinking of Cora – you've been great with her.'

I shake my head.

'Not at all. I wish I was more relaxed with her – with Bonnie and Daniel, it's more about containment and crowd control than anything else and you know me –

nothing a dyed-in-the-wool control freak likes more than having to keep everyone else in order. But Cora's so different – like a little adult in some ways – she reminds me – anyway, thanks for the pizza.'

'No sweat. Um, you do get kind of freaked out by lateness, don't you?'

'Do I? I'm pretty punctual myself, but I'm used to Ellen's being late all the time – mostly, I just grin and bear it.'

That lopsided smile, the questioning eyebrow, knowing when I'm being truthful and when I'm kidding myself.

'No, you're right. I really hate it. I think it's rude and selfish and—'

' – you *worry*.'

'And I worry. And, yes, I know it's not rational and, yes, I know it's neurotic and worrying doesn't make the person come any sooner or anything else. But I can't help it.' I wave him in. 'You'll be glad to know I've done the washing-up.'

'I could make coffee?'

'Would you? I feel shattered. Can I have peppermint tea instead please?'

'You can have whatever you like.' He starts getting out mugs and filling the kettle.

'Good. In that case, can I also have a Georgian house with huge windows and proper fireplaces and an enormous garden and off-street parking?'

He pats his pockets.

'Nothing like that on me, I'm afraid.'

'I was looking at estate agents yesterday – everything's so expensive.'

'*I?*'

I shrug.

'*We*. Of course.'

His back is to me as he delves into the box of tea bags.

'When are you planning to move?'

'Oh – whenever – however long it takes. No rush

really. Still – don't suppose I can put it off for ever.' I laugh feebly, as if I have made some kind of joke.

He doesn't reply, just passes me the tea in silence.

'Would you mind watching telly?' I ask him. 'I quite fancy a spot of rubbish – I feel wiped out today, don't know why.'

'Me too. Shall I turn the TV round a bit?'

'Actually, I normally pull down the bed and watch from there . . .'

'Do you now?' He tilts his head and gives me that look.

'Oh, behave – it's just more comfortable. It wasn't a subtle attempt to seduce you.'

'Thank God for that.' He grabs the cupboard knob and pulls down the bed. 'If you do ever decide to seduce me, by the way . . .' he sits down and starts taking off his shoes, '. . . don't be too subtle – I might not get it.'

'Fine.' I hurl over some extra cushions from the sofa at him. 'I'll hold up a huge placard.'

'Good plan. Have you got anything to nibble?' That smile again. '*Food* would do.'

'Help yourself. There's some good cheese and stuff.'

He gets up and starts poking about in the fridge while I sort out plates and a tray.

We sit side by side, propped up against the pillows, channel-hopping.

'This is nice,' he says, cutting up an apple and passing me a chunk. 'Do you think we'll still be doing this in forty years' time?'

Forty years. I attempt to gauge his expression without turning round to face him. He's teasing, of course he is. He must be.

'Surely I'll have found somewhere else to move to before that?'

'This really *is* rubbish, isn't it?' Leo changes channels

for the fortieth time. 'And not in a good way. Can't we play a game instead?'

'Such as . . . ?' I fold my hands neatly in my lap. 'I've only got cards and Scrabble, I think.'

He slides further down the bed, and turns on his side facing me.

'Too tired for Scrabble – you'd wipe the floor with me.' He yawns. 'Sorry.'

'That's OK. We really ought to go to bed soon,' I point out. 'School day tomorrow – I've got a client at nine.'

'We're *in* bed already. Well – on it.'

'To sleep,' I add.

'Of course to sleep.' He looks into my eyes, then slowly traces his fingertip across the back of my hand, making me shiver. 'What else?'

24

Wake-up call

In my dream a phone is ringing. It's all right, I say in
my dream and in my head, it's only the telephone,
someone else will get it. I roll over and snuggle up
closer to the nice, warm body next to me, curl my arm
over it, mmm, lovely soft material. Phone still ringing
then, close by, a clunking as a hand – mine? No –
scrabbles to pick it up, then a deep, sleepy voice says,

'Urgh? *Wha*—? Oh, *shit*.' Suddenly, said body is
sitting up right next to me.

'Ssh-ssshh . . .' I say. 'Lie down.'

'Georgia!' A hand shaking me. '*Georgia*,' Leo
whispers loudly, then, 'er, yes – she is actually – she's
right here, but—'

'It's Stephen.' He covers the mouthpiece for a
moment to whisper, 'I'm sorry – I forgot where I was –
I just grabbed it.'

Oh fuck. Fuck, fuck, fuck.

I swallow and sit up, suddenly one hundred per cent
wide awake.

'Oh, hi, Stephen – I—' Click.

Stephen has never, ever hung up on me before. Ellen
does it frequently and if I tell him he always says he
thinks it's incredibly childish.

'Oh, shit.' I look at Leo.

'I'm *so* sorry,' Leo says again. 'I didn't realize where I was. I'm an idiot.'

'Yes, you are, but it's done now. Still, at least nothing actually *happened*. We just fell asleep – it couldn't have been more innocent, really – ' I ignore the expression on his face. 'We're both still dresssed . . .'

'True – there was no getting naked, I'd remember that – and no fondling, not even any snogging . . .' He is smiling. 'What a terrible, terrible waste.'

'Oh, stop! Don't you dare smile! This is very, very serious. Poor Stephen, how he must feel – look what I've put him through.'

'But he trusts you, surely? As you say, nothing *happened*.' He shakes his head. 'I can't believe I fell asleep.'

I cover my face with my hands.

'What can I possibly tell him?'

He gets off the bed.

'The truth?'

'Don't be ridiculous. Help me strip the bed? The pillows will smell of you.'

'Cheers, Georgia – you really know how to make a man feel wanted.'

'Sorry, but come on. Think of something. Be helpful.' I grab the end of the duvet and start yanking open the poppers.

'Shall I do the pillows then?'

'Not that kind of helpful! But – yes! Don't stop.'

'Yes, ma'am! Now . . . why don't you tell him that I'd just popped round this morning?'

'But you sounded all groggy and sleepy and, anyway, why would you be answering my phone?'

'Because you were in the shower?'

'Oh, marvellous idea – Stephen, Leo was only answering my phone because I was lathering my naked body just a few feet away.'

'Perish the thought. Carry on, don't let me stop you. OK – I know – I answered it because you were dealing with a distraught client on your mobile?'

'I never give them the mobile number, he knows that.'

'I answered it as a joke?'

'Ha ha, ha ha.'

'Well – *you* think of something, smart-arse.'

I hurl the scrunched-up duvet cover onto the floor and stomp over to the hall closet for a clean one. A pile of stuff falls out onto the floor.

'Well, well, well . . .' Leo has come up behind me. 'So your cupboard's not exactly a model of order either – your dark secret is out at last.' I desperately try to stuff everything back again, but it's bursting at the seams. 'God, it's *worse* than mine! Unbelievable!'

'No, it is *not*!' I drag him away. 'Here, grab a corner and make yourself useful. Why don't I explain what happened calmly?'

'I suggested that already.'

'Yes, but a slightly *edited* version: we were talking about something to do with your work—'

'Until gone two in the morning . . .'

'Until *quite* late. And I'd had a very *tiring* day—'

'And we were both so relaxed lying on the bed . . .'

'*I* was on the sofa and *Leo* was on the bed right across on the other side of the room, *miles and miles away*—'

'We'd folded the bed down because we wanted to get more comfortable . . .'

'I'd only opened up the bed because the mechanism was acting up and Leo thought he might be able to fix it—'

'Apparently, he's rather good with his hands . . .'

'But he was being *so boring* that I couldn't stay awake a moment longer and I passed out on the sofa—'

'I begged him to have sex with me, but he said it wouldn't be fair on you . . .'

'Will you be sensible! This is *not* helping!'

We hold up the duvet to shake it out, but it's completely twisted inside, with the corners in the wrong bits.

'What am I going to *do-oo*?' I wail.

He digs his hands deep into the duvet and starts wrestling it into place, like a vet delivering a tricky calf.

'Tell him the truth – tell him that you wanted to make mad, passionate love with me but that you didn't because you're a decent person and you wouldn't be unfaithful to him so we spent an entirely chaste night together – unfortunately.'

'And you think that'll do the trick?'

He shrugs.

'There's a time and a place for complete honesty, Leo, and frankly I don't think this is it.' I slump back down onto the bed.

'Ah-ha!'

'Ah-ha what? Have you thought of a sensible excuse?'

'No, but look at what you said, Dr Freud – complete honesty – so you *do* want to have sex with me?'

I hit him with a pillow.

'No, I don't. Not even remotely. You're insufferable, deeply irritating and unjustifiably arrogant – but I don't have time to argue with you when I need to come up with something credible for Stephen.'

I look at the clock – 8.57 a.m.

'Oh, God! I've got a client at nine! I have to go!'

Vole agrees igloo

I ran downstairs, raking my fingers through my hair, and licking my finger to rub away any mascara smudges under my eyes. With any luck she'd be late and I could have a couple of minutes to tidy myself up a bit. I turned into the corridor. She was there, outside my door. Terrific. This was a woman with lateness issues – you would think she might just manage to act true to form and be late the one time I needed her to be, wouldn't you? Bugger it. That meant everything I said to her last time actually sank in. I checked my watch: bang on nine. I slowed my steps to a dignified pace,

312

calmly said hello and let her in. Her gaze flicked over my face – perhaps I hadn't quite erased all the mascara, so what? I took my seat sedately, though my heart was thudding away, and she sat down. I was desperate for a pee, but I crossed my legs – only fifty minutes to get through – and attempted to concentrate.

As soon as she left, I dashed to the loo, only just made it. I so nearly wet myself. Checked my face in the mirror. Oh. I see. That explains the look. My hair was flat on one side and kinked and frizzy on the other. Mascara and eyeliner smudged not just under my eyes but also at the sides and onto my cheeks. Worst of all, right in the middle of my forehead, there was a small G in blue pen where Leo had attempted to write my name until I grabbed his arm and stopped him and – ah, I remembered, I'd only managed to divert him to my arms. Yes – my upper arms: three games of noughts and crosses on the left one, some silly anagram on the right – VOLE AGREES IGLOO – I must get all this stuff *off*.

I had to scrub at the blue G to get rid of it and, even then, the pale ghost of it remained. I was desperate for a shower but, no, better ring Stephen first. I tried his direct line at work but it went straight through to his voicemail.

'Stephen. It's me. It really isn't what you think. Honestly. Please, please call me as soon as you get this.'

Then I rang the switchboard and spoke to the receptionist, who told me Stephen wouldn't be in all day, had called to say he was going straight to a meeting. So I rang to leave a message on his machine at home.

'Hi, Stephen. I tried to get you at work but you're . . . not there, er, you know that, of course. Anyway – look, I'm really, really sorry about this morning. It *so* isn't what you imagine.' An inspired thought suddenly popped into my head. 'Leo was just messing about – he happened to drop by this morning early to borrow a book I'd mentioned and I was looking for it when the phone rang and he grabbed it as a joke and pretended to sound groggy as if – well – he said he thought it would be Ellen and it would be a laugh – he was just being silly – honestly. Look, call him yourself if you want to check, here's his number . . .'

OK, I realize now that it did sound just a tad far-fetched but it was exactly the kind of thing Leo *would* do. Stephen had already made it all too blindingly obvious that he considered Leo to be an utter twat, so he shouldn't be too astonished, ha ha, just silly old Leo being daft. I really didn't think that he'd buy the 'we just fell asleep and it was all perfectly innocent' story. I mean, it was innocent, of course, and it's not a story, but it doesn't *sound* good, does it? This way, he might believe me or even just pretend to believe me but it would leave his pride intact – and that counts for an awful lot with Stephen.

I must warn Leo that Stephen might phone him. I was pretty sure he wouldn't, but just in case, better get our stories consistent, right? Pulled on a cardigan in case my arms got any funny looks in the corridor and ran downstairs, even jumped the last three, feeling inexplicably happy – I really thought I'd got the problem sorted. Banged on Leo's door.

'Corridor patrol! Anybody up?'

Leo opened the door.

'Hi!' His voice sounded strained, as if he had a pistol dug into his back and was 'acting normal'. He mouthed something unintelligible at me. I mouthed back, 'What?'

'*Stephen*,' he whispered, then, much louder, 'Great, you're here. Stephen's here.'

'Oh. Great!'

'Hi!' I tried to smile and look relaxed.

'Hi.' Stephen smiled back. 'Oh, darling.' He came across and hugged me. 'Leo's explained what happened. I'm sorry I hung up on you, but I—' A glance at

Leo. 'Well, let's go for a coffee, eh?' He took my hand and led me to the door.

'Er, yes! Fine! Lovely, let's do that.'

I looked back at Leo, trying to communicate a thousand questions with a single glance. He made a discreet thumbs-up sign and mouthed 'OK' at me. Not helpful.

A spoonful of sugar

'Two cappuccinos, please,' Stephen ordered. I was in dire need of a cup of tea actually, but I didn't think now was the time to be highlighting our differences. Besides, nothing delights Stephen more than when I utter those three little words in a restaurant: 'Same for me.'

'Lovely,' I murmured.

What the fuck had Leo said? Presumably not the truth, oh no, that wouldn't be interesting enough for him; he probably said we were just rehearsing a play and he'd picked up the phone as a prop – that's what people are always saying in bad sitcoms, that they were acting out a scene to cover up for some adulterous clinch, and it's never remotely credible. Or that I'd abducted him against his will and he'd grabbed the phone to call for help – I wouldn't put it past him. Or that I'd had some trouble with the phone and he was only trying to test it.

I sprinkled some brown sugar across the foam, watched it slowly sink in. I'd just have to be vague until I could work out what Leo had said.

Stephen reached across the table and took my hand.

'Why didn't you just *say*, you silly-billy?'

He waggled my hand about as if it were a floppy toy. I shrugged.

'Oh, well, you know . . . Anyway, you hung up before I could—'

'I know. Not like me. I thought for a minute – crazy, I know – you wouldn't do that.'

'No,' I shook my head. 'I wouldn't.'

Just thinking about it doesn't count, right?

Stephen tore open a sachet of sugar and measured it carefully into his spoon. He always does that, every single time. It doesn't make sense. Those packets contain a teaspoon of sugar – no matter which café or restaurant you go to, they're always the same. But, every single time he orders coffee, he goes through his routine: carefully tears off one corner of the sachet at an angle then slowly trickles the sugar into his teaspoon before tipping the spoon into the coffee. Sometimes I just want to snatch it from him, rip the top off and dump it in his cup – 'Look, it's been bloody measured for you already so you don't have to do it – cut out the middle man, why don't you, and just drink the sodding coffee!'

' . . . yes, quite an upheaval, with a kid and everything.'

Upheaval? With a *kid*? Something to do with Cora? How the hell could Leo have roped Cora into it? Why couldn't he just keep things simple? Isn't that what people say – that when you lie you should stick to the truth as closely as possible – it's easier to remember for a start.

Oh, shit! – the message! I left that message on Stephen's answerphone about it all being a joke with not a mention of an upheaval or Cora. OK, just keep calm . . . calm . . . calm. I clutched the handle of my coffee cup so hard I thought it might snap off. It's fine, completely fine. I know the remote code for Stephen's machine – I can delete it as soon as I get home. Calm, calm . . . completely calm.

'So, do you know when he's off exactly?' Stephen was still stirring his coffee, round and round – God, it must be mixed in by now. 'He just said imminently.'

'What? Um, I'm not sure. Quite soon, I think.' I took a sip of my coffee, starting to relax a bit, even enjoy it in a weird sort of way. 'Obviously, there'll be a lot of packing to do.'

Shit. Is Leo really leaving? He could hardly have lied about that – or he'd have to hide in his flat every time Stephen came over.

'Quite. And he'll have to sort out his plumbing problem before he goes.'

Plumbing problem? One minute he's talking about Leo dashing off somewhere with Cora, now he's talking about plumbing. And, when he says plumbing problem, does he *mean* plumbing problem? With Stephen's tendency to be euphemistic, he might mean Leo's having trouble peeing or something. I wish he'd be a bit clearer.

'Oh, I'm sure he will.'

'But there's no need for you to worry on that score at least, thank God.' Given how calm he was being, I figured he wasn't worrying about my having contracted VD from Leo during the night.

'No. No need to worry at all.'

I wish I had at least some idea of what was going on.

Stephen started doing up his jacket, he ought to be getting on, he said, had a client to see, but wasn't it naughty skiving off like this? Quite fun really. I don't think Stephen's ever bunked off in his entire life, not at school, not even at college. Even I skipped the occasional lecture.

He stood up.

I must, must, must talk to Leo.

A simple explanation

'OK,' I say, 'what the hell did you tell him?'

'Keep calm – you'll like this. I take it you managed not to blow it by saying the wrong thing?'

'I hardly said a word. Unfortunately, because I am nearly as much of an idiot as you are, I left a message on his machine saying you'd just been messing around, pretending to sound sleepy, and thought it might be Ellen on the phone – you know, that you'd done it as a wind-up? God, I must remember to delete it before he hears it.'

'Why did you say that?'

'Because I couldn't see Stephen going for the "we lay side by side all night like little lambs and didn't get up to anything" story.'

'But he *did*. He was fine.'

'You told him the truth?' I stand there, hands on hips. 'And he was fine with it? No. Not possible.'

'The plain truth,' he nods. 'But with a bit of garnish on the side . . .'

'Let's have it.'

Leo throws himself onto his sofa, then budges up to make room for me.

'I told him that I'd stayed the night at your place—'

'Because you'd missed the last train – to the floor below?'

'No, I don't think he'd have bought that, strangely enough.' Leo grins. 'I said it seemed as if my boiler was leaching noxious carbon monoxide and it was too dangerous to sleep there in case I was asphyxiated during the night . . .'

'Chance'd be a fine thing.'

'Shut up. You'd miss me if I was gone.'

'Only because you're such a rich and endless source of irritation – hang on a second, you don't have a boiler, do you? Isn't your heating and hot water on the communal system, like mine?'

'Yes, of course it is. But Stephen doesn't know that.'

'But he was right in your flat! He could have seen your, your . . .'

'Boilerless void? Yes. Fortunately, he's obviously no DIY expert or he might have asked to take a look at it.'

'But he must have thought it odd that you have one when I don't? That must have made him suspicious?'

'Georgia, I don't know. Maybe Stephen lies awake at

318

night contemplating other people's plumbing systems or maybe, like most men, he spends his idle moments thinking about sex, worrying about work, or wondering whether God is balding too or not looking not bad for his age . . .' He runs his figners through what's left of his hair. '*Anyway*, I thought he'd be a lot less uptight if I said I'd had Cora staying too – we're hardly going to be tearing each other's clothes off with her in the room – so, if he asks, you gave Cora and me the bed and you took the couch.'

'But what was all this stuff about an upheaval and your going off somewhere?'

'Ah, yes – well, after I'd told Stephen the stuff about the boiler, he was still acting kind of twitchy about the whole thing. He went over to the board there and started looking my prints up and down as if he didn't think much of them, then he said, "So, do you manage to earn a reasonable living by taking snapshots?" Fucking rude really. But I clicked what was bugging him – he needed to believe that I'm just some hopeless failure who's no threat to your domestic bliss. So I said I was short of work but going to Canada for a few months with Cora to do a job. I mean, you're hardly going to trail half way round the world with an un-successful photographer who barely earns a crust, are you?'

'Why wouldn't I? Is that how you see me? That I'd only love a man if he were rich and successful?'

'No – not at all. I thought *Stephen* might see it that way. Sure – from the outside you look all neat and tidy and sort of aloof – like you'd never deign to eat in a greasy caff and if you did you'd probably send the cutlery back—'

'I wouldn't!'

'Hello? Pay attention. I said you *looked* like that kind of person – not that you *are*. Not at all. God, if you could just let go of some of your hang-ups, your picture-straightening and your leaf-wiping, your "No, not that way, this way", your "Oh, no – just one glass for me, I mustn't overdo it," probably "No – just the one orgasm for me, thank you" – it wouldn't surprise me – if you could just *relax* for more than five minutes – long enough to accidentally enjoy yourself – you'd realize how amazing and extraordinary life can be when you don't keep trying to pin everything down the whole time – and you'd love a man for who he was. If you'd only tell your brain to shut the fuck up for two seconds and pay attention to your guts and your heart and—'

'Excuse me while I pick my jaw up off the ground.' I leap to my feet in anger. 'Who the *fuck* do you think you are? How *dare* you decide what sort of person I am or what I like or how many – how many orgasms I have? Why let the fact that you've known me all of five minutes stop you? Clearly, you're an expert on the subject of Georgia Abrams. I suppose you think I'm like some librarian in an old movie – that if I only let my hair down, you can say, "Gosh, you're beautiful after all" and I'll fall at your feet in gratitude? Well, dream on, buster. I'm extremely happy with the way I am, thank you, and I have many, many orgasms – often *several* at once.'

'Hey, hey! Calm down.' He stands up and lays a hand on my arm but I jerk away from him. 'I'm sorry – I didn't mean to patronize you. Shit. Why do I always say the wrong thing? Please don't go off in a huff. You might not see me for ages.'

'What's that supposed to mean?'

'What I said before – I'm thinking of going to Canada.'

'But wasn't that just made up to appease Stephen?'

'Not entirely. Why – would you miss me?'

'Not in the least. You're not really going?'

'I don't know. I really have been offered this major job. You remember that publisher I went to see a couple of weeks ago?'

'Yes, the guy you said was a complete wanker.'

He sighs.

'That's the one. Anyway, he's a complete wanker with a chequebook, so I'm beginning to see his more positive qualities. They're doing this new travel guide, covering the whole of Canada, and they're using some agency shots, but they need a load of new stuff too. The money's not bad, but it'll take three, four months at least, maybe more.'

'Three or four *months*?'

'Yup.'

'Congratulations,' I said flatly. 'It sounds great. But what about Cora? You can't take her out of school all that time, can you?'

He frowns, puzzled.

'Of course not. I couldn't *possibly* take her with me. I'll be working.'

I stand there, mouth half-open but silent, like a photograph. Who is this stranger in front of me? How could I have thought I even *knew* him?

He shrugs, watching my face. 'She's managed OK without me in her life so far . . .'

'That was before she'd even *met* you.'

'It's no big deal – it's only a few months. She's got her aunt, she's settling in at school—'

'You can't abandon her *now*! Not now you're a part of her life!'

'I'm not *abandoning* her. Don't try and pull a guilt trip on me.'

'Children need a rock-solid grown-up in their lives, someone who won't keep letting them down.'

'I *don't* let *anyone* down – you said that before and it's complete crap. What the hell do you know about it anyway? Is that some piece of counselling-by-numbers you picked up from a book? And *you* don't even *want* children, so excuse me if I don't come rushing to you for advice on how to be the *perfect* bloody parent, OK?'

'Don't tell me what I do or don't want! Fine – go on then – fuck off to Canada with your cameras! I hope you're very happy together. You're right – Cora will be a lot, lot better off without you waltzing in and out of her life as the mood takes you – ' I fling open the flat door so it bangs back against the wall, turn to face him once more. 'You can be her daddy by postcard. That should suit you down to the ground.'

25

The truth is out there

By the time I unlocked the door to my own flat my whole body was shaking and my arms were covered in goosebumps. I yanked off my cardigan and hurled it across the room onto the sofa. Looked at my arms again. I'd have to scrub them red raw to get all the stupid pen off. I can't suddenly start wearing a long-sleeved nightie out of the blue – Stephen may have gone for Leo's broken boiler saga but I think his suspicions might just be a teensy bit aroused by my suddenly refusing to bare my arms in front of him. Terrific. Bloody Leo. He's happy to be all flirty-flirty and amusing and isn't-this-fun-drawing-on-Georgia, but come the next day, look who's stuck with arms covered in pen. Canada's welcome to him. It makes no difference to me whether he goes or stays. I shut my eyes, recalling the feel of his fingers as he held my arm, drawing the grid for noughts and crosses . . .

'Love and kisses,' he said. 'That's what we call it in my family. Let's play love and kisses.'

'I can see the crosses could be kisses, but why do noughts represent love? Isn't that a bit sad?'

'Nope. It's from tennis – thirty – love. Love is nothing, see?'

I'd nodded, adopted a serious face.

'I suppose so, yes, love is nothing to most men.'

'Oh, shut up. That's so untrue. Come closer and say that.' His smile. His mouth, close to my face, too close. The feel of the pen on my arm, my nerve endings tingling.

'I know you want to seduce me, but in all honesty I think I'm too knackered.' He flopped back on the pillow.

'You shouldn't say things like that,' I rebuked him. 'What about Stephen?'

'What *about* Stephen? Does he want to seduce me too?'

I shoved him.

'*No-one* wants to seduce you, big-head.' I stretched out to get a bit more comfortable.

And then we'd had three rounds of love and kisses – noughts and crosses – all draws, inevitably, and had fallen asleep. I hadn't even been awake enough to put the pen top back on and some of the ink had marked the duvet cover. So unlike me.

I must concentrate. Time was ticking on. I must delete that message from Stephen's machine, and I must leap into the shower. I reached for the phone, but just then it rang. It was Stephen.

'Stephen – hi. I was just thinking about you.'

'Nice thoughts, I hope?'

'Naturally.' Well, not un-nice thoughts at least.

'Darling – do you mind if we take a rain check for tonight? My last meeting's been rescheduled for six tonight and I could be hours . . .'

'Of course not. That's fine.' God, what a relief – a bit more time for the pen marks to fade.

'See you tomorrow then? Come round and we'll have a quiet night in.'

Right. Please, no more distractions for the next two minutes, then I could wipe the message and dive into the shower.

I dialled Stephen's home number. It was engaged. Oh-oh. Someone else must be calling him. Maybe they'd hang up without leaving a message – lots of people hate answerphones. Or it could be something completely insignificant, something I could erase without a second thought. I stood by the phone, humming a tune in a carefree fashion, da-dee-da-dee-dee-dah, I'm perfectly relaxed. Calm and relaxed. Practised my deep breathing. Calm – calm. Hit the redial button. Beep-beep-beep. Still fucking engaged. Come on, come on, how long does it take to leave a message, for God's sake? It must be his mum, rabbiting on as usual, she's always doing it, uses up almost the entire tape. Even Stephen rolls his eyes and makes little wind-up, come-on, come-on motions with his hand when he listens to one of Trish's epic accounts – 101 Not Very Funny or Interesting Things that Happened to Me, Mrs Winstanley and Several People You've Never Met Before in the Twenty-four Hours Since I Last Phoned You.

Redial. Dring-dring. At last.

Stephen's outgoing message, then that annoying sing-song tune. I pressed the code number and the creepy electronic or digitized voice or whatever it is came on: 'You have *three* messages.'

The first one was mine. It sounded ridiculous, now I was listening to it as if it were a message left by someone else. I am such a bad liar. Then – surprise, surprise – there was indeed a message from his mother, telling him the astonishing news that she was planning a nice shepherd's pie for this evening and that her hairdresser had had a very nice holiday in Portugal and that she'd picked up a nice short-sleeved shirt for Dad, well two actually, it was a two-pack, special offer, and she'd seen some very pretty ready-made curtains for the downstairs cloakroom, floral, in an apricot and cream colourway, with ever such lovely tiebacks. I don't know why she bothered to tell him, I'm sure he could have found out all about it on *Newsnight* . . .

Then a third voice came on.

'Hi, Steve – it's me . . . um, Denise – obviously – ' This surprisingly familiar introduction was followed by a girlish giggle. 'I didn't want to leave a message on your voicemail at work for obvious reasons. Last night was . . . aah, really super! It really was. Super. Thank you. I'm feeling really, really excited about it. I know there are some obstacles, so I won't hassle you, but call me, OK? Byeee!'

I pressed the delete code, stabbing at the button with rather more force than was strictly required.

Steve? Aside from Ellen, and Stephen's squash partner Jason who thinks he's a bit of a wag, no-one, but no-one, calls Stephen anything other than Stephen. And – *me*? Who the hell is *me*? I'm *me*! I mean, the only *me* in his life is me. Denise? Who do we know called Denise? And just what are these obstacles, I'd like to know? Me again, I suppose. What am I doing? Here I am running round in circles, footling about with his answerphone and trying to cover my tracks as if I'm some kind of desperate criminal when all I've done is spend a completely innocent few hours *asleep* in the company of another man, a man who means absolutely fuck all to me at that, while Stephen's getting sneaky, secret messages from a giggly 'me' who has no right to call herself 'me'. I wish I had bloody gone ahead and slept with Leo – not that I wanted to – just to even things up a bit. But no, why relax and enjoy myself like a normal person when I could mess things up completely instead? Another impressive piece of wisdom from your local relationships expert.

'Stephen – I've got a bit of a confession to make,' I said at supper the following night.

'Nothing serious, I hope?'

I shook my head.

'Of course not. It's silly really, but I left this message on your machine, then I – I – rang up and used your code to delete it. Only you had a couple of other messages, too.'

'And you erased those, did you? I see.' He wiped his mouth firmly with his napkin. 'And what were the messages you decided I didn't need to hear?'

'One was only from your mum.' I poked at my pasta with my fork, pointlessly moving it around the dish. 'And the other was from some woman – Denise? Thanking you for dinner. Perhaps *you* have a confession to make too?' I sat back and looked him in the eye, then smiled to show that I can take these things in my stride, no need to get everything all out of proportion.

'Fortunately, I called Mum in any case so the one *only* from her was taken care of, though I think you certainly might have told me before. As for Denise, I believe I mentioned her to you – she's a PA in another department, but I want her to come and work for me. I took her out so we could talk away from the office – otherwise I could be accused of trying to poach her. Which is also why, incidentally, I gave her my home number, so she could call me and let me know if she's going to apply via the official channels.'

'Oh.'

'Quite. Is that the sum total of your confession? Or is there something else I should know about? Why were you so desperate to wipe your own message in any case?'

I felt as if I were about five years old, being told off by teacher: 'Did you take the red pen from my desk?'

'I wasn't *desperate*, I just . . . Look, you know when Leo stayed in my flat the night before last?'

'Oh, *Leo*. What a surprise that he's mixed up in all this.'

'He's not "mixed up" in anything. You make it sound like we're planning an armed robbery.'

'Huh. Well, you've certainly changed since knowing him.'

Yes, I thought. I have.

'Have I?'

'Yes.' He nodded and put his knife and fork together neatly. 'And not for the better, if you want my opinion.'

'Honestly, Stephen – you sound like some pompous Victorian patriarch! I'm the same person I always was.'

He said nothing.

'I'm sorry. I didn't mean to be rude.' I can't even open my mouth any more without upsetting everyone.

'Apology accepted.'

'It was only – my message – Leo ended up staying because we were talking and we were tired and we both fell asleep. That's it. End of story. We were both fully dressed and absolutely nothing happened, I promise.'

He remained silent.

'But I didn't think you'd believe me and I felt you were biased against Leo – I know you don't like him.'

Stephen gave a dismissive snort.

'I thought you'd be suspicious even though there was no reason to be.'

'And why shouldn't I believe you if you were telling the truth? Do you think I'm an unfair person?'

'No. Course not.' I slumped in my chair, suddenly feeling helpless and tired. Perhaps he would tell me it was all over and I could just walk out the door. I imagined myself sitting in a taxi, chatting away merrily to the driver, a carefree woman going home after an evening out.

'No. Quite. So why concoct that ridiculous lie? Yes, I did hear it, of course I did. I check my messages regularly. I picked them up not long after I'd left you at the café, on the way to my meeting. I only left it on the machine because I was planning to watch your face as I played it back in front of you so you could hear how crazy it sounded. And as for that absurd shaggy-dog story about his boiler . . . After I'd heard your message, I should have gone straight back there and – and jolly well sorted him out. I won't be made a fool of, Georgia. Now – just what exactly is going on with you and this – this clown?'

'Nothing. Absolutely nothing.'

'And you swear you've never – nothing's ever happened between you?'

A kiss. Who would count a single kiss? Just one kiss, relived in my head a thousand times. It seemed as if it belonged to another lifetime or as if it was a scene I'd once seen in a film. Now, we were no more than strangers. If we saw each other by chance in the street, would we even nod politely, or would we turn away, pretending to be fascinated by the contents of some shop window, or rushing past to some imaginary appointment?

My throat felt tight and full, as if I had flu. I shook my head in silence. 'By that I mean, in case there should be any doubt, that he's never touched you inappropriately, or kissed you other than in a purely platonic way on the cheek?' Stephen's wasted in management consultancy. He should be a lawyer or a judge. I thought maybe I should just plead guilty and let myself be carted off to the cells.

'He – I – we had one kiss. Once. Ages ago.'

'And that was it?'

I nodded.

He sighed heavily, theatrically. Now he would reach for the black cap, pronounce my sentence. It's all over. No mercy, no appeal. It would almost be a relief.

'And are you planning a repeat performance?'

'*No*. Of course not. It was nothing – a stupid mistake.' I looked into his eyes. 'I *am* sorry, Stephen. I wouldn't deliberately hurt you – I – I – he doesn't *mean* anything to me, it's nothing like that.'

I waited.

'Well . . . if that's really true . . .'

'It *is*.'

'Good. Promise me you'll never see him again then.'

What?

'That's ridiculous! You're treating me like a child – telling me what to do!'

'I'm *not*, darling.' He shook his head. 'I'm *asking* you, that's all. You do see I must be able to *trust* you, don't you?'

I nodded.

'You *can* trust me. This is all so unnecessary – he's moving out soon *and* he's flitting off to Canada, we won't be – it won't be a problem.'

'Well, I can't say I'll be weeping at the airport. It won't be soon enough for me.'

'Oh, don't go *on*, Stephen – I don't care about bloody Leo, I told you. Left to myself, I'd happily never see him again anyway.'

'Good – well, that's all sorted then. If you're happy not to see him anyway, I really can't see what the problem is. We both want the same thing, don't we, sweetie?'

'But I – ' What was the point? It didn't matter any more. Stephen was right, it would be better this way. Easier. Stephen's always right. 'Fine. Whatever. I said I won't see him, OK? Can we just . . .'

'Move on to the next square? Certainly. We've had our plans on the back burner for far too long. Let's crack on with selling our flats. You can move in with me in the meantime. Rent a consulting suite if you need to.'

'I—'

'Or not? If you don't want to be with me, Georgia, just say so. I'll get along perfectly well without you, you know. Otherwise, let's for Christ's sake just get married and get on with our lives.'

He folded his arms, waiting.

'Of *course* I want to be with you. It's just – my flat –

my office – everything – all at once. And it's almost Christmas – there's already so much to organize – I've had so much on, I've hardly even bought any presents yet and that's so unlike me – and . . . everything.'

'Well, it's not as if it's a surprise, is it, darling?' His voice softened. 'We have been planning this for a long time. Just move your bits and bobs in for now, then we can organize a van early in the New Year to bring the rest of your things. If Christmas is a problem, we can go shopping on Saturday, first thing, eh? You can help me choose something for Mum and Dad – from both of us.'

'Yes, of course.'

He raised his glass and motioned for me to do the same.

'To us then?'

I smiled and our glasses clinked, though I wasn't even aware that I had picked mine up.

'To us.'

26

Leo's friend

This morning there was a brief ring on my doorbell.

'Excuse me, dear?'

'Oh Mrs Patterson? Hello.'

She looked slightly taken aback that I knew her name, as if I might be a spy or had access to some secret file on her, although she's lived on the same floor as my office for decades. When I first moved in, I sometimes used to get some shopping for her then she'd always want to have me in for a cup of tea and a chat when I dropped it off. It was sweet of her and I did go in a few times, but then it was clear she expected it. After a long day, I want to be able to slam, sorry, shut my door on the outside world unless I choose to venture out there. Anyway, so on the next few occasions, I said I was a bit pressed for time and couldn't stop for a cup of tea and after that when I asked her if I could get any groceries for her, she said no thank you, she could manage perfectly well and our cheery 'Hello, how are you?' as we passed in the corridor soon became no more than a half-smile and the barest of nods.

'How are you?' I asked. I felt something more was called for, felt suddenly embarrassed, ashamed of the way I'd been so distant. 'I hope you're well?'

'Oh, you know, fraying at the seams!' She laughed, a frail, papery laugh. She's a small, very slight woman, who always wears a rose-pink mackintosh even on a gloriously sunny day. 'Now, you're Leo's friend, aren't you?'

I wondered if she'd forgotten me altogether. I felt slightly annoyed – I've lived in the building for nearly five years, so how come I'm 'Leo's friend?' How has everybody come to know him in such a short time?

'Well, yes, I suppose so.' Not something I could swear to with confidence, given that a) I haven't seen him for days, b) he's obviously not talking to me and who could blame him? and c) even if he were talking to me, haven't I just more or less promised Stephen not to see him? He must have left for Canada already. If someone had asked him if he were 'Georgia's friend', would he have still said 'Yes'?

'You see – he asked me to feed the cat while he's away.'

So he *has* gone then.

'Cat?' I must have sounded as puzzled as if she'd suddenly switched to a foreign language.

'Yes. Cora's cat. You know. Leo just got it for her, but her aunt's allergic.'

'But cats and dogs aren't allowed here.' It wasn't that I was bothered – he could have kept a sabre-toothed tiger in there for all I cared – it was just I wondered how long he thought he could get away with it before someone spotted it, especially if he'd let Mrs Patterson in on the 'secret'.

'You won't tell?' She shrank back a little.

I reassured her that I wasn't going to report the infringement to the pet police.

'The thing is, dear,' she leaned closer, 'as you know, he only went yesterday and he gave me the keys but I've looked high and low for them and they're not where I thought I'd put them. I put them somewhere safe you see, so I would be sure not to mislay them . . .

and then I said to myself, well Leo's . . . um . . . friend may have a set, so I . . .'

'I did have once, but not any more, I'm afraid.'

'Oh.' She clenched her tiny hands into fists. 'But it'll starve to death if it doesn't eat for a week!'

'A week?' I frowned, puzzled. 'He's gone to Canada for a week? But I—'

'Canada? I don't think so, dear, no. He's gone back to Scotland, to sort out his house.'

'Sort out his house?'

She looked at me as if I must be a bit simple. 'Of course,' I said confidently, aiming to reassure her so I could find out what the hell was going on. 'The house. Silly me. I'd forgotten. But the cat, we must—'

'Blossom.'

'Blossom, yes. Well now. Keys, keys. Have you checked with the porters?'

She shook her head and I suggested she return to her flat while I nipped down to the lobby.

What on earth was going on? What had happened to Canada? Was he still planning to go? And why had he gone back to Glasgow? Was he sorting out his house because he was moving back there? Or because he'd be away for so long? I didn't know and now I was having to pick up pathetic crumbs of information from Mrs Patterson because I was too proud to admit to someone else that I was so irrelevant in his life that I didn't know anything about his house, his cat, his plans.

I walked down the stairs, thoughts racing through my head. What if he really is leaving? OK, keep calm. Glasgow's not the other side of the world – it's, what? Only 400 miles or so from London. No distance, no distance at all. Five hours by train? Can't be much more than an hour if you fly. But too far to be popping in and out of each other's flats for cups of coffee, too far to call each other up and say, 'What're you doing? Fancy some pizza?' Too far for him to come banging on my door to ask my opinion of his latest photographs, a CD he'd just bought, an old shirt he'd found stuffed at the bottom of his linen basket – was it so dated that it had now come back into fashion once more? My eyes filled. Don't be silly, I bossed myself. What's it to you anyway? He'll never want to see you again after what you said. And you don't care, remember? Yes, but . . . I carried on in my head. It's OK, he'll still come down to London for work sometimes, you can still see each other. But it'll only be for the odd snatched half-hour, just one friend among many, an acquaintance even, our intimate conversations, sharing of secrets – silly dreams and crazy hopes – long forgotten. 'How's the family?' he'd ask politely. 'Fine, thank you. How's life in Glasgow?' A tight smile, a cursory peck on the cheek. 'Call me sometime.'

Down in the lobby, Barry, the porter, nodded at me.

'All right, lu—' he cut himself off short. 'Miss Abrams.'

I flushed, remembering that I'd once asked him not to call me 'love' – 'Georgia is fine, but not love, thank you.' I remembered my brusque tone, cool smile. How pompous, how uptight it sounded in my head. I knew what Leo would have done if I'd told him about it – he'd have called me 'love' every second word, would have said it built up my immunity to it or something. Now, here I am, having to imagine what he'd say, as if he'd died and I was some grief-stricken widow having conversations with him in my head.

'Georgia, please. I'm fine, thanks, Barry.' I smiled warmly. 'And you?'

'Back's playing me up again. Still, mustn't grumble, eh?'

I explained the problem, modifying the forbidden hungry cat for a collection of thirsty houseplants.

'Mr Kane. Flat 418,' I said.

'Should have a set for him, I took a package up only last week.' He went into the back room to check. 'Can't have our Leo's plants turnin' up their toes now, can we?'

Our Leo? Does everyone know him as well as I do? Did. I felt keenly, irrationally jealous then, a stabbing pain right at the core of me. Now I realized that I probably didn't matter to him, was no more than just another resident, all right for a chat and a cup of coffee, a pleasant enough person with whom to pass the time of day. Leo was nice to everyone, wasn't he? Maybe he even felt slightly sorry for me, thought I could do with the company like Mrs Patterson – 'Must pop in and see the uptight spinster in flat 411, poor thing, a smile that could turn water into ice – shame she can't loosen up a bit.'

Barry returned, jangling the keys.

'Course, I can't be handing over Leo's keys to just anyone . . .'

I dropped my outstretched hand.

'I could give 'em to Joan.'

'Joan?'

'Joan Patterson. In 416. You said Leo trusted her with a set?' His hand closed around the keys once more. 'P'raps I'll just check.' He reached for the phone. I stood there feeling like a child sent to stand in the corner by the teacher, untrustworthy, ashamed.

He spoke to her and then handed over the keys, with strict instructions to return them to him straight afterwards.

'And while you're there?'

'Yes?'

'Better feed his cat too, eh?' He grinned and gave me a wink.

A woman I've never seen before

'I'll come in with you, shall I? See if Blossom's all right?'

Mrs Patterson looked relieved.

As soon as I opened the door, the cat came running through, circled herself around Mrs Patterson's stick-thin ankles, and mewed plaintively. On the table were several tins of cat food, a huge box of chocolates, and a note:

'Dear Joan—
Thank you, THANK YOU, for being Blossom's personal chef for the week. Please can you top up her water too? You're a doll.
    Love, Lx
PS Chocs are for you, not Bloss. Save me the nutty ones!'

She smiled.

'A doll? At my age? That Leo!' She tutted, though she was grinning fit to burst. 'He always has the ones with nuts in, you see, when we have a few choccies. I can't manage them, not with my teeth. Now then . . .' She looked around vaguely as if not quite sure what to do next. I went and found a tin-opener and Blossom, unfaithfully, inevitably – immediately transferred her attentions to me, identifying me now as the potential purveyor of food.

With Blossom happily stationed at her bowl, I turned my attention to Leo's two wilting houseplants and gave them some water. I looked at the sofa we'd sat on together. I wanted to stretch out on it, be on the cushions where he had sat so many times, lay my head on the arm, smell his smell. Then I caught sight of the latest photos on his pinboard. Leo has a stretch of one wall covered with cork and he often puts new shots up there; he says he needs to live with the pictures a while before he knows if he really likes them. Also, he says they feel different when you have them pinned up from the way they are when you leaf through them in a folio or just glance at them in the pages of a magazine. These were all black and white prints, and I hadn't seen any of them before. There was one of Cora, looking sweet but desperately serious, a characteristic Cora expression, I thought, then one of Cora and me together in the park, when I was trying to remember the

337

clapping rhyme. I hadn't even realized he was taking shots – he always has a camera with him and I'd got so used to his taking pictures that I'd stopped noticing. It's a good photograph – he's shot it from one side so we're both in profile, facing each other. I'm taller, of course and it's not as though Cora and I especially look alike – why should we, after all? – but, because we're both concentrating and gazing intently straight ahead, at each other and our rhythmically moving hands, we look oddly similar so the effect is rather striking. Both of us are frowning slightly, me trying to remember the words and the hand sequence, Cora trying to learn them:

'Under the brown bush, under the tree . . .
Dum-dah-dah-dee, my darling, dum-dah-dah-dee.
We'll be together – and raise a fa-mi-lee . . .'

Another one of Cora, smiling shyly direct to camera, direct to Leo, her new-found daddy. How strange it must have been for her, having been told her whole lifetime that her father was abroad and couldn't see her, then suddenly being told that he was right there in the same country. God knows what it would do to her relationships in adult life, I thought, slipping into counsellor mode automatically. Oh shut up, I told myself, what she needs now is plenty of time with her dad – lots of attention from him, cuddles, conversation, play, reassurance – but, mostly, time. How could he go away and leave her? I thought again of what I'd said: 'You can be her daddy by postcard', and was stung afresh with shame. I bit the inside of my lip hard, wanting to give myself even a small punishment of pain. I was a vile person, mean-spirited, judgemental, unjust, unkind. I looked back at the board to take my mind away from myself, but there was another photo-graph of me, frowning again as I cooked. I remember that – I was just cooking some pasta when he'd phoned – he was nipping out for pizza, did I want to come or could he bring me back one? – so I asked him to join me, play guinea pig for a sauce I wanted to try out. The sauce, in the end, was only so-so – but it had been a lovely evening, the two of us lounging around, eating and talking and laughing.

And there was another one I'd never seen before – a woman laughing – I mean really, really laughing. Her eyes were all creased up so they looked almost closed and her mouth was open, showing her teeth. It was so unfamiliar that it took me more than a moment to realize that it was me. Not only had I never seen this particular photo of me, I'd never seen one even remotely like it. I've always disliked the rictus grins so beloved of amateur photographers – 'Say cheese!' – so in posed photos of me I'm usually offering no more than the barest ghost of a smile, a cursory acknowledgement that one is supposed to look happy in photographs. 'Come on, Georgia, smile! No – a proper smile! Heavens, it won't kill you!' So the picture didn't look like me, wasn't the me I recognize and know, because it was a face I'd never seen before.

I sensed Mrs Patterson hovering at my shoulder.

'Is that you, dear? The laughing one.' Her head tilted, assessing. 'That's a lovely picture, isn't it? Unusual really.'

'Mmm.' I nodded, unable to speak for some reason. 'Mmm.'

Blossom started mewing like crazy when we made motions to leave.

'I'd have her in with me, I like a bit of comp'ny, but it's the smell, you know . . .' Her voice tailed off as she looked down at the cat-litter tray in the corner of the room.

I was surprised she could smell it. Her own flat has the same kind of smell that pervades the whole block, the corridors, the lifts, the lobby – an odd interwining of aromas: a whiff of overcooked cabbage, the slightly sick-like smell of that particular floor polish they use for the lobby, and some strange, other scent that's hard to put your finger on – the smell of old clothes and musty wardrobes, mothballs and long-since-faded lavender sachets, of cooking, sad, lonely cooking – cod in parsley sauce for one, tinned sardines on toast, the once-a-week treat of a small syrup pudding with Bird's custard – overlaid with the tang of pine disinfectant and those round loo cleaner things that hang in the cistern that you thought no-one used any more – the smell of yellowed newspapers used to line drawers and the sudden, upbeat waft of hairspray as one of the old ladies passes by, proud to be out with her hair just done that morning, neat and silvery, so lacquered it's as stiff and unyielding as a hat – it is the smell of loneliness, of people who live alone by necessity rather than choice, each of us in our own box, battery chickens – clucking gossip and eating by the clock and waiting for night-time with its hope of sleep and the long, sweet hours of forgetfulness.

A hand on my arm.

'Oh, I'm sorry – I'm miles away.' Blossom smooched up against me, looked up at me with beseeching eyes. How can you resist me?

'I could take her up to my flat, I suppose. She must be lonely.'

'Would you? I could still feed her if you're too busy – with your work – or perhaps you'd rather not . . .' Mrs Patterson looked awkward, remembering no doubt my former chilliness to her.

'That would be lovely. I'll feed her first thing, then why don't you pop upstairs at four tomorrow? We can have a cup of tea together, too – if you want – if you can spare the time, I mean.'

She smiled warmly.

'I'd love to, dear.'

I dipped to pick up Blossom.

'Come on, Bloss. Come and sniff your new territory.'

I ran, naked and dripping wet from the shower, to grab the phone before the machine cut in.

'Yes! Hello! I am here! Don't hang up!'

'George – it's me.'

I felt my whole body sag with disappointment.

'Hi. What's up?' I can always tell when something's gone awry in Ellie's universe from the tone of her voice.

'It's Brian – he's refusing to sleep with me.'

'Ellen – I really don't have time for all this now. I'm—'

'You have to help – it's your job. Why won't he sleep with me?'

'Er, sorry, have I missed an episode in the non-stop soap of your love life? I thought you didn't want to sleep with him? Besides, aren't you off men for now, understandably, of course—'

'I know, I know. Will you just *listen*.'

'Sorry. OK, hang on – let me go grab a towel.' I zipped into the bathroom and back. Blossom curled round my ankles, a ring of black fur.

'You know, since I was attacked, I haven't wanted anyone to touch me – I mean, not at all, not to kiss me or anything.'

'That's only natural, babes. Don't rush it.'

'It's not natural for me and it feels weird. So – ' She paused, a rarity in itself.

'So . . . ?'

'So I thought, who do I really, really trust? Who could I sleep with and it would make it OK for me again? And I can get all that other stuff out of my system. Who wouldn't be too fast and gropey but would just take it really slowly if I want to?'

'Ah . . . Brian?'

'Of course. Brian. I trust him completely.'

Oh, dear God, can't you just picture it? Ellen, Queen of Tact, asking Brian if he'd help her out with her little

341

problem, as if she wanted a hand with working the espresso machine in the bar.

'And?'

'And so I explained about it and I told him I'd picked him and he said no!'

'Oh, Ellie – can't you see why?'

'No. You always told me he really liked me. Now I feel such a prat.'

'He *does* like you.'

'Well, he should want to sleep with me then.'

'What did he say when you asked him? Try and remember.'

'Oh, I don't know. He just said he couldn't do it and it would be bad and it would make it all worse and he didn't want to be like the others.'

'Ellen. Think back and remember what he said *exactly*.'

'I'm not like you – I don't remember things like that, every little itsy-bitsy word, what's the point? He just said no.' She sounded petulant. 'God, I'll try. Let me think – OK, I think he said, "I couldn't do that, Ellen," and I said why not and he said, "Because I'm half crazy over you as it is and making love to you will only make it worse," and I said why again and that's when he said that he'd end up on the discard pile with all the others.'

'Right. I see.'

'What?'

'You can be so thick sometimes.'

'Thanks a bunch, *counsellor*. Is that how you talk to your clients?'

'If only . . . Why don't you just stop for a minute and think about how he must have felt? He couldn't have been any clearer.'

'You mean I should have asked him in a different way?'

'I mean you should consider his feelings as well as your own. He's not just there for your convenience.' My mouth felt dry. 'Try to be a bit more considerate.'

'So I'm supposed to say sorry or what?'

I'm so glad she isn't one of my clients; I'd find it hard not to give her a good shaking.

'Now there's an idea. For starters. Did you tell him also that you wanted it to be him because you *trust* him – not just because he happens to be around?'

'Don't know. Can't remember.'

i.e. no she didn't.

'Why are you so anti trying to see how things would work out with him? Not just sex. A relationship.'

'That's the thing where you have less and less sex as it goes on, right?'

I laughed.

'Not necessarily. Besides, in theory the quality usually improves even if the quantity's not what it was. It's the thing where you talk and go out to dinner and phone to say sorry if you're running late rather than just assuming the other person will sit and wait – the thing when you lie awake talking and giggling in the dark the way you did with your best friend when you were eleven – when you find yourself looking at the person's face and thinking you'd still like to be looking at that face in ten, twenty, fifty years' time – when you know that if he were suddenly gone from your life you'd drift about like an empty shell, as if part of you were missing. And you put on a smile when it comes to meeting his friends, his daugh— his family, including all forty-three of his cousins because they're part of his life and who he is and you want to be a part of it too – and he cooks you a nice meal or you give him a back massage at the end of a long, hard day because you care about making each other's lives easier and better even when you're knackered yourself – and, God knows, it's also the thing when you say, "No, it's *your* turn to change the sodding bedlinen," – and you argue about who should phone the plumber or pick up the dry-cleaning or who used up the last of the coffee but didn't write it on the bloody board – and you find yourself lying awake worrying about whether he still loves you

343

because he hasn't told you for two weeks. You know – a real relationship. Real life.'

There was another pause.

'Ellie?'

'I didn't want to interrupt you – you sounded as if you were just getting into your stride.'

'Sorry – I didn't mean to lecture you.'

'It's OK. Do you really have all that with Stephen?' Silence.

'So, George – why have you stayed with him so long if you don't want to argue about the plumber with him? Or whatever. If you don't still want to be looking at his handsome face when you're eighty?'

I sighed and it felt as if I were letting out a long, long breath.

'Because . . . Stephen seems such a perfect match, you see? He *is*.'

'For you? But I never thought he was—'

'You don't understand. I *need* someone like Stephen in my life. I can't be flitting all over the place with a man who doesn't know what he's doing from one day to the next and who won't make proper plans for the future. I *can't* live like that. I know exactly where I am with Stephen – he wouldn't let me down. I have to have someone who's a hundred per cent steady and reliable.'

'And predictable. And boring.'

'Oh, shut up. That's just unfair. See – after Mum – you *know* what I'm like – I can't be around people who might just disappear at any moment.'

'But you've got us, too. You can rely on us – you know we'd be there if you needed us. Matt would, Dad would, I would. Quinn too.'

'I know.'

'You mean I'm right? That's a first.'

'No, it isn't.'

'It is, but what about my problem? Brian? Solutions please.'

'Give him a chance – bring him to brunch one

Sunday, then it won't be like a date and there won't be any unrealistic expectations – on either side. And we can all get another chance to stick our noses in.'

'OK. Thanks, George.'

'Anytime.'

'Are you going on Sunday? Dad wants to sort out Christmas.'

'Yeah, I suppose so.'

'And George?'

'Mmm?'

'You're OK, aren't you?'

'Yeah. I'm fine.'

'Promise?'

'I promise.'

27

Countdown to Christmas

For a man who supposedly doesn't celebrate Christmas, my father certainly frets a disproportionate amount about December the 25th. As early as mid-September, he starts making little whimpering noises about it, then as soon as we've got Ellen's birthday out of the way, he raises the subject practically every single brunch. It's not that he fusses about the presents or the food or any of that stuff. Quite the contrary. All he really cares about is having the whole family gathered together. For us, it's always been a strange mish-mash sort of festival. When I was small, we used to celebrate Chanukah, the Festival of Lights. It lasts for eight days and we had this beautiful menorah – an eight-branched candlestick – actually, it's nine because we used the ninth candle as a sort of service one to light the others; on each day, we lit one extra candle, so we had one on the first day, then two on the second and so on. Unc and Auntie used to come round with the cousins and we were given a small present each day. Sometimes Chanukah falls so it overlaps with Christmas and sometimes it doesn't, but it didn't matter because, either way, we still had roast turkey on 25th December and stockings to open in the morning. But then Mum died and we didn't do Chanukah any more. Dad said it was because Chanukah is really for children and we were getting too big, but Ellen was only four. I think – before – that Mum wanted to celebrate it for Dad's sake – and that he wanted to mark Christmas Day for hers. Quinn usually has some weird gaggle of her women friends round on the 21st December – for a Solstice get-together – and they each bring a dish, the only guidelines for which are – apparently – that it must contain chickpeas and/or brown lentils and look like something the cat sicked up.

A couple of times, I've gone to Stephen's parents for Christmas Day, the main advantages of which are that a) I don't have to do any cooking because his mother is even more controlling than I am and won't let you so much as cut up a carrot without standing over you and telling you that actually she prefers to cut them in thin, diagonal slices rather than sticks, they look that little bit nicer, don't you think? b) I get to chill out and watch crappy Christmas telly non-stop – which I find quite restful and a welcome change: Dad won't have it on because even on Christmas Eve, it's non-stop ads for the sales and he finds the whole buy-buy-buy mentality a little hard to take. Oh yes – and c) Stephen's parents always have one of those huge tins of Quality Street and I get to have all the lovely crackly purple ones because none of them eats nuts. But last year, my fleeing the family nest unhappily coincided with Matt whisking Izzy and the kids away to a watermill in Wales, which Iz said was lovely but the relentless sound of rushing water meant that they all never stopped wanting to go to the loo and it took them about five hours to load the car because they weren't sure what the rented house would have and Bonnie would insist on taking every single soft toy she owns in case the house was broken into while they were away and the 'burgulars stole them'. Ellen went home and so it was just Dad and Ellie and Quinn and Simone who you would have expected to be living it up on the slopes of Verbier or swigging champagne in some slick rich kid's penthouse in New York. Ellen said it was a dreadful Christmas. Quinn apparently spent the entire time fluttering around Simone like a moth round a candle flame, offering her herb teas, 'this one's very calming', scented oils, 'just a few drops in your bath, excellent for destressing both body and mind' and, as a last resort when these were inevitably spurned with a gracious 'I'm not fucking stressed, Mother, leave me alone!', Quinn proffered posh Belgian chocolates – 'I can't eat those, I'll look like a pig', and, finally, champagne – 'It's not that cheapo Spanish bollocks, is it? Haven't you got any proper flutes? These glasses are embarrassing.'

Dad, not surprisingly, withdrew ever deeper into his pile of Christmas books, occasionally peering over the top like a besieged man at the battlements who's down to his last arrow. Ellen said she only survived by challenging herself to break the Abrams family roast-potato-eating record, consuming twelve at a single sitting, then she plugged in her headphones until Dad begged her to talk to him.

Present tense . . .

No-one else in the family has ever mastered the art of good present-buying, finding the exact perfect thing for each person. Apparently, they all find the process as baffling and complex as they would if confronted with a dismantled car engine which they had to try to piece together. Matt, Dad and Ellen are, respectively, too busy, too disorganized and too lazy to devote the proper amount of energy, time and effort to it, so – surprise, surprise – guess who chooses and wraps most of the family's presents? Quinn, being Quinn and an ethical sort of person to boot, wouldn't dream of imposing on me in such a way and also prefers to select gifts from Fair Trade catalogues, Oxfam shops or to 'support' a number of her 'talented' friends. In a good year, this means you receive a basket packed with delicious coffee beans and nuts and slabs of chocolate all sourced from happy co-operatives where the workers are actually treated like human beings so you can stuff your face and still feel virtuous at the same time; in a not-so-good year, this means remembering to put on the Peruvian hat with earflaps as you near the house so that Quinn will believe you really like it or taking yet another aromatherapy oil burner (my fourth!), this time glazed in a singularly nasty sort of khaki shade with meaningless wafty shapes on it, to the Oxfam shop, so completing the cycle of giving and receiving.

Last year, for example, I bought a lovely thick towelling dressing gown for Dad, which Ellen enthused over in the way she does when you know it's not something she actually likes but she can't slag it off if she wants to pretend it's from her too.

'Ooh, can I go halvies with you? You know how hopeless I am at choosing presents.'

'You're not hopeless, you're lazy. It's not the same thing.'

'Whatever. Please can I? Last time ·I got him that purple inflatable chair and I know he's never even blown it up.'

'He did actually, but he said he was so scared it might burst under him that he couldn't relax.'

'See? I'm no good at this stuff. I thought it was lovely.'

'Yes. Lovely to *you*. Why don't you get that not everyone is Ellen?'

'Well, they should be!'

'Good grief – can you imagine? Still, it would save having train timetables because the drivers would just turn up when they felt like it but the rush hour would last all day because everyone would be tearing round in a frenzy the whole time. Marvellous.'

'Oh, shut up. So, can I go halvies?'

'Go on then. God, I'm such a pushover. Your half's twenty-five quid.'

'For a dressing gown? Couldn't you have got a cheaper one? I'll give it to you next week.'

And I end up saying yes because I am me and Ellen is Ellen and I always end up saying yes no matter how much I tell myself that this time I will say no.

Then Dad takes me aside and gives me an old, used envelope with cash in it, saying, 'Could you pick out something for Ellen? You know what she likes – a blouse or something.' Only my father could possibly not have noticed that no-one under the age of sixty wears 'blouses' any more and that Ellen in particular hasn't worn one since she was about seven and even then only under duress.

Then Matt rings up and says can I get something for Dad from him and, while I'm at it, for Ellen and Quinn too because Izzy's got her hands full with the kids and he never has any time, as it is he's not left work before eight all this week and Izzy's saying he never sees the children any more, what's the point of having them if you only see them for two and a half minutes a day and get them all stirred up and racing around just when she's trying to settle them down ready for bed.

So, when it comes to Christmas, I look at the stack of presents and know that almost all of them have been chosen and bought and, in many cases, even wrapped by myself. Sometimes, I wish they'd go the whole hog and ask me to choose my own presents too. Izzy, at least, always gives me something gorgeous – a velvet scarf the colour of claret, a photo album bound in watered silk, bath oil with the scent of bluebells in a twisty glass bottle. My father if left to his own devices would buy me some kind of art book that was too heavy to lift and would hand it over saying, 'Of course, the colour repro's not what it should be. Never is . . .' so that I'd be disappointed in it before I'd even opened it. Now, he always buys me something for the kitchen. In November, he says, 'So, have you thought what you might like?' and this is the cue for me to write on a slip of paper the exact item and shop: Le Creuset oval casserole dish, black, two-litre size. From John Lewis or kitchenware shop. Then Dad gives the slip of paper to Quinn and she braves the temple of Mammon one lunch hour from work. Ellen buys presents she wants herself then borrows them almost immediately. So it was that last year she bought Matt CDs by David Gray and Moby, a plan that backfired because he liked both of them, and Quinn a pink leather belt which, Quinn being Quinn and a stranger to sartorial elegance, she wore; the belt, which would have looked hip and funky on Ellen, of course was simply embarrassingly young on Quinn. I received a red feather boa which I managed to hang onto for all of six days until Ellen purloined it to wear to a New Year's Eve party and never returned it. She also gave me a surprisingly nice hardback note-book with a glittery purple cover. The notebook I keep out of sight, away from her acquisitive gaze and hands, because despite my tasteful, minimalist decor, I have a secret passion for all things sparkly, like a magpie. I use the notebook to record my dreams on the rare occasions when I remember them and I hide it tucked beneath the stretchy bands that hold my bedding in place when I fold my bed away each morning.

Family planning

Organizing Christmas is like planning a military oper-ation in our family, trying to arrange who is going to be where at what time and who is bringing what: the satsumas, the bubbly, the nuts, the proper Cheddar from the posh cheese shop.

'And is Stephen coming?' Dad asked, even though we'd already been through it more than once last Sunday.

'No,' I sighed, trying to keep the impatience out of my voice. 'Not until after lunch anyway.' We eat Christmas lunch at about four o'clock, so that meant we wouldn't see him for much of the day. 'He's hoping to turn up around six or seven, after he's spent the day with his parents.'

'But who will we tease if there's no Mr P-h?' Ellen leaned across me to grab a bagel.

'That's not actually his sole purpose in life, you know, to be a comic punchbag for you and Matt.'

'Isn't it? But he does it so well.' She leaned across me again for the butter.

'And the other thing . . .' Dad lowered his voice and I instinctively leaned towards him. 'Simone will be joining us.' Quinn was upstairs in the bathroom, and I knew he'd picked a moment when she was out of the room to tell us just in case Ellen complained without thinking.

'Oh, no! *Why* is she?' Ellen sounds like such a spoilt brat sometimes. 'Last year she was non-stop hideous from the second she walked in the door. And she was foul to Quinn,' she added, making her face the picture of outraged concern.

'Ha! And like *you're* not!' I shook my head. Unbelievable.

'Ellen. Any guest in this house is to be made welcome. She's Quinn's daughter and I expect you to be polite to her at the very least if you can't manage to be pleasant.'

Ellen pouted.

'Act your age, Ellen. Quinn is endlessly hospitable to you, and puts up with your teasing and your sulking and all sorts of nonsense. It's not much to ask in return that you behave half decently towards her daughter for a few hours, is it?'

'I was only protecting Quinny. Simone's always so horrible to her.'

Dad sighed.

'That doesn't give you licence to be horrible to Simone. Families . . .' He took off his glasses and tapped them against his open palm, the way he does. 'Who knows what goes on in them? You can't judge their relationship from the outside.'

Ellen rolled her eyes at me, expecting my complicit look in return, but I thought Dad was right and I looked away. Ellen's never had to navigate the potential minefield of mother-daughter tensions, so it's easy for her to think that everyone else is doing it all wrong.

'Huh.' Ellen sat sideways on her chair and gnawed at a piece of her bagel. 'Well, it won't be the same, that's all I'm saying.'

Dad smiled into his newspaper without looking at her.

'Change can be a positive thing. Just try to keep an open mind. There's plenty of good in Simone.'

Ellen snorted.

'Well, at least tell me you'll be doing the cooking, George.'

'Of course I will.'

Dad peered at me over his newspaper battlements, brows raised.

'I mean, if that suits everyone? If Quinn doesn't mind,' I added.

' – if Quinn doesn't mind what?' Quinn came back into the kitchen.

'Um – about Christmas dinner, would you like me to do— to help you with it or . . . ?'

'Goodness, I was hoping you'd do the whole lot, Georgia. I did it last year, you know, and the turkey was very dry, I don't know how you always get it to be so delicious, and my stuffing was . . . slightly peculiar, I think maybe I was a bit heavy-handed with the five spice powder, or perhaps it was the coconut that was the problem . . . I was trying for an Eastern sort of flavour, I don't know, it wasn't good, was it, dear?' She laid her hand on Dad's shoulder.

'I'm always overjoyed to be cooked for.' He smiled up at her. 'I think the occasion and the people matter rather more than the stuffing.'

'Your roasties were good. Really crunchy,' Ellen offered, attempting to redeem herself.

Quinn positively beamed.

I hate sharing a kitchen with anyone else and I hate trying to cook when someone else is fluttering around me, moving things which I'm just about to use or, like Quinn, using the chopping board with the edge hanging half off the worktop so you keep thinking it's going to fall off, but I thought I'd better make an effort. At least the kitchen's a decent size, or it would be if it wasn't so full of clutter.

'Why don't we share the cooking then? Quinn, you do your legendary potatoes—'

'And George can do all the rest.' Ellen's terrific at volunteering other people to do things.

'And what's *your* contribution going to be?' Dad asked her.

Ellen looked shocked, as if he'd asked her when she was planning to retile the roof, before or after lunch?

'Um – I'll – I could – well – I – '

Dad was still looking at her, and even went so far as to lower his paper.

'Maybe I could chop the carrots or something?'

Dad turned to look at me, questioning.

'I tell you what – I know you hate cooking and I don't mind, so why don't you do the table? Make it look nice and sort out candles and napkins and all that. But you've got to do it *properly* – not just any old how.'

She nodded, happy again.

'I *will*. Don't boss. What about Matt?' Ellen can't bear the idea that anyone else will get off with doing less than her, but given that her work-avoidance capabilities are quite exceptional, even Matt can only ever come a poor second. Dad would do all the clearing away and loading the dishwasher. That's his job.

'Matt will have the kids to look after.'

'But Iz can do that! It's not fair!'

'Ellen,' Dad sighed. 'Until you have children of your own, you don't realize how much work it involves.'

'Quite,' I said.

'What would *you* know?' Ellen turned on me. 'You haven't got any either – you're hardly an expert!'

'Ellen!' Quinn rebuked her, which she never does. We were all so surprised that we turned to look at her and were silent. She coloured slightly, unused to so much attention all at once. 'That's not very diplomatic,' her voice softened. 'A childless woman in her mid-thirties is bound to feel a little bit . . . *sensitive* on this subject.' She smiled sympathetically at me, the object of her concern.

I was outraged.

'What? Quinn – thank you for your intervention, but it's quite unnecessary – if you're referring to my ageing ovaries and my cobwebbed womb, let me assure you that I'm happy for them to atrophy with disuse – more than happy. I have no intentions of having children. Absolutely none.'

Quinn cocked her head on one side and directed a small, infuriating smile at Dad who, annoyingly, smiled back.

'Meaning *what* exactly?' I addressed both of them.

Quinn stayed silent.

Dad removed his glasses once more.

'What do you think it means?' he said.

'I have no idea and I'm not in the least bit interested.' I pulled one of the colour supplements towards me and started to leaf through it.

'Well, *I* want to know. What *did* you mean?' Ellen looked from Dad to Quinn and back again.

'Just – we'll see – that's all.' Quinn stood by Dad's shoulder and he smiled in agreement.

'Don't mind me, will you? It's only me and my life and my future and my innards you're talking about. I'm thirty-four, for God's sake – and more than capable of making up my own mind about what I do and do not want in my life, thank you very much. Why does everyone think they know me better than I do myself all of a sudden? If I say I don't want children, you're all just going to have to accept that a) I might actually be telling the truth and b) that it's none of your business in any case. OK?'

I stared back down at the magazine, apparently fascinated by a horrible pair of pointy fake-snakeskin boots which looked as if you'd have to cut off half your toes in order to squeeze your feet into them.

'But we all know that you *do* want them really . . .' Ellen reached across me again to grab the apricot jam.

'*Ask* if you want something, will you! Your table manners are dreadful. You don't know anything of the kind.'

'If you're going to end up with Leo, you'll have a child whether you want one or not,' Ellen plunged on, undaunted, and dug her buttery knife into the jam.

'Ellen, can't you use a spoon? You're getting the jam all buttery. I can't see how it can possibly have escaped your notice, but I am NOT with Leo, nor am I likely to be EVER – is that clear? And it's nothing to do with Cora – she's a really sweet child – but I have absolutely no interest in Leo in any case and, even if I had, there's no way I'd ever want to be a stepmother – what could be worse than being some awful, unwanted substitute and knowing that you're always going to be second-best and never—'

I'd been going to say about knowing that the children are only putting up with you and don't really want you there, then I was meaning to remind her about how I'm also, of course, with Stephen and entirely contented so she should just shut up talking about Leo all the time. I was about to explain all that when I realized what I'd just said out loud. The room was absolutely silent. I swallowed and stole a quick glance at Dad. He looked angry, very angry, his paper abandoned on the table in front of him. He was waiting.

Even Ellen was completely quiet, but then she looked at me and, inappropriate as always, mouthed a single word at me so that only I could see: *Fuck*.

Finally, I looked up at Quinn.

'Quinn, I'm really sorry – I didn't mean—'

'No, of course you didn't.' She tried to smile, which

made it worse somehow. She looked on the verge of tears.

'I really didn't – I just . . .' I was floundering, unable to find a way out.

'It's all right, Georgia dear. We all say things we don't mean sometimes.' Her hand flew instinctively to Dad once more and he reached out and squeezed it.

'Well, I'd best be getting on.' She looked up at the kitchen clock. 'I've got – some – some – things – to do.' She smiled once more, a valiant smile, then left the room and I heard her running lightly up the stairs.

The Queen of Tact

'Holy fuck,' said Ellen. 'And *you* call *me* Queen of Tact!'

'*Not* helpful, Ellie.'

'Oh, be like that then.' She picked up her coffee and flounced through to the sitting room with a section of the paper, sprawled full-length on the sofa, waiting, no doubt, for me to come and placate her. I ignored her.

'Dad – I'm so sorry—'

'Don't apologize to *me*.'

'I – I – wasn't thinking – you know I don't think of Quinn as a substitute mother – '

'As you made all too clear. Georgia. Honestly. How must she be feeling?'

'But Quinn's never tried to mother us – she wasn't even around when we were growing up . . .'

'Quinn's never tried to mother you lot because she's got more sense than that and she's always hoped you might let her into your lives a bit more. But you, you especially, Georgia, haven't let her get within a mile of you – emotionally, I mean. Half the time you treat her as if she's some comical cameo, getting in little clever asides about her cooking and her clothes – I haven't interfered because I hoped you were grown-up enough to moderate your own behaviour and see that it upsets

357

her. But I was wrong.' He looked down, away from me. 'I was wrong and I was stupid. Sitting on the sidelines as usual, hoping things will fix themselves.' He shook his head, but more at himself than at me it seemed, and, when he spoke again, he sounded suddenly much older, tired and defeated. 'No-one's saying she's a replacement for Joy . . . or that she's anything like her.' Our eyes met then and I knew what he was thinking, knew it with such certainty that I clamped my mouth shut to stop myself from crying out. 'And no-one is saying you've got to think of her as a mother. Of course not. But I will not have you talk to her like that. Quinn is my wife and this is her house too – don't look like that – *it is her house too,* and while you're in it, I expect you to treat her with the same respect you'd accord anyone else.'

I nodded dumbly, tried to swallow.

'Shall I go and apologize then?'

'Georgia, you're thirty-four. As you've only just been reminding us, you're supposedly capable of making your own decisions.'

I nodded again. Slowly climbed the stairs. Tapped on the bedroom door. Their bedroom door.

'Um, Quinn?'

A pause. A long pause.

'Oh. Georgia? No. I'm – just – I'm – changing just now.'

I leaned my forehead against the door, grateful for its solidity, something I couldn't damage so easily.

'I – wanted to say – I'm sorry – really sorry – I—'

'Thank you, dear.' Her voice sounded artificially bright.

'Can I come in for a minute?'

'Not just now. I'm having a little lie-down. I've got a bit of a – a migraine.'

'Oh. I'm sorry. Can I get you something for it?'

'No, thank you. I'm fine.'

'Well, OK. I'm sorry. Really I am. I – well. I'll be off

then I guess.' There was no response. 'Hope you feel better soon. Bye then.'

Still no answer.

I went downstairs and back into the kitchen.

'She can't talk to me now,' I said flatly. 'She says she has a migraine.'

'I'll go up.' Dad shook his head. 'It's not like you to be so thoughtless, Georgia. I expect better from *you*, you know I do.'

'I know.' I couldn't even meet his eye, I felt so ashamed. 'I'd better go.'

'I'll come with you, George.' Ellen sprang up from the sofa, forgetting that she'd been in a strop. 'You can drop me off, can't you?'

'If you like.'

Dad gave each of us a cursory kiss.

'Let yourselves out,' he said, then he turned away from us and headed up the stairs.

28

Moving in, moving on

Well, I've finally moved in with Stephen. I took over some of my clothes and my books and he cleared a whole section of his wardrobe for me – way more space than I needed for the things I'd brought. After all this time together, I can't believe that all I kept there before was a spare T-shirt and some knickers. Stephen's wardrobe is wonderful – its lights come on automatically when you open the doors and there are niches for shoes and jumpers and belts and ties. He divides his clothes, with work suits in one section, work shirts in another, then semi-casual shirts, non-work trousers, and T-shirts and holiday clothes. His boxer shorts are laid out neatly in one drawer, stripes and patterns on the right, plains on the left, and his socks are paired and balled in a drawer with a divider so that each pair has its own nest-like nook. I wish I'd had my wardrobe like that – then you can find exactly what you need in a moment. He wanted me to bring more things, a couple of my lamps or houseplants, but what's the point if we're going to hire a van anyway? Better to do it all in one go, much more efficient. Stephen agreed, he hates poor time management. I sleep at his place almost every night, but still come home each day to feed Blossom and – just to – to sort things out. Stephen thinks I'm looking after a cat for a neighbour. Which I am. Leo is a neighbour. Only I may not have mentioned that it was his cat. I know what Stephen's like – he'll only get all antsy about it and God knows there's no need. When Leo returns, I'll hand Blossom back and that will be that. End of all contact. I want to apologize for what I said. I will apologize. I don't know why I said it. All I seem to do at the moment is go round upsetting everyone I— everyone I know. At least I have no more sessions until January, so that's one less thing to worry about. Stephen thinks we should have booked to go away, says I'm looking tired and run-down, but I couldn't be away from my family for the whole of Christmas, I just couldn't.

'I fail to see the logic of that, darling,' Stephen said, when we talked about it. 'Your family don't really celebrate Christmas anyway – not properly.'

'Just because we don't have a tree and don't treat it as a religious festival doesn't mean we don't celebrate.'

'Don't get touchy, sweetie. I'm not attacking you. All I'm saying is – what exactly is it you imagine you're celebrating?' He'd smiled and drained the last of his coffee.

'We *imagine* we're celebrating the fact that we're a family and that we're choosing to spend the day together, talking and sharing a meal and giving presents to—'

'Huh! Well, there you are – you said David hates the whole commercial trappings side of Christmas, but you still all give each other presents!'

'Yes, we do. Not hundreds of expensive things. And the kids don't get showered with toys either. The idea is to give each person one thing you've thought about – to show you value them – and—'

'But no-one except you and Isobel gives the slightest thought to it whatsoever. Ellen always gives you things she wants herself!'

'Well, that's the intention – I didn't say we were any good at carrying it out.'

He smiled indulgently and kissed me.

'Come on – let's not argue. It's terrific having you here at last. We should have done it ages and ages ago.'

He's right, of course. It makes miles more sense this way. Once I've got all my things here, it'll be much easier – I won't have to keep going home because I've left behind my favourite shirt or the novel I'm in the middle of, I won't have to dart back to water my plants or pick up my post or catch up with my admin. Everything will be more orderly and organized. So much better.

Homecoming

Leo's back. He's been away for eleven days. It was supposed to be a week, but he phoned Joan to ask her if she could carry on feeding the cat a bit longer. Naturally, she told him I'd taken Blossom into my flat, to save messing about with the keys each time. I was hoping – I suppose I also thought that then he'd have to talk to me, wouldn't he? I mean, even if only to ask for his cat back. And that would give me a chance to apologize properly. He'd have to listen to me at least. But then I went home yesterday and found this note on my doormat:

'G –
I gather that you are in possession of something that belongs to me – i.e. one cat (black, white flash at throat, name of – but not necessarily answering to – Blossom – just in case you are in habit of collecting other people's cats and have a herd – flock? – of them to sort through). Kindly return same a.s.a.p.
 L'

That was it.

I phoned him, but got the machine, so I left a

message, but I was so nervous that I babbled away like the old lady in our block who sometimes travels up and down in the lift for as much as an hour, just so she can talk to whoever gets in with her. Another few years and that'll be me, buttonholing some poor person as they stagger in with their shopping – 'Ooh, been to fetch your groceries, have you? To the supermarket, was it? I went in there but they have people watching, you know – they follow you round – there was a man by the cauliflowers watching to see which one I wanted – I got a packet of frozen peas instead – and you don't get the personal service, do you? No. We used to go to the corner shop – my mother would put a coin in my hand and I'd trot off to the grocer's as happy as you like – it's not the same now – you can't let your children out on the street – have you lived here long? – ooh, just moved in – it's very slow, this lift, isn't it? – I've told them before but they won't do anything – oh, is this your floor? – the sixth? – which flat are you in, dear? – you must come and see me – I'm on the fifth – oh, yes, I've missed it – I'm always doing that – oh, well, up we go and down we go – you'd pay gold bars to do this at that Alton Towers – take care now – bye-bye – well, what a nice woman – very pleasant – some people are happy to chat and pass the time of day – they should do something about this lift – you can sit here for ages waiting – oh! – press the button – there we go – oh, yes, we're moving now . . .'

Anyway, I was in the middle of rambling on about Blossom and how she'd been and how sorry I was for what I'd said and I couldn't seem to stop. I probably would have carried on until I'd used up the whole tape, but then he picked up the phone and said,

'Hey!'

'Hi. I – I was just leaving a meessage.'

'Sorry – I didn't hear the phone – I've just come in.'

'I've got Blossom. Shall I—'

'You're not holding her hostage, are you?'

'No, of course not.'

'Hello? Joke.'

'Oh, of course. Yes. Right. I'll bring her back now, shall I?'

I picked up Blossom and held her close, resting my chin in the softness of her fur for a minute, stroking the back of her neck.

'Bye-bye, Bloss. I shall miss you. We'll have to come back up for your food bowl and litter tray, won't we?'

Dear God, here I am talking to a cat. Actually, I've been talking to her all week. I never really understood why people keep cats before. They're very beautiful but any attempts at keeping pets in my family have always resulted in their early demise, so you can't blame me for being reluctant. Every single pet I have ever owned has bitten the dust – Geronimo, the goldfish who got fin rot, Chips, the terrapin whose tank was topped up with boiling water straight from the kettle to warm it up because Mum said it was 'looking sluggish', Sally, the snail whose unnoticed escape bid across the kitchen floor was tragically curtailed by Mum's gold-sandalled foot, and Cleo, a young cat who turned up in our garden when a neighbour moved away without her, who was run over and found lying in the gutter by Dad. But Blossom has been a treat – she moves so beautifully, I could watch her for hours. I chat away to her while I'm tidying or washing up and it's wonderful – she doesn't interrupt or disagree or tell me I'm being ridiculous. Shame we're not allowed to keep animals here. I mentioned to Stephen I thought he might like a cat, but he pointed out that they shed hairs everywhere and it might sharpen its claws on his leather sofa and spoil it.

The agreement

A corridor full of people talking and clinking glasses. Music – Ella Fitzgerald? – emanating from someone's flat.

'Hey, you!' Leo appears in front of me.

'Hi. Here she is then.' I want to look at him, want to look into his eyes, but I cannot. I bury my face in Blossom's fur one more time.

'Thanks for looking after her.'

'That's OK. She's lovely.'

'Good. Bye then.'

'Oh. Right. Bye.' I put her into his arms, then turn to leave.

At the double doors, I feel a hand on my shoulder.

'What *are* you doing?' he says.

'Going back upstairs – oh, the litter tray and stuff – shall I get it now?'

'Are you mad?'

'What?'

'We're having a party – in case you hadn't noticed. Don't you want to be at it?'

'I didn't think I was invited.'

'No-one was invited. It just – happened. I got back an hour ago – saw Joan and she said let's celebrate you being back, so I got the wine and crisps and we banged on everyone's door at this end and now here we all are. Of course, there's no reason why you might want to stay, ask how I am, how my trip went, any of that stuff—'

'But you're not talking to me.'

'No. That's true. To the naked eye, it might look as if I'm standing here talking to you, but of course this is merely a sophisticated illusion and no conversation is in fact taking place.'

'You,' I say, 'are a very silly person.'

'So are you – only you're better at hiding it than I am. Why am I not talking to you?'

'Because of what I said, of course – about you – and

365

Cora – and I *so* didn't mean it – I'm so, so sorry – I felt terrible about it – wretched – it was mean and horrible and I don't blame you a bit for not talking to me – you're right not to – I wouldn't talk to me either if I was you – anyway – your note – I knew you were still angry.'

'Hello – are you awake yet? Note was a joke. Can't I leave you alone for a few days—'

'Eleven days.'

'Eleven days then – without your losing your sense of humour and your apparently all-too tenuous grasp on reality? Obviously I'll have to stick around to keep more of an eye on you. Look – yes, of course I was upset. Very. And bloody angry too – I'd have happily punted you off your balcony at that moment – but do you really think I'd hold a grudge all this time, you dope? How well do you know me? I can never be annoyed with anyone for more than twenty-four hours – even when I mean to be, something else happens and then I forget that I was supposed to be cross.'

'I didn't think. I just felt angry then guilty then completely and utterly crap. It's been horrible.'

'Well – *do* think. God – I could have milked this so much more than I have. What a lost opportunity. So much guilt – all gone to waste.'

'Don't.'

'Now, stop all that and come here and give me a hug and tell me how much you've missed me.' He puts down Blossom who coils around and between us, mewing for attention.

'One good thing did come out of what you said.' He lets me go and picks up Blossom again. 'It made me realize something. You know that Canadian job?'

'Yes?'

'I *was* seriously thinking of taking it – then you came out with your—'

'Nasty, snide dig—'

'Forthright and decidedly frank comment – and I

thought, what are you doing, you crazy schmuck? Me, not you. You were right.' He lowers his voice. 'I was scared, Georgia. Shit-scared. One minute I'm breezing along, my biggest worry where my next cheque's coming from – the next I've suddenly got this five-year-old daughter and I don't know what's hit me. I don't know how to be a proper parent. I mean I – I *love* Cora so much already – really, really love her – I never felt this way before – and it's bloody terrifying. Sometimes I lie awake at night, thinking of her at her aunt's and worrying that her uncle might not have stubbed his cigarette out properly and – and I see the flames – and her asleep in her little bed – or I picture her running into the road after a ball – or – shit – I can't relax any more. Then I thought of you. Just for a change. I know I had a go at you about taking risks, but I'm way worse than you – here I am – with this extraordinary, miraculous gift of a *child* out of the blue – and I was about to chuck it all out the window and not see her for months, making out this *job* was some amazing once-in-a-lifetime opportunity when the real opportunity was right here under my nose – only I couldn't handle it.'

'It *is* difficult. And scary.'

'So are lots of things. It's not going to get any easier if I run away from it, is it?'

'No. I'm glad you're staying. Not just for Cora's sake.'

'Did I mention how much I missed – Blossom?'

'No. Did you?'

'Yes. I missed – her – very – very – much indeed.'

'You could have phoned her.'

'Nope. I decided not to. I was trying not to think about her.'

'Why?'

'Because I'm never sure how she feels about me. One minute she's purring, the next she's sinking her claws into me. I figured if I didn't have any contact with her for a week or two, I might stop thinking about her. I thought it might help.'

'And did it?'

'Nope.'

I step slightly closer to stroke Blossom as she purrs there, cradled in his arms.

'She missed you a lot too. She used to curl up close to me just for comfort – because I reminded her of you.'

He smiles.

'And how's everyone else doing? Ellen? Your dad left me a nice message inviting Cora and me for Christmas – really kind of them. How's Quinn? Come on, give me all the news. What have you been up to? Been canoodling up on any rooftops lately? And, dare I ask, how's things with Stephen?'

Stephen. Oh shit. What am I doing? I promised I'd never see Leo again. But I had to return his cat, obviously. I couldn't help it. It's not as if I deliberately went out of my way to see him, is it?

'What is it? You've gone white as a sheet.'

He puts the cat down once more, touches my arm.

'Stephen – he – I – we. I said I wouldn't see you.'

'You *what*?'

'I *thought* I wouldn't. You don't know. I felt so awful and I *thought* you weren't speaking to me. I thought you'd never—'

'So you offered to drop me faster than a week-old haddock? Cheers.'

'No, no. It wasn't like that. He wanted me to move in with him and—'

'I see. And you're going along with that as well, are you?'

I drop my head.

'You've moved in already? Great. Well, that's wonderful, wonderful news – did I miss the fireworks and champagne? Boy, do I feel stupid.'

'No – it's – I didn't think—'

'No, you certainly didn't, did you? Fine – you just stay stuck in your good old trusty rut, it suits you.

Thanks for bringing Bloss back.' He looks down to find her, but she's scampered off along the corridor.

'No, Leo. *Please*.'

He turns his face away from me, holds his hand out as if to keep me at a distance.

'*Enough*. I've *had* it with all this. Just forget it. Forget *everything*.' Then he strides away, calling for Blossom.

I press my feet hard down into the floor, to anchor myself, to show myself that I am still here. What is left of me is still here, standing in a corridor, in a building, in a street, in a city. These are my feet in my shoes, though I cannot feel them. This is my body, this empty shell; this is the body of Georgia, the mind of Georgia, but there is no *me* anymore.

Joan Patterson comes up to what used to be me.

'Georgia, dear, you'll take a glass of wine, won't you?' Her thin fingers squeeze my arm. 'So good to have our Leo back, isn't it? Such a nice boy.' She laughs and pats me, as if reassuring me on the wisdom of my choice. 'You're very lucky, my dear, I wish I were your age again. Now, this is such fun, isn't it?'

'Yes. It's terrific. Really wonderful. But I can't stay – ' I back away. 'I've got – people – coming – any minute. Must go. Sorry. Bye now. Bye.' Backing through the doors, blind strides to the stairs, clutching at the banister, pulling myself up, half-staggering, the fifth floor – another neighbour, turning my face away, running, fumbling with my keys, shutting the door on everything behind me.

23 December, two days to go

I think my car's been stolen. I never bother taking it to Stephen's because it's all residents-only; Stephen says I should apply for a permit now that I live there, but there's no point fussing about it over Christmas.

And there's even less point if it's been stolen. At first I thought I'd just forgotten where I'd parked the bloody thing, so I spent nearly two hours wandering up and down the streets looking for it. Then – ah-ha! – I thought, I must have lent it to Ellen and she hasn't given it back. I rang her, but she said she hadn't used it for ages and ages, not for weeks.

'But didn't you use it for work the other night?'

'Oh, OK, yes, I did use it Thursday, but I gave it back first thing Friday, remember? *And* I put petrol in it. But George – ?'

'Yup?'

'If you do find it, can I borrow it tomorrow? Brian's invited me to a Christmas Eve lunch thing up in Highgate.'

'No, you can't – once I find it, I'm chaining it to the end of my bed. I can't be without my car over Christmas.'

'God, that's a point. How are you going to get home on Christmas Day?' Ellen still refers to Dad's house as 'home' even though she left ten years ago.

'I can walk if I have to – except I'll have loads to carry and . . . anyway, how will you get there? I thought I was picking you up first thing?'

'Yeah – no, I changed my mind. I'm going tomorrow instead and staying over. I know you – you'll be going too early because you'll want to get the turkey on.'

'Thanks for telling me. Anyway, I wasn't planning to leave here until half eight or so in the morning.'

'Exactly. Way too early after a day of boozing.'

I hate it when she talks like that.

'How could you have been planning to drink if you were wanting to borrow my car?'

'Oh, God, George – don't take everything so literally. Obviously, I wouldn't drink and drive. *Obviously*. I wouldn't have had more than a couple. I just meant, you know, at Christmas, everybody gets a bit drunk, don't they?'

I said nothing.

'Well, everyone except you and Stephen then. Every-body normal, OK?'

'Oh, shut up. I don't see why everyone thinks they have to be completely pissed in order to enjoy them-selves.'

'They don't. It's called relaxing and having fun. It wouldn't kill you to try it once in a while.'

'It doesn't agree with me. And it's not up for discus-sion.'

'Whatever. Sorry – OK? Come tomorrow instead and stay over.'

'Where?'

'Dunno. My old room?'

I laughed. Ellen's room has become a dumping ground for junk, an overflow for the rest of the house. It's the room where I hid under the camp bed when we played Sardines. The room where I lay on the floor with Leo, and with Cora, trying not to sneeze because of the dust.

'Where's Simone sleeping? Downstairs?'

'I guess so.'

My mother's old studio is now the guest room. It's not especially swish or anything but it's tidier than any other room in the house and at least there's a loo and basin down there. I didn't begrudge Simone the room, though; I never go down there anyway.

'And you?'

'In your old room. Well – I arranged this *weeks* ago.'

I knew she hadn't because only last week she was moaning about having to get up early to go with me.

'Come on, George, bunk in with me. We can talk in the dark like we used to.'

'Well, maybe we can find a spare mattress or some-thing to put on the floor.'

The bed's too narrow for two people even if you want to sleep squashed together, and it's definitely too narrow if one of the two people is Ellen because she thrashes around in her sleep and hogs all the duvet.

*   *   *

After I'd spoken to Ellen, I rang Quinn.

'Oh, Georgia! How are you? I'll just call David.'

'Actually, I was calling to speak to *you*.'

'Oh, well. Now. If it's about the other day, I'd virtually forgotten all about it . . .'

'I am very sorry. It wasn't what I meant to say at all. It just came out wrong.'

'Well, not to worry now. Anyway . . . ?'

I told her that my car seemed to have gone AWOL and asked if it might be possible to stay.

'Of course! No need to ask, this is your home too. Oh – but we've got Simone coming too, you know, and Ellen now as well. Perhaps Simone could move so you . . . ?'

'No, that's not necessary. Give her the guest room, please. I can sleep on the sofa at a pinch or the camp bed. Or is there a spare mattress and I can share with Ellen?'

'Well, if you're sure? I'll ask Tarka – she might have a futon we could use.'

A futon. My favourite. So comfortable.

Then I went round to the police station to report the theft of my car. They took the details, but said it's unlikely I'll ever see it again – unless it's been nicked by joyriders, in which case it might turn up totally trashed and with the ignition ripped out. Terrific. It's shaping up to be a wonderful Christmas.

29

'Tis the season to be jolly

Last night I ended up in my old room with Ellen.
She had the bed and I was in the camp bed set at
right angles, so we were forming a T. Tarka's hypo-
allergenic, gluten-free futon had already been promised
elsewhere unfortunately. The camp bed's fine – as long
as you don't want to do anything on it, such as sit up,
turn over or go to sleep. You have to lie there in a
straight line like an Egyptian mummy and you must
position yourself exactly in the middle otherwise it tips
over on its side and catapults you onto the floor. To be
fair, Ellen did offer me the bed because 'you're older
and more creaky', but I knew if I'd taken her up on it,
I'd then have had to listen to her complaining about
how uncomfortable it was half the night. We lay there,
talking in the dark.

'Did Mum used to do proper stockings?'

Ellen knows all this stuff, of course; she's asked me a
thousand times.

'Mmm, and she made wonderful little things to go
inside. One year, she made a miniature pillar box from
one of those little plastic pots that have paprika or
herbs in them. She painted it red and cut out a piece
for the slot, then she wrote some teeny-tiny letters and
postcards with Dad's thinnest pen. They were funny

and silly – one said, "Dear Miss Abrams, You have won a big, fat cuddle as the top prize in our competition. Please present this voucher to the nearest Mummy to redeem your prize." They were great.'

'Did I get one?'

'No. It was before you were born. I told you before.'

'So why did she stop doing them?'

I made a face in the dark, the way you do, forgetting that the other person can't see your expression.

'Hmm – well, I suppose she was more tired once there were three of us. So Dad did the stockings then, but . . . then Mum died and it was too much to do everything all the time so he sort of phased it out.'

'Oh. And you used to help with the dinner, right?'

'Yes. Even when I was only six or seven, Mum showed me how to smear butter on the turkey and which herbs to pick from the garden – thyme and sage and rosemary for the potatoes.'

'George?'

'Yes?'

'Do you really think you won't have children?'

I sighed.

'I don't know.'

'You always used to say no, definitely not.'

'Nothing seems definite any more.'

'George?'

'Ye-es? We really should go to sleep now.'

'Just a couple of minutes more. When you say nothing's definite, does that include Stephen too? Are you still going to marry him – I mean absolutely, no question, a hundred per cent definitely, definitely, as you would say?'

'George . . .?'

'Yup.' Saying it made me think of Leo. That's what he says – yup. Yup – an exclamation more than a word, like the bark of a puppy falling over itself with the excitement of being alive.

'Yup, you are going to marry him, or yup, you're still listening?'

'The latter.'

'Oh. So you might not?'

Sometimes, in the dark, it's easier to be honest.

'I don't know.'

'Oh. It's just, if you are going to and I'm your maid of honour or whatever, can I pick what I wear or do you do it?'

I laughed.

'Oh, Ellie! Here am I, agonizing about Stephen and fretting over whether I've been kidding myself for God knows how long and here you are worrying about whether I'm going to make you wear something you hate – you are funny.'

'I thought of a headpiece I'm going to make for your wedding.'

'Really?' I sat up in surprise, wobbling the camp bed. It's rare for Ellen to sound excited about her jewellery. Usually, she's whingeing that she couldn't get a stall in her favourite spot or that the catches she bought have turned out to be faulty. 'What's it like?'

'It's got all these tiny coloured crystals threaded onto really fine wires so they'll dance about with even the slightest movement of your head.'

'Sounds beautiful.'

'I hope so. It's just in my head at the moment, I haven't even drawn it.'

'Do I have to marry Stephen to get you to make it?'

I heard her turn suddenly towards me.

'No. Why? Have you got someone else in mind? – As if I didn't know.'

'Oh, shut up. No, I haven't. I was just thinking out loud, that's all.'

'You haven't mentioned Leo once today.'

'So? – Why should I mention him?'

'Because you always do – like, normally – whatever you're talking about, you *always* bring his name in somehow – you say, "Oh, yes, Leo was telling me about

375

this the other day," or "Leo has a shirt exactly that colour," you kind of work the conversation round to get his name in—'

'I don't! That's so untrue!' I tried to think back. It's hard to tell with Ellen, because she always exaggerates so much. 'Do I really?'

'Absolutely. We all think it's funny.'

'Which *we all* is that?'

'Me – Matt – Dad – Quinn.'

'I'm so glad to be a source of amusement for you.'

'Oh, hush – we're not laughing *at* you – it's funny and sweet. We all love him, you know we do.'

'Well, that's lovely – I hope you'll all be very happy together. But given that I'm engaged to marry *Stephen*, that's not a great comfort to me. Also – Leo and I aren't exactly on the best of terms right now.'

'Why?'

I sighed.

'Because I – I'm *unbelievably* stupid sometimes. It was all my fault. Oh, Ellie – I really have fucked up so badly. I sort of promised Stephen that I wouldn't see or speak to Leo – I thought it would make things easier. Better. I thought I wouldn't feel so confused all the time.'

'But you can't not see Leo! And you can't let Stephen boss you around – that's my job.'

I laughed.

'I know. Stephen wasn't bossing me. Don't blame him. It's just I thought Leo wasn't talking to me anyway and – I don't know – I've been faffing around all this time about Stephen and it's not fair on him. He's a good man, he's the *right* person for me, and I need to stop messing about and sort out my life.' I thought of Stephen and something he'd said. 'It's time to move on to the next square.'

Ellen snorted.

'Oh my God – you're becoming like him – oh, help! You'll go around calling yourself "Georgia with two 'g's" and wearing ironed jeans at the weekend and

376

frowning when someone says fuck. You'll be slurped into his family and we won't be able to take the piss out of you because you'll purse your lips instead of cracking back at us and you won't come to brunch and you'll eat bridge rolls instead of bagels and – and water biscuits instead of matzohs and you won't be George any more – you'll be Mrs Cooling – oh fuck – fuck, *fuck* – I can't stand it – you can't let it happen, George. I won't let them take you away.'

'Too late. I started moving my stuff in.'

'You didn't!'

'Yup. Some clothes, a few books.'

'Did you take – um – your plants?'

'No. Too awkward in the car. We're planning to hire a van in the New Year.'

'Did you take your favourite mug? The one with the red polka dots?'

'No – what's that got to do with anything?'

'Just wondered. Ah – did you take your shell box? The one Mum gave you.'

'No.'

'Ah-ha!'

'Don't go reading anything into that. I just wanted to keep it safe, that's all . . . Anyway, I wasn't trying to take every single thing, just make a start, you know, show willing etcetera . . . This is nice, talking with you. I miss this. It was great when you came to stay – I'm sorry I was such a pain in the arse to live with.'

'You weren't – I know I'm untidy.'

'Understatement of the century. But you can't help it. It's just the way you are.'

'It's crazy though – when I'm at the bar, I'm clearing up after other people all the time – you get so you do it automatically – the sight of an empty wine glass or a full ashtray on a table really bugs me.'

'Now that I do find hard to believe.'

'It's *true*.'

'Ellie?'

'What?'

'Has anything more happened with Brian?'

'What kind of anything?'

'Any kind of anything.'

'Sort of . . . he took me to this lunch party today and . . .' Her voice faded away.

'And what? Tell, tell.'

'And – nothing. It was really nice, we spent most of the time talking to each other – and – that's it. No snogging, no shagging. But it was good.'

'Good. We must go to sleep.'

'Night-night.'

'Night-night.' I turned over and the bed flipped onto its edge, tipping me onto the floor.

'For fuck's sake!' I shouted as Ellen burst into laughter.

Pieces past and present

I shut the alarm off quickly at eight a.m. so as not to wake Ellen, then came downstairs, put on a pot of coffee and brought the turkey out from the cool larder to start preparing it. For once, downstairs really did look nice. Quinn had made swags of greenery – laurel and bay with trailing strands of creamy-margined ivy – to go above the fireplace in the sitting room, along the shelves of the dresser, and over the big mirror in the hall. I nipped out to the garden to pick the herbs for the turkey, the way I had done whenever I was in this house for Christmas for as long as I could remember. Grated zest from a lemon and an orange. Peeled a couple of onions. I took a satsuma from the basket on the old wooden trunk to eat with my coffee. It was nice being here, in the calm before the storm, with no-one else making a noise or getting in my way – but also knowing that soon the others would be up and they'd drift in for coffee and toast, and ask if I was doing eggs.

In front of the fireplace, Quinn had set the massive old pot we fill with evergreen branches – Mum's pot, with its beautiful, unusual glaze, the colour not quite green and not quite blue, hovering between the two, the clay beneath showing through in swirls made with a wax-resist. There were branches of spruce and pine at the back, with gold-edged holly, thickly beaded with red berries, in front, and spotted laurel, its shiny leaves splashed with cheerful yellow-gold, looking like bright paint had been flicked on them with a toothbrush.

So I was standing in the kitchen with my hand halfway up the turkey, shoving in bits of onion and lemon and sprigs of thyme. I was feeling perfectly happy, completely relaxed in the way that you can only be when you are quite alone – and singing a sort of bluesy version of 'We Three Kings' when a voice right behind me said, 'Is there any coffee?'

Simone. Oh, hello, good morning and happy Christmas to you too. I'd forgotten she was even in the house; when people come down from upstairs, it sounds like thundering hooves, the carpet's so worn, but the stairs up from Mum's studio have that thick sisal stuff on them, so you can't hear a thing. Also, Simone had bare feet, toenails painted a dark red.

'Oh!' I said, making a bit of a thing of it. 'Hi. You *startled* me.' She didn't bother to apologize, just slumped into Dad's big carver chair at the end of the table. 'Happy Christmas,' I added, with not much feeling. 'Or do you go for Winter Solstice? Though we've passed that already, haven't we?'

She shrugged.

'My mother only pretends to be into all that Solstice shit because she's still desperately trying to rebel against the nuns – it's pathetic.' She looked over at the worktop, angling for some minion to come and supply her with her caffeine-fix.

'The nuns?' I took a mug from a hook and filled it with coffee.

'Yuh.' She arched a single eyebrow. 'Didn't Ma tell you?' She snorted, evidently amused. 'She went to convent school. I don't think her parents were even especially religious – they just wanted her to speak nicely and not mix with the nasty rough children at the state school – that type, you know?' She delved into the pocket of her silk dressing gown and came out with a packet of cigarettes. 'Ashtray?'

Honestly. I wish Quinn had sent *her* to convent school – at least then she might say please and thank you occasionally.

I handed her a saucer and she vaguely proffered the cigarettes in my direction.

'Oh – you don't, do you? I really should give up sometime . . . vile habit,' she said as she lit up, clearly with no intention of ever doing so.

'No. Quinn's never told me that. She never talks about her schooldays.'

And I don't think I've ever even asked her, I thought.

'No surprises there. A couple of the nuns were frightful, frustrated old bitches, if you ask me. One of them used to smack the girls over the backs of their hands with a wooden ruler. And they were always telling them to keep their hands on their desks. Ma thought it was because they weren't supposed to be writing girlish notes to each other or secretly un-wrapping sweets, but oh no—' She exhaled sharply.

'What? Wasn't that it?'

She shook her head.

'No. It was so the nuns would know that the girls weren't touching themselves – *down there*, as they used to say.'

'No!'

'Exactly. Who'd want a wank in a roomful of school-girls and decrepit nuns? Not my idea of a turn-on.'

'How bizarre.' I suddenly felt sorry for Quinn, picturing her for a moment looking young and holding out her hands to be struck, her eyes welling up with tears. 'Poor, poor Quinn. I didn't realize.'

*   *   *

380

I offered Simone some breakfast, reminding her that we don't usually eat the main meal till three or four in the afternoon.

'I never eat breakfast – not unless you count three fags and a vat of coffee. Better not say anything to Ma. She's quite ashamed of her past – anyone'd think she'd been in prison rather than a convent school. I think it's 'cause she's tried to reinvent herself as this right-on arty-farty earth-mother type and it doesn't fit with her being a repressed Catholic girl from a semi in the suburbs.'

'Well, we all react against our pasts, I suppose, don't we?'

She looked straight at me, unblinking.

'You mean me, right?' She took a deep drag of her cigarette. 'Fair enough. Still – better to be a stressed-out, materialistic yuppie shrew or whatever my mother thinks I am than an ageing wannabe hippy.'

'I wasn't thinking of you at all, actually.' I turned away to cut some bread and put it in the toaster. 'I meant just generally.'

'Really?'

'Well.' I shrugged. 'And me, I suppose.'

Her brow furrowed and she mashed out her cigarette firmly.

'I hadn't figured you for a rebel. You and your family—' She cocked her head on one side while she thought a moment. Just the way Quinn does, I noticed. 'You *fit* together – like a jigsaw.'

'Us?' I laughed. 'But we're always squabbling and interrupting and getting up each other's noses. Not exactly a pretty-picture jigsaw, is it?'

'So? At least you're all part of the same puzzle. You know . . .' She looked down. 'Many people would be kind of . . . envious of you lot.'

I stared at her incredulously. I couldn't imagine Simone's being envious of anyone. She's so successful, for a start. And she's clever and attractive and immaculately groomed. Besides, she's normally so dismissive of other people.

'Yuh,' she continued. 'Even when you're arguing – in fact, *especially* when you're arguing – you all mesh – like a real family. You're all different, sure, but you're at least all on the same wavelength. Shit, when I'm talking to Ma, half the time I feel as if we're not even on the same planet. As for my father – ' She paused to take out another cigarette and light up. 'He's just a complete arse basically. Still kidding himself he's an artist at the age of sixty. He is such a loser.'

She looked at me.

'That's not meant as a snide dig or anything,' she said. 'I mean, I don't see your dad as a wannabe. He's like a real designer, right? He earns a living and everything, he's not wafting around banging on about expressing himself.'

'Mmm.' I guess I must have looked a bit blank because she cocked her head in that assessing way once more and said, 'What? Your toast's getting cold, by the way.' She gestured over behind me with her cigarette.

I took out the toast, buttered it and cut it into triangles, then sat down and set it on the table between us.

'You're right. I always think of Dad as being hopelessly befuddled and incompetent – and, yes, he *is* vague and impractical and infuriatingly untidy – but he *does* earn a decent living and he managed to bring up the three of us virtually single-handed. And he's absolutely professional about his work, unexpectedly precise and fastidious in some ways about design details. Funny, isn't it? When you suddenly see someone you know so well in a slightly different light – like going round the back of a sculpture and realizing it's not at all what you expected from seeing just the front.'

'Ma said your mother painted, too. Have you any of her work?' She picked up a piece of toast and started eating it.

'Very little. She didn't just paint though – she did etchings, sculpted in clay and wax, made tapestries, ceramics, she loved to experiment – though the results were a bit erratic. She made that big pot in the fireplace, with the branches in.'

Simone went in to look at it then came back and crossed to the worktop to put on more toast.

'It's rather good, isn't it? Why haven't you got much of her stuff left? Did you flog it or what?'

'No.' I almost wished I hadn't started on this conversation, except that it was still so calm here in the kitchen and it suddenly seemed easy to be talking about this to someone I didn't know so well. 'A lot of it was . . . badly damaged. Well. Destroyed.'

That arched eyebrow again, but no comment.

'Got any Marmite?'

I laughed and pointed to the cupboard. I thought she'd just said it to break the tension.

'My brother, Matt – he went a bit ballistic after our mother died. He – he smashed up a lot of her stuff.'

'Christ. He doesn't look the type, does he? But wasn't he just a kid at the time?'

'Yes, not quite eight. After Mum died, Matt hardly spoke a word for days and then, on his birthday, Dad went downstairs and found him in the studio – surrounded by broken glass, smashed ceramic heads, busted canvases. With poor Matt in the middle of it all, curled up into a ball.' I felt at once relieved to have said it but also guilty for having told someone outside the family. 'Please don't say anything.'

'Whatever.' She shrugged. 'All families have their skeletons.'

'Of course. But he's so happy and settled now, he doesn't need to be reminded of that time. And also . . .'

Simone took another deep drag of her cigarette, and waited.

I looked down into my empty mug.

'Ellen doesn't know.'

Then Dad came shuffling into the kitchen in his slippers. Looked surprised to see us sitting there so cosily.

'Morning, girls. Happy Thingummyjig.' Dad doesn't like to use the C-word if he can help it. Normally, it drives me crazy, but now, this morning, it suddenly made me feel ridiculously tender towards him.

I stood up and gave him a hug.

'Happy Thingummyjig, Dad.'

'Yuh,' said Simone, waving her toast at him in what I supposed was some sort of greeting. 'Happy whatever.'

'D'you want scramblies? Lunch won't be for hours.' I took up my post by the turkey once more and started packing soft butter mixed with herbs under the breast skin.

'Love some. Thank you.'

'Let me just get this beast in and on the go.'

'I can peel potatoes or something if you want.' Dear God – Simone, volunteering to help. 'But I can't cook to save my life. I only use my microwave to heat up coffee.'

After a little while, Quinn appeared and came and kissed each of us on the cheek. Then I cleared the table of the breakfast things and started preparing the veg. Simone went off for a shower and returned looking wonderful as always, in a tiny red skirt and black cashmere jumper and gorgeous suede mules of the sort that I can't even seem to stand up in.

Eventually, Ellen deigned to make an appearance, wearing a big, baggy T-shirt and thick socks.

'Is there any breakfast?' She came over and looped her arms round me and gave me a kiss. 'Happy Thingummyjig, George.' Then she went and hugged Dad and kissed Quinn.

'Chef's off duty now. There's toast if you like.'

Ellen opened the fridge.

'Are there any eggs?'

'Please, please, please don't go making a huge mess, Ellie. I need the worktop clear to do the veg, and I've only just wiped the table.'

'Oh, fuss, fuss. I can do it again.' Stood there with the fridge open. 'Aren't you doing scramblies?'

'Not again, no. I've already done all that. It's nearly twelve.' She gave me a pleading look, like a forlorn puppy. 'Oh, for God's sake – how about a boiled egg then? Final offer.'

'Yes, please. Can I have two please? Thank you, thank you – you're the best sister in the whole world.'

'Don't go overboard. I'm not giving you one of my kidneys. It's only a boiled egg.'

'*Two* boiled eggs. And toast.'

'You do the toast. I'm not your slave.'

'It must be quite fun having a sister,' Simone chipped in. 'Sort of like a friend who it's OK to argue with.'

'George is my best friend, too. Always has been.'

'Am I really?' I felt ridiculously pleased. 'What about Vicky? You go out with her all the time, don't you?'

'Yeah, Vicky's my best *mate*. But you're my *closest* friend.'

I smiled and crossed to the toaster.

'How many toasts? One or two?'

'Two, please.'

Dad was shaking his head and smiling to himself.

'Ellen, you should be running the country – you can get anyone to do anything for you.'

Simone went downstairs to her room and returned with a bottle of champagne.

'It's not too early to open this, is it? I've had it chilling on the window ledge.'

'Never too early for me,' Ellen said.

'Just a tiny drop for me.' Quinn went to fetch glasses from a cupboard.

'There's fresh orange juice if you want to do Buck's Fizz,' I pointed out.

'I'll have it straight,' said Ellen.

Simone opened it with consummate ease and brought me over a glass filled almost to the brim.

'Oh thanks, but can I just have orange juice please?'

She frowned.

'Don't you drink at all? You didn't have anything last night either.'

'George is practically teetotal.'

'No, I'm *not*. I enjoy a glass of wine as much as anyone. I just don't like to overdo it, that's all.' I put the red cabbage on the chopping board and started slicing it thinly.

Ellen laughed loudly, too loudly.

'George's idea of overdoing it is anyone who has a second glass, Simmy – so prepare to be given a lecture if you dare to start enjoying yourself.'

'That's so unfair – I don't stop anyone else drinking—'

'You do. You had a go at me on my birthday.'

'Only because you were making a complete twat of yourself! You were *excruciatingly* embarrassing.'

'So what if I was? What's so bad about making a twat of yourself once or twice a year? Big bloody deal.'

Simone's head turned from me to Ellen and back again, as if she were watching a tennis match.

'Now, now, kids.' Dad spread his hands out, palms downwards, to signal us to calm down. 'Let's not get to the crockery-hurling stage too early in the day . . . there's still the afternoon and evening to get through – leave it till later and we can have it to look forward to.'

30

Peace and goodwill

Ellen proudly put on the pink glittery headband, her present from Bonnie, then barricaded herself in the kitchen, pulling the dividing doors closed so that we couldn't see in.

'I shall now prepare . . . the table,' she intoned. 'Do not enter under any circumstances – on pain of being pelted with squashy satsumas.'

The phone rang while I was unwrapping my present from Matt and Izzy, a beautiful, soft cream jumper that must have been bought by Izzy. Quinn answered it.

'Hello? Ah, hello, how are you? Happy Christmas to you too. Are we seeing you later? . . . Ah, I see. OK. I'll just get Georgia for you.'

Stephen, presumably, though I had already rung him earlier to say happy Christmas. Probably just confirming what time he was turning up later. I laid the jumper carefully over the arm of my chair and stood up.

'It's Leo,' she said.

I stood with my back to the others.

'Hello?'

'Hey, you. It's me. If you're really not speaking to me, just nod, OK?'

'And for those of you listening in black-and-white, the red cracker is the one to the left of the green.'

He laughed.

'Tell me you're having a good Jewish Christmas over there – good food, good jokes and good arguing, with not a sausage roll or paper hat in sight.'

'Well – more or less. The arguing's coming along nicely.' I dropped my voice, knowing that the others would be straining to hear every word. 'I'm glad you've rung. I – I really am. I wanted to say sorry. I never meant— God, I'm hopeless. Are you having a good time? How's Cora?'

'No, I'm not. I've eaten six mince pies out of sheer boredom. Cora's fine though. Look – this is crazy – this is supposed to be the season of peace and goodwill and here I am, being cross with you and cross with me and feeling like hell. Georgia – you *can't* not talk to me. It's not allowed. And if Stephen's not happy with that, well then he'll just have to see me about it – um – he's not as fit as he looks, is he?'

I laughed.

'Tell him we've saved two places at the table,' Dad called out.

'Did you hear that? . . . Of course he's being serious . . . yes, I'd love you to, too, you know I would . . . you must come . . . that's OK . . . it doesn't matter a bit . . . no, of course not, don't be silly . . . no, don't worry, it doesn't matter . . . yes, whenever. Good. See you then. Take care.'

I turned round and they were all looking at me except Bonnie and Daniel who were 'helping' Dad open his presents, ripping off the paper and throwing it around the room.

'Leo's coming too then, is he?' Matt said. 'Excellent.'

'Is he all right?' Quinn asked.

'Yes. Well, sort of. He's at Cora's aunt's and they're making him wear a paper hat and sing carols but he says the atmosphere's horrible – you-will-be-jolly-whether-you-like-it-or-not and Cora's got no-one to play with. They've had their lunch already, so they won't need feeding, but he's fretting because he hasn't got us presents.'

'But we don't mind about that,' Izzy said. 'Bonnie – Cora's going to come over. Do you remember her?'

Bonnie nodded.

'Do I have to give her a present?'

'You don't *have* to, Bonnie. But it would be nice if you did. You've got so many lovely things here, we could rewrap one of them for Cora.'

Bonnie thought for a minute, clearly wondering whether to give in graciously or throw a strop.

'OK. But not my Barbie.'

'Ellie?' I knocked on the dividing doors.

'Don't come in!'

'I'm not. But Leo and Cora are coming. Can you set another two places?'

'Aaaaaarrrrggghh! No! I haven't got enough napkins!'

'Use the ones in the dresser drawer!' Quinn shouted.

'They won't match!'

When has Ellen ever worried about anything matching?

'They'll have eaten already, but you never know, they might manage a nibble.'

'Oh, bloody hell!' I could hear her stomping over to the dresser. 'Don't tell me Mr P-h is bloody going to turn up too because then I really will throw a wobbly.'

'But you *know* he is,' I shouted.

'He's *not*!'

'Yes, but not till later.'

'Not for the meal? He doesn't need a napkin?'

'No.'

'Oh. Well, that's OK then. I can put up with the P-h as long as he isn't going to sit down or anything.'

'Ellie – I have to get in there to baste the turkey and turn the potatoes. Can you *please* hurry up?'

'Can't you do it blindfolded?'

'Of course – nothing I'd like more than to wrestle a fifteen-pound lava-hot turkey out of the oven and spoon hot fat over it without being able to see.'

'OK – you can come in – but no-one else.'

Knowing Ellie, I figured she'd come up with something, well, Ellen-ish. Gold glitter place mats and loads of pink tinsel. Can't you just see it? She led me in from the hall, covering my eyes with her hand.

'OK – ready?' She removed her hand. 'Open your eyes!'

Along the centre of the table was a line of six ivory candles, each one in a most unusual-looking holder, half sprayed gold and half left unsprayed –

'Oh my God – they're *bagels*!'

'Right. You like?'

'I *like*. This is brilliant!'

Around the bagel candleholders, trails of ivy entwined, with subtle touches of gold here and there on the leaves. The place mats were beautiful, some sort of wonderful dark green slate.

'And these?' I tapped one.

'Floor tiles – left over from when Brian had his bathroom done.'

The napkins were plain calico, secured in spiral coils of more ivy.

'It's beautiful, Ellie. It really is.'

'I kept thinking, all the time I was doing it, would Georgia like this or would she think it was naff? But you haven't seen the best bit. Look up!'

Suspended above the centre of the table was a mobile, with small pipe-cleaner figures dressed in coloured tissue, dangling from invisible threads.

'What are – oh God – Ellie!'

There was a male figure, wire hands clutching a miniature newspaper.

'Is that *Dad*?'

'Of course.'

One had wild curls and pink jeans and was holding three bags – Ellie. One had yellow-painted legs and ridiculous outsize earrings made of wire and tinfoil – Quinn. Another was tiny and hanging upside down as if from a trapeze – Daniel. Bonnie. Matt. Izzy. Even Simone. And there – right in the middle – was a Christmas fairy or angel. Except that it wasn't. It didn't have wings, just a tiny wand, with a silver star at the end. Aside from this one festive touch, the figure was plainly dressed, wearing black trousers and a white top.

'But why—?'

'Because you *should* have a magic wand – you're always the one who tries to make everything all right again – whether it's your clients or us.'

'God, I wish that were true. All I've done recently is make a total hash of things left, right and centre.'

'You haven't. You've just – ' She shrugged. 'Become a bit less Georgia-ish and a bit more like a normal person. It's *good*.'

*   *   *

'Hi, everyone! Happy Thingummyjig, happy Christmas, happy Solstice etcetera, etcetera.'

A burst of hellos as Leo goes round the table, saying 'don't get up' and kissing cheeks and shaking hands. He sets two bottles, port and champagne, on the worktop.

'Now, have I missed anyone?' Leo says, making out that he's about to sit down.

'Only the chef. No-one of any importance.'

'Auntie Gee!' shouts Bonnie.

'The chef? You mean I have to kiss the *staff*? Uch – these liberal households . . .'

He comes up next to me.

'Best not to get too witty while I'm wielding a large knife.'

He puts his arm round my waist then kisses my cheek in a chaste manner.

'Ohh,' says Ellen, 'call that a kiss?' She tips the last of a bottle into her glass. 'Pass that other bottle along, will you, Matzo?'

We eventually wind to a halt, weighed down with turkey and too many potatoes, and slump onto the sofas and cushions in the sitting room. After a while, Bonnie and Daniel start to get tired and fractious, so Izzy suggests taking them home. Dad, who hardly drinks at all, volunteers to take Matt back later. Cora, I notice, is also running out of steam, though she doesn't get stroppy like Bonnie. Her eyelids are drooping.

'And I see my little one is fading fast too . . .'

'Oh, don't go!' says Ellen.

'She can go to sleep in our room.' Quinn stands up. 'Then you can wrap her in a quilt to take her home. Or you're welcome to stay – we can all squash up.' Leo picks up Cora and Quinn leads the way upstairs.

The ghost of Christmas past

Ellen reaches across me for what must be the fifteenth time, knocking over my water glass to get to the wine.

'Ellen!'

'Oops! Sorry. Sorry, sorry, *sorry*! Relax – it's only water.' She dabs vaguely at me with a stray napkin, pours yet more wine into her glass.

'Don't you think you've had *enough* now?' I keep my voice low, so as not to embarrass her.

'Come on, George, light'n up, will you?' Her voice is slightly slurred but, as usual, clearly audible to anyone living within a mile's radius. 'You have another glass – it won't kill you. C'mon, have some with me.'

'I don't want any more. And you shouldn't either. You really have—'

'Why not, for fuck's sake?' She takes a swig, knocking it back dramatically to make a point. 'If you don't want to enjoy yourself, fine, but don't go spoiling it for everyone else. Get off my case – you're not my mother.'

'Ellen . . .' Dad says. 'That's enough now.'

I stand up to start clearing away the coffee cups to the kitchen.

'So . . . Leo . . .' Ellen says, loudly, and as soon as I hear his name I just know she's going to say something awful. 'Tell me, before the P-h arrives to spoil the fun – are you madly in love with my sister or aren't you?'

'Ellen! For God's sake!'

'Personally, I think you *are* . . .' she continues, ignoring me, 'and Matt thinks you're only hanging back because of Stephen – because you're a decent bloke, but Georgia—'

'Ellen. Just *shut up*. Right now.' I turn to face her. 'Leo.' I cannot look at him. 'I'm terribly sorry. Ellen's just being stupid and ridiculous—'

'It's OK. Really. Don't worry about it.' His voice is calm, but still I cannot bear to meet his eye.

'Because she's had way too much to drink and—'

The doorbell rings.

'Saved by the bell!' Ellen calls out, rolling her eyes at Simone, hoping to find an ally.

'That'll be Stephen. Ellen – don't you dare carry on like this in front of him.'

'Happy Christmas, darling!' Stephen puts his arms round me and kisses me on the lips. 'Are you all having fun?'

'We were, but Ellen's had too much to drink. She's behaving appallingly – please, please promise me just to ignore her if she gets too awful.'

'I'll do my best. But never mind, eh? She'll have a lousy head in the morning and say she's sorry, I'm sure.'

It's not like Stephen to be so laid-back.

'And also – now don't go mad, but Cora and Leo are here. Dad invited them ages ago, and they only decided to come at the last minute – so I didn't know, I swear. But can we please not get stressed out about it? It's Christmas – let's not spoil it.'

He nods, though he looks decidedly unhappy about it.

'All right. But we're not staying long.'

'Hello, everyone. Happy Christmas! Er . . . Happy *Thingummy* . . .' Stephen says, tailing off and sounding embarrassed. He nods at Leo.

'It's Thingummy*jig*,' Ellen says, 'Not Thingummy. Mr P-h – you don't know how much we've missed your sparkling company and dazzling repartee. Come and sit here and entertain me!'

Oh, God. Why won't she just stop?

Stephen takes a seat and I can see Dad attempting to hold a normal conversation with him, but with Ellen sitting between them, it's impossible.

'Isn't there any more wine?'

'I stuck another bottle of bubbly in to chill,' says Simone.

Oh, thank you. That was helpful.

'Will you have some, Stephen?' Quinn stands up and goes to fetch another glass while Matt opens the champagne.

'Thank you. I will. Just the one though as I'm driving.' The original plan was for Stephen to spend the whole evening with us before driving us both back to his place, but now I sensed we were in a rush to leave as soon as possible.

'Don't forget me, Matzo.' Ellen waggles her glass at him. Her eyes have that out-of-focus expression, as if she is looking at someone over Matt's shoulder.

'Why – not exactly dying of thirst, are you, Ell?'

'God – you're getting like George. Nag, nag, nag. It's Christmas and I've barely had a drop all day . . .'

'That's complete crap, Ell, and you know it.'

'Come on, Ellie. Have some coffee instead.'

Stephen is nervously watching us.

'Oh – will everyone just STOP getting at me!' Ellen stands up suddenly, knocking over her glass. 'I'm perfec-ly fine. Leo – you, you think I'm fine, don' you? Mr P-h? Let me tell you – you don' want to marry George – she won't let you have more than one drink at the wedding—'

'Ellen! Cut it out!' I step closer and grab her arm but she jerks away from me.

'Don' boss me! You're just cross 'cause I asked Leo if he was in love with you and he never answered!'

Stephen's face is as if carved of stone.

'*Ellen.*' Dad's voice is serious and deadly calm. 'You have clearly had more than enough to drink and you're now embarrassing our guests as well as yourself. I think you should go upstairs right now and have a lie-down.'

'Why's everyone havin' a go at *me*?' she wails. 'What've *I* done?'

'Oh, Ell. Give it a rest.' Matt sounds angry. 'You know something? You're turning into a real lush. Wake up for God's sake! You drink too much, OK? Just because Dad and Gee do their usual act of trying to pretend it's not happening—'

'Matt – no – *don't*—'

'*Matthew,*' Dad says, making it sound like a warning.

'No. It's ridiculous. Everyone treats Ellen like a child and that's why – what a surprise! – she still acts like one. You can't keep trying to protect her from everything. Ell – face it, you're nearly thirty – time to grow up! You can't go round getting pissed the whole time like some teenager. I think it's becoming a real problem and you should take it seriously—'

'No, Matt – please!' But I can see from his face that nothing can stop him now.

'Take it *seriously* . . .' he says firmly. '. . . Because

Mum – Mum – she . . .' His voice fades and he slumps into a chair.

Dear God.

Silence. Then Stephen looks at me, suddenly comprehending, utterly shocked. Leo, unsurprised, sends me a look of sympathy.

'What do you mean?' Ellen's voice is like a child's.

'Do you need everything spelled out for you? She was an alcoholic. How clear does it have to be?'

'But – she *can't* have been.' Ellen looks round at Matt, at Dad, at me. 'I'd *know*. George would have told me. Dad would have.'

'Would they?'

She turns to me once more, her eyes imploring, but I look away. Then she faces Dad. He sighs.

'We thought it would be easier for you not to know, Ellen. That's all.'

'But all the stories George told me about when we were kids.' Back to face me again. 'You never *said*!'

'She wasn't like that at first. Not when I was little. I wanted you to think of her the way *I* remember her, the way she was in the beginning – the way she was *before*.'

Ellen looks round the room, slowly turning, assessing the expressions of the others.

'*You* knew.' She accuses Quinn, who nods. Simone and Stephen are clearly dumbstruck; there is no doubt that it is a revelation to them both. 'And *you*.' She frowns, pointing at Leo. 'And Matt – is that why you never talk about her?' He drops his gaze and I can see that the enormity of what he's said is starting to hit home.

All these years and I have never been sure whether Matt really knew or not. Now, it seems impossible that I never asked him. Of course, it was clear that he didn't want to talk about Mum and I knew he remembered smashing up her studio because he was so angry with her, but I thought he was just angry about her dying, not about . . . everything else. I was never sure if he *knew*.

'I don't remember all of it, just bits and pieces.' Matt's shoulders are hunched. 'Her mood swings – her little naps to sleep it off – never being on time – lying – making promises she didn't keep – letting us down again and again – laughing so loudly that everyone turned to stare – embarrassing the shit out of us.' Dad hangs his head, Quinn's hand on his shoulder, a silent support. 'But Georgia bore the brunt of it, trying to hide the bottles when she found them, getting Mum up and bullying her to get dressed – she was running this household well before Mum died, any fool could tell that. Gee's been a way better mother to you than Mum ever was.'

The Last Christmas with Joy

For the last three years, Daddy has done the stockings, but he doesn't know what to put in them and he doesn't have time to make things like Mummy used to – miniature postboxes or a marble-look fireplace for her dolls' house or pipe-cleaner dolls with braided wool hair, just like proper plaits, or handmade little books telling stories in which Georgia is a princess, a glamorous film star, an international spy and Matt a daring pilot, a private detective, the owner of the world's largest lorry. Now, they get packets of felt-tips and new pencil cases for school and a small doll or a toy car, with a net of gold chocolate coins and a tangerine in the toe, nice things, ordinary things like other children get.

Georgia picks up her stocking and takes it into Ellen's room to open. Normally, by now, Ellen would have come bounding into Georgia's room, jumping on the bed and squealing with excitement. Ellen's chubby little fingers are not yet adept at the art of peeling the foil from chocolate coins, but she has opened the chocolate selection box sent by Aunt Grace and eaten half of the contents. The empty chocolate wrappers are scattered around her, along with a riot of torn tissue and paper. Ellen sits in the middle of it all, glassy-eyed, with chocolate-coloured vomit down the front of her pyjamas.

'Oh, Ellie!' Georgia takes Ellen's hand and leads her through to the bathroom, peels off the yucky pyjamas, runs a flannel under the tap and wrings it out. Ellen, sated with sugar, stands relatively still while Georgia wipes her down and gives her a toothmug of water.

Georgia and Joy are preparing the lunch. Joy is rummaging through the contents of the vegetable basket, saying she can't find the carrots.

'No, Mummy. We have to start the turkey or it'll be ever so late. We don't keep the carrots in there anyway actually.'

'Since when? Where do we keep them *anyway actually*?' Joy is smiling.

'In the fridge. But we *have* to do the *turkey*.'

The bird is sitting in a roasting tin, looking large and pink and naked. Spread out on the worktop are a packet of foil, the butter, two onions and a handful of herbs from the garden.

'It's no great shakes whether we serve it at one o'clock or three o'clock, is it? Besides, grown-ups are more than happy to relax with a little something while they wait for lunch.'

A little something. That's what she calls it.

'But it *won't* be *lunch*. It'll be *supper*. We *have* to put it in the *oven*.'

The oven is the kind that still has to be lit by hand – with a match if you're brave, stretching your arm right to the back to the scary dark gap from where the gas comes hissing like a snake, until it snatches the flame from your fingers and you yank your hand back fast as you can. Or you can make a long taper from a twisted sheet of paper, which you have to throw in the sink after and run the tap over. Georgia won't ask, but Joy knows she's waiting for her to light the oven.

'So bossy! I don't know where you get it from – ' Joy sighs and turns on the oven knob, then casts round for a match. There are none on the counter. 'Your father's side of the family probably – all those stern Russian matriarchs, God help us.' She crosses to the dresser, starts poking about in the big dish of coins and sugar sachets taken from restaurants. Georgia eyes the open oven door and holds her breath. 'I'm sure there were some in here . . .' Joy stretches up with one hand and starts feeling her way along the top shelf. 'Somewhere . . . ah, here they are.' Strolls back to the oven. Georgia sidles further away, to the far side of the big wooden table.

Joy strikes a match and chucks it casually into the depths of the oven. There is a loud *whoomph*. Even Joy jerks back slightly.

Georgia bites her lip, stays where she is.

'Oh, darling, don't look so cross. It's Christmas! Come on – come here and give Mummy a kiss.'

Georgia slowly comes forward to comply. Her mother hugs her tight, showers kisses on the top of her head.

'Let's dance! We should be enjoying ourselves, not doing boring old cooking!'

She seizes Georgia by the elbows and whirls her round the kitchen, singing, 'Deck the halls with boughs of holly! Fa-la-la-la-lah-la-la-la-laaah! 'Tis the season—' Stops as she catches sight of Georgia's face, slows to a halt, a final twirl.

'Well.' She draws back a pace. 'Perhaps we'd better get that bird in.'

It is not quite a quarter to twelve when Joy says, to no-one in particular, 'Well, it's Christmas – we'd better drink a toast, hadn't we?'

David gets out two sherry glasses and half-fills them.

'Down to emergency rations already?' Joy asks, laughing.

David doesn't reply, but goes to the fridge to get Coca-Cola for the children, a rare treat.

At half past twelve, Unc turns up with Auntie Audrey and the cousins. As well as presents, they bring chocolates and two bottles of wine to join the single bottle David has put out.

Unc is driving, so has just one glass. Auntie Audrey claims to get tipsy if she even so much as looks at a bottle of sherry, but she lets David pour her a glass all the same. The cousins, like Georgia, Matt and Ellen, are allowed one sip each, just to taste.

There are presents to be unwrapped, family stories to recount as they have been recounted for years – the Day David Won the Sack Race at School by a Fluke, the Day Unc Proposed to Audrey and She Said, 'Perhaps', the Time when Joy Burned the Carpet with Acid, the Time Matt God Stuck in a Bog and had to be Lifted Clean out of his Wellies . . . There is laughing, drinking, nibbling of crisps and cheese straws. The smoked salmon starter is devoured, then everyone leaves the table again for the turkey is still not cooked through.

At four o'clock, the immense turkey is finally brought to the table and David begins to carve.

Vegetable dishes are set out, but the table is too crowded for them to be moved so carrots, sprouts, peas are spooned across the table. Potatoes are relayed from plate to plate. Gravy is poured at full stretch.

'Won't you open some more wine for our guests, David dear?'

'Mmm . . .' he looks round, then sees the empty bottles on the worktop. 'Oh. Well – does anyone want any more?'

'Not for me,' says Unc. 'I'm driving.'

'Go on,' Joy urges Audrey, 'live a little.'

'Oh, I couldn't.'

'You must!' Joy insists. 'It's only once a year. Come on. God, you're all such bloody stick-in-the-muds, you lot – can't we just take the brakes off for once!'

Unc laughs, he can take a joke, his eyes avoiding his brother's. Audrey smiles awkwardly.

'Just a sip then. Only if you're opening it, mind.'

'Of course we are! Aren't we?' She gets to her feet.

David pauses a moment, at last carving some turkey for himself.

'Of course.' He puts down the knife and stands on a chair to open a high cupboard. 'Oh.'

'I'll get it!' Joy disappears into the hallway, can be heard clanking about in the depths of the clutter under the stairs. 'Found one!'

'That was lucky.' David's voice, sounding bright and jovial.

Mummy's voice gets louder and louder when she is being like this. She laughs when people say things that are not funny and when you look at her, her eyes are strange, all shiny like polished stones, or as if she is looking at something just beyond your shoulder and not really at you at all.

When Mummy is being like this, Daddy hides behind the newspaper, but now, today, all the family is here and the papers have been stuffed out of sight in the dresser. Daddy smiles and fills Audrey's glass almost to the very top when she is looking the other way. After the meal, when Georgia comes to sit by him, he pulls her close and kisses the top of her head, then smiles at her. It is the smile he does when he is not properly smiling, a smile that gives Georgia a funny feeling in her insides, as if she has swallowed a big piece of bread and now it is just sitting there in her chest, stodgy and stuck.

*   *   *

Unc starts singing, quietly at first, then his voice growing stronger, deeper, hamming it up a bit, signalling for David to join him – an old Hebrew song, the words at once strange and familiar to Georgia. 'Our Chanukah carol' Unc calls it, the song he and David and their sister Rachel had to sing as children for Chanukah, the Festival of Lights, though calling it a carol is just Unc's joke, of course. Then Joy joins in, for after all these years she knows the words almost as well as David does, her voice deeper than you'd think to look at her slight frame. A smile passes between her and her husband, a real smile, like the silver, heart-shaped locket that Georgia got as her most special present this very morning, small and precious and rare, something to treasure and keep.

And then the song ends and David and Unc give each other a big hug and Georgia and Matt and the cousins roll their eyes, already old enough to be embarrassed by their parents' singing and hugging.

'Another! Come on!' says Joy, although the moment has passed now. She always wants more, to go on longer, sing louder, dance more exuberantly than anyone else, doesn't know when to stop.

'Maybe later, hmm?' David firmly jams the cork back into the wine bottle, although it is virtually empty. Joy shrugs, as if she isn't bothered one way or the other, then dances across to put the coffee on, singing, without the words, a Christmas carol, 'Silent Night'.

Now, when it is like this, her father's arm stretched along the sofa behind her so she can tilt back her head at any second and know it is there, Georgia can make believe that everything is all right. Her mother is sitting on the floor, with Ellen sprawled across her knees – thumb in mouth, eyelids drooping. Unc is telling a long story but she does not hear the words, just lets the deep waves of his voice roll over her, wrapping round her like Granny's old eiderdown, safe and familiar and comforting. Georgia pushes her own thumb into the dip of a satsuma, holding it close to her face to sniff that first gasp of citrus, then easing off the peel in one piece if she can, holding the joins together, making the torn shell whole again so it looks almost like the real thing.

Suddenly, there is a loud snorting noise in the middle of Unc's story. Joy is snoring, her head fallen askew against the arm of the sofa, mouth gaping. The cousins laugh, look at that, their Auntie Joy snoring like a pig. Matt looks down at his shoes, undoes the laces then pulls them tighter, tying them in a careful double bow. Georgia bites her lip, folds her arms. Normally, when Mummy is being like this, Georgia just puts a blanket over her wherever she happens to be. She usually wakes up in a couple of hours and then she's all right again.

Unc laughs.

'So much for my skills as a raconteur!' He casts around for Audrey, brows raised. 'Anyway – we should be heading off soon . . .'

'No, really—' David begins. 'Joy's been up since the crack of dawn – cooking, you know.'

'Of course.' Audrey gets to her feet. 'It's a lot of work catering for the troops. Let's not disturb her, she looks . . . worn out.'

'Yes.' David nods. 'She's worn out.'

'C'mon, kids.' Unc marshals the cousins, who are nudging each other and making insufficiently surreptitious fake snores every two seconds. 'Stop that. Get your coats on.'

The hall is a buzz of activity then as jackets and boots are sorted out, bags found for the conveying of presents, hugs given. Georgia stands by her father's side, smiling, stretching up on tiptoe to kiss Unc and Auntie, thanking them for their gifts. Matt leans against her at such a sharp angle that he'd fall over if she stepped away, looking up at the ceiling, not saying goodbye properly; normally, she'd push him off, stupid Batzo-Matzo, but not now, not today.

In the sitting room, sprawled on the floor, Joy and Ellen sleep on.

31

A lifetime of lies

'Ellie?' I knock on the bathroom door.

'Go away.'

'Can I just talk to you for a minute?'

Silence.

'At least give me the chance to try to explain.' I rest my forehead against the door.

'What's to explain?' she calls back. 'And, by the way—' The door suddenly swings open and she stands there, red-eyed and smudgy-cheeked. 'Small intelligence test. None of these fucking doors have fucking locks on, remember? Nothing was stopping you coming in.'

She stomps across the room and plonks herself down on the bathmat on the floor. 'This should be interesting. We all know you're the Queen of Rational Thinking – but I'm just fascinated to know how you plan to explain away twenty-four years of lying.'

I shut the door and lean back against it.

'We – I – wanted to protect you . . .' Even to my own ears it sounds pathetic, one of the classic feeble excuses: we did it for your own good.

Ellen snorts with derision.

'Why? I'm not three years old any more, am I? OK – maybe, just *maybe*, that might have been some kind of excuse at the beginning – but all this time? Give me a break. Just when exactly were you planning on letting me in on this minor family secret – when they're wheeling me away to the twilight home?'

'I'm sorry. Of course, it's only natural for you to be angry—'

'Don't you *dare!*' She leaps to her feet. 'Don't you dare try and load any of that I'm-so-fucking-calm-and-reasonable counsellor shit onto me! It might work for you, but I'm not interested in your self-righteous rationalizing. You always do this! Everyone else is some sort of emotional fuck-up according to you – you're the only one who's perfect. Well – you're not fucking perfect, not even close, are you? Look what you said to Quinn, for fuck's sake – and you've been stringing Stephen along all this time when I don't think you even *like* the guy all that much, never mind *love* him – just think what bloody priceless pearls of wisdom you'd have dished out to me if I did that, hmm? And you'd have to be dead, blind or wilfully, unbelievably, bonkersly self-deluding not to see how you really feel about Leo. And Cora. Any idiot can see how you look at him. God – even Bonnie asked me the other day if I thought you'd let her be your bridesmaid – and, no, she wasn't talking about Stephen either – she said, "When Auntie Gee marries Cora's daddy" – she's *four* and she's got more nous than you. And then there's me, oh let's not forget me – it's easy to lie to little Ellie, isn't it? Ellen's clueless – everybody knows that. Ellen can't even manage to get from A to B without being an hour late. Ellen can't keep a boyfriend for longer than it takes him to get dressed again afterwards. Ellen – titter, titter – is still waiting to find out what she's going to be when she *grows up*. This wasn't some silly little lie to protect my feelings. You kept the truth from me about my own mother – year in and year out. I can understand Dad doing it, in a way – he'd rather hide behind the Review section than have to deal with anything real and messy – but *you*? You're

406

supposed to be dealing with this kind of crap all the time – you're always on about the importance of open, honest communication! How *dare* you?'

Her words whip against my face like sharp sand in the wind. I flatten the palms of my hands against the solid door behind me.

I wish I could be angry too – angry like she is – throw something, anything, back at her. But how can I when I know that she is right?

I shake my head, unable to speak at first.

'You don't know what it was like—'

'No.' She folds her arms and stands steady, straight and tall. 'Well, how could I as you've never told me? And – what about all our stories – ' She bites her lip, her eyes welling with tears. 'Those stories you always told me – were *any* of them true?'

'All true. I swear. But – I edited out the – the difficult bits – bits I thought you didn't need to know. I wanted you to have the perf— the mother you could have had, *should* have had – the way she was before she—'

'But what use is that? That's not how she *was*, is it? And who are *you* to judge what *I* need to know? You've fed me a fucking fantasy my whole life – and now I don't have a clue about anything any more.' She slumps to the floor again, huddling close to the bath. 'I never asked to have a *perfect* mother. I wanted to hear about Mum, about the past – but I didn't want stories – not really. I wanted to share your memories because I – I don't *have* any of my own. I thought you were *giving* me her as she really was. *All* of it. The crappy bits as well as the good stuff.'

'I'm sorry.'

Two words. Two words for a lifetime of lies. It is not enough. How could it possibly be enough?

She shakes her head then and hugs her knees up to her chest.

'Leave me alone.'

'Maybe I could—?'

'No.' She will not look at me. 'Just fuck off.'

Cold turkey

Stephen unwrapped the food parcels his mother had given him: cold turkey, ham, mince pies, swathed in multiple layers of foil and plastic bags.

'I can't believe you never told me,' he said, avoiding my eyes.

'It's not easy to tell. I felt . . . ashamed.'

'Why? It's not *your* fault.' He opened the fridge. 'Talking of which, 'scuse my black sense of humour, but do you want some wine? I've barely had a glass all day because of driving all over the place.'

'Yes, please. I will have a glass. You must be tired. I'm sorry you got dragged in to my family's – mess.'

He started to open the wine.

'What I don't understand, Georgia, is how come you couldn't tell me in all this time. Nearly four years.' He wanted to ask why I told Leo, and not him. I knew he wanted to know, but he was afraid to ask and I could not give him an answer, not an answer he could take. *Because I knew he wouldn't judge me. Or Mum. Because I knew he wouldn't give that little smug look on finding out about yet another of the Abrams' numerous flaws. Because I just came out with it one day and he listened. Because I knew I could trust him. Because . . .*

'I don't know. I was always scared you might – judge me somehow. I know you think my family are all hopeless. And you're right – we *are*.'

'Silly – you're not. Not at all. You're not to blame if your family are . . .' he shrugged, 'the way they are.'

'And you're so – so perfect sometimes. You never do anything wrong. Your family hasn't got any skeletons in the cupboard.'

'Oh, Georgia. No-one's perfect. And you make it sound as if there's something weird about my family being . . . just normal.'

'Sorry. I didn't mean that.'

He came closer and put his arms round me.

'Come on, sweetie. Let's not dwell on this. Forget about it for now. Let's have a bath and go to bed, eh?'

On Boxing Day, Stephen and I went to stay with some friends of his down in Sussex for a couple of days. It was good to get away from everybody and everything and not have to worry about my family for a change. I did almost nothing but read and sleep, as if I were convalescing from a long illness. When I returned to my flat afterwards, to pick up some more clothes to take to Stephen's, there was a message on my machine from Leo, so I rang him back and he came up for some tea.

'Hey – how are you doing? Have you managed to talk to Ellen?'

I shake my head and he puts his arms around me and just holds me.

'Listen – you're not to beat yourself up about all this. I know what you're like. You and your dad did what you thought was right.' He puts one finger gently under my chin and tilts my face up so that I'm looking into his eyes.

'But we were *wrong*.'

'You don't know that. Just because Ellen's angry about it – you can't possibly know how things would have been if you *had* told her. And even if you were wrong, it wasn't out of malice. You were only trying to do what was best for Ellen.'

'I can't let myself off the hook so easily.'

'OK. You're a vile, nasty, evil person – happy now?'

'Oh, *don't*.'

'Now, if you've finished with the sackcloth and ashes for the moment, can I demonstrate my usual chutzpah and ask if it's OK to stop by at brunch on Sunday? Or do you not bother with it over the break?'

'Of course you can, silly. You don't need to ask now,

you know that – you're part of— you're a regular. And Cora too. Always welcome.'

He smiles.

'How is she doing?'

'So-so, I guess.' A shrug. 'But she's so quiet. I told her I'm going to find a bigger place so she can come stay with me every weekend, have her own room, and I said she can choose everything to go in it and she smiled her funny, polite little smile and said "thank you" – as if I were a stranger.'

'You need to be patient.'

'Always my strong point, you know me . . .' He sighs, frustrated with himself as much as anything. 'I know, I know – don't tell me – it takes as long as it takes.'

I nod.

'She will come to love you and to *know* you as her daddy, I'm sure of it. But she just needs to feel . . . completely safe.'

He frowns.

'But she *is* safe. I'd do anything to protect her. Anything.'

'I know you would but that's not what I meant. She needs to *feel* safe. My guess is she can't risk getting close to you because she fears losing you as well as her mother. Who could blame her? It must be almost impossible for her to trust that you'll stick around – it's not your fault at all, but you weren't *there* before. How's she to know that you won't run off to – to Canada or wherever?' I laugh at myself then. 'Sorry – doing my counsellor schtick, you don't need that.'

'No. I do.' His eyes light up and he nods as if considering something. 'That makes sense.'

The sound of the wind

Sunday. A quiet brunch. No Matt and family. No Ellen. Brunch without Ellen. It's like smoked salmon without lemon juice. Dad phoned her but she said she didn't fancy it and wouldn't say any more than that.

I put on the coffee and chewed half-heartedly at a bagel. Simone was still there, surprisingly. I thought she'd have sloped off back to New York by now or gone to stay with one of her glamorous friends. She seemed to have come to some sort of ceasefire with Quinn and I noticed that they were falling over themselves to be polite to each other. It's a start, I guess. Ha! They could teach me a thing or two – what do I know about families? Ellen hates me, I'm still angry with Matt – I can't believe he was so stupid – and even though Quinn's doing her best to be nice to me, I can tell she's still upset. Full marks – have a fucking gold star, Georgia. How the hell will I be able to face my clients in the new year? I feel like such a fraud. I'm sure Stephen's seething beneath the surface too, deliberately not asking me the one thing he wants to know: why did you tell him, Georgia, and not me? The unspoken question hangs in the air between us, like some sticky cobweb suddenly caught in the light. We tread carefully, cautiously either side of it, afraid to step any closer.

The doorbell rang and, as Quinn was upstairs, Dad was hovering in an irritating way by the toaster and Simone showed no sign of emerging from behind the sanctuary of the Sunday papers, I went to answer it.

'Hello, Cora.'

She smiles shyly back at me, half-hidden behind Leo's leg.

'C'mon, Cora – say hello, hmm?'

I explain that Bonnie and Daniel won't be coming today as Matt and Izzy have taken them away for the weekend.

'It might be better,' I tell Leo. 'You know how dominating Bonnie can be.'

I try to draw Cora out a little more over brunch, but she remains almost silent and barely eats a thing. Dad fetches some paper and coloured pencils for her

411

and she sits there, quiet as a statue, drawing. Once more, she draws a girl standing alone in a garden, surrounded by grass and flowers.

Simone stands up.

'Just going outside.' She picks up her cigarettes. At least she's stopped smoking in the house.

She leaves the kitchen door open and also the back door to the garden, creating a huge draught. I roll my eyes at Leo.

'No-one in this family *ever* shuts the door.'

I leap up to close it, but then there is a sudden clanging noise, at once metallic and musical, like distant bells. Cora's head snaps up from her drawing.

'Cora?'

Her eyes are wide open, like a startled fawn.

'Do you know what that noise is?' I ask.

A silent nod.

'Do you want to come and see?'

Another nod.

Leo frowns and mouths, 'What?' and I motion for him to follow us. As we walk down the rear hall, Cora slips her hand into mine and I give it a small squeeze. Out into the garden now, the wet grass slicking our shoes.

'Oh, hi. Come to join me?' Simone says, puffing away.

'You left the door open.'

'Oh. Sorry.'

'No – it's good.'

Another sudden gust of wind. That sound again. Quinn's much-maligned wind chimes, hanging from the old apple tree at the other end of the garden.

Cora points, then runs towards them, laughing. She stops under the bough, her face tilted upwards, transfixed. I bend down to pick her up, hold her close so she can touch them, make them chime. Her face is serious now, thoughtful.

'Did you used to have these?'

412

She nods.

'Yes, but not the same. In Mummy's room. By the window. They're called wind chimes you know. They're very lucky.'

It is more in one go than she's said all day.

'Yes. Do you know where yours are now?'

A shake of the head.

'Shall we get you some more then?' Leo says. 'Would you like that?'

Quinn comes out to the garden, wondering where everyone has gone.

'Quinn – can we take down your chimes for a sec? Just to show them to Cora?'

I put Cora back down on the ground, but she stays on the same spot, looking up at them.

'Certainly. Here we go – ' Quinn unwinds the wire from the branch. 'Here, Cora – why don't you have these? They're a bit weatherbeaten, I'm afraid, but you're more than welcome to them.' She hands the chimes down to Cora, who looks up at Quinn, then round at Leo, then at me, as if checking that it is all right.

'Thank you.'

'Don't worry, Quinn,' Leo says. 'I can get her some.'

'You'll need two sets anyway, won't you? She can have one at her aunt's.'

He nods.

'Well, thank you. That's very kind of you.'

Cora holds the chimes high up in front of her as she goes back inside, like a flag borne aloft in victory.

'Quinn?' I touch her arm, as Leo and Simone go on ahead.

'Yes?'

It is hard to meet her gaze.

'I – what I said – that time—'

'Oh, that's OK. It's all in the past.'

'No. No, it isn't. I just want to say that I am really and truly sorry – I know I've never treated you – properly – like a – a – but I—'

'I've never tried to replace your mother, Georgia. No-one could do that.'

'No. I know. But that doesn't mean I—' I look down at the rough lawn, then force myself to meet her eyes again. 'I do know that I've teased you – and been kind of – well, mean, really – and it's unfair and I'm sorry. I do – I really do appreciate how – how much Dad loves you and how good you are for him – how good you've always been for him. He's much happier now than – than before. And I do – I do actually like you. And I'm really fond of you. I just – don't know – how – how to show it.' My hands fall to my sides and I look down once more. Why don't I know how to do this properly?

'Well, here's a secret – I like you too. I must confess I've always been a little scared of you – but I do like you.'

'*Scared?* Of me? Why?'

'Oh, Georgia – do you have any idea how you come across sometimes? You're so efficient and capable. You're so good at everything – even when you cut a slice of bread, you do it with such ease and grace. And I've always been so clumsy – my mother was always telling me off for dropping things – so I feel like an awkward girl of twelve again when I'm around you and I feel as if you're judging me and waiting for me to make a mistake . . .'

I try to swallow.

'I *am* very judgemental. I know that. Leo says I give people a hard time.'

'I know you're harder on yourself than you are on anyone else.'

I shake my head.

'That doesn't excuse it. It's just—' I shrug my shoulders, defeated. 'I've been like this for so long now I don't know how to be any other way any more.'

'Be patient with yourself. Everything takes time.'

I exhale a long breath, nod slowly.

'Friends then at least?'

'Yes please.' I suddenly want to hug her. All these

414

years and we've only ever exchanged polite cheek kisses. I stand there awkwardly. Perhaps it is too late, it would be too strange after all this time.

But she opens her arms wide suddenly, like a bird about to soar, unafraid to take the risk. I half-crumple against her.

'I don't know what's wrong with me,' I mumble into her shoulder. 'I seem to keep driving away everyone who matters most to me.'

'Sometimes it's easier that way. Safer.'

'Why is it?' I ask, although I already know the answer. It's so easy to be wise about everyone else.

'Because then we don't have to worry so much about losing them – if we don't let anyone too close in the first place, we think we won't miss them when they're gone.'

'But it doesn't work that way, does it? You miss them anyway.'

'That's right. Because you can't really stop yourself from loving people – not if you're someone like you, you can't.'

She fishes out a crumpled tissue from the pocket of her patchwork jacket. Her pockets are always full of old tissues. Used toothpicks, pens that don't work, and crumpled tissues.

I laugh and wipe my eyes.

'That is such a *Quinn* tissue.'

She laughs too then, and we go back inside for a pot of tea and some of her raisin bread, thickly spread with butter. Even Cora has a piece, despite the fact that it has bits in it, and Simone admits that it's 'not bad for one of Mother's culinary endeavours' – high praise indeed.

A child's job

'We'd better be off,' says Leo. 'I'm taking Cora to the Natural History Museum to see the dinosaurs. Fancy tagging along to help fend off the raptors?'

'I'd like to, but I want to stay here a bit longer. I need to talk to Dad.'

'Go on, Cora – will you go and get your coat – we put it up on the bed, remember?' She runs upstairs and he turns to me. 'That's a shame. Shall we bring you back a little rubber tyrannosaurus to go on the end of your pencil?'

'Don't know how I've lived without one all this time.'

He smiles and leans forward to kiss me on the cheek.

'What are you up to tomorrow, by the way – for New Year's?'

'I'm seeing Stephen. We're having people over for a dinner party. We do it every year.'

He steps back.

'Oh. Right. I thought you might spend it with your family.'

'No. Dad and Quinn are having a couple of friends round and they're babysitting Bonnie and Daniel here. What are you doing?'

'Oh, you know me. This and that. Been invited to a couple of things. See what I feel like tomorrow.'

'Ah, yes – last-minute Leo. Don't you ever plan anything in advance?'

His face is unsmiling.

'I don't like to get too attached to plans in general. They seem to have a way of not working out.'

'I didn't mean—' Cora comes running down the stairs again. I am about to help her on with her coat when Leo takes it from my hands.

'C'mon, Cora – off we trot.' He opens the door. 'Say bye-bye now.'

'Bye-bye.'

'Bye-bye. Have fun with the dinosaurs!' I stand on the front step and Cora turns to wave at me. Leo, clutching her hand, stares straight ahead, heading for his van.

Back in the kitchen, I poured myself some lukewarm tea and sank into a chair. Look on the bright side, I

416

thought, now you've alienated pretty much everyone you know, at least you're running out of people to offend. Dad was deep in the paper as usual and murmured a vague thank-you when I topped up his mug.

I asked Dad if Ellen had phoned him but he shook his head.

'But it'll be OK,' he said. 'You know Ellen – she can never stay angry for long.'

'Yes – but, Dad?'

'Hmm-mm?' he said, still keeping one eye on the paper as if it might make a dash for it if he dared to look away.

'Do you think we were right?'

He put down the paper and sat back. Took off his reading glasses.

'Not to tell her?'

'Mmm.'

'Hindsight is always 20-20, of course.' He tapped his glasses against his palm. 'No. I think I was wrong – *I* was wrong, Georgia, not *we*. It shouldn't have been up to you at all. None of it should have been. You – you always seemed so grown-up, you see? It was easy to think you could cope with anything. If someone had asked you to carry the world on your shoulders, you'd have said, "Make sure it's strapped on properly." And then you'd have soldiered on. But it wasn't your *job*. A child's job is to play, to learn, and to be loved – that's all. You shouldn't have had to worry about – anything else. I – *failed* you. I know I did. Very badly. I *wish* – it's too late to go back – but I wish so much . . .'

I reached forward to pat his hand, then perched on the arm of his chair and looped my arms around him.

'No, Daddy, *no*. You didn't fail me. Or us. Never, never. You were always the best dad in the world for me. *Always*.'

32

Six days to change the world

Ellen hasn't spoken to me since Christmas Day and now it is New Year's Eve. Six days. Just six days and I am living in a different world. A world without Ellen. Again and again I find my hand reaching for the phone, forgetting that I can no longer reach so casually for one of our endless, aimless chats, talking and giggling and interrupting and snapping at each other – our butterfly calls – that's what Stephen said they were, as we flitted from subject to subject in apparent non sequiturs, the links unspoken – unguessable to anyone other than us.

It's the longest we've not spoken since – ever. Even when I was away at college, when Ellen was still living at home, I phoned at least a couple of times a week, and when she was backpacking around Europe she often called, and not only when she'd lost her traveller's cheques, her money, her passport, her friends – she'd call from a youth hostel or a *pensione* or a lone phone booth in the middle of a village square, ringing to ask me what was the Italian for 'Please may I use your loo?', the French for 'Do you sell Tampax?', the Spanish for 'Meet us in this bar tomorrow.'

Dad tells me Ellen won't listen to him either, but he's sure it will be all right. Dad always says it will be all right. That was what he used to say about Mum. Quinn believes we must just give Ellen time, we must be patient and wait. Stephen thinks I am making a fuss. It won't have done her any harm to know, he says, help her grow up a bit, understand that the real world's not all clothes and bars and multiple boyfriends, still angry that I didn't tell him either.

New Year's Eve. For the last three years, Stephen and I have had a dinner party for a few friends, just eight or ten of us for a quiet meal and a civilized champagne toast at midnight. Nothing wild. Ellen usually pops in with her man of the moment to pick at whatever I'm cooking or stay for one course before dashing off to some raucous party. Sometimes we all declare our resolutions out loud, unless they're too embarrassing. I still have last year's list in my purple notebook, the sparkly one that Ellen gave me last Christmas. Looking at it now, it seems pathetic: the most ambitious resolution there is to tidy out my hall cupboard – and I haven't even managed to do that. At least I have sort of technically moved in with Stephen, I suppose that's one significant change. Except that it wasn't on the list, so it doesn't really count. Aside from that, the only resolutions I have even vaguely kept are remembering to pumice my feet periodically and polishing my bathroom taps. Marvellous. What dazzling achievements to look back on in the year gone by. Imagine my epitaph:

GEORGIA ABRAMS
She had lovely, shiny taps and
sometimes pumiced the rough bits on her feet.

Terrific.

I open the purple notebook, my Ellen notebook, at a fresh page. This year, my resolutions should be ambitious, adventurous, challenging. I sit there for maybe half an hour, alternately sipping my coffee and

419

chewing the end of my pen. In the end, the best I can come up with is this:

1. Get new life.

Yup. That just about covers it.

A civilized occasion

This evening, the dinner party is at Stephen's flat – just us and three other couples, a neat number. I wanted to ask my friends Emma and Susie, but Stephen said it spoils the balance if you have odd singles when all the other guests are couples. Also, he has eight matching dining chairs, so he'd have to use the two odd ones from the kitchen and it wouldn't look right. The menu is virtually identical to last year's; I couldn't seem to set my mind to thinking of anything else and Stephen said he thought it best to play safe in any case, you don't want to try anything new when you're cooking for a proper dinner party, do you? So here we are again, a whole year on, looking forward to hot vichyssoise followed by poached salmon, then lemon tart and flambéd fruits. Fruit bonfire. A cafetière of coffee and a dish of dark truffles. A toast at midnight, champagne in chilled glasses. Here's to next year, here's to us. And then next year? And the year after that? If, ten years from now, I find my list of resolutions, will I even be able to tell when I wrote it? Perhaps I'll just take it out each year, smooth out the creases, and pretend I'm starting afresh?

The vichyssoise I made yesterday and now it's in Stephen's fridge, waiting to be heated up once the guests arrive. The bubbly is chilling. The lemon tart is already on its blue glass plate, ringed with raspberries placed just so, sprinkled with an artfully artless dusting of icing sugar.

*   *   *

This is the first year of my life when I haven't known what Ellen is doing for New Year's Eve. All I know is that she won't be popping in for an hour or two, won't be getting in my way as I fuss at the stove, dipping her finger in the soup, nicking the carefully positioned raspberries, leaving her telltale fingerprint in the icing sugar, knocking back my glass of champagne as soon as she's finished her own.

Alongside the two bottles of bubbly in the door of the fridge there are another two bottles of white wine. A rather expensive Chablis, the one Stephen always buys when we want something 'classy' to drink. Stephen prefers red wine, but he never buys it when we have guests in case they knock over a glass and it spills onto his beautiful pale carpet. He's had it for two years and managed to keep it looking almost brand new, so you can't blame him really. Dad once told me that, in Hungary, as soon as the guests are seated round the table, the hostess tips some red wine straight onto the tablecloth – so that everyone can relax and not worry about 'spoiling' anything.

My car still hasn't been found and I seem to have mislaid my memory as well. I forgot to bring my fish kettle over so I am poaching the salmon the way my mother used to do it. You wrap it loosely in foil and put it in the oven in a roasting tin with a little water and wine in it. Once you open the wine, you can have a glass of it too, of course. Chef's perk – that's what Mum called it, only in her case it was a perk even if she was only making two slices of toast. It's too good for cooking really, this wine – perhaps I'll just use lemon juice on the fish. I tuck a couple of bay leaves around it, a sprig of expensive out-of-season fresh tarragon, chuck a few green and pink peppercorns over it, rub some sea salt into the slit along its length.

*   *   *

A little more Chablis for the chef is in order, I think. Chablis-dabbly. Plenty of time before anyone arrives. I'll put the salmon on now, anyway, then I can skin it while it's still hot and serve it warm or cold, so there's no fussing at the last minute. Last year, Ellen came early – I think she was going to a party miles away – and she helped me cut 'fish scales' from slices of cucumber. They're supposed to be so thin that they're translucent, and you can see the pale pink of the salmon through the green of the scales, but the ones Ellen cut were much too thick, so she and I stood in the kitchen, eating them while I sliced some more. We got the giggles and started being silly, doing impressions of everyone we know and suddenly saying 'penis' loudly every now and then to annoy Stephen.

I take the cucumber out of the fridge and tear open the plastic covering with my teeth, cut off one end. Try to cut a slice but the knife slips, leaving just a misshapen sliver. 'Penis,' I say loudly, but it is not the same. I don't think I'll bother with the cucumber now. Or I could just put the whole thing out on a plate with a knife and people can cut their own as they like, thick or thin, whatever.

I wonder what Leo's doing tonight. He's probably going to a wild party. He'll do his stupid embarrassing dancing and get very drunk, I bet, then go back home with some equally pissed woman. Well, good luck to him. If that's what he calls having fun when he's nearly forty, then he's never going to grow up. Cora will be at her aunt's. She'll be tucked up tight in her bed at midnight, dreaming, while the adults downstairs drink sherry and pass round bowls of peanuts and stuffed olives. When we were kids, Matt and I told Ellen that green olives were the eyeballs of witches' cats and that the ones with the red stuff in them were like that because it was all the blood and gunge you got when you took them out of the cat. When Mum had two of her good old drinking pals round the next evening and set out a dish of olives, Ellen went screaming into the midst of them and clung onto Mum's legs, saying, 'No, no, no! Don't eat them, Mummy! Don't! Don't!'

It's really not at all bad, this wine, though I hadn't realized I'd used so much of it in the fish. I don't even remember adding it, I must have done it without thinking, it's so easy to do that when you're cooking, you just switch on to autopilot, don't you? There's barely a glass left in this bottle. Anyway, there's still the second one and we won't run short because everyone brings a bottle or two, don't they, and at least we won't have Ellen around drinking us dry.

Now, look, here's the salmon still sitting in its tin on top of the hob. That's not going to get us very far, is it? Put it in on the upper shelf. There we go. Good. Turn on the cooker hood thing so no fishy smells. That's that sorted. Now, with salmon, some people say cook it on high but very briefly and some people say cook it on low but very slowly. I haven't cooked a whole salmon since last year. One year ago today. I could check it in a book, I suppose. I can't remember which way I did it last time. I'm sure Stephen must have some cookery books somewhere.

Midnight at eleven

Ah-ha. Stephen's back.

'Hi, sweetie. How's it all coming along?'

I nod and smile.

'Fine. Fine. It's all very lovely.'

'I'd love a glass of wine. Shall we open a bottle now, do you think?'

He comes into the kitchen, sees the empty bottle on the counter.

'Good God – did you use all that for the salmon? Rather extravagant, surely – it's a very decent wine.'

I nod again.

423

'I'm really sorry. I couldn't find anything else.'

He sighs.

'I wish you'd waited. I've heaps of other wine in the rack.' He sighs again heavily and goes through to the sitting room. Returns with two other bottles to chill. Takes out the second bottle of wine from the fridge.

'Fancy a glass, darling?' He is looking at me in a slightly odd way, as if discovering that the glass he is about to drink from has a chip in it. 'Are you all right?'

'Fine. Yup. Fine. Bit of a headache, that's all.'

'Oh. Do you not want any wine then?'

'No, I'll have a drop. I've taken a tablet.'

He pours himself a full glass, and a third of a glass for me, then goes through to the sitting room. I hear him settling himself on the sofa, putting his feet up on the coffee table.

'Mum and Dad send their best and say Happy New Year,' he calls through to me, as I take out the salad stuff from the fridge, top up my mingy glass of wine. 'But I'll phone them later anyway, so you can wish them a happy new year properly then.'

'Great.'

'Remind me to phone them at just on eleven, will you? Mum says they don't like to stay up so late, so they're going to put the lounge clock forward an hour and celebrate at eleven instead.'

Did I hear that right?

'They're havin' midnight at eleven?'

'That's right. Rather clever, isn't it? You should tell your dad – he might appreciate the tip.'

Excuse me? He's sixty-two, he's not dead yet.

'You'll be calling him later, will you?'

'Prob'ly. Yup.'

It's funny because the label on this wine's the same as on the other bottle, but it tastes a bit different. It's hard to tell because the other one's all gone now, but I think I liked the first one more. Have just a little bit more of this one, just to check.

'God, it's nearly eight now!' Stephen goes through to the bedroom. 'I'll just change my shirt and shave.'

I don't need to change because I put on an apron while I was cooking. I only need to take it off.

The doorbell goes. Jason and Sandra. Stephen's friends. They are terribly, terribly nice. I know they are nice because Stephen told me so. Also, Sandra did a sponsored slim for starving children in Africa so she is definitely a nice person. They thrust bottles and chocolates into my arms and kiss me somewhere near my cheek. Jason holds me a few seconds longer than he needs to. As they come in, Stephen emerges from the bedroom.

There is much kissing and patting of backs and 'great to be here's and 'let's make a night of it's. Then, in quick succession, Liz and Mike and Tim and Jools arrive. More kissing. Stephen opens bottles and fetches glasses and gives me cross looks.

'Darling? Where are the nibbles?'

They should be on the coffee table. That's where nibbles live, everyone knows that. They inhabit small, detached dishes with no balconies or off-street parking and they have no ambitions and no adventures and no dreams. Life is very simple when you're a salted pistachio.

Stephen comes into the kitchen, spots the bowl of olives on the counter, the nuts and rice crackers bafflingly still in their packets, the empty dishes alongside.

'I thought you were doing these,' he says.

'I *am*.'

'Darling?'

He is standing in front of me, looking at me with his serious face on. This is the face he uses when he is telling his clients what is wrong with their management structure and how much they will have to pay him to make it all lovely and nice; this is the face he uses when members of my family phone after eleven o'clock at night; this is the face he uses when he thinks I am being silly.

I am not going to laugh. It is very, very important not to laugh when Stephen is doing his serious face.

'Darling,' I say back.

'You haven't been . . . drinking, have you?'

I half-suppress a sudden snort. Clearly, the idea is absurd. Ridiculous. Everyone knows that Georgia doesn't drink. Georgia has one glass of wine. Just one. It's a rule she has. Like Ellen said, and she should know. She's known Georgia since – forever. Georgia doesn' drink. Georgia doesn' have fun. Georgia doesn' have a life. People who drink are embarrassing and awful and out of control.

I have had a little bit, tiny bit to drink, to taste the wine while I was doing the food, but Stephen looks so cross, I'm not sure I should mention it.

He comes nearer.

'Breathe on me.'

I shake my head.

'Come on, I think you've been drinking.'

I shake my head again, then get a fit of the giggles.

'It's not funny, Georgia. We've arranged this nice evening here with all our friends—'

'Your friends.'

Still got his serious face on.

'So that's how you see them. Well, that *is* nice.' He clicks the kettle on. 'I think you'd better have some coffee, don't you, if you're not to ruin the evening completely.'

I nod. Prob'ly best to have some coffee.

'Cannive a truffle too?'

He turns his face away from me. I wasn't going to have all the truffles. I only wanted one. They're to go with when you have coffee.

From the sitting room, I can hear him explaining to our guests. His guests.

'I'm afraid the chef's started seeing in the New Year a bit ahead of time . . . Georgia's had a drop too much . . .' Laughter, a single whoop from Jason. Someone calls out, 'We'd better catch up with her then.'

Stephen comes back in.

'Have you had a coffee? God – I'll do it.' He pours hot water on some instant coffee in a mug, pushes it into my hands. 'Drink that. Where's the soup? For God's sake, Georgia, haven't you done anything?'

I point to the fridge and he opens it and takes out the big pot of soup.

'I thought we were having it hot? How do we heat it? Does it go on top or in the microwave or what?'

'Vich-soise,' I say. 'Serve chilled.'

'Out of this? Is it supposed to be in a dish? For Christ's sake, Georgia, come on!'

I point to the big white bowl on the counter, the ladle ready by its side. Stephen attempts to tip the soup into a bowl, slopping it onto the worktop, the floor, his good black shoes.

'Oh, Georgia! Honestly!'

Resolutions

I follow him through to the sitting room, where the guests are already seated at the dining table.

'Georgy!' shouts Jason. 'Stevie says the chef's been at the sherry! You naughty girl!'

'Sack the chef!' someone calls.

'Promote the chef!' Jason shouts back.

Stephen nods for me to sit at the other end while he tries to transfer soup from the big bowl into several small ones, which involves quite a bit of spilling and swearing. I press my napkin hard against my mouth and reach for my wine.

'It's very tasty,' Liz says quietly.

'It's better hot,' says Stephen, looking daggers at me.

I make a face and Jason laughs.

'What are your resolutions then, Georgia?' asks Jason. 'Go on the wagon for a bit, eh?' Everyone laughs, except Stephen.

'Mine is to have more sex,' shouts Tim. 'Some of it even with Jools!' Jools simpers by his side, to show that she has a really, really GSOH.

'I'm planning to raise funds for people who've lost one or more limbs,' begins Sandra, 'by doing a sponsored hop.'

Jason spurts out a mouthful of wine as he laughs. I stuff my napkin into my mouth. It must be a joke, right? A sick, sick joke, but a joke. But no, it is Sandra. Not a joke then. She looks from Jason to me, then back to Jason, then sniffs loudly and looks down at her soup.

'I'm going to go to the gym twice a week and lose a stone,' announces Liz, though no-one is listening really. She has the shape of a ten-year-old boy as it is and can toy with a small salad for over an hour before declaring herself 'stuffed'.

'My resolution . . .' I begin.

Suddenly, everyone stops talking and looks at me, as if I am about to say something important. I look at Stephen. His lips are pressed firmly together and he is frowning, worrying that I'm going to embarrass him.

'My resolution for next year . . .' I take another gulp of my wine '. . . is very simple, actu'ly in fact. My resolution is to *live*.'

'What?' says someone.

'How do you mean?'

'Georgia's not ill, is she?' someone half-whispers to Stephen.

'To live?'

'Yup.' I nod. 'To *live*. Really *live*. Not just exist. I'm going to eat ice cream on rooftops and sing when I'm walking down the street when I want to – I shall cry in the cinema and do my teeth for less than two

428

minutes and eat spaghetti bolognese without a napkin – and I'll laugh loudly in restaurants and get drunk every now and then and let myself fall in love . . .'

There is a silence, then Jason says, 'Sounds like an excellent plan to me. I'll drink to that.'

Stephen has got up from his seat and is now at my side. He bends to speak in my ear.

'Go and drink your coffee.'

Slowly, I get up and go back through to the kitchen. Stephen comes in, carrying some of the empty soup bowls.

'I hope you're happy now that you've made me look like a complete fool.'

'Mmm?' I am definitely not going to laugh. Clamping my lips shut and doing my sensible face.

'If you can't get your act together, you'd best go and lay down while we eat our dinner.' A small noise escapes through my nose, but it is not at all funny. Absolutely not even one little tiny bit. And by the way, it's *lie* down not *lay* down, you ignoramus. I remember to think this and not say it out loud.

'I suppose I'll have to clear the table and everything. For Christ's sake, Georgia, this *isn't* funny. I would think that you of all people would take this very seriously indeed – given your *background*.'

He strides out of the kitchen, back to the sitting room. I stand stock still for a moment, then lean heavily against the counter. Did you know that Stephen has polished granite worktops? You can almost see your face in them, they're so shiny. I am very, very fortunate even to know a person who has such civilized, shiny worktops, given my background. It's astonishing that I've never thrown up on them or danced naked on them or passed out on top of them. Quite amazing, when you come to think of it really.

The timer buzzes – that's right! Come along now!

I open the oven door, reach in to pull out the salmon.

Jump back as I touch the tin, realizing I should have used the oven glove.

But I'm not burned. It's not even warm. The oven's not on.

Oh-oh.

It's important, when you're doing the cooking, to put the oven on. Otherwise, the things will not be as hot as you want them. Or cooked.

I can hear Stephen clattering the dishes, his friends telling jokes.

'No, I've got one – listen to this. There's this Englishman, an Irishman and a Scotsman, right . . .'

I tiptoe out to the hallway and take my coat from the rack, pick up my handbag from beneath the chair there, where I always leave it. Then, quietly, I ease open the door and let myself out, and then I'm tottering down the street, pulling on my coat, the night air fierce and cold on my face, stumbling in my high heels.

There is no way I'm going to see a cab just gliding by with its light on on New Year's Eve. I don't care. I can walk. Or get a bus.

On the main road, I get a portion of chips from the greasy takeaway that Stephen says is guaranteed to give you food poisoning, you can tell it's dirty just by looking at it, he says. The chips look clean enough to me. I smother them in salt and vinegar. As I come out, I see a bus and I run to the stop to flag it down, leap on.

'The West End? Oxford Circus?' I hold out a handful of change.

'That's the other way, love.'

'Where's this going?'

'Up the Finchley Road, then Hendon. Come on, love, on or off? Make up your mind.'

Finchley Road. Where Ellen works. The Warm

South. Brian's wine bar. Ellen.

'Finchley Road then, near Fortune Green.'

He pokes through my palm for the right money.

'Happy New Year, love. Sit down before you fall down.' He smiles and winks at me then. 'Any chance of a chip?'

I'm staring out of the window and it's only when the conductor calls to me that I realize it's my stop. I would have sailed straight past it.

'Here you go, love. This the right one?'

'Yes! thanks!'

'Mind how you go now. Happy New Year!'

'Happy New Year!'

Belonging

The Warm South. The windows are lit up, and as I press my face to the glass, I can see it's packed with people. There is a bouncer at the door.

'Got your ticket?'

'No. I – I left it at home.'

'Ticket or guest list only.'

'I'm a friend of Brian's.'

'Yeah – isn't everyone? Wait here.'

He opens the door a fraction then squeezes his considerable bulk through the gap. It is easier for a camel to pass through the eye of a needle than for a fat bouncer to . . .

Brian appears.

'Georgia! Brilliant! Sorry – didn't know you were coming or I'd have put your name on the door. Ellie didn't say. Come in, come in.'

I blow the bouncer a kiss as I waltz inside.

Brian thrusts a bottle of beer into my hand and kisses my cheek.

'Have this, I've not touched it yet – or do you want wine?'

431

'Whatever.'

'Are you OK?' Brian takes my hand. 'You look a bit – funny.'

He points to the stairs.

'They're all up there. I'll join you in a sec.' He moves through the throng with ease, stopping to say a few words here and there.

They?

I climb the stairs. One of last year's resolutions. Always walk up the stairs unless carrying something heavy. The bottle of beer and my handbag are not all that heavy. Also, there is no lift in any case actually.

'Oops – steady as she goes!' says a man coming down the other way, bumping into me.

At the top, I cross the landing and enter the main room. It is very crowded and fairly smoky. I can't see Ellen and there is nowhere to sit down. I lean against the wall for a minute and take a swig of my cool beer, close my eyes. Just having a little rest.

'Georgia!'

I open my eyes. There is a man standing in front of me. He looks like Leo, very like Leo. This is a dream. I think I have drunk a little bit too much and now I am dreaming what I want to see.

'Georgia! Are you all right?' He has such a nice face, I bet you've never noticed that about him, but he has a lovely face.

'You've got a lovely face,' I say, as I start to cry.

'Thank you. So have you. Why are you crying?' Gently, he smooths away my tears with the pad of his thumb.

'I don't know. Can I have some wine?'

'Of course. Come and sit down. We're over here.'

He takes my hand and leads me to a table in a corner.

'George!' says Ellen.

'Hi,' says Simone.

'Gee-gee!' says Matt, getting up to come and hug me.

'Hello,' says Isobel. 'What's the matter?'

'You're all here,' I say, which is true. 'You're here without me.'

'You're here now,' says Leo.

'We thought you were at Stephen's,' says Izzy.

'I was. I ran away.'

'Not really?'

'Yes really.'

'What did he say?'

'I don't know. I didn't tell him I was going.'

'Holy shit,' says Ellen, handing me a glass of wine. 'I wish I'd been there.'

'No, you don't,' I say, drinking my wine. 'It was horrible.'

'Oh, George – don't cry.' Ellen comes round the table and puts her arms around me. 'Please don't cry. Please don't. I can't bear it if you cry.'

'I ca-can't help it. You won't talk to me an' I messed everything up.'

'I am talking to you, George. I *am*.'

'No, you're only sayin' that to be nice.'

'No, I'm not. I promise.' She touches the tip of my nose with her finger, the way we make a promise. I reach up to touch her nose, but I am slightly off-target.

Ellen laughs.

'I've never, ever seen you this pissed – I think we've swapped places.'

I shake my head.

''m not pissed. Just had a little tiny bit wine for cooking. Chef's perk.'

'Yes, I think we've gathered that.' Leo puts his arm round me. 'Did anyone ever tell you that you're dead cute when you're tipsy?'

A new beginning

It is very noisy and we are talking and drinking. Matt puts his arm round me.

'I'm sorry about what happened at Christmas. I

shouldn't have said it. You know I love you, Gee?'

'I love you too, Batzo-Matzo.'

I lean across to Ellen and say, 'I'm sorry, I'm so sorry,' and she says, 'Sh-sssh, it's OK now. Don't worry about it now.' She pulls me close for a hug.

'Am I still your favourite sister?' she asks.

I nod.

'Am I yours?'

'Always,' she says. 'You'll always be my favourite sister.'

Brian weaves between the tables but always comes back to us, resting his hand lightly on Ellie's shoulder for a moment, leaning over her as she stretches to say something in his ear.

'Two minutes to go, folks!' Brian calls across the room.

Leo.

He is looking at me and I am looking at him. It is all right to kiss someone on New Year's Eve at midnight. Even a total stranger. It's practically compulsory. It doesn't have to mean anything, everyone knows that. It can just be a kiss, two sets of lips touching for a few seconds, barely more intimate than a handshake. It doesn't have to mean that you love this person, does it? Love him so much that you're getting tears in your eyes just thinking about it. Love him so much it makes your ribs hurt. Love this face, this face you could look at for a lifetime. This is the face you want to see on the pillow beside you. This is the person you want to talk with, make love with, laugh with. This is the person you even want to argue with – Whose go is it to empty the dishwasher? – Who didn't replace the empty loo roll? Did you call the estate agent today? The building society? – For God's sake, why did we move these bloody wooden carvings if neither of us actually

434

likes them? Shall we paint the baby's room sky blue or primrose yellow? The baby's room. With this person, life would never be the same again. With this person, you could be the person you were always meant to be, the person you never dared dream you could be, the person you really are.

And it *is* terrifying. Of course it is. But it is also too late now, too late to turn back, to inhabit a life that no longer fits me, a life I no longer want.

'Get ready!' shouts Brian to the room.
   'Ten!' Leo's eyes lock on mine.
   'Nine!' Everyone shouts, sort of together.
   'Eight!' Brian steps nearer to our table.
   'Seven!' My brother puts his arm around his wife.
   'Six!' Brian lays his hand on Ellen's shoulder.
   'Five!' I look down at my hands, resting in my lap as if they do not belong to me.
   'Four!' I look back at Leo.
   'Three!' My heart is thudding.
   'Two!' Leo takes one of my hands between his own and cradles it as if it is something infinitely precious.
   'One!' He gathers me to him and I tilt my face up to his.

In some part of me, I can hear the shouts and the whoops, the cheers and the 'Happy New Year!'s. But that is there, outside of us. Here, there is no noise except the beating of my heart. It seems to me as if I can hear the roar of my blood as it rushes round my body, quick and hot, red and full of life. It seems to me that I have been waiting my whole life to notice the simple fact that I am alive.

One minute past midnight. A new day. A new year. A very good time to begin to *live*.

Epilogue

L'chaim

I wore red in the end. You know, I had a whole folder of clippings I'd cut from magazines and sketches I'd done of the Ultimate Dress. Elegant. Classic. But – when it came to it – I'd gone off the whole idea of the sophisticated ivory satin number. It just seemed so – well, like vanilla ice cream. Nice. Inoffensive. Bland. And then we organized the whole thing in one hell of a rush so there wasn't time to mess about having something made. Ellen came with me and banned me from even looking in the same three shops I normally use. Used to use. We found this dress made of deep red velvet – off-the-shoulder and quite low-cut.

'That is so *you*!' she said as I stood there, tentatively stroking the fabric. 'What are you waiting for? Try it on, try it on.'

When Leo sees me in it, he just stands there with his mouth open for a few seconds.

'Now *that* – ' he says, moving closer, 'is what I *call* a dress . . .'

'That's because it *is* a dress.'

'What would I do without you to point out these things?' He steps towards me. 'Aren't brides supposed to look demure and virginal?'

'A little late for that, don't you think? Aren't the happy couple supposed to wait till *after* they're married before they wear each other out with wild sex?'

He puts his arms around me, then squeezes my bottom.

'This feels gorgeous – *you* feel gorgeous.' He strokes me through the soft velvet. 'I don't suppose we've got time—?'

'Not unless you can go from nought to ecstasy in twelve seconds – and you won't be put off by having eighty people just the other side of those doors?'

'*I'm* not the *noisy* one – so who'd be the more embarrassed, do you suppose?'

We decided to forego the formal sit-down affair and just have everyone free to roam and mingle and sit wherever they damn well please. The buffet tables are laden with food, whatever we fancied, so it's an eclectic mix of cultural treats. No poached salmon. No coronation chicken. No rice salad. There are bite-sized potato latkes and deep-fried fish balls, four sorts of bruschetta, garlicky chicken tapas, huge piles of crudités with falafel and houmous and tsatziki, platters of chicken on skewers with pesto dip, spiced lamb meatballs with tomato salsa, tiny hamburgers in buns with relish, thin pancakes filled with crispy duck and hoisin sauce, miniature bagels with smoked salmon and cream cheese, poppy seed plaited chollah and sweet-sour cucumbers – we even had trays of mini pizzas (no leeks, no black pepper).

I look round the room then, catching my dad's eye. He smiles and raises his glass and mouths: '*L'chaim*' – to Life. His arm rests along the back of Quinn's chair. Her earrings sway madly as she bobs her head, deep in conversation with Unc, her big sleeves trailing into her food. There is Anne, Leo's mother, bright and animated in her emerald silk dress, nattering away to Simone. And Leo's sisters – Rebecca, being chatted up by the dishiest member of the band, and Linda, helping to push back the chairs to make more space for dancing. Beyond the open French windows on the lawn, there is Matt, whirling Daniel round and round, screaming with delight. And Daniel's loving it too. Izzy is watching Bonnie who has tucked her long bridesmaid's dress into her knickers and is being a ballerina, leaping across the grass in exhibitionistic *grands jetés*. And there is Cora now, running at full pelt to join her, then twirling round and round in pirouettes, her bridesmaid's dress swirling round her, her sash flying out as she spins, then falling over with dizziness, laughing with Bonnie, rolling over and over down the grassy slope, shrieking with joy. And there is Ellen, stationed by the buffet, picking out the biggest, plumpest strawberry she can find – clamped between her fingers – turning now and feeding it to Brian.

And here, by my side, is my husband, with his lovely, much-loved face and his thinning hair. He smiles then and the sight of his chipped tooth stabs me with such love and tenderness that my eyes fill with tears.

'You look *so* beautiful,' he says, laying his hand on the swell of my tummy, already starting to show. 'My bride with a bump.'

He takes my hand and nips it softly with his lips, twists the ring on my left hand, my wedding ring. White gold, inscribed: Song of Solomon, II.16.

My beloved is mine, and I am his.

'We've some family between us, hmm?' he says.

We look round together at them all – talking and arguing, eating and drinking, offering each other prize morsels and trying things from each other's plates, the children shouting and laughing and pushing each other, the adults – well, doing pretty much the same.

Leo shakes his head.

'*What* a bunch . . .' But he is smiling.

'Mmm. But, you know what?' I cuddle up close to him, rest my head against his shoulder.

'No. What?'

'I'm beginning to think I like it like that.'

THE END

Acknowledgements

Many thanks to everyone, including those who chose to remain anonymous, who gave me help and support while I was working on *I Like it Like That*, and especially the following:

My mother Pat, for her patience, enthusiasm, help with research and many editorial suggestions.

My sister Stephanie, for her ceaseless support and help – always my favourite sister.

My extraordinary man Larry and his wonderful extended family, including a quite unbelievable number of cousins, but especially Harry, Ron, Jenny, Josie and Susannah – for welcoming me so warmly into the fold.

Dr Paul Barnett and HAGA (Haringey Advisory Group on Alcohol) for help with research and medical advice.

Ruth Shane, counsellor, for her insightful and constructive comments on the text and for being a great friend.

Gillian Andrews, for her honesty and highly valued friendship.

Suzie Hayman, Relate-trained counsellor and broadcaster, for her help and amusing e-mails.

Jane Taylor, for giving me a fascinating insight into an architect's life – sorry I didn't end up using it.

Ben Murphy, photographer, for providing a picture of a freelance photographer's life.

Presley Warner, because he really thinks it's about time he made it onto the acknowledgements page, even if I didn't use the stuff about the stickers.

Everyone at Transworld/Black Swan, who always impress with their tremendous warmth and professionalism.

My editor, Linda Evans, for making the editorial process such a pleasure.

My agent, Jo Frank – it's great to have a fairy godmother. Now please can you work your magic to get me a Jacobean farmhouse, a vintage Bentley, and a multi-million-dollar movie deal? Thank you.

LOVE IS A FOUR LETTER WORD

Claire Calman

Sex. Yes. She remembered that.

Wasn't that the thing that happened somewhere between the talking-and-going-out-to-dinner bit and the sobbing-and-eating-too-many-biscuits bit? Still, Bella was sure she could handle some – preferably before her as yet unopened packet of condoms reached their expiry date. She must be practically a virgin again now, all sealed over like pierced ears if you don't wear earrings for too long.

But the 'L' word? Uh-huh. No way. She never wanted to hear it again. There were things in her past which needed to be put well away, like the 27 boxes of clutter she'd brought from her old flat. And having changed her job, her town, her entire life – the one thing she wasn't about to change was her mind.

'SIMPLY WONDERFUL! I WAS TOTALLY
ENCHANTED'
Fiona Walker

'A WARM AND FUNNY FIRST NOVEL'
Elizabeth Buchan, *The Times*

'FUNNY, CLEVER AND MOVING'
Sunday Mirror

0 552 99853 2

BLACK SWAN

LESSONS FOR A SUNDAY FATHER

Claire Calman

'TOUCHING, HILARIOUS AND DISARMINGLY
ACCURATE'
Red

It's never too late to grow up

This is the story of

Scott, who finds his belongings outside in a bin
bag one day and realizes he may have made a
Big Mistake . . .

Gail, who wishes her husband were under guarantee
so she could send him back and get a refund . . .

Nat, who discovers that growing up isn't all it's
cracked up to be . . .

and **Rosie,** who just wants her Dad back – or if not,
then at least some new glitter nail polish.

**Four lives, one story
of love, loss and learning to be a grown-up.**

'THIS BOOK IS A *TOUR DE FORCE*'
Daily Express

'A MASTERPIECE BY A WRITER WHO
UNDERSTANDS THE HEARTBREAK AND JOY OF
THE HUMAN CONDITION LIKE NO OTHER . . . FOR
INTELLIGENT READERS EVERYWHERE'
William Kowalski, author of *Eddie's Bastard*

0 552 99854 0

BLACK SWAN

SOMEWHERE SOUTH OF HERE

William Kowalski

My name, for what it's worth, is William Amos Mann the Fourth, and I arrived in Santa Fe on the back of my steel-gray 1977 Kawasaki KZ1000, bringing with me only what I could carry on the back of it: an antique typewriter, some books, and a few articles of clothing. I'd just turned twenty, or so I assumed – my exact date of birth, like my origins, was unknown, so my grandfather had had to invent one on my behalf.

In search of the mother he had never known, Billy is flying south on his motorcycle, to her last known address, a side street in Santa Fe, New Mexico. There he encounters as vibrant a cast of characters as the world can offer, including Eliza and her crazy daughter, and Consuelo, a beautiful gypsy Latina.

Consuelo sings at the Cowgirl Hall of Fame bar. She is waiting for stardom, but Billy comes along first. When finally she gets her big break, Consuelo wants him to leave with her for Los Angeles. But Billy has still not told Eliza his secret – that he is the baby she deserted twenty years ago. Life is all about choices and now Billy is faced with the biggest choice of all: Eliza, whom he must know in order to know himself, or Consuelo, the woman he loves more than anyone else in the world.

'WILLIAM KOWALSKI MAKES STORYTELLING SEEM SO RIDICULOUSLY EASY. HIS SIMPLE WORDS GENTLY WIND THEIR SPELL, DANCING LIGHTLY AROUND YOUR HEAD'
The List

0 552 99936 9

BLACK SWAN

PERFECT DAY

Imogen Parker

Can one day change your life?

If we were a song, what song do you think we would be?

On a perfect spring morning, Alexander catches an early train into London, but he never reaches work. Instead, he spends the day with Kate, a waitress he has met the previous evening, a woman so unlike anyone he has ever known, she makes the world shimmer with possibility.

Such a perfect day, Nell takes her child Lucy to the seaside, hoping that the sea air will blow away the doubts she has about her life.

As Nell ponders why falling in love is so different from loving someone, Alexander allows himself to imagine leaving his old life behind and starting afresh. And by a strange turn of fate, there's an opportunity to do just that – if he chooses to take it . . .

0 552 99838 5

BLACK SWAN

A SELECTED LIST OF FINE WRITING
AVAILABLE FROM BLACK SWAN

99588	6	**THE HOUSE OF THE SPIRITS**	*Isabel Allende*	£7.99
99734	X	**EMOTIONALLY WEIRD**	*Kate Atkinson*	£6.99
99860	5	**IDIOGLOSSIA**	*Eleanor Bailey*	£6.99
99853	2	**LOVE IS A FOUR LETTER WORD**	*Claire Calman*	£6.99
99854	0	**LESSONS FOR A SUNDAY FATHER**	*Claire Calman*	£5.99
99686	6	**BEACH MUSIC**	*Pat Conroy*	£7.99
99836	2	**A HEART OF STONE**	*Renate Dorrestein*	£6.99
99925	3	**THE BOOK OF THE HEATHEN**	*Robert Edric*	£6.99
99898	2	**ALL BONES AND LIES**	*Anne Fine*	£6.99
99851	6	**REMEMBERING BLUE**	*Connie May Fowler*	£6.99
99759	5	**DOG DAYS, GLENN MILLER NIGHTS**	*Laurie Graham*	£6.99
99890	7	**DISOBEDIENCE**	*Jane Hamilton*	£6.99
99847	8	**WHAT WE DID ON OUR HOLIDAY**	*John Harding*	£6.99
99883	4	**FIVE QUARTERS OF THE ORANGE**	*Joanne Harris*	£6.99
99796	X	**A WIDOW FOR ONE YEAR**	*John Irving*	£7.99
99867	2	**LIKE WATER IN WILD PLACES**	*Pamela Jooste*	£6.99
99936	9	**SOMEWHERE SOUTH OF HERE**	*William Kowalski*	£6.99
99738	2	**THE PROPERTY OF RAIN**	*Angela Lambert*	£6.99
99959	8	**BACK ROADS**	*Tawni O'Dell*	£6.99
99938	5	**PERFECT DAY**	*Imogen Parker*	£6.99
99909	1	**LA CUCINA**	*Lily Prior*	£6.99
99645	9	**THE WRONG BOY**	*Willy Russell*	£6.99
99952	0	**LIFE ISN'T ALL HA HA HEE HEE**	*Meera Syal*	£6.99
99819	2	**WHISTLING FOR THE ELEPHANTS**	*Sandi Toksvig*	£6.99
99902	4	**TO BE SOMEONE**	*Louise Voss*	£6.99
99864	8	**A DESERT IN BOHEMIA**	*Jill Paton Walsh*	£6.99